A Dangerous Land . . . a Daring Woman . . . and a Limitless Horizon

KATE BURKE is "the red-haired woman with the red dog" who cuts such a distinctive figure in Sioux Falls, South Dakota, in the spring of 1891, that everyone from newsboys to Indians knows her. Camera always at the ready, she is clearly focused on what she wants . . . and she never blinks.

BILL BURKE is the petty schemer and traveling photographer who wedded a woman half his age, twice his intelligence, and three times his talent. He knows Kate accepted his proposal only because he promised to take her west. And yet she has such a hold on his heart, he's driven to desperate measures.

COLONEL ELLIOT GEORGE is a hero, acclaimed in the nation's newspapers as the man "who ended Indian wars forever." Believing that no one wants to know how a soldier does his nation's dirty work, he sees nothing wrong with covering up the gruesome truth—even if it requires killing the troublesome Mrs. Burke or anyone else.

POWERS T. NOCK is the odd but charismatic lawyer with the impossible case. His client, an Indian, shot an army officer in front of witnesses. Everyone expects he'll hang, until Nock turns his trial into an assault on the nation's conscience . . . and tops that with an assault on Kate's heart.

RICHARD HOUSTON is the son of a wealthy eastern business tycoon who was attracted to photography by Kate's father. Now, equally captivated by Kate's photographic vision, he becomes both lover and sentinel—guarding the secret of her past.

WOMAN-WHO-DREAMS is the seer and last leader of the quillworkers, whose dream art is dying. Long ago she saw a vision of "a red-haired woman with a red dog." Now it will take an act of courage for Woman-Who-Dreams to entice Kate to her destiny, yet she has no fear—and neither does the red-haired woman.

JERRIE HURD

KATE BURKE SHOOTS THE OLD WEST

POCKET STAR BOOKS

New York London Toronto Sydney Tokyo Singapore

This book is a work of fiction. Names, characters, places and
incidents are products of the author's imagination or are used
fictitiously. Any resemblance to actual events or locales or persons,
living or dead, is entirely coincidental.

An *Original* Publication of POCKET BOOKS

A Pocket Star Book published by
POCKET BOOKS, a division of Simon & Schuster Inc.
1230 Avenue of the Americas, New York, NY 10020

Copyright © 1997 by Jerrie Hurd

ISBN: 0-671-51910-7

First Pocket Books printing January 1997

10 9 8 7 6 5 4 3 2 1

POCKET STAR BOOKS and colophon are registered
trademarks of Simon & Schuster Inc.

Cover art by Kam Mac

Printed in the U.S.A.

*This one's for the
pioneering women photographers
of the last century.*

Acknowledgments

The author wishes to acknowledge the sustaining interest and generous help of Nat Sobel, whose influence is felt on every page, Eric Paddock, who helped with the photographic information, and Jon Hurd, for all the reasons only he knows.

Author's Note

While the December 1890 massacre at Wounded Knee and subsequent trial of Plenty Horses are historical events, the characters and incidents depicted here are entirely fictional.

1

April 1891
Sioux Falls, South Dakota

The buffalo charged straight at Kate.

She'd never seen a buffalo except in photographs. Then grouped together, the animals had looked small and slow-moving against the wide expanse of prairie and sky whitened from overexposure. This one was a huge hump of brown, matted fur, black eyes, black nose, black horns, and flared nostrils blowing a fog ahead of itself. This one was close enough to smell and coming closer. And worse, it was dragging the Indian.

Kate steadied her camera against the fence railing and worked quickly—aperture, focus, slide the plate in . . .

Townswomen grabbed their children and ran. The Wild West exhibitioner who owned the buffalo climbed the fence, whip in hand. Other Indians leaped to the fence top whooping and hollering. All around people exclaimed the insanity:

"He'll be killed."

"Damned crazy Indian . . ."

"Fool thing. What does he . . ."

"I've never seen . . ."

But Kate had seen. She had watched a tremor rack the

Indian's body as he threw himself against the startled wide-eyed bull in what could only be called an embrace—his fingers clawing the shaggy mane the way hers now clutched the fence top. And she knew . . . the Indian was not crazy. She couldn't explain it. Sometimes she saw things like that with a clarity that invaded her dreams, the images burned into her soul; and sometimes when she was lucky, she captured them on the gelatin of her photographic plates. She lived for those moments.

The Indian, a thin, crooked-armed man, past the prime of his life, threw back his head and sang out sharp and high-pitched, "Hey, ya na hah . . ." or some gibberish like that, and she thought again: maybe, this was crazy. Then it happened—the perfect orchestration of light and shadow, form and frame, even the angle of the sunlight on the dust roiling up under the beast. How many chances did one get to capture the image of an elderly Sioux warrior hugging a buffalo? She clicked the shutter.

Then the animal slammed against the opposite side of the fence, where she still clung. The force was enough to split the top two rails. One broken rail punched her in the stomach and sent her flying. She threw her arms around her camera to protect it from the fall and landed flat on her back, the wind knocked out, her own focus blurred. She couldn't immediately catch her breath, and her dizziness grew. Still she worked her fingers over her camera feeling its various parts, checking for damage. The camera seemed to be all right. That was about as important to her as breathing. Good cameras were hard to replace, in her case, next to impossible.

Just as she was on the verge of losing consciousness, she became aware of her husband leaning over her, shaking her. He was a graying, slightly rotund man with short, wide fingers that were now digging into her shoulder. His vocabulary included a range of grunts she'd learned to interpret with great accuracy. The one escaping him now was embarrassed frustration, but with a slightly higher pitch than usual—aggravated, embarrassed frustration, she decided, adding it to her catalogue.

2

Kate knew that Bill Burke considered her handheld "snaps" a nuisance, not to mention the fact that his first wife would never have gotten herself flat on her back in the middle of a public fairground. But Kate had never promised ladylike decorum and, in general, doubted he had any notion what he was getting into when he asked her to marry him. Thus his ever-expanding range of nonverbal expressions. The fact that she could amuse herself with that observation served to assure her that she was all right and not about to pass out. Then, finally catching her breath, she sat up.

Bill grunted irritation, a second grunt of impatience; his fingers were still dug into her shoulder. He reached around with his other arm to steady his own camera atop a tripod.

He had been using the open space of the fairgrounds to pose a picture that recreated a scene from the recent Ghost Dance Uprising. Nearby tents were being erected for a Wild West show. Both activities had attracted plenty of onlookers. Then several buffalo caused a commotion as they were unloaded from a train. No, she thought, not the buffalo. It was the Indian who'd caused the disturbance. Seeing the buffalo, one old Sioux warrior had jumped to the top of the fence and then thrown himself around the neck of the largest.

Kate closed her eyes, remembering that, and heard the bustle of Sioux Falls in the background—the noises of the coming age—the hum of the electric generator on the opposite side of the river, the clack-clack of a trolley crossing the bridge, a factory whistle. It might have given the impression of being settled, almost urbane, if she hadn't known that only four months earlier the Ghost Dance Uprising had ended with the death of three hundred Indians and twenty or more soldiers at nearby Wounded Knee Creek. Now soldiers, Indians, reporters, lawyers, photographers, and interested individuals from all over the country had converged for the trial of Plenty Horses—including this Wild West show complete with seventeen buffalo.

The idea of trying Plenty Horses struck her as odd every

time she paused long enough to think about it. He'd killed an army officer. No one disputed that fact. But why was that one killing deserving of formal justice and none of the hundreds of others? she wondered. Obviously, the young Indian had crossed some fine legal line beyond her comprehension, but not beyond interest. The trial had sparked national attention.

Her dog, a large, red mongrel named Homer, pushed his nose into her face and licked her chin. She opened her eyes and rubbed his neck in the spots she knew he liked while waiting for the last of her dizziness to pass. He whimpered little sounds of pleasure.

Then her husband's fingers dug into her shoulder again and his hand caught her under her arm. "Get up," he told her. "Get up. Soldiers are coming."

It wasn't "soldiers" who caused the tautness she recognized in his voice. It was one particular soldier, Colonel Elliot George, an angular man with thin lips, deep-set eyes, and a manner so commanding she'd known her husband to break into a sweat just talking about him.

The third time Bill said, "Come on, get up," she took his hand and pulled herself to her feet. Just in time. Suddenly the colonel and half a dozen soldiers rode up on horseback, swirling a new cloud of dust across the fairgrounds. They immediately took positions around the corral, their guns drawn.

Kate turned and half hunched her shoulders round her camera, hoping to protect it from some of the newly raised grit, and at the same time gave a quick glance in the direction of the broken fence wondering about the Indian. Several men were bent over his form as it lay just inside the corral. She hoped he wasn't hurt too badly. All around, the rest of the townsfolk were retreating from the fairgrounds as the colonel ordered the Indians "rounded up."

That got Bill. He stomped in the colonel's direction, one hand raised, as he shouted to the man on horseback, "Now how am I supposed to get my picture if you send my Indians packing?" Bill gestured at his camera and props.

The colonel turned his horse in a tight circle, seemingly taking in the whole situation for the first time. Then he barked back, "Take it outside town. This trial's enough trouble. We don't need more reasons to have Indians wandering the streets of Sioux Falls."

Any excuse to hassle Indians, Kate thought, but kept that thought to herself. She hadn't liked the colonel from the first time she met him. On that occasion, he'd barked back at Bill, "She won't last two weeks." He meant Kate, and she'd lasted all winter—stuck to it the whole time Bill and the colonel and his soldiers were out on the prairie chasing ghost dancers. Not that she'd gotten any respect for that fortitude. But she had gotten some fine photographs, which is what mattered to her.

Suddenly Kate's thirteen-year-old Indian serving girl, named Mary by the nuns at the reservation school, ran up and ducked behind Kate's skirts as if she thought that would hide her from the colonel and his soldiers. Kate handed her a box of photographic plates that needed to be kept out of the dirt and whispered, "He doesn't mean you."

The colonel returned to his soldiering, barking orders left and right. Bill swore quietly and then began packing his camera, other gear, and stage props. No photograph today. His Indian subjects were being marched away, three mounted soldiers at their rear. The soldiers he'd hired for his tableaux were now scrambling to mount their own horses and join in executing the colonel's orders. Playacting one moment, drawing their guns for real the next, Kate didn't pretend to understand things like that.

She folded her camera and was pulling her cape over her shoulders when the colonel swung around and halted his horse directly in front of her.

"I'll have that picture."

She was so startled, she wasn't sure what he meant. Then the realization of it spread over her like a blush. Why? she wondered. He'd never shown an interest in any other pictures she'd taken all the time she and Bill had traveled with him and his Seventh Cavalry documenting events being called the end of Indian wars. Why did he care now? It was just a silly picture of an Indian hugging a buffalo, or at least she expected that was the way he would think of it.

His horse, heaving short breaths, was standing so close, she felt its edgy energy and found it hard to raise her eyes from the animal to the man above. When she did, she caught an unmistakable look of practiced arrogance. Colonel George plainly enjoyed keeping the horse under him wide-eyed and quivering in nervous anticipation. He expected the same of her, a quick, quivering compliance. What's more, that's all he cared about, she realized. The picture meant nothing. He hadn't seen the way it had posed itself before her camera, the action coming straight at her such that she'd likely stopped even the flip of the Indian's hair. He just wanted to prove he could have it, the way he could march Indians in any direction he decided.

Kate tried feigned innocence. "What picture?"

"The one I hear you took of a fool Indian."

Kate swallowed. How long had it been since a Sioux warrior had seen a live buffalo? Ten years? Fifteen? To her way of thinking that image captured more of this time and place than all the pictures her husband had posed in the last eight months—another thought she didn't give voice. In fact, she didn't give voice to any thought. She was too awash in indignation to speak.

The colonel leaned over his saddle horn bringing his face closer to hers. "I don't think anyone needs a picture of a drunken Indian, do you?"

The Indian in her picture hadn't been drunk. She was sure of that. There'd been too much knowing awe in his face as he hung to that shaggy beast, like embracing an old friend. She gave another quick glance over her shoulder. Several men were still bent over him. At least he wasn't dead. A body would have simply been carried off by now. She was glad for that. She'd seen quite enough of dead Indians lately.

Then her husband nudged her from behind. "Give him the plate."

Of course, he wouldn't side with her. Bill's business

dealings with the colonel included paying him a percentage of every photograph he sold in exchange for the privilege of being allowed places off limits to other photographers. Given the interest this Ghost Dance Uprising had generated in the eastern press, that had proved a lucrative arrangement for both of them. Trouble was, the colonel could work out that same arrangement with most any photographer, and there were plenty of them around. She considered all she owed Bill. Not trouble.

"Give him the plate." Bill nudged her again.

"Yes, give me the plate," the colonel repeated. He'd straightened atop his horse and let a grin spread across his face. He thought he had her.

Why didn't he ask her to pluck out an eye and hand it over? No big thing. She had another eye. But he didn't have her. She knew what to do. Still she hesitated. If the colonel didn't know that her plateholder held two plates, Bill did. Working the mechanism at the back of her camera, she chanced it. She slid out the blank, not the picture, and offered it up.

The rest happened quickly. The colonel took the plate, broke it over his knee, and tossed it back into the dust in front of her. Typical, she thought. If there had been an image on that plate, it was ruined the moment it was removed from her plateholder, but the colonel was a man who didn't stop at ruin. He ground things into dust.

The Indian girl bent and immediately began picking up the shards. Her dog growled. The colonel turned his horse, paused as if he intended to say something else but didn't. He rode off instead.

She felt her husband relax. "You know better than to take pictures of Indians. Stick to your other pretties."

She made no reply. Picking up her skirts and calling her dog, she stomped off the fairgrounds.

Bill Burke watched Kate leave with such a mix of fearful fondness his stomach churned. She'd slipped the colonel the wrong plate. He'd watched and said nothing. He couldn't believe he'd allowed something like that. It was more than foolish; it was dangerous, but that's how much he wanted to please Kate, not that it helped. No matter what he did, it was never enough to please that woman. His silence hadn't pleased her, he knew. He supposed she had expected him to speak up for her, confront the colonel. She was that young.

He felt his pockets looking for his roll of liver pills. He hadn't experienced heart palpitations and stomach upset before marrying Kate.

Looking up again, he caught the way she kicked her skirts out of her way as she climbed aboard a trolley headed for town, her camera tucked under one arm, her cape flapping off her other shoulder, her dog and Indian girl at her heel. She was a short, small-boned bundle of energy topped with such a wild profusion of curly red hair, she somehow never looked entirely tidy. Didn't matter. Anyone meeting her was immediately captured by her bright green eyes and wry smile. He'd watched how people looked at her and then looked at him wondering how they'd ever gotten together. Sometimes he caught himself marveling at her laugh and his own good fortune. Then she'd do some fool thing like almost letting a bull buffalo trample her. If that fence had given away completely . . .

He found it was better not to think about things like that. Most of the time he felt like an oaf in her presence and tried not to think about that either. He was too old for her. Old and a bit too fleshy and a lot too dowdy. She was the daughter of his longest and best friend. He'd literally watched her grow up, develop. He knew damned well she'd have never married him if she hadn't needed to escape a bad situation. He'd been familiar and conveniently available, that's all.

He popped the pill and felt its bitterness sting his tongue before it slipped down his throat.

Somebody had to keep Kate's exuberance in bounds. She had no idea the nastiness of this Indian business, for example. He couldn't let her meddle in that, alienate the colonel. He might as well slit his own throat when it came to his business. Nobody was going to respect him for doing that, not even Kate. She, at least, understood the necessity of "livelihood." He just wished she didn't always force him to act more like a father than a husband.

Bill popped a second pill and crushed the empty package in his left hand. Since coming to Sioux Falls he'd been going through three packages a week of these nasty liver pills. When they were out on the prairie with the troops, Kate had mostly kept to herself. Then the only questions put to him were friendly gibes about "having his bride along." Nothing serious. One look at her and every man out there knew why he "wanted his bride along." But since they came to Sioux Falls, the colonel had begun to question why she was always taking pictures. He'd probably assumed she was amusing herself before. Now it bothered him. "Why doesn't she go shopping like other wives?" the colonel had complained recently.

Bill shook his head. His father had warned him about "expensive women." His father had meant the kind who needed baubles and fine clothes—the kind that had to "go shopping." They were the worst, he'd told Bill. "Suck the life right out of you," his father used to say. Bill tossed the pill wrapper into the dust. His father should have met Kate. A woman with a passion was worse than the expensive kind.

On the other side of town, Kate stepped off the trolley and straightened the cape over her shoulder. Then she started up Phillips Street on her way to Tony Amato's photography studio. To her annoyance, her dog kept up a chorus of guttural noises as they moved along. He alternated those with rumbled warning growls whenever someone on the boardwalk moved too close. She told him to shush.

She was already thinking how she would develop and print the plate of the Indian and the buffalo. The problem was always how to hold the subtle spectrum of grays. Contrast defined a photograph, but too much contrast resulted in sooty shadows and chalky high values.

Her dog was still growling. She tried shushing him again, but Homer wouldn't be quieted. She looked around, saw nothing, continued. She stopped, looked around, still saw nothing. The third time she repeated that sequence, she saw the objects of Homer's unease—two Indian women working their way up the street on the opposite side.

She stopped and gave a glance to her girl, Mary, a young reservation child who'd been to Catholic mission school but still dressed mostly native. She was staring at the ground. Kate looked right and left and back to the trolley stop. The women were obviously keeping Kate in sight. Had they been waiting for her, knowing she frequently came to Amato's studio?

Her dog growled lower, longer.

She didn't understand the sudden rush of fear that gripped her, except that there were rumors everywhere. Rumors of remote hostilities, secret ceremonies, other strange doings among the Indians that the army hadn't yet quelled despite their protestations to the opposite. The very air of Sioux Falls rustled with such tales as if belying the safety of a city with five railroads and a new four-story hotel advertising a telephone in every room. She shook herself. She wasn't going to be part of the local paranoia. The town was in no danger.

She'd been rubbing elbows with the "slayers of Custer" for some time now, and, in her opinion, there had never been any danger from them. This whole uprising wouldn't have amounted to anything, if not for the colonel. She'd watched him repeatedly turn a bit of excitement into a full-blown confrontation, the way he had at the fairgrounds. It made him a big man, kept his name in the newspapers. Of course, as her husband was quick to point out, no one was asking her opinion, and supposedly she didn't understand such things anyway. Indian troubles couldn't be allowed to fester, no matter how seemingly inconsequential, he'd told her.

At first, she'd considered the possibility that he might be right. She'd never been West before coming with him. But after months of watching the colonel and his men, her unease had grown and broadened as a slow widening arc of discomfort she couldn't quite name. There was something wrong with all of it. Very wrong.

Lies, she decided, slowly, quietly forming her own opinion as she took her pictures and hid them away. It was all lies. And lies based on lies that made it into the press and were believed. Needed justification for sending in the soldiers, she knew, but couldn't condone.

She was a photographer. She'd trained herself to see, and from what Kate had observed, ghost dancing had never posed a threat to anyone. It had been nothing but a strange religious hysteria—a messianic movement that had swept through the tribes offering hope to the hopeless. Diseased, defeated, hungry, and disillusioned by the government's failure to keep its promises, proud nomadic peoples newly confined to reservations began to believe they could dance their troubles away.

Believing in the visions of an Indian prophet who promised them a better future, they had gathered in open spaces and drummed and danced and fasted in hopes of hastening the coming of those "better days." Some fell into trances and reported talking with their ancestors who, like the prophet, promised them the buffalo would return. And the people believed and danced and danced and danced until the local white population, who equated all Indian dancing with "war dances," demanded that they stop, that the soldiers come and "subdue them." And the soldiers came and "subdued" the Indians—many of them right into their graves.

All that had happened because the Indians had danced until the "ghosts," their ancestors, came and gave them comfort. Nothing more. But it was dangerous to speak that truth, Kate knew. Almost no one did.

Homer growled again.

The Indian women now crossed the street, coming directly toward her. She put her hand on Homer's collar and commanded him to be still. His growl grew quieter but not silent.

The Indian women sidled around to Kate's side opposite her dog and approached carefully. Both were wrapped in government issue blankets draped over long calico skirts. Only the moccasins were traditional. The younger woman's hair flowed over her shoulders in what appeared to Kate an unruly mess. But her face was scrubbed, her cheeks highly colored, her eyes dark and quick. More of the older woman's face showed, her hair having been pulled back and braided. The skin around her mouth was lined.

But when they got to Kate, they didn't stop. They passed by and offered her a beckoning gesture so slight she almost missed it. Then they stepped off the boardwalk and disappeared into an alley.

Kate paused. She glanced around and thought twice about following them. Contrary to her husband's most common complaint of her, she did use caution sometimes.

She took Mary's shoulder. "Who are those women?"

The girl shrugged, said nothing.

Kate glanced up and down the street again. Then she stepped into the alley.

At first she didn't see the women. She continued down the passageway, past the back entrance to a barbershop, past a coal chute and several garbage bins. The light was dim from the closeness of the buildings. A cat started, hissed, and scurried under a back step. Kate grabbed Homer before he could give chase. Then hearing another noise, she whirled.

They emerged from shadow and, while still at arm's length, the older women pulled a leather pocket pouch from between the folds of her skirt, unhooked it from her belt, and extended it to Kate. She motioned a second time with a gesture unmistakably meaning that Kate was to take the bag. She did. It was about six inches square with decorative fringe and what Kate recognized as an intricate quillwork design. This was a rare piece. Most Indian women had given up the more difficult porcupine quillwork for stitching beads. She turned it over. The back included a tuft of hair. Kate hoped it wasn't human.

Kate had always been short and slight. These Sioux women of the plains towered over her. She looked up, catching the shy glance of the older woman as well as the wide brown eyes of the younger one. They nodded in unison, and the younger said, "It's beautiful?"

Kate nodded and again glanced at her hired girl hoping for some helpful hint. She got none.

"Woman-Who-Dreams makes it special for you," the younger woman said in hushed, almost reverential tones.

Kate let her eye follow the quilled pattern—geometric lines, bands, bright colors. Engaging and subtle, yet powerful in its ability to draw the eye deep and then deeper into the design. Kate's head swirled again. For an instant she wondered if she'd been more injured at the fairgrounds than she thought.

"Woman-Who-Dreams makes this special for you," the older woman repeated. "She knows you have Double-Woman in you."

"Double what?" Kate looked up.

The younger woman was now nodding vigorously while the older woman continued, "Those who know Double-Woman see her not only in the dreamtime but in the shadow the wind makes when it passes over the prairie. Grass and Double-Woman know things. Important things."

"You will come to our camp?" the younger woman now asked.

Kate shook her head. What was this about?

The older woman stepped closer. "You are invited. It is an honored invitation."

That explanation was hardly enough to answer Kate's mounting confusion.

The older woman fingered again between the folds of her skirt and pulled out another pocket bag. Without removing it from her belt, she indicated the finely worked design showing it to Kate. It was plainer but still eye-engaging. Now the younger woman did the same, pulling out a pouch that hung from her belt and showing it.

Kate thought she understood. They wanted her to come to their camp and buy handiwork from them. But she had no money. She said, "It's beautiful, but I'm afraid I can't." She offered the pouch back to them.

The older woman shook her head slowly. "It is made special for you, a gift."

13

Now Kate's confusion was complete. She couldn't imagine why these women would want to give her such an item. It was valuable and there were at least a dozen relic hunters in town willing to pay for it. What's more, it was common knowledge that the government gave these Indians barely enough to eat, less when there was trouble as now.

"It's beautiful," Kate repeated. "But you cannot mean to give it to me."

"Are you not the red-haired woman with the red dog?" the younger asked.

Kate nodded. She could hardly deny the description.

"Then it is for you, and so is the invitation. Day after tomorrow, the women who quill . . ." she paused and again pulled her bag forward for Kate to see. "The women who quill," she repeated, "wish you to be their guest on the south side of Indian camp."

Kate shook her head. Indian camp was a temporary cluster of teepees set up at the edge of town to accommodate the Indians who'd come to Sioux Falls for the trial, many of them witnesses who would be testifying, all of them guarded by the colonel's soldiers.

"Woman-Who-Dreams calls for you," the older woman intoned in a voice deeply mellow. "You must come."

"I can't," Kate said and again tried to return the quillwork. More than the colonel and his troops, a white woman, respectfully married, did not wander out of town and into an Indian camp by herself, not if she expected to come back with any decency left to her name. And since Kate already lived at the edge of what was considered respectable for a woman, she had even more reason to avoid this, or she just might find herself completely outside polite society. It was a delicate balance she'd chosen for herself.

"I'm sorry, but I can't," she repeated.

Homer growled.

The two women stepped back but still refused the quillwork.

The younger woman looked to the dog, then back to Kate. "You must come. If you cannot come day after tomorrow, then please, you must come soon after that. It is honored, important."

Homer growled once more, and the women fled.

Kate looked at the pocket bag again and shook her head. Then she glanced up and down the alley to see who might have minded this strange encounter, and caught Mary crossing herself.

2

The horse, a gray with four stocking feet, was tied to the only woody bush within miles. Richard Houston rode up, dismounted, and looked around for the owner. He expected to see some lanky farm kid out for an early morning rabbit shoot inasmuch as the gray was a harness horse that had been bridled and ridden bareback. Instead, he saw Kate Burke's red dog flush a prairie chicken from a thicket of tall grass and then circle, barking as the bird took to the air. He didn't see Kate.

That struck him as odd since the prairie stretched nearly treeless in every direction. He tied his horse to the same woody bush and then ran his hand down the neck of the gray. It was still a little sweaty, which meant it had to have been ridden within the hour. Daylight wasn't much older than that. Mrs. Burke was up early, he thought, now recognizing the horse as one of a pair of grays Bill Burke used to pull his equipment wagon when he was working in the field.

Richard had worked a project with Bill Burke two summers ago. They hadn't parted on exactly friendly terms, but they'd since found it useful to be civil. He'd met and exchanged pleasantries with Mrs. Burke on several occasions. Never when Bill wasn't around.

Richard lifted his tripod from the rifle holster of his saddle. He attached his camera to the stand, and then, holding the tripod by the legs, he slung the camera over his shoulder and started up the hill. Still he didn't see anyone.

Sioux Falls, South Dakota, lay in the curve that glacial ice and the Big Sioux River had cut into the prairie, leaving a half circle of bluffs to one side and an expanse of boggy bottomland to the other. It was the sloping backside of the biggest bluff that Richard climbed until, reaching the edge, he paused to take in the vista of the city below. Mostly inspiring to the civic boosters who'd hired him, it was a crisscross of railroad tracks and telegraph lines drawn from all directions and focused amid mills, livestock yards, and hotels. He framed the scene with his hands and then moved along the bluff trying different angles.

Kate's dog trotted over and, while wagging his tail, sniffed Richard's feet. Richard bent and rubbed him behind his ears saying, "How you doing ol' boy? Where's your mistress?" The dog shook himself and then wandered off again, parting the buffalo grass but detouring around any patches of blue or arrowfeather with thicker, tougher stems. A bee buzzed. A meadowlark sang.

Richard drew a deep breath. It had been a mild winter. Already the ground plums, pasqueflowers, and buttercups had begun to bud offering a hint of the color about to burst upon the prairie in broad swatches of early spring. Except for a bit of chill in the air, it was a near perfect morning for a lady to take an outing with her dog. Only Kate wasn't her dog.

He shrugged and shaded his eyes to check the rising sun. He preferred early morning light before the sun had a chance to wash the shadows from the landscape. But if he was going to catch that light, he needed to work quickly. With his camera shouldered, he moved on thinking to try the view from the highest point, where the bluff dropped into the river as a nearly sheer rock wall.

It was while climbing that last rise that he nearly stum-

17

bled over a box of five-by-seven photographic plates from Seeds of St. Louis, according to the label. Beside the box was a neatly folded pile of petticoats held down by a pair of lady's shoes.

Mrs. Burke's, he guessed.

Then he considered for a moment why that didn't surprise him. There was a restlessness about the woman that far outpaced Bill Burke. It was obvious in even the most casual encounter. In fact, encountering her was a little like running into a dust devil—all stirred space and grit. He chuckled to himself. Rolling around in the grass with a lover would certainly explain why he hadn't spotted her earlier. He should have considered that possibility, he told himself, as he stepped back intending to remove himself discreetly from the scene.

That's when he heard a cascade of rock rattle down the nearby cliff followed by a surprised whimper.

It took him a second to put some meaning to those sounds. Then with one continuous forward motion, he swung his camera off his shoulder and lay it down even as he strode forward and threw himself to the ground. He reached with both arms. Failing to grab Kate on his first try, he scooted forward, extending his body out over that empty expanse, and reached again for her where she lay sprawled across a narrow ledge a couple of feet down.

To his astonishment, her arm came around in a rearward swing that knocked him aside with enough motion to leave them both rocking. A breeze washed across his face, bringing with it a sense of the emptiness under him and his own precarious balance. He froze, swallowed, then scooted himself back six inches. A moment later he swung around and sat up, his legs tucked under him, his back turned to her. He thought he owed that much polite deference to her somewhat unclad condition.

"Are you all right?" he managed to say.

"I'd be better if you stayed clear of my light," came the answer.

"But you cried out."

"Only because I got surprised when a piece of the ledge broke off."

Only because the ledge broke off! he thought.

He was still trying to assess the situation. Chancing a glance over his shoulder, he noted that she was lying on her stomach along a rock shelf wearing a brown calico shirt-waist and matching skirt that she'd tied between her legs to make bloomers. Her camera rested on the rock ahead; her bare toes stubbed the rock behind.

But what was she doing?

"And if you think I should be embarrassed, I'm not. Nobody in her right mind would crawl out on this ledge in high-button shoes and three petticoats."

He didn't think anyone in her right mind would crawl out on that ledge at all. It wasn't two foot wide and narrowed toward her head. But then Kate had been something of a curiosity from the time she arrived in town. Richard had heard the talk—all the wonder that such a "pretty, little thing" had spent the whole winter with nothing but soldiers and wild Indians and Bill Burke. The part about Bill Burke was rarely spoken. He knew Bill wasn't all bad, even if he did regularly live up to his reputation of being a ne'er-do-well—ever chasing fast money and loose women. He'd heard folks wonder out loud how Kate had gotten "hooked up" with him.

Then he spotted the baby birds, and things began to make sense. The birds were young prairie falcons that were just beginning to sprout gray downy feathers over their pink backs. But they were huddled so deep in the shadow of the rock, it was hard to tell if there were three or four of them. He shook his head. "You'll never get any light on that nest." He gestured at the rock all around. "No matter the angle, there's always going to be something to shade that particular spot."

"Oh, but of course," Kate returned, her voice full of the exasperation of an older sister. "Even a bird knows better than to leave its babies in the sun. Besides, who wants a picture of ugly half-formed fledglings. I'm waiting for the adults to return."

He thought he ought to go. He didn't care for the tone of her voice. "They're not going to like your being that close," he told her and started to stand up. He had his own picture to take.

"Oh, I hope the birds don't like it one bit—wings wide, talons flexed, eyes focused, and nothing but sky behind."

He saw the picture she was hoping to get. It flashed to the back of his mind with such a dramatic, stark simplicity, he sat down again. He'd been reminded of the photographs in Kate's father's last exhibition. That show had changed the direction of Richard's life, determining for him that his interest in photography would be his life's work. Then he shook his head and thought better of Kate's immediate plans. Moments after she got that shot, the birds were likely to dig their talons into her flesh.

He glanced out over the vista again. He was losing the light for his own picture. "You might have to wait a long time," he said.

She raised a pocket volume of poetry to where he could see it. "I once read the entire *Midsummer Night's Dream* while waiting for a particular shot," she told him.

He shook his head again and thought about excusing himself. He had work to do, and she plainly didn't appreciate his presence. He could understand that. When he was trying to line up a picture, he preferred a singular concentration, but her situation was precarious, and he greatly admired her father's work.

He cleared his throat. "Your father was truly one of the pioneers of photography," he told her, and then haltingly tried to explain just how much her father's photographs had meant to him.

Her father, she thought, and the cascade of feelings that followed was enough to leave her speechless.

"It was your father's last show in New York that I really liked," Richard continued. "The one that won the Gutzmann-Heinz prize."

"You particularly liked that one?" she asked. "Did you go to many photographic exhibitions?"

"As often as I could."

"William Henry Jackson's show?" she asked. "How about Eadweard Muybridge's work on animal locomotion?"

"Oh, that one! Yes, yes, it was like I'd never seen a horse run before I saw those photographs. Imagine, all four feet off the ground at the same time. It took a camera to really see that."

"And curiosity. Muybridge had to want to know what a horse really looked like when it ran. That's just the thing. We don't see the things right around us, like horses running. My father packed up his things and went off every summer to take photographs in places faraway in the West or the Orient. My husband thinks he has to be where history is being made so his camera can record it. But mostly he recreates his pictures. Muybridge's genius was seeing what we'd all looked at and never seen. That's what photography does best if you let it."

There was a noticeable pause. Kate imagined she'd said too much. She had a way of running on about photography that left people with nothing to say in return, she knew. She didn't understand. To her even the tiniest technicalities of photography were more interesting than the weather or other pleasantries. But she'd obviously overdone it again. She half twisted around to look at him.

He'd been playing the gentleman, staring off into space rather than looking at her as they spoke. Now she caught him glancing over his shoulder. Their eyes met. There was an instant of curious engagement. Then Richard seemingly remembered she was a woman. He flashed her the wide smile that was practically his trademark as a known "ladies man." He said, "I heard Muybridge did it because of a bet."

She wanted to throw a rock at him. They'd been discussing fine photography, a thing that meant almost more to her than life. She'd even thought there had been some hope of a serious conversation on the subject, and now he'd reduced all that to a smile and a bit of banter concerning Muybridge's alleged bet.

"We don't bet on what we don't care about," she returned.

He paused again, his smile slipped, and then slowly he nodded. "You're right."

She was getting a nasty kink in her neck from twisting around enough to watch him over her shoulder. She wished he'd go away. He was a man who too obviously took care of himself—clean-shaven, hair fashionably trimmed. He wore clothes a cut above the common and wore them well. Neither too tall nor too short. Neither too broad nor too narrow of shoulder. It was hard to find much wrong with him except maybe the chin. Below the light brown hair and blue eyes there was enough chin to give his face a massive look. But on second thought, she decided he even wore that well. Any jaw less wide would have hardly held his smile. But she wasn't impressed.

He was the kind of man who knew he was handsome, and it was her experience that handsome men expected that every attention bestowed on a lady would be returned with a disproportionate amount of female flutter. She didn't have the patience for it and didn't intend to satisfy Richard on that point. She turned back to her birds and her poetry book without further comment.

He cleared his throat again. "You must have been skipping school to go to those exhibitions."

She nodded but didn't offer more. Skipping school had angered her mother. Now she wondered if her mother had been angry at the lack of lessons or the fact that her father preferred having his daughter on his arm when he received the accolades of his peers. Just the opposite, her grandmother, the former actress, had always been excited for her, wanting to know where she'd been, who she'd met, and all the details of what people were wearing and drinking and talking about. Of course, later she would throw all that up to Kate's mother, reminding her of what she'd missed. Somehow Kate had never figured out how to not play into their battles. The only thing that ever worked for her was escape into her father's photography studio—into the darkness

22

and the smell of acidic chemicals that could be contained in rows of neatly arranged glass bottles.

Not put off by her silence, Richard chuckled. "So was I. I left the Massachusetts Institute of Technology after only one year because my professors thought photography a mere novelty while I thought I'd been introduced to the whole world by looking at photographic exhibitions."

"Like train windows," Kate said, bringing her thoughts back to the moment.

"I beg your pardon?"

"I thought of the pictures as being like train windows. My father and I used to take the train in to New York from New Jersey, and I loved how the scenes outside the window flashed by—rows and rows of houses, factories, the river, children looking up from their play to see us go by. When we arrived, I walked down the halls of the exhibitions, passing the photographs, and got the same feeling. Only it was wider, as if it was . . ."

"The whole world," he finished for her. "I know what you mean."

"No, not the whole world," she said with enough quickness she caught herself. She was going to ramble on again if she wasn't careful. She fingered her camera.

"Go on," he said. "I'm intrigued."

She considered whether he might be humoring her. She hated the way some men encouraged a woman's talk only to then bandy her expressions like mere flirtatious trifles, but she supposed she owed him some explanation.

"Time. They were like little glimpses of time, little moments stolen from other people's lives. I told you, my father liked travel and the exotic, but I like details. I like photographs that look like photographs—the ones that can't be sketched because there is more than lines of composition, light, and shadow. I liked the work of photographers who weren't afraid to shoot for the moment."

She chanced another glance over her shoulder and was surprised to find that he'd dropped his eye-averting gentlemanly pretext and was openly studying her. She couldn't read his expression. At least his too wide smile was gone.

"I think I know what you mean," he said more softly. "Photographs that could never be taken again because even if the place was still there, the time had changed."

"Exactly, you do understand!" And a warmth came over her in spite of herself.

Richard hemmed. "Your father must have enjoyed having someone who shared his interest in photography."

That stopped her. Even her father's encouragement had been limited to a bemused indulgence of a daughter's whims. He had called her his "his sweet muse," "his inspiration," and then pined for a son who might have continued his work. She couldn't remember having shared her ideas with him. Like Bill, he called her pictures "pretties."

"What happened to his studio?" Richard asked.

She choked up. That wasn't like her. She prided herself in keeping her wits about her and never needing help from anyone. But her mother had sold her father's studio the same day as his funeral, hoping to keep Kate from an unwomanly occupation, and it had felt like losing him twice. She didn't know how to begin to explain that. So she said only, "Everything was auctioned off except for the camera he gave me." She indicated her Scoville view camera with a double swing back and cone bellows. It was a good camera with a fine German-made Goerz lens, but old. It was even missing one gear knob. Then, because she didn't want to talk about her father any more, she asked, "But what are you doing out here so early in the morning?"

Richard gestured outward. "The city fathers think that will be the next Chicago. They want a picture that will sell investors on the notion."

She glanced in the indicated direction with real reluctance. She only managed her perch by keeping her focus on what was solid, but she didn't want to let him know that. So forcing herself, she looked and saw the bend in the river, the town straddling it, and, just beyond that, a cluster of Indian tepees, a good-size camp of Sioux having come to town for the trial.

She knew the kind of photography he was doing. Her

husband referred to it as "local work." It didn't pay as well as working for the big national companies. Bill's photographs went to Edward Anthony, editor of *Anthony's Journal,* one of the most prolific and widely distributed publishers of stereographs and "views of America," a fact Bill liked to make known everywhere he went. Richard's pictures would appear in local brochures that sold for two to twenty-five cents. Tourists bought them to send home. Local boosters sent them other places. It was respectable work, the place a lot of photographers got their start, but hardly the same thing. Besides from what she saw, he had a problem.

"I doubt your employers are going to want tepees in their picture." Actually she more than doubted it. The city fathers of Sioux Falls had been all but denying the recent Indian troubles, all the Ghost Dance Uprising business, shrugging it off now as if it had been nothing. Yet last fall they were the ones who'd screamed for protection. Now that things were calm, they complained about the soldiers almost as much as the Indians. They were that sensitive about their city appearing too wild and too western.

"I know, I'll have to paint them out," Richard told her.

"Ever been to Indian camp?" she asked.

He shook his head. "Mostly I do landscapes. But I understand you and Bill spent all winter . . ."

"With the army," she finished for him. "We were always with the army. I imagine it must be quite different to go into an Indian camp without soldiers along."

He shrugged. "I suppose so."

"Would you go if you were invited?" she asked. A curiosity concerning her strange invitation had been gnawing at her.

"To Indian camp?"

"Yes."

"I don't know. Is there some importance to this question?"

"Only that a man can decide things like that rather casually, don't you think? If you wanted to go to Indian camp . . ."

Suddenly another piece of the ledge broke off. Nothing

serious, just a bit of the edge crumbling away and noisily rattling downward. But it scared her. She sucked air audibly and stubbed her feet tighter against the rock behind. Her fingers felt for something solid.

In the midst of that excitement, she realized Richard had flipped over and grabbed her bare ankle. That startled her more than the falling rock. No man had ever put his hand on her that way. She couldn't even remember Bill showing any particular interest in her ankles. He was a fanny man, and besides, the only time her and Bill's love turned to passion was when they quarreled. She suspected that was why they quarreled as often as they did. It was in the vain hope of igniting some lasting spark.

Richard's grip was something else. Beyond spark, it was enough to make a woman forget herself. Kate felt like laughing, maybe a bit hysterically. She, who'd always prided herself on the fact that she never had any use for handsome or interesting men, was feeling a surge of the hots. There was really no more polite way to describe the sensation. But then drawing a second breath, she recovered her sense of balance. She was no sentimental silly. She knew what she wanted, which was to take fine photographs, not entertain some "too handsome" man who was likely to forget her as quickly as light moved across a landscape, giving its glow to new features practically moment by moment.

"I'm fine now," she told him. "You can let go."

Richard had already thought about letting go. His hand simply wouldn't loosen its grip even though the awkwardness of the situation had come to him full force. He couldn't think of another time or place when he'd found himself holding a woman's ankle. His own mother considered legs so sacred, she draped her parlor tables to the floor in layers of ruffles to keep their wooden "limbs" from suggesting anything untoward. But he couldn't let go. He wondered if she had any notion how immobile he was. He was so lost in her, the very thought of her danger shivered his stiffened arm.

He looked up and away hoping to break the spell. His own situation was more than awkward, it was painful. There was a rock poking him under one rib, and he'd skinned his arm reaching for her. That scrape was beginning to burn. He was still holding her ankle when she half turned again and said, "I know what I'm doing."

He was sure she did. It was the advisability of what she was doing that puzzled him. No, it was more than that. This woman with her wide forehead, green eyes, and perpetually pink cheeks was an enigma—a beauty for whom flirting should have become second nature, but who obviously preferred the direct over the coy. This wasn't the first time he'd experienced her bluntness.

So he returned some of it. Pressing her ankle tighter, he said, "Maybe I know what I'm doing as well. A gentleman . . ."

She groaned. "Oh, please don't tell me what a gentleman will do and not do. I refuse to resolve the chaos of life into the sweet nothings of gentrified conformity. If I can't think how to make life more of an adventure than that, I hope I fall off a cliff."

The bite in her words startled him. He brought his gaze to hers and connected with an anger that further confused, an anger deeper than this situation—deep enough that his eyes slid away unable to take it in. He saw, instead, that she'd tied a kerchief round her head in an old-fashioned style, like a milkmaid or a farmer's wife on her way to the field. But the hair, redder than the dog, was too full to be contained. It frizzed around her forehead and fell in long strands along her neck and back. Worse, he noted that her makeshift bloomers rippled revealingly over the roundness of her rear. That only served to stir him more. He swallowed hard and couldn't think of what to say. He still couldn't let go.

Then out of the corner of his eye he spotted the adult falcons swooping down at what might have been a hundred miles an hour. She saw them, too. She grabbed the camera and rolled over on her side.

He nearly lost his grip both because she squirmed suddenly and because he was startled when another shower of rock sounded down the cliff, having been knocked loose by her foot. He scraped his other elbow and felt the rock under his rib poke deep and hard enough to make his breathing shallow as he struggled to hang on. Despite all that, he noted with some wonder how deftly her hands worked the camera.

Taking handheld pictures was not generally considered an easy or beginner's branch of photography. You had to make too many technical decisions all at once, and with a sinking feeling, he thought she wasn't going to get this picture. The birds were coming too fast. Then just when he'd despaired of her getting anything more than a blur, the birds fanned their feathers, both wings and tail, and hung almost motionless for a moment.

Now! he thought.

Still she didn't click the shutter.

He sucked air and held it. He heard the river below and the sound of a distant train, but other than that, it was as if the whole world were holding its breath.

Now! he thought again almost sick with tension. What was she waiting for? The time, the chill, the risk of hanging off this cliff was all going to be for naught if she didn't do something.

Then the breeze coming up the face of the rock lifted the birds ever so slightly and drifted them apart. For one brief instant they hung in perfect parallel before folding their wings and diving straight down, screaming as they streaked past. Yet he'd become so attuned to listening for her shutter, that was the loudest sound he heard. She'd gotten the picture!

Just like that, it was all over—except that her dog was now standing at the edge of the cliff barking at the screaming birds as if he thought he was the sole reason for their retreat.

Richard extended his free hand. Kate took it and pulled herself to the top of the bluff. She untied the bottom of her skirt and patted her dog. Then reaching up to pull the kerchief from her head, she gave her hair a shake and said, "I suppose I should thank you."

He thought so but shrugged modestly as if a scraped arm, a bruised rib, and his own morning's work wasted were nothing.

But then she didn't offer any thanks. She started talking excitedly about the picture. "Did you see it? They were almost wing tip to wing tip."

He nodded. He'd seen it.

She was brushing the dirt from her sleeves now. That combined with the shake she'd given her hair filled the air with such a scent of her, it nearly took his breath away.

"There's always a moment—a perfect moment. You just have to wait for it."

"Always?" he questioned.

She looked up and this time caught his gaze. In that instant, it was as if their very beings were hung in suspension like birds, wing tip to wing tip in an updraft. "Always," she repeated, not much above a whisper.

He knew then that she'd felt something. He could see it in her face, which was flushed with excitement, and he didn't think it was just from the birds. Her eyes were too bright, her cheeks too colored.

He waited for her to say something, anything that might give him hope.

"Spontaneous photography is all a matter of timing," she said with more strength of voice.

That wasn't what he wanted to hear. He had an urge to reach out and touch her again, if only to brush her cheek ever so lightly.

"Carefully posed pictures, of the sort my husband takes, are going to be a thing of the past. The future belongs to the quick, to the photographer who can compose in the moment," she went on.

Photography! he thought. This was about more than photography. Didn't she know she was losing the feeling of this moment?

And there was something else. He was used to a polite deference from women even if it was feigned. In the thrill of having caught the picture of the birds, she'd completely forgotten herself. He saw in her excited self-assurance that she considered him superfluous, a distraction, maybe even a nuisance.

That hit him harder than the rock that had bruised his rib. He bent and slapped the dust from his own clothes as he wondered what it would take to impress this woman. A whole hell of a lot, he suspected. It angered him that he even cared. She was Bill Burke's wife.

He picked up his camera and shouldered it. "I hope you'll let me see the picture when you've got it printed." It was the polite thing to say.

"Oh, yes, of course," she said, also the polite thing to say.

Then with the briefest of good-byes, she tucked her petticoats under her arm and was off, her skirt sweeping across the grass as she wove her way to the horses. Her dog followed, stopping once to snap at a fly. Neither of them looked back.

When she was gone, Richard shook his head wondering at the mix of his feelings. He wasn't used to being ignored by a woman. In fact, he couldn't remember the last time he'd failed to turn the head of a member of the fairer sex once he put his mind to it.

He sat and swung his legs off the cliff. He thought about climbing out on that ledge if only to prove he could do it. But the river swirled below, and the birds circled above, and his own head took a whirl. He tottered with indecision. Then he quickly drew back, telling himself she was really a lot shorter, smaller.

3

Her petticoats tucked under her arm, Kate rode astride down the back of the bluff and around the bend in the river. Her dog ran ahead of the horse. She trusted he would bark if he saw anyone, allowing her time to swing her leg over and assume a proper sidesaddle position. Sidesaddle was particularly difficult riding bareback with a camera and box of slides. She could do it but didn't see the need if no one was looking.

At the edge of the river, she slid off the horse, and setting down the box and camera, she pulled her petticoats on— the black sateen with wide flounce, then the striped gingham with flounce bottom and finished ruffle, then under that the basic black underskirt finished with ruching round the bottom. She worked the fastenings and pulled the drawstrings. Then she shook her skirts and jumped up and down a few times to let all the ruffles fall into place. In her opinion, layers and layers of petticoats, corset covers, and sashes all tucked and tied required far more dexterity than handling a camera on a ledge. She never managed them without feeling a flush of the same frustration she had experienced as a child every morning before school when

31

she wanted to get going and couldn't because there were too many details to her dress—the evenness of braids, the straightness of stockings.

When she felt she was reasonably presentable, she picked up her camera and box of plates and walked the horse the last quarter mile. Her destination was a makeshift corral made of fresh-cut poles that a pair of enterprising young brothers had put up next to the river to accommodate the horses of the extraordinary number of visitors who'd come to town for the trial—the town stables being already filled to overflowing. Arriving, she found the brother currently on duty was the younger, a fair-haired, broad-shouldered sixteen-year-old who liked to say the words *lady photographer*.

Seeing her, he pulled his hat off and drawled, "Well, if it isn't our lady photographer. Where have you been so early this morning?"

"Out taking pictures," she said. His brother had been on duty when she picked up the horse. The brother was older, taller, more laconic. She preferred him.

"Taking pictures of what?" this brother asked.

"Birds," she answered.

"Birds?" Then he shook his head. "Didn't know they could be made to stand still long enough for a portrait unless, of course, they was stuffed." He chuckled.

She handed him the reins of her horse without comment.

He wouldn't let it go. "Bird portraits. Who buys bird portraits from a lady photographer?" Then he stood there, holding the horse, waiting for an answer.

It was the wrong question, phrased so that any answer sounded trivial. "Other ladies," she said, being deliberately coy, not that this fellow caught on. He was too young and full of himself. He led her horse away mumbling about "birds" and a "lady photographer."

She called her dog and continued toward the clearing a little farther up river where Bill had parked the "tourist wagon" they called home when they were working in the field. It was a combination portable studio and sleeping quarters built onto the bed of a wagon that could be expanded with a tent that rolled off the back to provide additional living space. It was considered the latest in travel convenience, short of having a maid in starched uniform and a private Pullman car.

She came upon the horses first, two of them tied in the shade of a cottonwood tree. From the way they stood with their heads down, resting one foot as they slowly switched flies, she guessed they'd been there for some time. She recognized them as military mounts, more specifically as belonging to Colonel George and his aide.

She drew a deep breath. It was a practiced bit of breathing. As a child, she'd paused and drawn breath like this every time before entering her own house, unsure of what she might find there. Before she was born, her mother and grandmother had engaged each other in jealous acrimony. From the time she first remembered, their angry dance had been so all-consuming, it threatened to engulf all who came near. As a result, she never, never knew what level of drunken fever she might find inside her own house and so always paused to breathe and prepare herself for the fray. It struck her as strange that she'd escaped that only to find herself having to similarly steel herself before plunging into her husband's world.

Out on the prairie last winter, with not much else to do, Bill and the colonel had been drinking buddies, sitting around the wagon for hours back-slapping and pouring. Lately, to her relief, the colonel hadn't come around as often. She supposed, now in town, he had other places to go, other people to see.

She checked again the sash at her waist and the way the ruffles of her skirt lay. Then, sending Homer off to amuse himself, she crossed the open ground. The first thing she heard was Bill's laughing loudness. Then, lifting the tent flap, she saw him dressed in a silk brocade dressing coat, the long, full sleeves flapping as he gestured. The colonel and his aide followed that movement with mouths slightly open. Her husband could tell a story, except in pictures. When it came to photography, Bill was mostly old school, posing his pictures according to textbook rules of aesthetics. The result was invariably wooden stock shots. It was all she could do to add a little interest in the printmaking.

She paused in the entrance, watching Bill as he continued speaking. She recognized the rituals of male companionship—the swelled chest, the loud voice, the gesture that brushed the other man's shoulder. In that pause she also caught the drift of the conversation. Bill was talking about the upcoming trial of the Indian Plenty Horses and his expected public hanging. What else? That was the reason they'd all come to this town: Bill, Kate, these army officers, Richard Houston.

Again, considering the amount of killing that had gone on lately, she wasn't sure why one young Indian having shot an army officer merited all the attention of a trial. More because he'd shot the officer while he was supposedly talking peace with the Indians, his "crime" was being called heinous in newspapers as far away as New York. She wasn't sure things were quite that clear-cut. But, as usual, she kept her opinion to herself. Her ideas on must subjects tended to annoy Bill, and she'd managed to frustrate Richard going on and on about photography this morning, she knew.

She set her camera and plate box down.

That drew the men's attention. Her husband suddenly let his arm fall to the top of the fold-down table where he was seated. The coffee mugs and plate of fresh biscuits jumped.

She started.

"Where have you been? That girl's worthless, left alone."

Kate gave a glance to Mary, a shy, slight child with a round face and long black hair. At the moment, she was standing so far behind the stove she could barely reach the sizzling bacon with a fully outstretched arm and long-handled spatula. Like many of the Indians, she was terrified of Colonel George, a fact Bill didn't appreciate.

He continued, "She can't find the preserves, and chewing on biscuits without something sweet is like looking on the River Jordan and not being baptized." His voice boomed. When he was entertaining, he had no quiet tones. "No one looks on the River Jordan and stays dry," he explained in an aside to the colonel's aide. "You ever been there?"

The aide, a fair young soldier, already beginning to bald, shook his head.

Her husband smiled broadly. He enjoyed making it known that he had traveled.

The colonel stood and offered Kate a gentlemanly bow. That movement caused the Indian girl to drop the spatula with a clatter. Kate acknowledged him with a wave of her hand, implying that such formalities were silly—especially in these tight quarters. In fact, he'd never troubled himself that way before. Did he think a little politeness would make up for yesterday?

To her husband Kate answered, "There's jelly in the storage boxes. I'll get it."

As she brushed by the colonel, he observed, "You're out early this morning."

"I walk the dog," she answered.

"For more than three hours?" he asked, and gave a glance to her husband.

Bill was busy telling the aide about the River Jordan and his trip there.

She replied, "He's a big dog. He requires some exercise."

The colonel raised an eyebrow and let his gaze wander over her. It was a look not leering but not completely respectful of a lady either. Kate stiffened, wondering at his interest, not that he hadn't looked at her before with some of the same leer. It was just that those looks had accompanied his elbowing Bill, not his questioning her.

She pushed past him and, pulling her skirts together, climbed into the wagon. She opened a storage drawer under the sleeping platform and pulled out a jar of plum jelly. She spooned some into a serving bowl.

Her husband had returned to talk of the upcoming trial. "The higher you hang them, the better the example," he was telling the colonel with enough voice that he sounded quite the authority. "Six stairs high, at least," he concluded with a flourish of his arm. "And in costume, a feather coming up the back of his head. That way no one will ever mistake who it is a-dangling from that rope."

The colonel nodded.

His aide mimicked that motion.

Kate paused. The casualness of such talk never failed to startle her. She didn't know what she'd expected when she followed Bill to this western prairie to photograph the "last great Indian uprising," but she hadn't seen anything glorious or heroic. Soldiers doing a job, Indians with no place to run, and this callused casualness in everything from the talk to the killing.

She stepped down and set the bowl of jelly on the table.

"And what do you think about hangings?" the colonel asked her.

"Me?" Kate voiced, wondering if her thoughts had been transparent. Deep down, she wanted to believe that there were always possibilities—hope. But no one believed the outcome of this trial was in question.

"Yes," the colonel continued. "How about an Indian hanging on a gallows at least six stairs high? Think eastern ladies will want to buy such a photograph for their parlor picture books?" he asked, nodding towards her husband.

Kate, too, gave a glance to Bill. His face had settled into a scowl; his eyes darted between her and the colonel. She knew the look. He was nervous about what she might answer. She embarrassed him sometimes with her lack of appropriately wifely platitudes, "Oh, I don't know," or "You better ask my husband about that," or "I just don't worry about such things, I'm afraid." At least Bill wasn't given to underestimating her as the colonel had, especially if he thought his question was some test of her squeamishness. The only thing that made Kate squirm was an overstuffed parlor—pillows on every sofa, layers of lace on every window. Like petticoats, all those layers only served to entangle and complicate. She thought a dose of reality, such as a picture of a hanging, might improve such furnishings.

She shrugged. "I imagine such a photograph might be quite a conversation piece."

At that, the colonel let loose a laugh, belly-deep, then just as suddenly he stifled his mirth and took another sip of his whiskey-fortified coffee. Unlike her husband, Kate could be amusingly unexpected at times. How was it that until yesterday he'd missed the danger of her?

Still he could respect a good bit of witticism. He raised his cup to her and echoed, "Quite a conversation piece, indeed."

At that, her husband relaxed noticeably. She acknowledged his gesture with a nod and then went to the stove where she took over from the Indian girl who kept dropping things, the spatula, the spoon, the pan lid, with enough clatter to make them all jump and turn in her direction.

He watched as Kate shoved a bucket at the girl and told her to get some water, obviously thinking to get her out of the way and remove her clattering annoyance. It didn't work. The girl stood as if paralyzed, except that her eyes darted left and right. Then, rather than pass by the men, she slid off the back of the wagon and rolled under one side of the tent, dragging the water bucket after her.

The colonel let loose a second laugh, belly-deep, and got a look from Kate. He didn't care. He enjoyed scared Indians. This one was skinny and not quite woman enough to be really interesting except for the level of her terror. It especially amused him to think he could frighten someone who'd literally encircled herself in the stars, birds, and other symbols of ghost dancing. They were painted all around the neck and waist of the girl's shirt and were supposed to be magical and protect the wearer from soldiers and their bullets. But as if the girl couldn't make up her mind what to believe, she'd also hung a Christian cross round her neck.

All this ghost dancing nonsense was crazy like that. It had started farther west, out near California, with an Indian named Wovoka, who claimed he'd had a vision. He began telling Indians everywhere that if they danced this new ghost dance, all their dead would return along with the buffalo and the Messiah. He meant Jesus. The Messiah was supposed take the white people away and give the land back to the Indian, because it was the white people who killed Jesus like they were killing the Indian. A silly harmless hallucination, he supposed, until it spread from reservation to reservation until men, women, and children by the hundreds were dancing, dancing, sometimes for days, their frenzy becoming wilder and wilder. Not that he'd ever actually seen any ghost dancing. Somehow that had always eluded him and his soldiers.

It didn't matter. He'd put an end to all that craziness anyway. He'd ended Indian trouble once and for all. That's what the eastern newspapers said. They called him "the man who had ended two hundred years of Indian wars in America." He liked the sound of that. He wasn't sure Kate Burke agreed, and he wasn't sure why he cared except that after the incident yesterday, he'd begun to be haunted by her. She knew too much. Bill Burke knew too much, but he could be handled. But he wasn't sure he trusted Kate to keep her opinions to herself.

He watched as she poured fresh coffee all around. Unlike the Indian girl, she was woman enough to be of interest. Quite a bit of interest. His own spanned more than one level.

He suspected she was deep. The fact that she was smarter and all around too much woman for Bill Burke was obvious, too obvious. That worried him because it meant he couldn't count on her husband to keep her in her place.

It had been a mistake to have her along. Women didn't belong in the field. He'd tried to discourage Bill from bringing her. Bill had insisted, and he'd thought it was because the old boy couldn't bear to be separated from his new young bride. He looked around. Bill's wagon didn't strike him as a cozy little love nest.

In fact, he couldn't imagine why a woman of proper upbringing would choose to live as Kate did. There was a thin mattress that rolled out over a sleeping platform inside the wagon. Next to that was a bench with a chamber pot and next to that the stove, its chimney poking through the wagon's rounded tin-topped wooden roof. A canvas extension gave shelter to the foldout table and chairs. It could also be arranged to become a photography studio complete with draped backdrop, he knew. Either way, nothing about it was glamorous. He imagined Kate had to miss the indoor plumbing and the gas, now electric, lights she must have grown up with. His own wife never left Boston and the damask-draped home she'd inherited.

Bill Burke was repeating some story about photographing Sitting Bull before he went to England with Buffalo Bill's Wild West Show. That old Indian had become famous over in Europe, where Indians were a novelty not a nuisance. Then the colonel reminded himself of how he'd taken care of Sitting Bull the same way he'd taken care of ghost dancing—with bullets. The old chief's body had been riddled with them before he and his soldiers finished. Now they'd see who got to be the more famous in the end. He took out his pocket flask.

Without interrupting his story, Bill slid his cup over, expecting the colonel to add a shot.

He did, noting with some pleasure Kate's look of disapproval. But she didn't say anything. The colonel and Bill went back a few years. He knew Bill's first wife would have said something. Bill's first wife had been scrappy and loud until pneumonia got her. Why was it that Kate's sullen silence bothered him more?

He watched her return the coffeepot to the stove and wipe her hands down the sides of her skirt.

Maybe it was the fact that she didn't much like soldiers or him, he knew. He wished he knew what else she didn't like. With most men, it didn't much matter what they liked or didn't like. Women were different. Women couldn't think past their passions. An uncontrolled, brooding woman who knew too much in a town where too many questions were being asked was not a situation to be tolerated. In short, he had good reason to keep his eye on Mrs. Burke and not because of her better womanly attributes. She'd plainly become something of a loose end.

He turned back to her husband with a new idea. "If we dismantled that house where Sitting Bull was killed, think some Wild West show would buy it?"

Bill shrugged, then after a moment's thought nodded encouragement. "Of course, of course," he said. "Why didn't I think of that?"

* * *

Kate listened as the men seriously discussed how to sell the two-room frame house where Sitting Bull died—was killed by the colonel's soldiers. They discussed how to dismantle it, where to ship it, whether they might add a few bullet holes to the front door for effect. From what she'd seen, this war didn't need any added effect. The images were so vivid as to haunt her.

Neither Bill nor the colonel had allowed her near any battlefield. Being a woman, she needed to be protected from "too much reality," they'd told her. So she'd stayed with the wagon developing and printing the plates Bill brought back, including pictures of contorted, frozen bodies, sometimes piles of them—photographs so graphic, her husband had her touch them up before he sent them East because they clearly weren't "parlor pictures." But she'd not only seen them, she'd watched them emerge like ghosts from her developing baths.

All the bodies in the pictures were Indian, many women and children, and some had been photographed miles from any battle site—a fact she found inexplicable unless the Indians had been hunted down by the soldiers. But when she'd asked about it, Bill had accused her of womanliness, suggesting that a man wouldn't raise such questions. Men understood war. She supposed that was true if some kind of military mind-set was assumed. As near as she could tell, that was the purpose of a soldier's rigid discipline. It supplanted the need to know, the child's constant question, "Why?" But not just soldiers. There were many ways to step outside oneself, embracing ignorance, when knowing was too painful. She'd watched her father practice ignorance all the years she knew him, never once acknowledging the tensions that had their whole family tied in a Gordian knot.

The colonel was now ordering his aide to wire William Cody and offer him Sitting Bull's death site as an "authentic stage prop." She had no doubt it would create interest.

The Indian girl returned with the water. She hesitated at the entrance and then, drawing herself up tight, she slid along the far side of the tent as she passed by the men who were now back to discussing the trial.

40

Kate directed the girl to some water on the stove to warm for washing dishes.

The colonel finished his coffee, pocketed his whiskey flask, and exchanged a last bit of banter with Bill. Then he stood to leave.

"Fine fixin's. Good coffee," he said, addressing Kate. "But I'll be taking that Indian girl with me."

The girl began to quiver all over.

Kate stepped in front of her. "Why?"

"I'm putting her under arrest."

"What for?"

From behind the colonel, Bill was signaling for her to shut up and get out of the way.

"She's wearing a ghost shirt," the colonel explained. "You know anything having to do with ghost dancing is strictly illegal."

Kate shot a glance over her shoulder.

All she could see was the girl's eyes. They were so wide, they almost filled her face, and Kate wondered how the colonel could see anything but those eyes. Yet when she managed to shift her gaze, she saw it was true. The girl's rough cotton, loose-fitting blouse was painted blue at the neck and decorated with a row of painted moons, stars, and birds around the waist. Kate swallowed. "She's such a poor child, I'm sure it's because she hasn't anything else to wear."

The colonel smiled broadly. "She pulled it on when she saw me. They think those shirts give them some kind of protection."

He chuckled and turned to Bill. "The braves think they're bulletproof. Did I tell you about the time one old Hunkpapa wearing one of those shirts strutted past my soldiers? He taunted them. He dared them to fire at him. Then he accidentally shot himself in the arm mounting his own horse."

Kate whispered to the girl, "Take it off."

She shed the shirt and gave it to Kate crossing her arms over her naked budding breasts.

When the colonel turned his attention back to them, Kate

41

handed him the shirt. "I'm sure she won't wear one again. She's just a child."

The colonel rolled the shirt and tucked it under his arm. A relic hunter would pay handsomely for it, Kate knew.

The colonel shrugged. "I'll let her go this time, but I was right, Mrs. Burke. You *are* fond of Indians. Mind it doesn't get you in trouble. Mind you and your dog don't wander too far." He reached over and touched her curls. "Indians love red hair."

Kate felt her scalp crawl and not because she was afraid of Indians. Never once in all those months when they were chasing renegade bands had she ever felt afraid of Indians. But she had felt fear.

4

Later that day, Richard Houston entered the Queen City Photography Studio and slid several plateholders of exposed plates across the counter. The proprietor, Tony Amato, held up a hand indicating he would get to Richard in a moment. Meanwhile he continued shouting invective-punctuated instructions about the handling of albumin print paper. It had a short shelf life, something Tony was clearly determined his newest, now red-faced, assistant was not going to forget.

Lately, almost every time Richard came in, Tony had been shouting at yet another new assistant. He'd taken over some warehouse space in back and had a crew working early morning until late at night trying to keep up with the sudden swell of demand from all the photographers in town for the trial. Richard listened with detached amusement, thinking that when this was all over, Tony was going to discover he'd trained his competition. That was more or less how they'd all gotten their start in this business. Except Kate Burke. She'd learned working at her father's side. He envied her that. He wished he'd had a chance to train with someone even half so good.

43

Tony finished with his assistant and turned back to Richard with a broad smile that lifted the corners of his bushy black mustache—an obvious pride, having been waxed and curled. But he still wasn't ready to get down to business. He slapped the counter in front of Richard and exclaimed, "What terrible luck! You just missed Emmaline and Georgalene."

Tony was referring to the grown but unmarried nieces he'd raised since they were babies—a history everyone who came to the shop knew sooner rather than later. So far as Richard knew, Tony started every conversation with a reference to Emmaline and Georgalene. While Tony went on about them, Richard mused on the fact that his luck was probably just fine if he'd missed the pair. One was about as broad as a moose. The other had a mustache that nearly rivaled her uncle's.

Tony continued, "They're off shopping. I'll be in the poorhouse by nightfall. Mark my words."

Richard doubted that. Tony had the only commercial photography studio in Sioux Falls, and he was making a killing. His prices were just short of outrageous. Like Richard, most of the visiting photographers had studio wagons that could be converted into dark labs by dropping light curtains over the ends, but the working conditions were cramped and nuisance enough to be practical only in the field. Tony had priced himself so he was dear and yet just cheap enough that most of the visiting photographers weren't going to resort to that inconvenience. He was a man who understood opportunity. But his face had taken such a serious set, one might have thought he was facing complete disaster.

"This trial had better last a year," he moaned.

It wasn't expected to last the week, Richard knew.

"This trial better last a year and a half if my nieces are off shopping," Tony went on. "Oh, but look who I'm talking to. What would you know about poverty?"

Quite a lot, Richard thought. Being the only son of an East Coast manufacturing mogul didn't mean much if your allowance had been cut off. Richard's father still labored

under the illusion that photography was his son's hobby—
one he was determined not to support.

Tony turned and ordered his new assistant to take care of
something in the back. Then he beckoned Richard over to
the end of the counter, where he reached under and pulled
out a couple of Stanhopes. He slid them over to Richard.

"Seen these?" he asked with a wink.

Besides the studio, Tony owned a truly amazing collection of Stanhopes, pornographic photographs attached to
tiny lenses and then affixed to a key ring or letter opener or
other small object. They'd been the rage eight or ten years
ago but were now considered out of favor. The two he'd slid
across the counter were cuff links.

Richard lifted them and saw two poses of the same nude.
In the first she was bent at the waist facing the camera, her
hand raised as if to wave. In the second she was bent at the
waist, broadside to the camera, looking coyly over her
shoulder. The poses were uninspired, and the woman
herself was not so much beautiful as voluptuous, the epitome of the hourglass figure, full both top and bottom, but
given to some sag. She was not particularly young. And
there was something more about the photographs that
bothered him. He turned them into better light and studied
them a moment. They were lit from beneath, he realized,
probably with footlights as on a stage. Pictures lit from
below never appeared natural, although the lighting in this
case had given a certain definition to the appropriate
curves, he had to admit.

Tony misinterpreted that interest. He pulled out half a
dozen more Stanhopes and slid them across to Richard.
Then he leaned over the counter and said, "But there's not
one here whose beauty can match my Emmaline and my
Georgalene. What's more, they're good girls, churchgoing
every week."

Richard never knew how to answer that kind of comment. From the moment his voice began to deepen, he'd
endured an almost continual parade of young women whose
virtues had been enumerated by anxious mothers, fathers,
aunts. Richard wasn't bad looking, he knew, and he could

be charming when the occasion called for it, but he also knew those qualities weren't the main consideration. All his life he'd been measured by one thing, his father's wealth. In part he liked photography because his father's money couldn't compose a picture or judge the light. He was on his own for that.

Richard muttered something vaguely complimentary about Tony's nieces and slid the Stanhopes back. Then, not waiting to be asked, he gave instructions for the plates—nothing special, just orders to develop them and print a sample to be sold locally. It was virtually the same work that Tony was doing for everyone in town for the trial. Developed plates were more stable for shipping East to the big photographic houses that made multiple prints under near-factory conditions that would get a more national distribution, but everyone sold prints locally, as well. Photography was becoming big business. One national house advertised two hundred photographs of "The End of the Indian Wars." The entire set was selling like hotcakes. He'd never broken into that market, and it didn't help that he'd had a falling out with Bill Burke, who might have given him an introduction.

Richard paused. A larger truth was that producing the kind of commercial pictures Bill Burke made didn't really appeal. He'd been inspired to pursue photography by reading the adventures of early photographers. Things had changed since men like Kate's father, working with wet plates, had carried an entire studio on their backs—sixty pounds of chemicals, equipment, and a changing tent because the plates had to be coated on site and developed immediately. And some of their glass plates had topped eighteen by twenty-two inches each. The remarkable thing was that many of those men had chosen to picture places remote and dangerous. Maybe Kate came by her fearlessness naturally, he thought. Maybe he was fated always to be "second generation."

Amato was still trying to interest Richard in his collection. And his nieces. "Seen this one?" he asked. "It's a real beauty—dark like my Georgalene."

Richard lifted one more to his eye. At the moment, the only woman he was really interested in was Kate. He asked, "Does Mrs. Burke bring her work in?"

"Oh, that one," Tony said. "More like she brings herself in."

Richard lowered the Stanhope. "She brings herself in?"

Tony rolled his eyes upwards. "Almost daily. Insists on using the dark lab herself. Makes her own prints. Drives my assistants crazy. Everything has to be this way. Everything has to be that way. I would tell her to take her work someplace else, but she gives the place a bit of class, if you know what I mean." Tony paused and looked around, his one hand on his hip, the other scratching his head. "I got some of her pictures here. She left them to dry. She'll trust me to dry her prints, but that's all."

His looking had became more serious. He was pawing through piles of prints, pushing aside boxes of plates. The only space in Tony's studio that wasn't congested was the draped area under a window where he did his own portrait work. Suddenly Tony snapped his fingers and turned and pulled a package from a shelf behind him. He handed it to Richard. Then he excused himself while he poked his head through the curtained door leading to the back of the shop and yelled something to an assistant.

Richard undid the brown paper folded over Kate's photographs. The top one was of a pair of longhorn cows. Immediately he detected Kate's father's influence in the composition, the arc of the horns dominating the picture in an unexpectedly truncated pattern reminiscent of a fine Japanese print. The second was of a coyote moving through tall grass, every hair on the animal's back distinct. The third captured a killdeer in the act of preening, one wing spread, the other folded.

Tony finished yelling new instructions to his assistant and now leaned over the counter to look with Richard. He chuckled. "If the lady would only apply herself to subjects that amount to something."

Richard knew what Tony meant. It wasn't obvious that these "snaps" had any commercial value. A stereograph would have some parlor appeal, he imagined. These were not stereographs. Nor were they art photographs, at least not as Richard had been taught to think of such things. Kate's work captured detail with directness. Photographers who pretended to art usually preferred a soft focus. In short, he wasn't quite sure what to make of her pictures except that he couldn't deny a certain power to them.

Tony was now complaining about how Kate had to have fresh developing baths whenever she came in and platinum paper. Once on a subject, he was hard to stop.

The next few pictures in the pile were carefully constructed tableaux. Bill's work. Next to Kate's spontaneous shots, they looked ludicrously false, and yet even these were remarkably better than any of Bill's work Richard had ever seen. Kate's platinum prints had added subtlety, and he suspected she'd improved the composition with cropping. The edges had become interesting. He'd never known Bill to even think about how a picture came to the edge.

"I do good work," Tony said. "If she'd just let me do my work, she wouldn't have to be perfumed by photographic chemicals all the time," he went on. "Can't understand why a lady would want to be perfumed by developer."

Richard shook his head as if he couldn't understand that either and flipped to the last photograph. It was of an Indian hugging a buffalo. He stopped. It was good. No, it was better than good.

The buffalo almost reared out of the picture, which had been framed in the dust that had roiled up under the animal and rolled over its back, blurring, but not rendering indistinct, the railroad cars, corral railing, and spectators in the background. But the moment was most embodied by the Indian's face. That visage had such an eye-arresting look, the viewer instinctively searched it as if seeking to memorize it, the high cheekbones that gave shadow to the eyes, the aquiline nose, the slightly parted lips, and the almost unearthly expression, like rapture, that contrasted the animal's startled wildness.

He wondered when she'd taken that photograph and

would have marveled at the luck to have captured such an image if not for this morning, when he'd watched with what patience and precision Kate worked. He was a landscape photographer. He knew about waiting to catch the sun at just the right angle as it moved across a cliff or canyon. He had experienced the serendipity of a rainbow, rain curtain, or other unexpected phenomena suddenly adding interest, but it had never occurred to him to try and capture something like that at the speed at which expressions changed across the architecture of the human face. He'd always thought of faces as subjects for portraiture, and while he wasn't exactly sure what kind of a picture this was, he knew it was well beyond mere portraiture.

Tony was still going on about how much Kate inconvenienced him, but his tone had assumed the same exasperated fondness he used when he spoke of his nieces. Even Tony recognized something special about Kate, Richard realized. Enough that he favored her with his indulgence.

Richard set the other photographs back on top of that last one. He folded the brown paper over them again. Then there was nothing left to do but face what he'd been avoiding: his opinion of Bill Burke.

"Bastard" about summed it up. The man was a bombastic old windbag, twice Kate's age, and Richard felt sure Bill was completely incapable of appreciating Kate even to the degree that Tony did. On the other hand, Richard had no doubt the old boy saw the advantage Kate's printmaking gave his work. Bill Burke had almost a sixth sense about anything that could be turned to cash. It was as if he smelled money—the cheap, quickly turned kind.

Richard wished that were the worst of it. But there was more. Bill Burke, despite his national reputation as a photographer, was still basically a petty cardsharp. That's how he'd started his career, and he still fancied himself a slick operator. He liked to drop names—the fact that he worked for Anthony's, the largest photography distributors in the country, and drank with the colonel. But he lacked the genius to really take advantage of that. He continued to scheme as if he were still in some back room and, as a result, made trouble for himself and anyone unfortunate enough to get mixed up with him. Richard knew that firsthand.

But how had Kate gotten hooked up with him? She wasn't stupid. She didn't seem desperate. Surely, she could see through him. He wasn't that hard to figure out. So why was she willing to spend her time making Bill Burke's prints look good? Not to mention whatever else being married to the man required of her. More, what kind of trouble was he likely to draw her into? Given the current circumstances— this time, this place, the army, the trial, ghost dancing, he thought the possibilities were truly worrisome.

On the opposite side of town, Kate wrestled with a swell of little girl feelings that made her want to grow smaller, fade, disappear. It was the way she'd felt every time her grandmother, the former actress, made a scene in a store or restaurant. Unfortunately, Bill shared the same penchant for inappropriate dramatics whenever something didn't go just as he thought it should. At the moment he was shouting overloudly at the two young soldiers who'd been sent to dress up this photograph session, neither of whom could do anything about the situation.

Bill didn't want to understand that. He used the colonel's name repeatedly as if he expected that to help: "Colonel George isn't going to like this . . . Colonel George will want to know who let this happen . . . Colonel George will demand to know why . . ."

Kate glanced around at the crowd that had gathered, attracted by Bill's loudness. He was embarrassing himself. Most everyone in the crowd seemed to know that, their eyes averted, and yet taking it all in. Except Bill. And maybe the Indian.

Plenty Horses, twenty years old, with a smooth brown face that made him look even younger, stood straight-backed and absolutely stoic in the middle of it all. Not a flicker of emotion had crossed his face, that she'd noticed, from the time he was marched out of prison to now as he stood next to a cannon that had been mounted as a public monument at the edge of Sioux Falls River Park. He was waiting to have his portrait made, and Kate couldn't help thinking he must feel as she did, that he wanted to melt into the earth or take leave of his body and fly away. But then she corrected that thought. She didn't know if she could possibly understand how it felt to be Plenty Horses, a prisoner about to be tried and hung. But first he had to stand in this public place and let his picture be taken.

The soldiers were making excuses. "Control of the prisoner has been turned over to the local authorities," the first explained when Bill gave him space to speak. "We've been sent to pose with the killer, that's all," the other responded, an edge of testiness creeping into his own voice.

At that Bill swore, his "God damn" loud enough to make some of the ladies watching give audible gasps. Kate looked around. A part of her had little sympathy with anyone so easily shocked. Another part of her just wanted to get on with this before the crowd swelled any more. It already included farm families in for a day of shopping, city officials, other soldiers, Indians, reporters, kids on bicycles, and one old Indian woman selling cheap wares, including hastily made and probably fake ghost dance shirts.

There were also five other photographers voicing their own complaints but with less rudeness. They were content to merely mutter about the situation being "not satisfactory," as the subject wasn't "Indian enough." Still they were setting up their tripods and cameras. Preferring to be busy, Kate fussed with Bill's equipment, getting it into position.

Now Bill turned on the sheriff demanding that he "do something." The sheriff, obviously unimpressed by Bill's continued use of the colonel's name, barked back that he'd already done everything that was required of him. He'd brought the Indian out. More, he told Bill that he could hurry up and take his picture because he wasn't going to bring "the little red bastard" out again.

Now ranting, Bill worked the crowd looking for some errand boy he could pay to go and get the colonel. But no one was willing to take the job, except three young Indian boys who stepped forward with hands out and grins on their faces. Bill dismissed them as "not trustworthy."

The other photographers were already taking their pictures. Bill stormed over to where Kate had his equipment set up and shouted, "Get out of my way."

She was more than happy to oblige. There was no reasoning with Bill when he was in a mood.

Picking up her own camera, she quickly backed away from the scene her husband and his big voice were making and lined up a different view. She framed not the Indian, who seemed wooden enough to be a cigar store statue, but the photographers half circling him.

She cocked the shutter, tripped it, and immediately heard a tooth-sucking noise behind her loud enough to rival her husband's rudeness. She turned to see a short but well-built young man in a bottle green suit who was not only sucking his teeth but picking them with a short knife that he folded and put in his pocket before he said, "A photograph of photographers. Is that supposed to be like a play within a play?"

Under her breath, Kate cursed her luck. There were probably fifty people gathered to watch, and who did she bump into but another embarrassment—an oaf who thought he was clever. She wanted to just ignore him, but there was something about his appearance that didn't allow that.

Besides the bottle green suit, he was wearing a string tie and wide-brimmed governor hat. The tie and hat were at least ten years out of date. The suit color had never been stylish. Yet despite that outlandish dress, the man looked pleasant enough, especially about the face. His expression suggested some sort of perpetual amusement.

He continued. "Really, you're to be complimented. Anyone with an eye can see this scene is more about the photographers than the photographed."

He was right, but Kate still wasn't sure what to make of him. His direct manner of speech, no beginning pleasantries, no polite introductions, struck her as being as odd as his dress. But she liked his eyes. His eyes suggested a quick intelligence and, no question about it, there was an amusement that twitched noticeably about his mouth. If she had to sum it up, she would have called his appearance almost clownish, except that his gold watch chain suggested seriousness, if not prosperity. Then she had to look again. He had two gold watch chains draped across his vest.

He saw that she'd noticed that oddity and pulled one pocket watch from his left vest pocket and another from his right vest pocket, flipped both open and said, "It's always best to check and double-check one's facts, I believe. One fourteen and thirty seconds if you want to believe my right watch, One fifteen and two seconds if you want to believe my left. I never can get them to agree completely. Reminds me of my parents before my father died. God rest him."

Again the frankness of his comments startled her. Her own parents had never agreed on anything, either. In fact, their disagreement had been so complete, they never even discussed most things. The silence in her family had grown to cover almost everything. But that was not a fact she volunteered to strangers in casual conversation. Yet she also sensed that his comments were hardly casual. He meant them to be understood in the larger context of the controversy still unfolding in front of them.

"Who are you?" she asked.

"Powers T. Nock, at your service," he answered, and tipped his big hat.

"The Indian's lawyer," Kate muttered. And then her interest really was piqued. She glanced back at Plenty Horses, still expressionless as he let himself be posed, first one way and then another. Always standing straight, never smiling, his eyes barely moving to take in the scene and general excitement around him as the crowd continued to grow and gape, people pushing and pointing at him. No matter how she tried, she just couldn't see him as the monster the local newspapers made him out to be. Yet his crime was considered so heinous, so unprovoked, no one had wanted to defend him until a week ago. It was thought that there was no defense for what Plenty Horses had done.

Even the Indian Rightsers Organization, saying it was a waste of money, had refused to pay for a lawyer. Then this man had stepped forward and offered his services for free. She'd read about it in the papers.

"Yes," Nock responded. "I'm the Indian's lawyer. But at the moment I'm mostly pleased to make the acquaintance of the famous Mrs. Burke and her dog."

Homer was sniffing his feet, circling him.

"Famous?" Kate questioned.

"Oh, yes, when a beautiful lady photographer appears in town, trailing rumors of having spent the winter with the army hunting ghost dancers, she's bound to be the subject of some curiosity. It's expected that you've seen things, done things, experienced things somewhat more exotic than pouring tea and framing Christmas presents. I suspect the reality was more that you've shivered through a lot of cold nights."

And hard work, she thought, remembering how she'd helped Bill pack his plates in trunks for travel over rough roads and then changed them into holders in a changing bag or in the tent at night. She'd processed his pictures by night as well, developing them in the dark, printing them by daylight under conditions that required her to warm the plates and chemicals first. It had been exciting. But suddenly in the middle of that reverie, she understood the present situation.

She turned to Nock. "You dressed the Indian in that fancy suit."

She was referring to the black worsted, three-button, cutaway gentleman's suit Plenty Horses had showed up wearing that afternoon—the suit being the cause of her husband and the other photographers' complaint that the prisoner "didn't look Indian enough."

Nock now smiled so broadly, he seemed likely to embarrass himself. He ducked his chin and cleared his throat but couldn't hide his pleasure in the fact that she'd figured it out. "Never do the expected is my motto," he answered, and then pointing to her camera, he added, "Perhaps that's a philosophy we share."

But then he immediately sobered and shook his head. "I had to argue harder to get him to put those clothes on than I expect to have to argue to save his life." He punctuated that comment with a soft chuckle and another shake of his head.

Had she heard right? He expected to save the Indian's life. And then more than ever she wanted to know why he'd taken this supposedly hopeless case. He didn't seem foolish, which was the way she'd heard Bill and the colonel describe the Indian's lawyer—"young and brash and foolish." They'd boasted that the case would ruin his reputation. Any lawyer who defended an Indian found it hard to get other business. But they believed defending Plenty Horses would mean his having to move as far away as California if he hoped to continue his practice. She wanted to know . . .

All of a sudden he grabbed her and her camera with enough force to wrench her arm. In the same moment one of the soldiers' horses reared beside her, its hooves slicing the air so close to her head, she stiffened, expecting to be hit. She'd have been knocked down if Nock hadn't pulled her aside, she realized.

Then Homer decided to enter the fray, standing on his own hind legs and barking at the horse. Kate worried that he'd be trampled and shouted at him even as Nock pulled her even farther back, the two of them flattening themselves against the park's bandstand as the horse dropped to four feet again, snorted, and then plunged wildly into the crowd, sending people shouting and shrieking in all directions.

Then the other soldier's horse thundered past, holding its head at an awkward angle to keep from tripping on the bridle reins that were dragging in the dust. Her dog lunged at that animal, sending it skittering several steps sideways.

Behind the horses came the three Indian boys, none more than ten years old, waving their arms and whooping and hollering, making enough noise to be ten times their number. They were followed by the soldiers giving chase, their own shouts adding to the confusion, then the sheriff and four or five others. Too late. There was no stopping the pandemonium that erupted and followed the horses down the street, creating a chain of havoc starting with the wagonload of beer barrels upset at the first intersection. The barrels rolled across the street, stopping traffic and tripping another horse, its rider jumping clear as the animal went down. Farther on, another pair of horses suddenly reared and tore loose of their harness.

"I trust your camera is fine," Nock said.

She shifted her attention from the commotion in the street to her immediate situation and realized she and Nock were both clutching her camera, holding it tightly between them. Clutching her camera in moments of excitement was something she did instinctively. It surprised her that he'd taken the same care.

He let go and asked, "And how are you?"

"Fine," she answered and marveled at the order of his concern—her camera and then her. She couldn't help being impressed but thought it might seem odd to comment on the same.

She thanked him and glanced down the street again to where more and more men had joined the chase. But Homer had given up and was trotting back, his tail wagging.

She looked back, and thanking Nock again, she quickly folded her camera and went to check where she'd left her box of plates, expecting that they'd been knocked over in the excitement. They were fine, but a couple of the other photographers hadn't fared as well. One had his tripod knocked over, his camera damaged. Another had a box of plates trampled by one of the horses. It was smashed. Bill was folding up his equipment, swearing as he wiped the dust from it.

She returned to the shade of the bandstand to find Nock hadn't moved except to squat next to her dog. He was rubbing Homer behind his ears as he watched the action down the street and chuckled softly.

"Did you put those Indian kids up to that?" she asked him.

He shook his head. "No, but I wish I'd thought of it."

Farther down the street, she saw some men catch the Indian boys and hold them, despite their flailing arms. She'd half hoped they would get away. Someone else had stopped the horses. "Well, I guess it just means boys will be boys, no matter."

"Oh, in this case I think it means a whole lot more than that." He allowed himself another chuckle and then added, "In this case, these boys will be men when the soldiers finally let them go and they get back to Indian camp."

"They've done a brave act, proven themselves," he continued when she looked at him quizzically.

"It's brave to scare off a couple of horses?" she questioned.

Down the street she could see the beer barrels being rolled out of the way. Soon everything would be just as it was before.

He gave her dog a couple more pats, then stood and answered, "It's coup-taking. Those boys will become men for taking coup—for creating chaos in an enemy's camp. The Sioux and many other Indians believe it is better to embarrass an enemy than to kill him. If you kill him, he's dead. If you embarrass him, he has to live with that embarrassment."

"That's not a philosophy your client chose to follow. Is it?"

To that he cocked an eyebrow and shook his head. "I'm afraid my client knows more about reading Latin than being an Indian. He's been in government boarding schools since he was five years old, most of them in Pennsylvania."

"Why are you defending him?" she asked, finally getting the question out.

He directed her attention to where a couple of deputy marshals were putting Plenty Horses in shackles before taking back to jail. "He needs a friend, don't you think?"

She nodded then shook her head. "Everyone says it's a lost cause."

"Oh, but I think I'll have to win this one."

"Why?" she asked.

"You ever seen a hanging?"

She shook her head.

"Me neither. I'm told they're rather gruesome. I'm told the defending lawyer is required to be a witness." He

57

hemmed. "I really don't think I want to witness a hanging, so I'll have to win this one." With that he gave her another tip of his big hat, and brushing her camera with his hand, he added, "I'm awfully glad we met and nothing came to harm."

"Yes, thank you again," she responded. She could appreciate a man who thought it as important to keep her camera out of harm as herself. More, he truly engaged.

Then she watched Nock cross the square to join the group leading Plenty Horses back to jail and couldn't help noticing how everyone else watched too. Talking to him, she'd almost forgotten how outlandish he looked. Not that he seemed to mind. His shoulders were straight, his walk jaunty. He waved cheerily to someone he recognized. When he reached the prisoner's side, Kate saw him put his hand gently on the Indian's back and lean close to speak to him. But even for Nock, Plenty Horses didn't give any response. Didn't move his head. Didn't give any indication he'd even heard.

The two of them made quite a pair—the short lawyer in his green suit and big hat next to the tall, bareheaded, nattily dressed Indian. Until that moment, she hadn't had much interest in the upcoming trial, figuring it for a mere formality that had somehow become necessary before killing one more Indian. But now, considering how Nock had stirred up this photograph session, she thought it might be interesting to see what he could do to a courtroom. Still, stirring things was a different matter than turning them upside down. She didn't really believe he could save Plenty Horses. For that he'd need to be more than shrewd; he'd need to be a miracle worker.

Then Kate's serving girl, Mary, ran up, grabbed Kate about the waist, swung herself around, and ducked behind Kate's skirts, causing her to have to brace herself to keep her balance. The girl, still clinging to Kate's skirts, now peeked around and whispered, "Where are they taking them?"

She meant the Indian boys who were being roughly dragged off by the soldiers.

"I don't know," Kate answered thinking city children the

same age would probably have been scolded and sent home, but she was truly ignorant of what punishment might await boys both Indian and mischievous. Perhaps a whipping. But would welts on their backs only prove them even more men? Then feeling the girl quiver, she added, "But I'm sure they'll be all right. It's only a little mischief they've done."

Then keeping herself low and partially hidden, Mary handed Kate the package of photographs she'd picked up at Amato's photography shop.

Kate took the package and stepped into the shadow of the bandstand, away from the crowd and out of Bill's sight. She pushed back the brown paper and flipped through the pictures until she got to the one of the Indian hugging the buffalo. She hoped the dry print retained the qualities she'd seen in it wet. She was not disappointed. Even though it was her eye that had framed and taken this picture, she studied it. That was the marvel of a really successful photograph. It always contained more than the eye could see in the second it took to snap the shutter.

In fact, she believed a good photograph was not to be looked *at* as much as looked *into*, letting the details, forms, and values present themselves like endless little revelations of reality, the wealth of which could never quite be appreciated unless first stilled in some comprehensible unit of time and place, a moment.

The girl tugged at her skirts. She looked up and heard her husband's bellowing voice again complaining about the soldiers, the Indian, the chaos, the morning wasted. All the photographers were packing up now. None were paying any particular attention to Bill, and she certainly didn't see any reason why she should either.

The girl tugged at her skirts again. That had become annoying. She turned to say something only to become aware of another presence.

Presence was the right word, Kate thought suddenly meeting the unguarded gaze of an older Indian woman. Tall, even with a slight stoop, the woman looked down on Kate with eyes deep and dark, and yet the gaze was not unkindly; if anything, it appeared curious. The face itself was aged but pleasant with a broad brow, straight nose, and wrinkles like fine etching. Kate glanced up the street to where she'd seen another old Indian woman selling cheap goods. She was bent and worn. By comparison this woman seemed seasoned like a piece of fine cherrywood, well rubbed.

"He is called Crooked Arm," she said, pointing to the print Kate held.

Kate looked down at the picture as if she'd forgotten it. Meanwhile, Mary edged around behind Kate's skirts opposite the older woman. But Kate's dog was curiously quiet. She gave a glance in his direction. He was sitting on the tail he was wagging. That struck her as odd. He usually checked out every stranger who came near her. He'd sniffed Nock.

"You know the man?" Kate asked indicating the picture. "I hope he wasn't hurt badly."

"A no-good Indian, but tough. He lives," the woman said with a rise to her voice. She reached over and took the picture from Kate and brought it close to her face. "More than buffalo and man is here." She tapped the picture with a long finger crooked slightly at the middle. The nail was thick and yellowed. "Vision work here."

Unprepared to respond to such a notion, Kate said nothing.

"Dreamwork," the older woman added.

"You sent the pocket bag."

"Yes, I am called Woman-Who-Dreams."

Kate fumbled in her satchel. "It is beautiful. But I don't understand . . ." She pulled it out of the pouch and offered it back. "It is far too fine for you to give away." It was true. The work was so delicate it resembled moose hair embroidery, except for the shiny surface of the quills.

The woman glanced quickly around. Then, stepping closer into the bandstand's shadow, she reached over and turned the quillwork in Kate's hand. Nothing of the pattern appeared on the back. "See, smooth, all smooth. Not many do such work any more."

"Yes," Kate said. "I know."

"You do not know the dream." The older woman turned

the piece again. "Long ago, in the dreamtime the Grand-mothers learned to steal and stitch our sister porcupine's quills. We blend our beauty into things we touch every day—pocket bags, cradleboards, pipestems, moccasins. Makes all sacred. This we learned from Double-Woman. You have the Double-Woman Dream also."

"The Double-Woman Dream?" Kate asked.

The older woman nodded. "She is here." Her finger again tapped the photograph.

Kate looked to Mary. She only ducked farther behind Kate's skirts. "I don't understand," Kate said.

The older woman's gaze took on distance. "Double-Woman is water and sky and your own reflection staring up from deep water. Untouchable. She is large like sky. She is small like sparkle on ripple. She is everywhere. Many cannot see her. You do. You catch her here." She again pointed to the photograph.

Kate didn't know what to say. In a strange way, she thought she knew what the woman described—not as Double-Woman but as moments of clarity when what she was looking at through her camera suddenly formed a picture.

Woman-Who-Dreams said, "Now you know?"

Kate drew back a step and almost tripped over Mary.

"Now you understand?" Woman-Who-Dreams asked again.

Actually, Kate wasn't sure. The world was such a swirl of incongruous detail, most of the time she didn't even try to make sense of it. Sioux Falls, soldiers of the Seventh Army, ghost dancing, coup-taking, photographers, reporters, a strange little lawyer in a green suit . . . her husband, her camera, her dog . . . the upcoming trial, the expected hanging, the girl clinging to her skirts, and now this woman with her talk of dreams and Double-Woman beauty. It was more than she could focus into anything meaningful. She didn't want to. She just wanted to take a few snaps.

At that moment Amy Farnsworth, a wealthy, well-known Boston matron who headed a delegation from the Indian Reform Movement, swished by on her way through the park. Kate and Woman-Who-Dreams both fell silent and turned away to let her pass. At the same time, Kate thought: Why me? There are others who have a better interest in things Indian.

After the other woman had passed, Kate pushed the quillwork toward Woman-Who-Dreams. "Really, I can't keep it. It's far too fine."

Woman-Who-Dreams shook her head. "It is a gift. Now, please, you will visit Indian camp? I have much else I will show you."

Kate offered the photograph. "Then take the picture. It is my gift to you."

"Thank you," Woman-Who-Dreams said with a nod.

"But I cannot come to Indian camp."

"No? Why is this?"

Kate drew breath. "Too many soldiers guard Indian camp. The colonel . . ." She paused not knowing how to explain what she didn't fully understand, but the incident of the colonel trying to destroy her picture hadn't been a whim without meaning. There was a danger here she sensed more than knew, and she had no right to drag Bill into it. He wasn't the best husband, but he'd been decent enough, and he'd already indulged her when he kept quiet while she fooled the colonel with that blank plate. She shook her head. "It would cause trouble. Too much trouble."

Woman-Who-Dreams slipped the blanket off her shoulders. It was a faded gray with a single red stripe at each end, army issue. She looked around. Then, seemingly satisfied that no one was watching, she handed the blanket to Mary but spoke to Kate. "Wrap yourself in this," she said. "The soldiers will not see. Nothing is so unseen as a woman in squaw blanket." Without waiting for a response, the older woman turned, and slipping out of the shadow of the bandstand, she blended into the crowd that was breaking up now that the excitement of seeing Plenty Horses was over. And she was gone.

Kate grabbed Mary by one arm so she couldn't duck away. "Who is Woman-Who-Dreams?"

The girl crossed herself and fussed with the end of one braid.

"I know you can tell me," Kate said.

The girl fidgeted, twisting one foot.

"Who is she?" Kate repeated.

"She's a witch."

"A witch? What do you mean?"

"A witch. Sister Mary Agnes says we shouldn't even talk about her."

Kate considered what "a witch" might mean to one of the teaching nuns at the reservation school. Possibly only an unrepentant pagan. But something shivered near Kate's spine, and she looked again to where she'd last seen Woman-Who-Dreams disappear into the crowd.

That evening Richard Houston crossed the dining room of the Cataract Hotel. It was late, only a few diners lingered over coffee. He was interested in something stronger. He pushed through a pair of doors in the back and entered the men's lounge, where he was greeted by smoke-laden air and a low rumble of voices, the most boisterous coming from near the billiard tables. Richard made his way to the bar, hung his foot over the railing, and ordered an Old Gideon.

While he waited for his drink, he turned and surveyed the room. There were potted ferns, heavy mahogany chairs arranged around matching tables, thick carpets, thicker air. The smell of cigar smoke permeated everything. Overhead the fancy chandeliers gave uneven light to the surroundings. Hard to photograph, he noted mentally, then wondered who'd care enough to want to picture the place anyway. It was not much different from similar lounges in similar hotels all across the West, most of them self-consciously cheap imitations of the clubs his father frequented.

Less democratic than this western watering hole, his father's clubs required ties, coats, and memberships. In them decisions concerning banking policy and presidential candidates were made, a reality the men in this room understood but rarely voiced except as snide asides about "eastern interests." Their frontier impotence took refuge behind the Sharps derringers and single-shot pistols they packed in their pockets.

The Old Gideon arrived. Richard put it back with one gulp. He'd learned to drink that way since coming West where stuff worth tasting, like one-hundred-year-old Scotch, was as rare as anything else of that vintage. He set the empty glass on the counter.

It wasn't the power of his father's world that Richard disliked. It was the uneven light, hard to expose. Not that Richard was any kind of populist. In his opinion, the men of his father's club were more fit to run the country than this crowd—more experienced, at least. He just didn't like what it took to get in their game. In his case, it required that he become his father the way a soldier putting on a uniform became his country.

Warmed by the alcohol, Richard wandered to the back of the room looking for a card game. He depended on poker winnings to supplement his income between bigger photography jobs. The local stuff barely paid his boardinghouse bills.

As he passed the billiard tables, he paused. Near the back, Bill Burke was dealing poker to four locals, and he was cheating. Richard knew his moves so well, he'd spotted the cheat in an instant. Not that spotting Bill's cheat was all that hard. Bill wasn't that good. Richard couldn't help wondering at the man's good fortune. A clumsy cheat like Bill should have been shot in a bar like this long ago.

Richard considered turning around and coming back another night. But he didn't. Pulling a roll of money from his pocket, he approached the table. His bankroll was impressive. It was also padded with newspaper, but the locals didn't know that. More, his East Coast, upper-class mannerisms got him remarkable deference. In fact, the only place his obvious breeding hadn't been good for credit was in a mud-hut village near the Mexican border. There, having never met an upper-crust New Englander, they'd mistaken him for a priest.

These locals sized him up and quickly agreed he could join the game. Bill squirmed, then grunted his assent. What else could he do? Richard pulled up a chair. Then, glancing across the table, he gave Bill a look they both understood: This game had just become honest.

An hour later, Richard was winning. Wasn't hard. The locals gave themselves away with a myriad of tics and nervous mannerisms. Richard had three of them learned. The fourth had proved harder, but he was also drinking more than the others and generally not playing as well. Bill had only to be watched—something Richard had learned to make a habit after trying to work with the man.

As they finished one hand, Bill elbowed the man on his right. He was a lanky divorce lawyer dressed a bit flashy—one of dozens who'd hung his shingle in this town. A low residency rule had made Sioux Falls the "quick divorce capital of the country." It was also the only thing to give the town any class. Wealthy matrons, the only women who could contemplate legal separation, demanded high fashion and real opera.

But the lawyer wasn't paying attention. He was concentrating on his cards and rubbing three fingers along the edge of the table, something Richard recognized as meaning he had a possible good hand but not high counters. He was trying to decide if he was going to bet it.

Bill nudged him again. "Did I tell you? Anthony's has three agents on the road all the time just selling my photographs of this 'Last Indian Uprising.'"

The lawyer looked up, shook his head, returned to his cards. He wasn't interested in Bill's brag.

"Anthony's can hardly print my photographs fast enough to keep up with those agents. They're selling my photographs everywhere, I tell you." Bill gave the lawyer another elbowing. "Bet you didn't know a man could make big money off of pictures, did you?"

The lawyer shook his head and folded his cards.

"How about you?" Bill asked one of the other players, a cattle buyer in need of a haircut. "Ever think a man could

65

make his fortune in photographs? Gold mines, maybe. Cattle, maybe. A rich daddy. Now there's a sure bet." Bill looked across the table at Richard.

So did everyone else. They'd all figured out by now that there was more than a friendly game of cards between him and Bill.

That was fine. Richard figured a little tension helped most card games. But he wasn't going to let himself get rattled. He laid out his cards and won another hand. As he reached for his winnings, he said, "Getting the money is one thing; keeping it is another."

Bill visibly stiffened.

Richard would have smiled, except that he'd put his poker face on an hour ago. But they both knew Bill's tendency to spend money faster than he could make it. He bought barges he was going to float down the Colorado River and camels he was going to sell to the army. None of those wild schemes ever worked. It was like good money wasn't good enough for Bill. He had to have slick money maybe because he thought that proved he was smart.

Richard folded his next hand. No cards worth playing.

That's when one of the barmaids came over swinging her rear as she circled the table asking if anyone wanted another drink. Bill suddenly grabbed her arm and pulled her down into his lap. Then tickling her ribs, he slipped a coin down the front of her dress for which he got her to kiss his cards and agree to stay in his lap a few minutes. "For luck," he said.

Richard watched, thinking this cheap buxom beauty was more Bill's sort than Kate, but he didn't say anything. However, when Bill lifted her hair and kissed the back of her neck, he couldn't help himself.

"Met your wife this morning," he said as he tossed a pair of winning cards on the table to show just how much luck Bill's barmaid had brought him.

Bill grunted and continued tickling the woman and popping coins in her dress.

"She was photographing falcons up on the ridge. Got a

damned good picture of the birds, too. Caught them in midair."

Bill grunted again. In his opinion, Richard talked too much. Richard had nagged him like a woman the whole time the two of them had tried to work together. He'd gone on and on about Bill's "better" work, about how he didn't have to do "stock shots" all the time, about how he could use his reputation to "improve" the whole industry, raise it above "illustration." The irony was that this rich boy had never gotten half the price for one of his photographs as Bill got regularly. Pretty pictures didn't put food on the table or quarters down the bosom of a barmaid. Richard didn't like him doing that. So he kept on doing it, practically filling the woman's cleavage.

He guessed Richard's feelings came from something interesting that happened out on that ridge with his wife and the birds. Bill would have been jealous, except that Kate was so in love with her camera, he was sure she gave Richard almost no notice. Probably that bothered him. He was the kind of man who was used to being noticed, especially by the ladies.

"I understand you worked with your wife's father," Richard continued.

"No," Bill grunted.

"No? I understood you were friends for years and often worked together," Richard stated again.

"Oh, you mean the man Kate calls her father. Yeah, we worked together. We even went to Japan together once. But he was never really her father."

Richard's poker face slipped. "I don't understand."

"What's so hard to figure? Kate's mother was a slut. I'm sure things like that happen even in your social circles."

Suddenly Richard was speechless. Bill enjoyed that. He leaned across the table and added, "I rescued her. I'm her hero, her knight in shining armor."

"Rescued her from all what?"

"Her mother, her grandmother, the reputation of the

67

women in her family. There's a reason why Kate spent so much time in a smelly old photography shop. No one wanted their little girls mixing with her sort, if you know what I mean. But I took her away from all that to where no one knows her past."

"Except those you tell," Richard added.

Bill pinched the woman's arm. "Nobody cares around here. You don't care, do you, sweetie?" Then turning back to Richard, he added, "Believe me, Kate appreciates what I've done for her."

"I'll bet," Richard said, folding his cards again. "I'm sure it's every woman's dream to live in a camp wagon and spend the winter on the open prairie."

"That's exactly it. You may have met my wife, but you don't know her. My old daddy used to like expensive women, even though he warned me about them. Kate's an expensive woman not because her tastes were dear but because everything about her is dear. She's a little too dear even for you, I'm afraid."

Richard's anger flashed. What was this? Why was Bill taunting him, daring him, almost inviting him to flirt with Kate? No man could be that sure of a young wife of less than a year. Did Bill do that with other men? How about all those soldiers out on the prairie? What about the colonel? Did he dangle his wife in front of the colonel? Was that how he'd gotten in with the man?

Kate deserved better.

And then in a second flash he suddenly wondered if that's what it took to impress Kate—rescuing her. What if he rescued her from Bill?

Richard stood up from the table. He wanted to do more. He wanted to tip the table into Bill's lap, but his lap was already filled with the giggly barmaid. Nevertheless, he'd lost his edge and figured he might as well pack it in for the night.

As he was picking up the last of his winnings, it hit him what had happened. Bill had wanted him away from the table so he could cheat. He'd bided his time and then engineered this whole thing just to get Richard to leave. That was the most damnable and frustrating thing about the man. He didn't have to be the scoundrel. If he could read people that well, he didn't need to cheat. Richard pocketed the money and looked at Bill. "Best hand you've played all night."

The man had the audacity to smile. "Kate's my ace."

5

Kate was on a curved staircase, always climbing. It was a recurring dream where she climbed and climbed trying to escape the noise of the constant bickering that flowed up the staircase from below. The voices were familiar: her mother's, her grandmother's. The voices never grew faint, no matter how far she climbed. They went on and on, both the stairs and the voices. The voices argued about the stairs—who had been helped up the fanciest stairs by the finest gentleman, who had lived in the better house with the longest curve of stairs.

Stairs, stairs, stairs. Kate kept going up and up. Her legs got weary. She could hardly move them. She became anxious. Why wouldn't her legs move?

She tried to run faster and faster, pausing only to pound on walls and try locked doors. Her danger was inside. It lived with her. It stalked her in her sleep. It followed her like her own shadow gliding up the stairs behind her.

She woke with a start and sat up. Then, drawing her knees under her chin, she shivered off the dream's lingering haunt.

Her husband slept beside her, making soft gurgling noises

almost like a baby. He'd come in late, smelling of smoke and whiskey, as he had frequently since they'd gotten to Sioux Falls. A lot had been different since the days when they were out on the prairie. Kate drew a deep breath and considered how their lives had become layered in deception. She never told him half of what she did and wanted to know even less of his affairs. That struck her as ironic considering how painfully direct she'd been the day of her father's funeral when she'd told Bill she'd marry him if he'd take her away, any place, traveling.

She simply couldn't stay another day in her mother's house or listen to another word about stairs. That was an oddity of her family—the importance of stairs. Her grandmother had run away at a young age and joined a troupe of actors, swearing she'd have a proper house with stairs someday, not the poverty and rented back rooms of her childhood. She'd gained some renown, played some fine places, had a daughter, but never married, never gotten her stairs. Kate's mother had married Kate's father mainly because he owned a house with a curved staircase. She'd then made it the subject of every morning's conversation.

"Hope the stairs weren't too much for you," Kate's mother would say to Kate's grandmother as she poured coffee.

"Seventeen are not so many," Kate's grandmother would answer. "You should be invited to a palace someday." And those were frequently the only civil words said until the next morning when they would start again with the stairs.

Without her father, without his studio as a place to escape, that would have driven Kate mad. With no effort at all, she could imagine herself dusting doorknobs or something equally obsessive, humming the same tune over and over so she wouldn't have to listen. Or embracing a wilder insanity, she might have put the drapery aflame one night.

Bill moaned and turned over without waking. With rare exceptions, no matter where he was, Bill always found solace in his sleep. Not her. For her, sleep plunged into a whirlpool of swirling images from which she could only emerge fully awake. The result was that she slept fitfully and always woke early as now.

In the raw morning, her thoughts touched her core. She did not regret marrying Bill. Except for the dreams, she'd escaped, and coming West with him had been all the adventure she expected and more. It was as if the landscape gave one courage to do whatever. She blamed the sky. Too wide and clear, it gave too broad a view.

She got up and dressed in the near dark; then, taking her dog and the blanket Woman-Who-Dreams had given her, she tiptoed out to where the Indian girl slept rolled under the wagon. Kate shook her awake. Still groggy, the girl threw back her quilt, picked up her own blanket, and followed.

They started down river, passing the falls, a quarter-mile cascade of water that rippled over layers of rose quartz like rippling stairsteps. Stairs! Kate shook her head, clearing it of the dream, and lifted the blanket over her red hair. Then, tucking the stray strands of her hair under the edge, she clamped the blanket tightly under her chin.

The girl, Mary, imitated each of those actions, also pulling her blanket over her head, also tucking her hair under. Now fully awake, she was also muttering the "Our Father," as she trotted along behind. She muttered it softly, almost inaudibly, but repeatedly. It was enough to drive Kate crazy, but she didn't say anything. She had larger worries.

To get to Indian camp, she had to go into town and cross the Eighth Street Bridge. There were soldiers and extra sheriff's deputies everywhere because of the crowds the trial had attracted. To avoid them, she paused at street corners and sometimes backtracked or slipped through an alley. Always she kept to the shadow side of the street, away from the pools of light made by the gas lamps.

Darting from building to building in that fashion, Kate, the girl, and the dog passed the Union Trust Bank, the Odd Fellows Hall, and a row of shops. It was chilly enough to make Kate shiver under the blanket, and quiet enough to hear the creak of the wooden walks under her feet. Sometimes it sounded to her that the noise of the walks was as loud as a train clacking down a track, but no one else seemed to notice, and it didn't help to tiptoe. She'd tried.

A milk wagon crossed from a side street. Kate grabbed Homer and the girl and stepped into the shadow to let the wagon pass. At the bridge she paused for twenty minutes or more, waiting for just the right moment. When all was clear, she picked up her skirts and fairly trotted across. The girl stumbled once keeping up with her. Homer streaked ahead.

So far, so good, she thought. But her biggest problem lay ahead. She would have to pass within sight of the army camp.

On the other side of the river, where the stockyards, packing plants, mills, and machine shops were clustered, Kate picked an alley beside a blacksmith shop. She paused, glanced all around, and then ducked into its darkness, nearly stumbling over a drunk.

Homer barked once before she could grab him and pull him back. The drunk only rolled over and drew himself up closer to the backside of the forge where the bricks gave off warmth.

Holding Homer by his collar, Kate stepped around the drunk and beckoned for the girl to follow. She did. Midway down the alley, Kate paused beside a coal bin. She lifted the lid, easing the unoiled hinges upward with care to keep them quiet. She managed it with only a slight squeak.

The drunk drew his knees up to his chest and moaned.

Kate held her breath until he was settled again. Then, directing the girl to hold Homer, she reached inside the bin with a rag and wiped coal dust from the side. Holding the blackened rag at arm's length from her own clothes, she knelt next to the dog and began rubbing him all over. She'd traveled with the army for months. Even if they didn't note a woman under a squaw blanket, the soldiers were likely to recognize her dog.

Homer didn't like the smell of the coal dust and tried to back away, but she grabbed his collar, helping the girl hold him tight. Then she rubbed and rubbed until only his ears and tail remained red. In fact, they looked slightly redder than usual in the rosy glow of the growing dawn and something about that struck the girl as silly. She began to giggle softly, trying to hold it, but not succeeding entirely.

The dog cocked his head and then sneezed.

Kate sat back and had to agree. He did look comical. She reached up to get enough dust to finish the job and suddenly froze. Silhouetted at the end of the alley was a man, tall, wearing a broad-brimmed hat and heavy mackinaw. She didn't recognize him, but that hardly mattered. Anyone catching her in that alley rubbing black coal dust on her dog would want to know why.

She crouched lower, grabbed the girl and dog, and pulled them as far into the shadow of the coal bin as was possible. "Quiet, Homer. Shhh," she whispered.

The drunk moaned.

The man stepped into the alley and stood for a moment examining the curled-up figure. He lit a cigarette, ground the match into the dirt, and then kicked the bottom of the drunk's boots.

A moan, nothing more.

The man took another couple of puffs and again poked the drunk in the ribs with the toe of his boot. The drunk only moaned and curled tighter. The man flicked his cigarette onto the drunk and moved on.

Kate stood and had to hold the edge of the coal bin while a bit of faintness passed. The question she had expected still rang in her ears: "What are you doing?" She could almost feel the rough grab of her arm that would have come next.

What would she have said?

Sometimes she imagined Judgment Day as silence—her silence. God thundered, "Why?" and she offered nothing. Closing her eyes, she drew another deep breath. This was just one of those things she had to do. She didn't know why.

The girl was back to muttering prayers.

Kate finished dusting her dog and they left the alley.

Then, as if that weren't excitement enough, farther down river where the less desirable elements were camped, she passed a "chicken outfit"—a smelly operation catching and killing quantities of prairie hens for city markets. A man with a clubfoot was already up building a fire under a boiling pot. When he spotted Kate and Mary, he dropped an armload of firewood and took several steps toward them. Homer growled. Mary whimpered. Kate grabbed the girl's arm and, pulling her along, kept walking straight ahead as fast as she could without breaking into a run.

At the same time, Powers T. Nock took his first sip of morning coffee and hadn't even swallowed yet when his mother wordlessly set a lady's button on the table in front of him. She expected the words to come from him, some explanation.

He swallowed his coffee and looked up from his breakfast. His mother was short and, while not heavy, she was thick enough through the waist to appear matronly. Her hair was white and pulled back in a bun. Her face was lined, but softly, and at the moment there was such a twinkle in her eye, he almost wished what she was thinking was true.

"You met someone," she said. "A nice someone, from the looks of it, but maybe a little spendthrifty."

His mother was referring to the quality of the button, a fancy carved mother-of-pearl, an inch in diameter, and slightly smoky in color. He knew those details without looking. He'd already given that button more attention than it deserved.

His mother went on, "When it comes to buttons, cheap is as good as dear. They both get the job done, I say. But there are those who prefer to be showy, even in the fastenings of one's dress. I'm not one to say that's wrong, mind you, but it's exactly those kinds of matters one must settle before the nuptials. A spendthrifty woman can send her husband to the poorhouse in no time, no time at all."

Nock set his coffee cup down and waited for her to run out of breath. His mother made leaps like this. One button and she had him married. He was not even in the habit of collecting love tokens, a lady's glove, a lace handkerchief. This was a mere button.

First time she paused, he said, "It's not like that. The button belongs to a lady, a married lady. I saw it had been

75

lost and considered it gentlemanly to return it, which I will next time I see her." That said, he turned his attention back to his coffee and biscuits.

His mother said nothing. For Clarissa Morgan Nock to be speechless, even momentarily, was an event. Nock looked up to see if she was all right.

Her expression had shifted to a stern glare. "It's not that good a button."

"I beg your pardon."

"The button isn't that good," she repeated. "It's not cheap, but it can be readily replaced, ordered from a catalog."

"I'm sorry. I guess I don't understand buttons."

"This button is not worth a gentleman's attention," she went on. "So the lady must be."

Nock started to take another sip of coffee but paused with the cup in midair. Was his mother calling him a liar? And then he nearly flushed because she'd hit a truth he hadn't even admitted to himself. Still he denied it. "Oh, there you go imagining things, again. You need to get out more. Join a social club."

That was a bit of banter he often exchanged with her. Her focus on him had become absolute since his father's death. He'd have felt smothered by her attention if she weren't wrong most of the time. In fact, his mother was remarkably unobservant for someone who considered it her duty to check his pockets regularly and not just on laundry day. She missed the big things, like the fact that he was too short and not nearly handsome enough to turn most women's heads. He didn't imagine that Kate Burke would remember him as anyone but an eccentric.

His mother continued. "It's you who should join a social club. Go dancing sometimes."

Nock chewed the last of a biscuit as he listened to her go on. He remembered that just before the young Indian boys startled the soldiers' horses yesterday, a stableboy had paraded a mare in heat by them. It was a trick photographers used to make the stallions prick up their ears and stand at attention for the picture. Made a better photo-

graph. It also made the horses edgy and easily spooked—
something the Indian boys had certainly taken advantage
of. Nock slid his chair back. No, what he really remembered
was how Kate had done the same to him. From the moment
he first saw her, she'd made him feel edgy and all at
attention. He'd never known another woman to affect him
quite that way. That, however, was not something he was
going to try and discuss with his mother. She was still going
on about where he should go to meet "nice unmarried
girls."

He excused himself saying, "I'm sorry, Mother, I'd like to
sit here long enough to discuss every eligible young lady
you've seen lately, but I've got to wind my clocks and
prepare for the trial." With that, he got up from his
unfinished breakfast and went to his study.

Leaving his breakfast unfinished was going to worry his
mother even more than the button, he hoped. She was going
to think he was feeling poorly. By evening she would believe
him to be dying of some slow but incurable illness. He
trusted he could brush that aside with more ease than this
business with Kate that he didn't understand himself.

No good. She followed him into his study still yammer-
ing, now with a focus on the fact that she didn't have
grandchildren. And she wasn't getting younger. And her
friends all had beautiful grandchildren.

Normally she wouldn't step foot in his study because she
hated his clocks. He had lots of clocks: both an oak and a
walnut cabinet clock, five parlor clocks, a cuckoo from
Germany, an acme queen cathedral gong, an iron clock,
several eight-day clocks. He also had a collection of alarms
and a cabinet full of pocket watches.

"Mrs. Andrews down the street has six grandchildren
already," his mother went on. "Five of them are boys. Every
one of them smart."

"Please, mother," he said. "I need to prepare for the
trial."

"Oh, that. You'll do fine," she returned. "Ask me, that
poor boy couldn't have a better lawyer."

"I'm the only lawyer who'd take the case," he said, trying

to put some reality into her thinking. "John Burns of Deadwood, who's known to be a friend of the Indians, wouldn't even take this case."

Nevertheless, he was relieved that they'd gotten back to familiar ground, namely his mother's unfounded belief that as a lawyer he was a genius. She hadn't figured out that his genius, if he had any, ran to stirring things, not making a career. It was a sure bet he wasn't going to improve his career with this case.

"My client shot an army officer in the back in front of witnesses," he said, not as explanation, but as statement, as though he needed to hear it himself. "But he's not guilty of murder."

"I know, dear," his mother said, as though there weren't some enormous incongruity in what he'd just said. "I know. You always said this was a difficult case, but . . ."

His Seth Thomas weight clock started to strike. He checked his pocket watches. The Seth Thomas was fast, but not by much. Soon the room would be filled with a cacophony of gong, strike, and chime.

His mother threw up her arms. "Oh, I can't talk with all those clocks making their noise. I don't understand you and all those clocks. What do you need them for?"

So he'd have at least one place he could go and be free of her chatter, he thought, but offered a different explanation. "Maybe they're better than collecting buttons."

She lowered her eyebrows and gave him a glare. "You better concentrate on your work," she said. "You've got a man's life in your hands." Then she fled the room before it erupted in a chorus of time.

He stood there a moment feeling like a little boy who'd just been scolded. Then, looking down, he realized he had the button between his thumb and first finger. That startled him. He didn't remember picking it up from the table, but he must have.

"Wrong time," he whispered.

"Wrong time," he repeated out loud.

He didn't mean the Seth Thomas that was slightly off. He

meant the feeling he had about himself, that he was somehow living in the wrong time.

If he'd met Kate a year ago . . .

If he were trying this case fifty years into the future . . .

The right time made all the difference. As it was, nothing he did seemed to fit exactly. It was as though he were in a time vortex, as though all the ghost dancing had raised enough spirit so that nothing quite fit. Or would ever be the same again.

He shook his head. That kind of thinking wasn't helpful. He had to keep his wits about him. Even concerning Kate. Maybe especially concerning Kate.

Meanwhile Kate, the Indian girl, and Homer had come to the spot where the U.S. Seventh Army was camped on the county fairgrounds, their rows of white tents, flagpole, hastily assembled supply depot, and stockade squatted next to a weathered grandstand. Beyond that, Kate could see Indian camp, with its tepees made of the same white canvas, now that buffalo robes were scarce. Indian camp occupied an open space of prairie between the tracks of two competing railroads. Both camps included temporary live-stock enclosures not unlike the one where Kate had left her horse the morning before.

This morning she was on foot, hoping that made her less conspicuous, as if a woman, a dog, and a child making their way along river in the early dawn weren't of any note. Looking over the camp, Kate hesitated. She thought about going around, swinging wide, and circling across the prairie, but that would take time and might also draw attention. Still she wasn't sure she believed Woman-Who-Dreams when she claimed the soldiers wouldn't notice a woman in a squaw blanket, but she decided to risk it. Adjusting the blanket one more time, she plunged forward, and it worked. The soldiers paid Kate no mind, not even the sentries, though she imagined that might have been different if she were trying to enter the camp rather than pass by.

It was entirely different at Indian camp. There approaching, she was immediately greeted by dogs and children who appeared from everywhere. The dogs sniffed Homer. The children giggled and pointed at Kate, their sparkling eyes so much like coals in a fire, she wondered if the origin of "savage" came from such deep, dark aliveness. Mary, too, suddenly became more animated. Her hands took up gestures Kate had never seen before as she chatted their language.

Then Woman-Who-Dreams emerged from one tepee near the center of the camp. Her two long braids fell over a bright blue calico shirt and skirt pinched at the middle with an elaborately decorated belt. She was pulling a blanket over her shoulders not much different from the one she'd given Kate. Seeing her, Mary stiffened, got silent.

A gust of wind swirled across the camp, and Kate glanced up and around, startled at a strange hollow clacking. That's when she noticed the strings of deer hooves hanging from the tepee tightening ropes. Wind chimes, she thought, and then, listening closer, found the noise quaintly pleasant.

Behind her, a couple of dogs snapped at Homer. Kate whirled, expecting a fight to erupt.

One Indian woman yelled. Another trilled a sharp whistle. The other dogs slunk away.

Homer followed the retreating dogs a few steps, growling. Kate chased after and grabbed his collar.

The Indian women found Kate's dog amusing, including the two who'd first given Kate the quilled bag. They laughed loudly. Then one hunched over and walked heavily, clowning. "Your dog has the spirit of a wolf?"

Kate had to smile. The woman's motion was a remarkable imitation of Homer. She was still holding her dog when Woman-Who-Dreams stepped forward. "You return my call. That is kind."

Return her call? The thought jarred Kate. She certainly hadn't considered this returning a call—not in the same sense that women back in her hometown called on each other, sharing tea most afternoons.

Then right behind that thought, unbidden, came a remembered bit of wisdom her father had shared after a trip to Japan. There, he said, it was believed that beauty was embodied in the tea ceremony. That all the ways we have of shaping life, stories, maps, alphabets, wine bottles, and ships' hulls were really teacups, finely made vessels for holding what we know.

Kate shook her head with a slight sense of confusion. She hadn't thought of that in a long time.

To Woman-Who-Dreams she said, "Mary told me you were testing me to see if I would come. I came."

"You couldn't not come."

"I beg your pardon?"

"You are much curious. You had to come. I know this. I look when you walk. With your dog, you let your spirit free."

Now the hair stood up on Kate's neck. It was true. Alone, except for Homer, she often skipped across streams on stones that didn't care how high she held her skirt and swung from tree branches and . . . "You mean you spy on me."

The older woman shook her head. "Those are Coyote words—twisted truth."

Kate leveled her gaze. "But not so twisted as to not be the truth."

Woman-Who-Dreams broke the gaze. She looked Kate over while the suggestion of a smile crossed her own face. "You were born regular?"

"I don't know what you mean?"

"No caul, no twin?"

Kate shook her head.

The older woman rubbed her chin. "Powerful spirit." With that she motioned for them to follow her inside, but she paused as she lifted the tepee door and pointed to Kate's dog. "Also creature of strong spirit, but too dirty to come in."

Kate hesitated, but not long. It was true. She'd known she would come from the moment she'd been given the quill-work bag. She couldn't deny the curiosity deep inside her that drove her like a thirst. She had to do things, go places, dare the unconventional because anything less felt like slow death. Having admitted that to herself, she commanded Homer to wait. He lowered himself to his belly with a groan.

Inside, the first thing Kate noticed was the way the strings of deer hooves sounding in the breeze echoed through the tepee, creating an odd muted music. The smells were pleasant, too. A small fire burned in the center with a pot simmering over it, giving the air both warmth and the scent of a stew. Above that were bundles of fragrant herbs hanging from the tepee poles. A larger medicine bundle hung from its own tripod at the back. Stacks of parfleches, large leather pouches known as "Indian baggage," held down the bottom edges of the tepee liners. The floor was covered with tanned robes, the hair facing upward. Cowhides, from government beef issues, Kate decided. One still had a brand showing.

A child, with a birthmark on one cheek, had entered ahead of Woman-Who-Dreams. She rolled a robe over a backrest for her elder. Woman-Who-Dreams squatted to the ground, leaning against it while the young girl arranged similar robed backrests for Kate and Mary.

"My great-granddaughter," Woman-Who-Dreams said as the girl finished and came around and sat close enough to snuggle under the older woman's arm.

The girl cradled a red quilled pouch in her lap.

"She keeps me company," Woman-Who-Dreams continued. "We call such old people's children. They become quite spoiled or else quite wise. This one will be wise."

The young girl ducked her head in shyness. At the same time, Kate wished Mary would quit fingering the cross at her neck.

"Do you have children?" Woman-Who-Dreams asked.

Kate shook her head.

"In time, perhaps."

Kate didn't think so. Bill's first wife never had a child. She doubted she would, either. Actually, having Bill's child wasn't part of her plans. It was hard to explain, but photography came alive in her, and that's what she wanted to do with her life—take pictures, fine pictures.

Now Woman-Who-Dreams took the pouch from her

great-grandchild's lap and motioned for her to go. The girl slid away from the older woman, stood, and beckoned to Mary.

Mary gave Kate a glance. She nodded, and the girls left together. Outside, Kate could hear other children at play.

Woman-Who-Dreams opened the pouch. She pulled out a short pipe also decorated with quillwork. She pressed tobacco into the bowl. Then, holding the pipe up and pointing it in the four directions, she said, "The nuns make Mary ashamed of the old ways. They turn her spirit into Rabbit's. Rabbit runs from hole to hole, always frightened. She was foolish yesterday morning when she put on her ghost shirt. You were kind to protect her."

Kate wondered how Woman-Who-Dreams knew of the incident. Then she realized that wasn't the real question. What she really wanted to know was how much of her life was familiar to this woman. But she said only, "I'm sorry the colonel took the shirt."

Woman-Who-Dreams breathed a puff of smoke into the air. "He is nephew to a famous senator. I will not honor his name with my breath. I say only the senator took money from cattlemen. The cattlemen wanted half our reservation for their cows. He got them our land. What does one expect from a family of thieves?"

Kate hesitated, not knowing how to respond to that.

"Such talk troubles you?"

Kate shook her head. She had heard the colonel mention his uncle. "I can't help you with that," she responded. "I have no influence with the colonel."

Woman-Who-Dreams shook her head. "I seek no such help." She slid forward and lifted the lid of the cooking pot. She stirred. "Red squirrel. I caught it in a net yesterday. I will boil it all day. Then it is very soft and easy to chew." She chuckled softly. "It is old woman's dish. I am old. I eat like old. But I eat. Most of my people are hungry. I do not say this because I want your help. Only that you understand. Too many of my people have forgotten the old ways or are ashamed like Mary. They do not know how to catch red squirrel, so they die of pneumonia. It is the pneumonia that comes with slow starvation, you know. Big Foot had pneumonia at Wounded Knee, but a bullet got him first. I am sure he was pleased to die a warrior."

Kate knew the image. Right after the conflict at Wounded Knee Creek, a snowstorm had moved in. It was two days later before Bill propped up the dead and frozen body of Big Foot and took his portrait.

She remembered trying to print that plate. The weather had been cold enough to interfere with her chemicals. They'd refused to change the brown for purple. She hadn't been entirely sure why but thought the gold solution had lost its strength from continuous freezing. So she'd thrown it away, washed the bottle, and made fresh, mixing it strong. Only then had she been able to fix Big Foot's face. She couldn't say that contorted visage had looked pleased to have met with a bullet.

The older woman went on. "Not many die as warriors anymore. They will hang Plenty Horses."

Now Kate was really confused. Red squirrel stew, a senator, starvation, and her own remembered images. She didn't know what to make of any of it. Didn't know what to say.

Woman-Who-Dreams suddenly passed her the pipe.

Not knowing what else to do, Kate took it. She fumbled turning it, then raised it to her lips. At first the smoke was not unpleasant. Then it was as if her throat had closed. She tried not to cough. She feared that would not be polite. Being offered an Indian pipe was supposed to be some kind of honor, she believed.

But trying not to cough only made it worse. She coughed, and then the more she tried not to cough, the harder she hacked. She couldn't help herself. The older woman finally got up and got Kate some water from a canteen hanging from one of the tepee poles. Kate gladly exchanged the pipe for the cup. With the water and some effort, she composed herself.

When her throat had cleared, and her eyes had stopped watering, Kate saw that the older woman was puffing on the pipe while she stirred the stew again. More, she saw that

Woman-Who-Dreams was obviously amused, chuckling noises escaped from her twitching mouth.

"Sorry," Kate said.

Woman-Who-Dreams put the lid back on the stew. Then she pulled out Kate's photograph of the Indian hugging the buffalo. She tapped the photograph lightly with one finger. "I read about this." Then, as explanation, the older woman rolled back the floor robe next to her and pulled out a newspaper. She tossed it in front of Kate. "See. They say he is crazy, gone loco from ghost dancing." She pulled out a second newspaper. "This one says he stampedes the buffalo. He want to scare folks. Cowboys bragging in front of a saloon tell better stories. Truer stories." She leaned close to Kate. "The truth is in this picture you take of him. It is a sacred thing Crooked Arm did, hugging his old friend. You see that."

Kate picked up the first newspaper and glanced at the story of the arrival of the buffalo. It was front page and sensationalized. She'd seen it before and shrugged it off. Yellow journalism, that's all.

Now Woman-Who-Dreams rolled back another floor hide. She tossed out several more newspapers saying, "Not true, any of it. Lies and more lies."

Intrigued, Kate rolled back the floor robe next to her and found a layer of old newspapers. She reached farther to her right and rolled back another robe. Under it were still more newspapers, one from Chicago. She looked up, a sense of confusion having returned. Who was this old Indian woman who spoke surprisingly good English, read newspapers, and had an ermine skin hanging from one of her braids?

"I collect them," Woman-Who-Dreams continued. "Others bring newspapers to me. Sometimes they're pretty old before I get them. Sometimes I get only part. That don't matter. I read them. Then I put them under my robes. They make my floor soft."

"That's how you know about the colonel being related to the senator," Kate commented.

"Right here in my floor." She patted the cowhide next to her.

85

Kate shook her head some more. She had no idea what to make of this interview. She'd been taught to think of Indian women as living little better than mules, always doing grunt work, drudge work. Yet a part of her knew better. Her serving girl, Mary, was the fourth generation to be educated in mission schools. Still Woman-Who-Dreams was hardly what she'd expected. She was becoming truly fascinated.

Now Woman-Who-Dreams opened a satchel and took out three photographs. She spread them in front of Kate. They were Kate's, not necessarily some of her best work, but hers. One was a picture of a trainload of soldiers arriving in Chadron, Nebraska, at the start of the hostilities. The other two were pictures of local scenes. Since they were more documentary than not, she'd simply mixed these photographs in with Bill's pictures. Some of the prints had been sold locally. The plates had been sent East for wider distribution.

She picked up the photographs. "Where did you get these?"

"People bring them to me. Same like they bring me newspapers."

"How did you know these were mine?"

"I see your eye working here. I know." Woman-Who-Dreams touched Kate's hand. "I am Woman-Who-Dreams. I suck the quills of my sister porcupine. When they are soft, I bend and stitch them. I make dream patterns, dream pictures. Not pictures like this." Her finger again tapped the photograph of the Indian and the buffalo. "This needs no song, no telling. Anyone who can see truly, can see this."

Kate finally figured it out. "You want me to take photographs."

Woman-Who-Dreams nodded. "Pictures of the women of the Sacred Quillworkers. No one had done it. No man ever could. No men ever come where the women do the dream-work stitching. It has ever been so. It is an honored invitation, no?"

Kate understood the part about the honor. She knew of other photographers who'd worked for years before building enough trust with a particular Indian tribe to be allowed to photograph sacred parts of their culture. But she couldn't say she understood much else. "Why me?" she asked.

Woman-Who-Dreams didn't answer immediately. She lifted the lid and stirred her red squirrel stew slowly. "Before you were born, I dreamed. I saw in my dream a red-haired woman with a red dog. When I saw you, I remembered my dream. But now I am confused. Since I left the mission school many years ago, I do not ask a white woman for anything. My spirit will not be as Rabbit's. Then I saw the pictures. These pictures make me wonder. Then I saw this photograph, and I knew." Her hand came back to the picture of the Indian and the buffalo. "You are Double-Woman touched."

A strange mix of feelings welled up in Kate. Every spring when her father left for some faraway place to take photographs of people and things never photographed before, she'd ached to go with him. When he was gone, she daily climbed to the edge of a railroad trestle near her home just to look at the track running over the river, going westward. Now she was being offered her own chance. She knew she ought to be excited. Yet part of her was afraid.

Mary had called this woman a witch. Kate didn't believe that, and yet she'd heard stories of Indian medicine, secret chants, powerful spells, dreams. As a child, she'd skipped rope to a jingle:

> Fearsome warriors in the glades of green
> Steal away children who've been mean . . .

How did she know what she was getting into? She was not a missionary or an Indian reformer who could come and go in Indian camp at will. She was supposed to be a properly married woman, and she was quite sure Bill would not see this as an opportunity.

Kate shook her head. "There must be someone else."

The older woman studied Kate. "No. I have looked. Much that was my people is gone. I did not want this to disappear also. First, I looked for someone to write it. There was one other, a woman from a scientific society. She was honored, but she had no courage."

87

"I, too, am honored, but I don't know if I can do it."

Woman-Who-Dreams shook her head. "You are the one. I was disappointed the other woman had no courage. I did not understand my dream. Now I know." Woman-Who-Dreams extended her pipe. "You like try again? Can be soothing. Can help you think."

Kate hesitated, then took the pipe and put it to her mouth. She took a small puff. That was fine. She puffed again and coughed, but only once. She passed the pipe back. And it did seem to help her think. In fact, she thought she understood the larger sense of what Woman-Who-Dreams was doing—the longer vision here.

When the sound and the fury of the moment stilled— when this last Indian uprising passed into history, the trial was over, and ghost dancing was no more, what would remain? That which appeared inconsequential now—the weavings of the Navajo, the pots of the Hopi, the quillwork of the Sioux, women's arts all, traditions so old and enduring as to transcend the immediate even if the immediate included the near destruction of Woman-Who-Dreams' own people. To document that . . . No, she corrected herself, not document the way Bill took portraits of soldiers and recreated battle scenes but to photograph, truly capture this . . .

Kate swallowed. Deep down she felt as if her whole life was trying to focus. Her drive for "straight" unposed pictures grew out of a belief that photography was uniquely suited to the recording of detail—the trivial by painterly standards, but detail that once recorded somehow became elevated to formal history and, thus, the true preservation of tradition. She could hardly imagine a more perfect union of subject and photographic style. It was almost as if this was what she'd been preparing for ever since she was five years old and her father first showed her how to slide a plate into a camera.

The pause grew long. Then Woman-Who-Dreams flipped the newspapers over. "Next to your pictures, these lies look like Coyote droppings. No?"

Kate shook her head, not because she didn't agree but

because her husband intended to stay in South Dakota only until the trial was over. Then he wanted to go to California. To not go with him would be to repeat the pattern of the women of her family, willful and unwise. She couldn't remember the times she'd promised her father she'd be "good." She'd agreed to that long before she'd understood why he asked. Long before she'd understood the importance.

"You must meet the women of the Sacred Quillworkers. I will fix it. I will fix it that you go hunting with them," Woman-Who-Dreams continued. "They will see you have the Double-Woman spirit. They will know you are sister."

"I don't know if I can help you," Kate mumbled, now thinking of the colonel. If taking a single picture of an Indian had upset him, what would he think of this?

Woman-Who-Dreams smoothed the calico dress over her legs. "You are not like other women. You know you have a hidden part that must live. This is good. This is the way of Double-Woman. It makes you face the truth. It gives you courage."

Kate shook her head. "I don't think you understand. I won't even be here long."

The older woman passed the pipe back to Kate. "Smoke. Think. Find a way, or your spirit will not rest."

6

Next morning Kate discovered that the whole city of Sioux Falls had taken on a festive air. Rough-looking frontiersmen in broad-brimmed slouch hats and wearing pistols mingled with farmers, townspeople, and eastern tourists, all of them taking in the trial like a holiday. Merchants propped their doors open and pushed barrels and boxes of their wares out onto the boardwalk with special "trial day sale" signs on them. Others draped red, white, and blue bunting across the windows in front of their establishments and advertised free coffee. Street vendors were hawking everything from bags of roasted nuts to yesterday's newspaper. On one street corner an Indian woman spread a blanket and set out her souvenir wares, beaded bags and child-size feather headdresses.

Overall, Sioux Falls had a bustle of prosperity. Church bells and factory whistles mixed with the repeated clack-clack of trolley cars and horse-drawn carriages sounding across the newly laid cobblestone streets that distinguished the downtown section. Those sounds were the same Kate had grown up with in New Jersey, and in some ways all of Sioux Falls struck her as an odd transplant that had not so much grown up where it was as been transported there. In contrast to the broad, treeless plain all around, Sioux Falls was a tight grid of straight streets and tall buildings, most of them at least three stories. They shaded the narrow streets beneath and cut the sky into ribbons glimpsed between rooftops. The storefronts and boardwalks were fashioned after storefronts and boardwalks in more established cities like Chicago or New York, as if some collective consciousness sought to deny Sioux Falls its newness or its westernness.

At least those were the thoughts that fluttered at the back of her mind as she wove her way through the city's increasingly crowded streets, a feat made more difficult by the fact that she had a folding display easel tucked under one arm and a bulky satchel flung over the other. Mary followed carrying a box of photographs. Homer ran ahead.

She took Eighth to Phillips Street, the boardwalks growing more and more congested as she approached the site of the trial. She paused at the corner of Tenth and Phillips to let a wagon pass. On the other side of the street a group of reporters lifted their hats. "Morning, ma'am. How's your dog?"

She returned the greeting while Homer wagged his tail in recognition. This same group of reporters had been following the story of the so-called Ghost Dance Uprising since last November because news of Indian trouble sold newspapers. They'd anticipated a big story from the first. After all, over three thousand troops had been ordered to South Dakota—the largest concentration of military force since the Civil War. But then when nothing happened for the first few weeks, these reporters had been disappointed. Peace talks and the surrender of one tribe after another hadn't made exciting press. She nodded her head as she recognized three Nebraska scribblers, the man from *Harper's Weekly,* another from the *Washington Evening Star,* a third from the *New York World,* and Frederic Remington, who was sketching for *Frank Leslie's Illustrated Newspaper.*

The New York reporter tipped his hat again and asked,

"What do you think? Anything interesting going to come out of this trial?"

Kate didn't know why he asked. He expected something interesting or he wouldn't be here. None of them would—she and Bill either. Like it or not, they were all making a living off this. But she knew the kind of polite answer he expected and saw no reason not to give it to him. She smiled and lowered her eyes. "Oh, I don't know. I just sell my pictures and leave the politics to those who know more about it."

"Good decision," the New Yorker responded. "My colleagues might consider the example." He elbowed an Omaha man who returned, "I believe the lady was speaking to you."

With that, Kate pushed on, leaving them to their banter. She found a space just outside the door leading to the upper floors of the Masonic Temple, a three-story redbrick building with a white clock tower, where the trial was set to begin. Two marshals guarded the entrance. Retail shops occupied the ground level. The third-floor lodge rooms had been appropriated for the proceedings. Sioux Falls had a courthouse under construction at Sixth and Main. One day it was expected to be the biggest building in the state, or so some liked to brag, but not yet.

She opened her easel and began arranging a display of photographs while Mary pinned other pictures to the skirt and sleeves of Kate's dress. Even before all the pictures were pinned in place, a crowd gathered to look them over. Why not? She had a fine selection of Bill's documentary photographs, Indian camps, army troops, battle scenes, a portrait of Sitting Bull, not to mention her own pictures.

Business was brisk—soldiers buying pictures to send home, people come to town for the trial wanting souvenirs. A Negro shoeshine from one of the hotels asked if she had a picture of Troop K, Ninth Cavalry—black soldiers. She did. The black Ninth Cavalry had saved the Seventh Cavalry in a skirmish following Wounded Knee, a fact the shoeshine knew and shared with her. Someone else wanted a picture of Sitting Bull's horse, a dapple gray circus pony trained to do tricks. That horse had been given to him by Buffalo Bill. She got it for him.

She sold five-by-seven unmounted photo-book prints for fifty cents each. An eleven-by-fourteen print, suitable for wall hanging, cost $2.75. Not cheap. A fancy lady's hat cost about the same. But photographs were the current rage. Every decent up-to-date home had parlor books full of them, racks of stereographs, and at least one wall covered with photographic views.

Leaving Mary to take care of the display board, Kate moved through the crowd, pausing every few steps to turn, her arms held wide, her skirt swinging with a swish and a bounce. The soldiers liked that. They followed her down the street asking her to turn first one way and then another. Having asked that favor, they almost always felt obligated to buy something. Older men, too. They would bend to examine closely one or more photographs and then purchase several.

Her strutting and turning were not exactly appropriately ladylike. She imagined a local matron might have gotten booed off the street for similar behavior. She only got away with it because she was a "traveling woman," and that was one of the reasons she liked being a "traveling woman," why she had married Bill on the condition that he take her "traveling." Even the scandal that trailed her grandmother had never tripped her until she'd been forced to "settle down."

"What's this?" a well-dressed gentleman with a British accent asked, and felt his breast pocket, obviously looking for his glasses.

He was pointing to a picture pinned to the back of Kate's sleeve. She held her arm out so he could get a better look. She knew the picture. It was one of Bill's, an image that struck many of her customers as strange—rows and rows of uniformed Indian men standing at attention with tin stars on their chests, Remington pistols strapped to their waists, and Springfield rifles slung over their shoulders.

"I don't know when I've seen the like," he was saying,

now looking through his spectacles. "Are they truly Indian?"

"The Pine Ridge Indian Police Force," Kate answered.

"An Indian police force," the gentleman said, now drawing back and rubbing his chin.

Most of her customers regarded that photograph as some kind of unnatural dress-up. In fact it was the other way around. Most photographers, including Bill, required their Indian subjects to dress "native," even to the point of supplying the costumes from trunks that they carried with them. Truth was, a lot of Indians didn't own anything truly "native" anymore.

Truth didn't sell. Except for this one photograph, which sold as an oddity, no one wanted to buy pictures of Indians that didn't look "Indian." That was one of the problems with taking photographs of the quillworkers.

Kate had thought of little else since her visit with Woman-Who-Dreams. And the more she thought about taking those pictures, the more impossible it seemed. She wanted to take the pictures. She believed the older woman was right. Someone needed to take those pictures if for no other reason than preserving history. But who would buy them? Never mind the fact that Bill wanted to go to California soon, she couldn't afford to take pictures no one would buy. She barely managed to keep herself supplied as it was, and then only because she was willing to parade herself and her wares on street corners.

"Not much good are they?" the British gentleman said.

"I beg your pardon?"

"These Indian police," he said pointing to the picture. "They aren't much bloody good, are they? I mean, if you had to call in a whole army to stop a little ghost dancing, these Indian police or whatever they're called must not have been much good."

She knew the answer to that. Because of the objections of local ranchers, the Indian police hadn't been issued rifles until well after ghost dancing was considered out of hand. But that wasn't what the gentleman wanted to hear. She clicked her tongue a couple of times and shook her head. "I know. Isn't this whole business strange?"

He liked that. He smiled and nodded and bought two copies of that picture saying, "Nobody is going to believe this back home."

She knew what he meant. Nobody was going to understand quillworking or Indian women's sacred societies unless someone put together a whole series of photographs illustrating the complete subject. Such a collection might be sold with lecture notes or bound together. But for a project of that size, she would need more than her one aging camera, a ten-year-old gift from her father, and the limited supplies she could manage by selling photographs on the street.

A young soldier asked, "Do you have a picture of Lieutenant Casey, the man Plenty Horses shot?"

She did. The picture showed him in dress uniform mounted on a coal black mare. It was pinned to the bottom edge of her skirt. As she turned to show it to him, she caught another young soldier enjoying a glimpse of her ankle. When their eyes met, he hastily ordered a copy of the same photograph.

"The lieutenant was a good man," the first soldier commented. "I sure hope they hang his killer."

She nodded not because she agreed but because that was easier than disagreeing. Besides, she wasn't entirely sure of her own opinion. She didn't think what Plenty Horses did was right, but . . .

A shout went up; the crowd parted. Kate looked around and saw Plenty Horses being escorted up the street by four law officers, obviously on his way to the trial. On her board she had a print of him as he was posed with the soldiers two days ago, his arm leaning against a Hotchkiss gun that had been supplied as a prop. She wasn't sure why. A Hotchkiss gun was a breech-loading cannon that fired an explosive shell measuring 3.2 inches. There had been four such guns at Wounded Knee, and later one had been used to blow a hole in the frozen ground large enough to make a mass grave. She thought that made it an odd prop. But then the picture on her board was odd in more ways than one. It had been taken just before the horses were spooked and showed Plenty Horses in a suit and long hair. But obviously Nock had decided against continuing such shenanigans. Today he had Plenty Horses wearing a faded blue blanket covering a cheap red shirt and well-worn trousers. On his feet were plain buckskin moccasins. His braided hair was tied with strips of red flannel. Powers Nock was beside him wearing a plaid suit and round black hat. The double set of watch chains still crisscrossed his vest. Plenty Horses' father followed behind. His face was soft with wrinkles, his arms crossed over his broad chest holding his blanket. As they stepped up onto the boardwalk beside her, the father reached out and patted his son on the shoulder.

Someone touched Kate's shoulder. She started and turned.

It was Richard Houston. "Good morning," he greeted her. He was smiling his usual broad smile, his hat pushed back, his hands poked into his pockets. She felt his eyes studying her. She couldn't imagine what he expected to see. She was fully dressed today. Maybe that didn't matter. It was said that Richard had "an eye for the ladies." In other words, he was a known flirt. But as far as she was concerned, he could cast his eye someplace else.

She returned his greeting.

Then when she offered nothing else, he bent and patted her dog. "Irish setter mixed with some larger breed, I would guess," he commented. "Extraordinary like his owner."

"I beg your pardon."

"Extraordinary women don't have to beg anyone's pardon," he said, and left off petting her dog.

"I'm sure I don't understand your meaning," she replied.

"I think you do," he answered, and then suddenly straightened and reached across to tug a photograph from the bottom corner of her display board. It was the one of the birds floating wing tip to wing tip. He stood there in the middle of the boardwalk and studied it long enough so that she began to feel embarrassed. When he looked up again, his glance lacked some of his usual cockiness. But she wasn't fooled. He was just dabbling, having a frontier fling. Everything about him spoke to finer things. She pitied the woman who was the current object of his attentions. It wasn't wise to get involved with a man while he was "sowing his oats."

But now with a different tone he asked, "This turned out rather well, don't you think?"

She nodded. She was pleased with it. The composition was simple, the lines clean, the detail so fine every feather was distinct. More, the suspension of the moment was so tense, it was as though the photograph itself could be shaken and startled, sending the birds off. That's what arrested the eye—the feeling that if you looked away even for a second, the birds would be gone.

"I'll buy this one," he said, and pulled his other hand out of his pocket holding coin.

"Why?" she returned.

"Why?" he repeated. "Do you ask your customers why they buy your pictures?"

"No," she answered, thinking he was right. That was not the expected response, but it was the one she wanted answered. "Most of my customers don't have the means of making their own," she added.

"Oh, I'm not likely to duplicate this one," he said. "Ask me, this is really too good to be sold as a street souvenir."

She didn't know how to answer that. What else was she going to do with it?

"It ought to be in an exhibition, maybe shown in London or Vienna," he went on, his voice assuming its usual breezy banter. He held the picture up and away from him as if it were hung on a wall.

Kate felt a confusion rising in her. She understood the flirtatious little game she played with some of her customers, but she couldn't think why Richard wanted to flatter her. "Do you know of an exhibition that would welcome a woman's work?" she asked.

That got him. He paused, the picture still held out. Then he seemed to become aware of his overly dramatic stance and dropped his arm. "No, but Julia Margaret Cameron must show her work someplace."

"Julia Margaret Cameron's pictures are nothing but pretentious fuzziness, the kind of sentimentality expected of my sex," she told him, because she thought if he was going to compliment her, he ought to know better than to make that comparison. The woman, a Britisher, deliberately photographed her subjects out of focus to create "impressions." Kate considered that kind of photography entirely "too precious."

But he seemed not to understand. He paused, as if puzzling over her comment, then he shook his head and said without much conviction, "Perhaps you're right. What does your husband think of this picture?"

"I don't know."

"You haven't shown it to him," he guessed right.

She shrugged.

"Too bad. That's his loss."

"I'm sure I don't know why."

"I'll say it plain then. I don't think your husband has learned to fully appreciate his young wife."

Kate felt the heat rise to her cheeks. She had always blushed too easily. It was the curse of being fair-skinned and redheaded, but she was not going to let that embarrassment render her speechless. "I beg your pardon," she said. Then, lowering her voice, she added, "I'll have you know holding my ankle while I was out on that ledge does not give you license to assume familiarity."

"Actually, I thought maybe it did," he said, matching her half whisper. Then he quickly added, "But don't let anyone tell you this isn't good." He indicated the photograph. "You're far more woman than you pretend to be." With that he tipped his hat to her and mounted the steps on his way to observe the trial.

She was left shaking, partly from temper, more from hoping he was right. But then she didn't know why she needed to be impressed by his flattery. She'd known she was good since she was fifteen.

A man had come to her father's studio one day to buy

pictures. She didn't remember his name now, only that her father was agitated and more anxious than usual that the man be pleased. She was under stern orders to stay in the back and not disturb their meeting. Only the gentleman had taken it upon himself to wander into the back, and seeing her work, he mistook five of Kate's pictures for her father's. He exclaimed over them and bought them, never the wiser.

She and her father never spoke of the incident. Didn't matter. It was only one of a myriad of things they'd never articulated. It had simply become woven into the vast mosaic of quiet behind the raucous surface of her family. But he'd given her the camera shortly after that. And she'd known. Without it ever being spoken, she'd known from that day that she was a photographer, a good one.

Still she couldn't help turning and watching as Richard disappeared into the building behind her.

"Pretentious fuzziness," Richard mumbled as he climbed the inside stairs to where the trial was to begin.

The man in the gray suit ahead of him suddenly stopped and turned. "Did you say something?" he asked.

Richard shook his head. He hadn't thought his mumble was that loud.

The man, a beefy fellow with highly colored cheeks, looked Richard over. Other people pushing past on their way up the same narrow stairway offered their own disapproving glances. Then the beefy fellow shrugged and continued on.

Richard turned sideways and pressed himself against the stairway wall as he wondered why it was that every encounter with Kate left him not only feeling like an idiot but acting like one.

He wasn't particularly fond of Miss Cameron's work either; and he couldn't say Kate's description of it wasn't apt. He just hadn't expected such a direct opinion. He'd only brought her name up because Julia Margaret Cameron was the one famous lady photographer he knew, and he'd thought it would lead to a bit of conversation. He'd counted on Kate to say something like, "Oh, that is an interesting notion . . ." or "I suppose so. What do you think?"—things that would allow him to continue to talk. Her bluntness practically left him tongue-tied. That was not his style. In some quarters he'd been faulted for his "smooth talk."

Having worked off that much of his peeve, Richard continued up and into the assembly hall. It was a large room, open in the center, but surrounded on three sides by a row of pillars holding up the balcony. The pillars had been painted to look like marble, the railings were carved, the woodwork wide and ornate. The floor was carpeted, but a canvas had been rolled over the carpet to protect it from the crowd now filling the room.

Richard pushed through that crowd, making his way to the front where he found a seat. The day before, during jury selection, he hadn't even gotten in. He wondered why this trial mattered to so many people. But clearly it did. Curiosity seekers packed the room as if they'd come to see a Sunday opera where all the characters took a bow at the end of the performance. This was going to end with a hanging.

Then he spotted Ethan Johnson, the general manager of Buffalo Bill's Wild West Show. He was sitting four rows over talking animatedly with a young man in buckskin. Seeing him, Richard wondered again about how much this was justice and how much was just opera, an extravaganza. Only a month ago, Buffalo Bill had been in town himself hiring ghost dance leaders for his show. Now Richard couldn't help wondering who Mr. Johnson was hoping to recruit: the witnesses as soon as they'd finished testifying? That was the likelihood. Buffalo Bill liked to advertise himself as "authentic," a "troupe of real players from the real West."

A shoving match erupted in the section roped off for reporters, and all heads turned in that direction, but it was quickly broken up. Richard took his seat. His own interest was purely coincidental. In a couple of weeks he was to join a survey team mapping the Colorado River. Meanwhile, having found himself in Sioux Falls with the trial about to begin, he'd thought he might as well watch this bit of history. He guessed from the level of animated discussion going on all around him that his was a detachment most of the spectators in that room lacked.

He turned his gaze to the balcony where the colonel, his aide, and several other soldiers sat with a row of Indian army scouts, many of whom would be testifying, he knew. Scattered around the rest of the room were other soldiers, town citizens, politicians, and their ladies. Directly in front of Richard sat Sam Spencer, South Dakota's biggest cattleman, and his wife. A few days ago, Mr. Spencer had cornered Richard in a bar and harangued him about how no one would be safe until the reservations were broken up, sold, and all the Indians dispersed. Richard didn't agree but suspected that would happen anyway eventually. Men like Sam Spencer and Richard's father usually got what they wanted. This whole trial reminded Richard of how the men in his father's circle did business—like gentlemen, the form carefully maintained, the outcome understood.

Richard's gaze came around to Plenty Horses. He sat at the defense table, his shoulders squared, his eyes forward. Next to him was a colorfully clad gentleman Richard guessed was his lawyer. His case was hopeless; everyone said so, but Richard thought the man might have at least made an effort to look the part of a lawyer, not a carnival barker. At the next table over, District Attorney Sterling and his assistant sat with their heads together such that he couldn't make out much more than their identically combed parts. A military lawyer sat with them, supposedly as an observer.

Then he spotted Bill Burke. He was seated on the lower level near the far wall with his tripod and other photographic equipment leaning into one corner. He was saving an empty seat. For Kate, Richard guessed and suddenly remembered the photograph he was still holding in his left hand. He pulled out his handkerchief and wrapped it around the print. Then he slipped it inside his jacket next to his pocket flask. When he looked up again, Kate was taking her place beside Bill.

She was alone. He guessed she left the Indian girl to tend her dog and other things. She'd also removed the photographs from her skirt and shirt. Without them, her attire looked remarkably unremarkable, a brown, pin-striped walking skirt, a cream-colored shirtwaist trimmed in some kind of embroidery, a fitted Eton jacket pulled over that. Good quality clothes, but nothing his mother and sisters would have considered stylish, if he understood such things. Still she turned heads. Except Bill's. He didn't even look up as she took her seat beside him and clearly hadn't noticed the other looks she got. Richard thought that strange. If she were his wife . . . What a thought!

The judge entered, and Richard turned his attention in that direction. The judge was a man gone to paunch and gray hair from his mustache to his eyebrows to the top of his head. He sat and took out a pair of glasses that he fitted over his ears and adjusted on his nose while the clerk announced the current case.

Then the Indian's short, plaid-jacketed lawyer stood and, in doing so, spilled his papers across the table. A muffled chuckle spread across the room. The lawyer scooped his papers back into a pile. He looked at the jury, then around at the spectators. He had a pleasant enough face, Richard thought, and then noticed with a start that as he scanned the room, his eye rested a moment on Kate. But there was more to the look than just a passing appreciation. They knew each other, Richard decided, although Kate made no gesture of acknowledgment.

When the courtroom quieted again, the Indian's lawyer composed himself, cleared his throat, and then made a motion for dismissal.

The judge peered over his glasses. "Dismissal?"

The Indian's lawyer cleared his throat again and offered an explanation. It took Richard a moment to figure out what he was saying. Seemingly that was the case with nearly everyone in the courtroom. There was a pause of quiet expectation as everyone leaned forward, listening. That was followed by a moment of silence as the Indian's lawyer finished speaking and everyone paused to take in what he'd said. Then there was an eruption of talk. Richard looked around. All across the room ladies' heads were bobbing up and down as they chattered, that motion exaggerated by their hats. Men punctuated their speech with gestures. Reporters scribbled in their notebooks. The mayor sent his assistant scurrying out the door. The colonel and his aide had their heads together, huddled, and Sam Spencer nearly choked, having swallowed his chew.

Unlike the rest of the crowd of spectators, who were now on the edge of their seats, Richard settled back with a new respect for the Indian's short, oddly dressed lawyer. He tried to remember his name but couldn't. In any case, he'd clearly misjudged him and now fully expected he was going to enjoy this courtroom charade.

War, Kate thought. But, of course, they were at war.

Yet for some reason, Nock's saying so had raised a spasm of nervous tics in her husband. He slid forward, he squirmed, his breathing grew quick, his eyes darted between the colonel and Nock and back again.

Kate's own gaze went to Nock, who was rather matter-of-factly checking one of his pocket watches, almost as though he weren't aware of the uproar he'd caused. Although she did catch him taking a peek at the jury as if to see how those twelve men were reacting. Much as everyone else, she noted. They, too, acted surprised and confused.

If she understood Nock's motion, he'd merely questioned whether this court had jurisdiction. Since the lieutenant and Plenty Horses viewed themselves as belligerents in a state of war, the incident between them could not be regarded as a criminal offense within the competence of the civil courts. That wasn't the same as claiming his client was innocent or ought not to hang. In all likelihood, she thought a military court would sentence Plenty Horses to death just as quickly. That didn't seem to be the point. It was the word *war* that had rippled across the room, changing expressions, even the judge's. He was now drumming his fingers on the table in front of him while he waited for his clerk to pound the court back to order, the gavel sounding sharp and repeatedly, wood against wood.

When the room was quiet again, the judge gave a quick

look in the colonel's direction; then he said he would take the motion under advisement. For now they would proceed. That got a wave of hushed comment, although Kate had the feeling no one in the room was exactly satisfied with the judge's decision. Except Nock. She didn't know him well, and yet she could have sworn he was satisfied, as if that was exactly what he'd expected.

And so the trial began.

After the opening speeches, the first witness called was, Bear-That-Lays-Down. He was an army scout and an uncle to Plenty Horses. Sam Williams, a half-breed army scout, was called next. His testimony was practically the same. Crooked Arm, the Indian she'd captured in her picture, was the next witness. He had a bandage across one side of his forehead and limped a little. Otherwise, he didn't appear any worse for having hugged a buffalo. More startling was how different he looked wearing his army scout uniform, but he told the same story.

Lieutenant Casey, whom most of the Indians liked and affectionately called Big Nose, had ridden to the top of a hill near where Red Cloud's band of Indians were camped. He was stopped by a guard but requested a meeting with someone from Red Cloud's band. A little later the son-in-law of Red Cloud came up from the camp and spoke with the lieutenant. None of the witnesses could testify as to what was said. Either they hadn't heard or they didn't understand English. They were all testifying with the aid of an interpreter, a stocky half-breed with his hair greased back and close to the sides of his head. But on the question of who killed the lieutenant they were all of one opinion.

Bear-That-Lays-Down did not see the shot fired that killed the lieutenant, but when asked directly who had murdered Casey, he replied, Tsunka Waka Otta (Plenty Horses). Both Sam Williams and Crooked Arm expressed surprise at what had happened, saying they had not thought Casey would be shot. He had come in peace and was still talking to Red Cloud's son-in-law when Plenty Horses lifted his rifle and fired.

As the day wore on, Kate became aware of a faint odor of

hair tonic and men's boots. Some of the boys sitting in the windowsills got restless and slipped out. A fly buzzed. The testimony sounded convincing, especially coming from Indians, even relatives of Plenty Horses. And after his first dramatic flurry, Nock seemed subdued. He asked only a few questions:

"Were the Indians in a warlike condition?"

"Did Lieutenant Casey know he was approaching hostile ground?"

"Would the army have shot a spy who rode too close to one of their camps?"

He was ghost dancing, she realized, circling round and round the same tree until the vision came. He was doing with words what a good photographer did with camera and plate. He was framing the picture, getting the focus, waiting for the right light. She didn't know how else to explain the charisma of this short man in his plaid suit and shabby tie. His socks didn't match. His voice was nasal. Clearly, he believed what he said, but so did the prosecuting attorneys. It was larger than that.

It was as if Powers T. Nock weren't really talking to the jury, the judge, or the roomful of spectators. His focal length was set at infinity. He was speaking to history. It was the same thing she'd sensed about Woman-Who-Dreams.

She scanned the courtroom, taking it all in again: the judge scratching his ear, the soldier shifting his weight. She saw a woman fuss with her skirt and a man sneak a sip from a bottle hidden in his jacket pocket. The temptation in life was to diddle around, keeping your ankles covered and your throat wet. But the world was wilder than that, more dangerous and bitter, more extravagant and bright. Powers T. Nock knew that, she realized. His strength came from refusing to raise mere arguments when he could address the collective conscience.

Later, after court had been adjourned for the day and the room had emptied except for a few hangers-on, the Indian army scouts lined up for a group portrait. Seven of them— the three who had testified and four more who were scheduled for tomorrow.

They stood there, half at attention, for fifteen minutes or more while Bill got ready. He spread the legs of his tripod, mounted the camera on the tripod's head, turned a cogwheel to raise the camera, and turned a second cogwheel to extend the bellows. Then he disappeared momentarily beneath the black cloth, fine-tuned the focus, emerged, and set the aperture. He pushed a plateholder in, pulled the slide out, grasped the Indian rubber bulb at the end of the cable, and then changed his mind. Looking over his subjects, he decided he wanted them arranged differently—in a row, but with their arms clasped across their chests, the tallest in the center.

That didn't please the scouts.

At first, they refused to move. Then they began shoving each other. Bill shouted for the interpreter. He was in the back of the room, but rushed forward and plunged into the growing melee, shouting and shoving his way to the middle. A few minutes later when everyone began to calm down again, the interpreter turned to Bill. He tried to explain that the scouts had some sense of their own ranking, and it had nothing to do with height.

Bill wouldn't listen. He simply barked back at the interpreter that it was his job to get those Indians lined up "properly," and he wasn't going to hear any excuses. The result was a row of stiff-backed, grim-faced Indian scouts with more space between their shoulders than Bill wanted. But he gave up trying to get them to move closer and handed Kate the flash bar.

She hated flash bars. Her father had made something of an early reputation taking indoor pictures, but that was at a time when such photographs were a novelty. And even then, her father had known the difference between a novelty and a good photograph. But she had no hope of getting out of that makeshift courtroom anytime soon unless Bill got his picture. So she raised the flash bar above her head.

Bill was out of temper. He barked that she wasn't holding it high enough, and he didn't like where she was standing. With a flash bar, it didn't matter as long as it was generally up and in front. The light was going to be flat anyway, like noonday sun. Besides, she hated lighting the powder, hated the pop and the smell, hated getting the sparks in her hair when it went off. But she stepped closer and put it higher, which was what he wanted.

That was what she hadn't liked about the testimony she'd heard all day. It had reminded her of how Bill arranged pictures—always according to some predetermined notion as to what he considered right. As he ducked under the black cloth behind his camera, she said, "If you ask me, it was a war out there."

He popped back out from under the cloth. "What are you talking about?"

She shrugged. When Bill annoyed her, she made it a practice to return annoyance. Besides, she really wanted to know what it was about Nock's talk of war that had so startled him and the colonel. She'd never seen the colonel so discomforted. She hadn't known he could be distressed by much of anything. Tramping across the plain with him and his men last winter, he'd always been in charge, the one giving orders, no questions, never any hesitation.

"There were too many soldiers," she continued. "Ask me, anytime that many soldiers are called out, it's war."

"Nobody is asking you about anything," Bill told her. "Besides, it has nothing to do with soldiers. It has to do with the fact that a bunch of renegade Indians cannot declare war on the United States of America." With that, he put his head under the cloth, focused, and in a poof of false light took the picture.

It was dark and quiet. Then there was a sudden pop and the sound of breaking glass.

Powers T. Nock sat straight up in bed, having identified the sounds even before he was fully awake. Still semiconscious, he pushed back the feather tick, felt for his slippers and found them, grabbed the robe off his bedpost, and stumbled to the door of his bedroom.

It was a little after two o'clock in the morning. He knew because even in his sleep he heard the muffled marking of the hours from his collection of clocks downstairs and noted the passage of time. Now, finally throwing off the last of his deep sleep, he took the steps going down at a near run and flipped on the parlor light, a single electric bulb behind a shade installed in the ceiling. The room leaped out of shadow to reveal a good-size rock sitting in the middle of the carpet amid a splash of glass from what had been the front-room window.

He could hear his mother feeling her way down the stairs behind him. She was bumping into things, the umbrella stand, the foyer table.

"Put on the light," he called to her. "The excitement's over."

No answer.

"Everything is all right. Just put on the light," he said again.

Still no answer.

He turned to discover she'd made it to the bottom of the steps, holding a gun unsteadily between both of her hands. He jumped back. He recognized it as an old revolver belonging to his father. Worse, she had the thing pointed as much at him as anything.

"God damn," he swore in surprise. "What do you think you're going to do with that thing?"

"Don't you take the Lord's name in vain," his mother told him, now moving the gun up and down like a finger she was shaking at him. "I won't have you being disrespectful. No, I won't."

First things first, he thought and asked, "Is that thing loaded?"

"Oh, I always keep it loaded," she announced. "Your father told me to never, never be in the house alone without a loaded gun. And I never have been."

"You're not alone. What am I? A mouse living in the woodwork?"

"But you won't touch a gun. Your father tried to teach you, God rest his soul. You couldn't learn."

Wouldn't learn, he corrected her sub vox. By the time his father got around to lessons in the manly arts of shooting a gun and throwing a punch, he'd already figured out he could outsmart all the playground bullies and anyone else who thought to give him trouble. What did he need with guns and fisticuffs. Besides, by that time it was clear he was never going to have any height or weight to throw around. In fact, it was that lack of size that had made his father put off such lessons until Nock was past needing them. So he'd feigned clumsiness while his mother made excuses for him: he was small for his age, or his health was delicate. He didn't care as long as it freed him to return to whatever book he was reading at the time.

"When you couldn't learn, your father taught me," his mother went on. "We would go out in the afternoons while you were in school and practice. I would shoot cans and bottles until I could hit at least as many as I missed. Your father said somebody in the family, besides him, needed to know how to shoot. He said . . ."

Nock shook his head. He hadn't known that and found it hard to imagine his father teaching his mother about shooting. Yet in another sense, it was absolutely typical of his father to insist he had to teach someone. Once he had gotten an idea in his head, there was no dislodging it. None. Nock reached over and took the gun from his mother's hands without interrupting her ongoing narrative about how she'd learned to stand and sight her shots. He opened the chamber. He looked and then had to look twice to be sure.

"There's only one bullet in here," he said.

"That's all I ever keep in it."

"One bullet?"

"Well, I didn't want to have anything too big and awful happen if I ever had to actually use the gun."

He never had been able to follow his mother's logic completely, even in the best of circumstances. This, however, was a new height of singular thinking. Bullets were not like shots of whiskey where more than one in short succession multiplied the effect. History had been changed by a single bullet. More than once. Plenty Horses had fired a single bullet. Look where that had gotten him. But rather than try to talk any sense on the point, he removed the bullet, set the gun on the foyer table, and said, "I'm going to check outside."

She grabbed his arm. "Wait until morning. Wait until it's light. You aren't the kind who should be expected to . . ." But she didn't finish that thought before she spotted the broken glass on her Turkish rug and gasped.

There were certain things of such importance to Nock's mother, she didn't tolerate any mischance in connection to them. The Turkish carpet was one of those. She rushed forward and began picking up the largest of the shards saying, "Oh, what if this should get worked in? What if it cuts the fibers?"

Leaving her to that worry, Nock opened the front door and peered into the darkness. He wasn't expecting to see anyone. And he didn't. It was when he turned to close the door that he saw the smear of red paint. It read, "Indian lover."

His mother was suddenly beside him again, gasping again. "Oh, Powers, what does that mean?"

He thought the sentiment was fairly self-explanatory. He tested the wetness of the paint with one finger and said, "I think it means I'm getting someplace with the trial."

His mother suddenly stiffened. "Oh, now, you can't let them make you afraid. You have to buck up. Your father would want to know that you bucked up, that you showed them all a thing or two. You can do it."

Indeed, he could. He'd already hit a nerve, and that, to his way of thinking, represented considerably finer marksmanship than hitting a front window.

7

Homer barked.

Kate woke with a start.

"Shut up, you damned mangy monster," Kate heard Bill say loudly and slurred. "Shut up, I tell you. A man shouldn't have to be barked at in his own home—his palace."

Someone else giggled, a woman. "I don't think your dog likes you."

"Not my damned dog," Bill stated, and gave a grunt. "My wife's damned dog."

"Your wife?" The woman's words were slurred, but not as badly as Bill's.

Kate sat up and swung her feet out of bed. It was dark, but she sensed it was close to dawn. Bill hadn't been home all night. Homer was still barking.

"Damn that damned dog," Bill was going on. Then Kate heard him kick at Homer. His feet scuffed against the canvas covering the ground. She heard him stumble. He must have fallen. There was a thud against one of the wardrobe trunks, and the woman exclaimed, "Oh, dearie, oh, dearie, did you hurt yourself?"

Homer was still barking.

Bill oofed a grunt and must have bumped another trunk. Kate heard the two of them bump against each other. If he kept it up, he was going to knock the whole tent down, she thought. She called Homer. He scrambled up onto the bed just as she stood and pulled a robe around herself. Homer turned a circle, bumping her twice and growling once. He squatted silently at the edge of the mattress, his nose pointed outward, his noise reduced to a low threatening rumble. By that time Kate had gotten the lantern lit and trimmed. She raised it to the hook at the end of the wagon, and "Bill's Palace," as he called it, took on enough glow to show him pulling himself to his feet while he leaned on one rocking wardrobe trunk as if he were at sea, swaying back and forth with the waves. His lady friend was supporting his arm. She was a thin blond with a scar on one cheek. She was wearing a frilly evening dress with such a big pink ruffle, Kate wondered if it had been stitched from a bed covering.

Then the woman's eyes went wide, and her lips almost touched Bill's ear as she whispered, "Who's that? Is that your wife? You didn't tell me you had a wife."

"Don't most men?" he answered her.

"Well, I mean, I thought she must be away. You know, stayed back home in the East or something."

Bill grunted. "My wife's a most original woman. She don't believe in staying home. That would be too much the lady, staying home and stitching couch covers or something. She thinks that's boring. You two should get along famously."

"Hey, I'm not staying here," the woman told him.

"I don't know why not. I invited you to breakfast. By damn, I'll give you breakfast. Kate's got this Indian girl who makes decent biscuits. Kate'll wake her up. Won't you, Kate?"

Kate stirred up the fire in the stove herself, not that she intended to make biscuits. She intended to be warmed by more than the slow burn of her anger. Besides, Bill didn't want biscuits. He wanted her to scream and shout and maybe threaten him with the stove poker. He found that arousing, but she wasn't going to satisfy. A deliberate calm would worry Bill more, she knew. It would even sober him some.

Meanwhile, Bill's lady friend backed toward the door. He shuffled in her direction and grabbed her arm.

She protested. "Really, I must go. It's been fine, but I'm not that hungry, and . . ."

He wasn't listening. He shoved her into a chair behind the fold-down table between the end of the wagon and the tent side. Then he flopped himself down beside her, leaving her wedged in with no graceful way to escape. He thumped the table with his fist and looked around at Kate. "We need some coffee. My friend here named Edweena or something."

"Edith," the woman prompted.

"Yeah," he said. "My friend here, named Ed-wee-ith, and I need some coffee."

Kate agreed and scooped a double portion of grounds into the pot that was beginning to warm. If he wanted coffee, she'd give him coffee strong enough to dissolve his guts.

"Don't mind my wife," he told Edith. "I promised her I'd take her traveling. Didn't have to promise her nothing else, just traveling. She had to go traveling, traveling. Respectable women don't much take to traveling. I do believe that's how it normally works, don't you? But then my wife didn't come from no respectable family. That's why she married me."

"I really need to go," Edith said. She nudged Bill as if she thought he might move out of her way.

He didn't. "Of course, that was nothing but a silly promise," he continued. "A silly promise made late at night on a moonlit porch. But my wife stood before a preacher and at least one hundred good churchgoing citizens and promised to love and obey. What do you think of that?" he asked Edith.

"It's not the same thing," Kate retorted before Edith could answer. "A personal pledge is not the same as some ceremony."

Immediately she regretted saying that.

"You better believe it," he told her, letting a self-satisfied little grin creep across his face, marking the fact that he'd scored. "Your promise was legally binding." Then, as if he wanted to rub it in, but couldn't reach Kate, he slid his hand under the table and tickled Edith.

She pulled her arms close to her sides and twisted away from him. She was no longer interested in his silly games. In fact, she'd stiffened to such a straight-backed primness, Kate was reminded of a peppermint stick, the color and swirl of her pink ruffle accounting for most of the effect.

"You're no fun," Bill complained. "I thought you told me you were ticklish everywhere."

"Not here."

Kate lifted the lid and added a handful of salt to the coffee.

She had no real idea what Bill expected her to make of him when he acted like this, but she was quite sure his object wasn't jealousy. If Bill had thought her capable of jealousy, he might have let her find a woman's handkerchief in his pocket or discover a bit of lily-white face powder on his jacket. This rudeness was more the ilk of a child misbehaving to get attention.

"Kate don't care. Ask her," Bill went on. "Even if she did, a man needs to put a woman in her place once in a while. I mean, it's a well-known fact that a woman who doesn't suffer becomes unsexed."

Kate slid the coffeepot across the stovetop, making enough noise to silence him, but only momentarily.

He looked around and continued, his voice large. "It's a known fact," he repeated. "Unless a woman suffers, she becomes too bold, too brazen, too unwomanly. She's unsexed."

Kate came down the steps off the wagon and thudded the coffeepot onto the table in front of Bill. "Pour your own," she told him.

He slammed his fist against the table. "See?" He looked round at Edith, but she refused to return his glance. He turned back to Kate. "See, there you go. You're not even thinking like a woman. A man brings another woman home with him, and his wife should be all aflutter with neglected attentions hoping to win him back." Glancing at Edith, he asked, "Ain't that so?"

Edith looked away, staring at the blank tent wall, which had taken on a slightly rosy glow from the coming day.

Bill grunted, shrugged, and continued. "Everybody knows a man's soul has to expand to be great. A woman's has to be squeezed, refined. Kate don't act like a woman, most times. Ain't been made to suffer enough."

Kate was not going to let him get her again. She turned back to the stove wordlessly, but not before she saw him nudge Edith. He said, "Kate's father was disappointed by all the women in his life. His once-famous mother-in-law gone charity case. His unfaithful wife gone drunk. His daughter who was everything he wanted in a son. Two weeks before he died, he said to me over a beer, 'If Kate had only been a son, *my son*.' Not that Kate didn't try to be a son to him, taking up photography and all. But that only turned her unwomanly, like I said."

Bill knew her quick. Drunk he hit it every time. Not that she ever let on, ever gave him satisfaction. Now she didn't even turn around.

But he knew he'd scored. His voice loud with self-satisfaction, he added, "Me, I don't expect much. Cuts down on the disappointment."

Kate groped for an answer sufficiently witty and cutting. But no words came before the air was suddenly shaken by the sound of a snore. She looked around. Bill had tipped forward onto the table and fallen into a loud sleep.

Edith giggled a little self-conscious noise. "Guess the evening was too much for him." Then, gathering her skirts, she clutched the pink ruffle to her chest and tried sliding out between the table and the tent. There wasn't enough room.

"Oh, don't rush off," Kate said, a tone of sarcasm in her voice. "Have some coffee."

Edith sat back down not so much because of Kate's invitation as being baffled about how to extricate herself from her corner. "Oh, I don't care what he says," she returned with her own note of incredulity. "You're not that original, and I know how this part goes. The wife acts all nice and then out comes the Bible. No, thanks, honey, I've been reformed once. Baptized and everything."

Kate laughed and then sat on top of the steps going up to the wagon. She straightened through her hair with her fingers. "You don't have to worry about me. I don't own a Bible. And this isn't the first time he's done something like this." She paused and shook her head. Then she said more softly, "My mother did enough Bible reading for our whole family. She was determined to do it right. She got herself married to a respectable man with a nice house with seventeen stairs. She settled into housekeeping and tea parties and Sunday afternoon buggy rides. It didn't work."

"Because she fell in love with another man," Edith said, pouring the coffee. "Honey, I've heard that story so many times, I don't need to hear it again."

Kate thought about that. She'd never considered the possibility that her mother's story might not be unique.

"Ask me, it's the other way around," Edith said, and thumbed in Bill's direction. Then, relaxing her shoulders to a rounded slump, she reached for the coffee.

"What do you mean?"

"The part about being unsexed. He's got that all wrong. It's the other way around. Most wives ain't got no boldness, no brazenness, no sex left. They done had it all suffered out of them. Beat out of them is more like it." She poured the coffee, and then lacing her fingers around the cup, she raised it to her lips.

Kate wondered at her. Besides the scar, she had a worn look around the eyes.

Edith sipped the coffee and pulled a face. Then she noticed Kate looking at her. "I used to be pretty, before this." She fluttered her fingers at her face where the scar was.

"What happened?" Kate asked.

116

Jerrie Hurd

"Oh, nothing much. It weren't even a boyfriend. Just a customer in a bad mood."

"I'm sorry."

"I don't need nobody being sorry for me, thank you."

Kate didn't say anything to that.

Edith tried more coffee and acted as if she wanted to spit it back in the cup, but didn't. She swallowed hard. "What did you do to this? It's salty."

Kate shrugged. "He didn't marry me for my cooking."

The woman looked over at Bill. "Why do men marry?" she asked.

Kate didn't know what to say. The question hadn't been asked as though the woman expected an answer.

Edith fingered along her scar. "Like I said, I used to be real pretty. Men noticed me. Oh, they still notice me. But mostly it's the clothes." She flipped the pink ruffle. "And what they imagine is under the clothes."

Kate didn't know what to say to that, either.

Edith went on anyway as if she were talking to herself. "I used to worry about being noticed. I read lots of novels. That's when I was a girl. Read all those romantic sagas of young women smitten with love. In story after story the men were callused beyond feeling until their true loves reformed them. You know the books I mean?"

Kate nodded.

Edith shrugged. "Everybody knows the books I mean. Some preachers call them 'temptations.' In my case, I was tempted to too much patience. Got so I didn't care how badly a man treated me because I knew in the end I was going to be his sweet salvation. I knew I'd suffer him until he loved me. Bound to happen, I believed. Never happened. They left first. It were all lies. Most of love is lies, you know. Not just the sweet nothings we get told but the sweet nothings we want to believe."

Kate offered no comment. She wasn't suffering Bill out of misplaced affection. Bill at his worst was better than living with her mother and grandmother. She could never go back to that. No matter what.

Edith chuckled and pushed the coffee away. "I did more

117

than read those novels. I memorized bits of dialogue and practiced swooning in front of a mirror only to discover that I was too tall to faint beautifully. Add that to my disappointments." She straightened the ruffle around her shoulders. "I think it was the swooning that confused me. I thought men wanted helpless women—the kind of pale pretties who needed someone to take care of them. Truth is men want most any woman they can get, even if she has a scar on her face. Except yours. He wants you."

"Me?" Kate laughed and looked over at the rounded back and face flattened against the table that was her husband. His shoulders twitched between snores. "If Bill wants anything, it's to annoy me."

"Nevertheless, he fancies you—really fancies you. Only mostly he can't figure how to get you to notice."

Kate shook her head. In some ways Bill had grown on her like a misfitting shoe—still rubbing, only with a certain comfortable irritation. But in the end, she suspected he didn't want much more from her than from this woman. His wedding night discovery of her buttocks was example enough.

She'd rather awkwardly undressed under the bedcovers and then to her surprise found him stroking that part of her she'd always thought most disgusting. He stroked and stroked until in the warm, close quilts and darkness, she'd began to quiver in a way she hadn't known possible. In those first moments of her married life, inexperienced and dazed, she'd almost hoped for some sweet exalted union.

But then Bill had to be Bill. He lit a lamp, insisting that his eyes had to feast upon her. His warm embrace withdrawn, he'd ordered her to stand in the light, the cold, bare floorboards under her feet. He commanded her to turn, round and round, her arms away from her body, so he could see "what he'd gotten."

She turned, once, twice, three times. In the lamplight, she watched his eyes flow over her. She saw no repulsion, but there was no particular delight either. His smile was the smile of a man who'd made a good deal on a horse.

To Edith, Kate said, "I think you imagine things are more

romantic than they are. Probably comes from reading those novels, like you said."

"Yeah, well, not owning a Bible don't make you smarter than them what does, you know. I see what I see."

What Kate saw was a woman drunk enough she was holding her head between both of her hands.

"You ought to get him away from here." Edith thumbed at Bill.

"Oh, it won't hurt him to sleep it off there." Kate said, and then remembering Edith's predicament, she added, "The table folds. You can lift your side and slide out anytime you want."

The woman slid her coffee onto Bill's side and tried lifting her part of the table. She swung it up and down on its hinge and evidenced some amazement at the device.

"I mean you should take him and get away from this town."

"What?" Kate asked. "Why?"

"It's trouble of some sort. Colonel George came by the house today and offered fine money to any girl who went with Bill and got him to talk."

"Talk about what?"

"You."

"Me?"

She nodded. "He described Bill as a windbag with only one subject—his wife. And he wanted to know everything he said about you. He was right, you know. 'Cuse me for saying so, but that man can go on and on about you. Only I thought it was lonesome talk—that he was missing you. I mean, you'd think a man who talked about his wife that much would stay home with her if she was home." Edith paused and pursed her lips. "It don't make sense."

Kate shook her head, remembering her own recent concern about the colonel's interest in her. But then she tried to excuse it. "Bill and the colonel do business together."

"This weren't business. I gets the willies. Ever since I got cut, it's like I got another eye. I can see trouble, and it gives me the willies right away. I see trouble in this. The colonel had a look about him."

"What kind of trouble?" Kate asked, a second wave of worry washing over her. She had no idea what to make of this.

"I don't know. Ain't trouble all the same really?" Edith asked.

Kate nodded. "Thanks for the warning," she said. And then she again tried to shrug off her foreboding because she never looked for trouble; she looked for pictures. And as if to prove the point, she glanced up and was startled to see Edith looking almost radiant in the morning light filtering through the tent. It gave a glow to her pink ruffle and cheeks such that Kate was willing to believe she was a real beauty once.

"Would you let me take your portrait?" she asked.

"Why?"

"Just because I like to take pictures."

"Not with this scar."

"I thought it was your third eye."

"Third eyes should be invisible."

"I could paint it out. I touch up all of Bill's pictures. Did the same for my father. All it takes is a steady hand."

The woman studied Kate with eyes half squinted, then with a shrug she said, "I never had my portrait made."

That same morning, Richard Houston crossed town going in the direction of the river.

"Jack the Ripper moves to New York City," a newsboy sang out. "Got the whole grisly story here." He waved his paper.

Richard wondered what kids in New York City were calling out to catch their customers. "Read all about the trial of the century in Sioux Falls. Will they hang the savage?" he guessed. New Yorkers were likely as touchy about Jack the Ripper stalking their streets as Sioux Falls citizens were about the recent Indian "unrest." Neither was good for local real estate.

He threw a couple of playful punches at the kid, ruffled his hair, and grabbed three of his papers.

"Hey, mister, you can't do that."

Richard tossed the folded papers in the air and juggled them, flipping them end to end.

The kid brought his hands to his hips. "Hey, that's great. You teach me to do that?"

"Another day," Richard answered, catching the papers. According to his father, juggling was another one of the "useless bits of learning" Richard had acquired. He slipped the kid a nickel, but kept none of the papers. The only thing he wanted encumbering him at the moment was the missing gear knob for Kate's camera.

In the middle of the night, he'd suddenly sat up in bed, remembering how Kate had worked one camera adjustment with her bare fingers twisting the raw threads. He had a spare knob of the right sort tucked away in his travel wagon. He was sure of it. So sure he couldn't go back to sleep for thinking about it.

Unlike Bill, he didn't camp in his wagon when he was in town, a practice he considered cheap. He lay there in his boardinghouse bed listening to the quarterly chime of the church bells. He kept telling himself it was silly to get up, get dressed, and go out in the dark to where his wagon was parked. Morning was soon enough. But when his mind wouldn't let it rest, that's exactly what he did, taking a lantern with him.

The knob wasn't where he first thought. He was disappointed, but didn't give up. He continued to rummage through his equipment boxes. He found a knob that was too small and one that was too large. Then he found it—the one he was looking for. The discovery came with a flush of excitement. He had something she wanted. With Kate, he'd found that was no small feat, not that he intended to make over much of it. He just wanted to hear her gush a little thanks once. The knob tightly clutched in his hand, he curled up on the bed in the wagon and waited for daylight.

Now making his way to the river, he hummed a cheery ditty. That is until he reached the edge of the clearing where Bill Burke had his wagon parked. There he swallowed the tune and finding a low branch where he could sit and watch, he waited. Last thing he wanted was to run into Bill again, but he had a hunch Kate took her camera out most mornings.

Not long, and he was rewarded for his wait. Kate, her dog, and her camera emerged from the tent. She tossed her dog a biscuit. Then, shouldering her camera and other equipment, she started off in the opposite direction. He followed, but lost her. The path came to an open area where the trees thinned, and she was nowhere to be seen. He cursed his luck, put the gear knob in his pocket, and was about to return to town when he heard her dog barking. He hurried in the direction of that sound.

He ran back along the path, then out onto the prairie and over a little knoll. There he found her flopped on her belly in the middle of a prairie dog town. Her dog was running around and around, chasing the prairie dogs down their holes only to have them pop back up and do a yipping bounce before going down again. Kate was hovering over one hole. Suddenly its occupant popped up, saw her, and got so excited it did a complete back flip. He heard her shutter click. Then she rolled over, sat up, and pulled her plateholder.

Sitting there in the dust, she looked up and spotted him. Her expression changed, taking on surprise. He was fascinated by the flutter of her changing expression. It was enough to raise the mischievous in him. He cupped his hands to his mouth. "Hope you stomped the ground to scare the rattlesnakes away."

"Rattlesnakes?" she asked, and twisted around, pulling her skirts closer to her.

"They crawl down the holes looking for nests. You never know when one will come up." Then, stomping the ground hard enough to raise little clouds of dust, he crossed to where she still sat, her camera in her lap, a box of plates beside her. He offered his arm to help her stand.

She didn't take it. Sometime while he was crossing that open space, she brought her hands to her hips and let her face form around a pout. "Rattlesnakes?" she repeated this time with more snip than surprise. "On a morning like this, I should think all the rattlesnakes would be out sunning themselves."

He shrugged and studied her for a moment, looking for a possible flaw, a weakness that he could use to excuse his feeling for her. No help. He even enjoyed the smear of dirt on her left cheek. He gestured a casual indifference and said, "The locals call them 'contrary critters.' My guess is that's because you never can be sure."

"Well, I don't know about their being contrary," she answered. "But I do know a rattlesnake can barely move until it's warmed, much less strike out of a hole."

At that, he put his hands up in mock surrender. "You caught me. I mean, rattlesnakes do hunt in prairie dog holes, but no doubt you and your dog have more than made enough noise to keep them away. I just couldn't resist offering a lady my arm." He poked it out again.

She ignored him again. Instead, she fussed with her plateholder, readying the camera for another shot while her dog trotted up and pushed between them, wagging his tail hard enough to beat against Richard's leg.

She looked up again. "How long were you watching before you couldn't resist extending your arm to a lady? Did you really think I'd believe you just happened on me again this morning?"

"No," he answered, and held out his hand. The gear knob was in it.

"Oh," she said. And then sitting up straighter, she took it from him. "I'd despaired of ever finding one. My camera's old, and being way out here where the biggest supply shop is Tony Amato's. Well, you know what I mean."

"May I see if it fits?" he asked.

She handed him the camera and the knob.

He lowered himself to the ground beside her, cradled the camera between his knees and examined the mechanism. "Did you get the picture?" he asked.

"What?"

"The prairie dog doing the back flip."

She laughed lightly. "I haven't been quick enough for that one. My seventh try, and I doubt I caught more than his tail disappearing down the hole."

"You can try again when I get this fixed."

"No, they only get that excited at first. Then they go down their holes and stay. I'll try again tomorrow."

He cleaned the threads, using his pocketknife at one point. Then he attached the knob, tried the mechanism, and being satisfied, handed the camera back.

She tried the mechanism herself and was obviously pleased. "Oh, much better. How can I thank you?"

This was the moment he'd been waiting for, and he was suddenly tongue-tied. That surprised him. He'd not met many women he couldn't immediately impress with his practiced charms. But then he'd not met any women quite like Kate. He wondered if she had any idea how singular she was. He shook his head and said, "Forget it. It's nothing."

"No," she said. "This was truly kind."

There was a new lilt to her voice that pricked his ears. He looked around and caught her gaze, caught her scent, mixed with the smell of the earth and the morning air. He had to swallow and ask himself why he was doing this. Partly he wanted to spite Bill Burke, satisfy himself that the old boy ought not to be so smug about his pretty wife. But there was more, much more. Something had happened out on the ledge the other morning. He knew it, and he thought she knew it. The danger here was in not exploring something that vital and living to be forever haunted by it.

Kate wasn't at all sure of her feelings. They'd been in some turmoil since Bill and his lady friend woke her that morning. They'd been in even more turmoil since Edith delivered her warning. Now Kate didn't know what to think of Richard and the kindness of his fixing her camera.

She knew one thing—she didn't want him to pity her. For that reason she worried whether he'd seen Edith leave, but then decided he probably hadn't. After taking the woman's portrait, Kate had cleaned up and gotten dressed. It had been more than an hour between the time Edith left and when Kate took her camera and went out.

Taking her camera and going off by herself was her usual answer to sorting out any confusion. But in this case, her confusion had become compounded. She genuinely appreciated the gear knob. But Richard's interest in her was neither appropriate nor kind if he cared for her reputation. They both knew that.

On second thought, she doubted either of them were the sort to worry overmuch about reputation. What they both knew was the palpable attraction they felt.

"Would you let me show you something?" he asked.

"What?"

"It's not far from here."

"Well, I'm not sure," she said and meant it. What concerned her were the consequences of abandoning oneself to one's feelings. That's how her mother and grandmother had lost themselves. And she had no desire to repeat that spiteful spiral of disappointment mounting more disappointment if she could help it.

She brushed the dirt from her dress. Maybe she couldn't help it.

"No one will see us," he said, and she wondered if that was supposed to reassure. She had expected him to try and prick her sense of adventure, daring her to the embrace of a flirtatious escapade, not invite her on a walk.

Looking up, she caught his gaze and suddenly felt naked under the analysis of his eyes. Naked and breathless. What was it about him? This time he hadn't even had to touch her ankle. There was no way he could know about her mother and grandmother, but still she wondered if he'd sensed in her the weakness that tormented the women of her family and known she'd be unable to refuse.

She was unable to refuse.

But he was a complete gentleman. He carried her box of plates, indulged her dog when he dashed off to chase a rabbit, and took her hand when they needed to cross a muddy spot, all the while keeping up a charming bit of banter about the weather, the scenery, her dog's continued antics. Safe subjects, but falsely safe. She detected a nervousness that tempted him to overstatement. He found the day "marvelous," her dog "clever," the air "most wondrously fresh." Then, coming over a little hill, Richard stopped, took his hat off and exclaimed, "Don't you just love a perfect spring day?"

She paused. She'd never heard a man use the word *love*. She didn't know if Bill could say the word, and she'd never heard her father utter it even in a casual context such as he "loved" licorice or "loved" the opera. In fact, she considered that one of the useful things she'd learned from him— how to be steady, detached, wrapped up in one's work. That's how he'd managed to keep himself sane while her mother and grandmother hadn't. And she'd so convinced herself as to the wisdom of that course that she could almost believe love was the vain imaginings of poets or the writers of those romantic novels Edith had talked about. Now what did Richard mean when he said he "loved" a spring day? She wondered.

She looked around. She saw greening grass and rolling hills in every direction. She could smell the earth warming in the morning sun. A meadowlark sounded once again. And she thought maybe it wasn't too exuberant to "love" a moment like this.

A little later, as they approached a rock outcropping, he led her upward around a slant pile of loose shale. Homer ran ahead. Together, she and Richard climbed to where a sheer rock wall became bloodred. Then taking her hand, he pressed it against the rock.

She pulled back, startled. Then more gingerly, she felt the surface again.

The sunlight had made the rock warm. More. Her fingers detected tiny ripples unseen by her eye. That, added to the warmth, made the rock seem almost living. It had been enough to take her breath away.

Looking closer, she recognized it. This was red pipestone, supposedly the sacred rock of the Sioux. She'd seen curios for sale made from this stone—miniature Indian heads, totem animals. Yet it was hard to connect those knick-knacks and this monolith.

Richard was rubbing his hand over the rock.

She copied his motion and then, throwing back her head, she looked up to where the red rock pierced the blue sky, and she thought no expression no matter how exuberant could quite catch the sensation. Her face must have said it all.

"I was hoping you'd like this place," he said. "The Indians say this is the lifeblood of the earth. To touch it is to touch life itself."

She looked around at him. The wind lifted the hair on his forehead. She saw mischief in the way the corners of his mouth curled around his words. He was, indeed, enjoying her delight. That startled her. She honestly couldn't say she'd ever been aware of someone taking such an interest in what pleased her. That aroused a vague tenderness even as she reminded herself of the devil in him or was it in her?

"How did you ever find this place?" she asked.

Richard laughed. "I have a friend who is a mining engineer. He's fond of such curiosities, but he's not much of a romantic. He just thinks of this as old rock. He matter-of-factly describes it as the oldest exposed rock in all the Dakotas. I doubt he's ever really met a wonderment." And then in his exuberance, he slipped. He added, "Like you."

It embarrassed them both. The unspoken spoken.

He ducked his head and muttered, "I meant that in the polite sense. You're unusual, you know, for a woman. Delightfully so."

But the words came too fast to carry conviction.

She answered, "Of course," as if she hadn't felt his words, as if her whole body hadn't tightened to them. Then she did what she always did in such situations. She switched the subject to photography.

"I truly believe no one really appreciated light before the invention of the camera. Don't you agree?"

"Not even the poets?"

"The poets?" she echoed, wondering what poetry had to do with photography.

"The poets," he repeated. "You know, the ones who named light 'God's oldest daughter,' 'the firstborn of creation,' 'the white radiance of eternity.' Those poets."

"Oh," she said, and then marveled at how deftly he'd directed her words away from her "safe subject." She drew another breath. "I can't imagine any poet sitting for hours waiting for the tide of light to wash in and lift the world out of shadow, splashing just the right definition . . ." She caught herself. That wasn't exactly the imagery she'd intended. Or had she?

He moved a step closer.

"I mean, photography can be tedious work."

"Most tedious," he agreed. "Especially in the dark lab where there isn't any light."

She never got witty about photography. "You're wrong," she told him. "Light is almost tangible in the studio. It's creation all over again, light from darkness."

His look shifted from the amused to the quizzical.

She hurried on. "In the dark lab you can almost feel the light as it emerges out of the slick wetness of fine papers being manipulated by chemicals." She paused. She wasn't handling this situation very well.

Turning slightly, she indicated the vista behind them with an expansive gesture. "What I meant to say is that it's all a wonderment, you know. All of this. As a child, I used to be curious as to why my father went West every summer to take pictures. I mean, the pictures he brought back were marvelous, but I thought surely there were vistas worthy of his camera closer to home. I think I was a little jealous of how much he enjoyed being gone so far away. When this Indian business came up, Bill tried to discourage my coming. It was winter, he told me. We'd be traveling with the army. It would be hard and maybe dangerous, but I knew I had to come."

Richard enjoyed her stammering frustration until she mentioned Bill. What did he care about Bill and their days following the army? What did he care about Bill at all? He was having trouble thinking of them together and let her chatter on because he didn't trust himself. He didn't know what to say, had no idea what he might do.

"It's so enormous, it overcomes everything," Kate was saying. She meant the sky.

"One day in the dead of winter when we were out with the army," she went on, "the sky was so bright and clear from the sunshine and so cold that the light appeared brittle, like ice on a stream. That's when I knew. It's the sky that drew my father West every summer. There's just so much sky here."

For want of something else to say, he muttered about how universally overexposed the sky was in photographs of the West. It was hard to capture something that large, that blank without overexposing, he complained. "It always comes out mottled," he added.

She shook her head, and with a new kind of excitement in her voice, she began to explain how to avoid such mottling by using a diluted developer rotated with water baths— thirty seconds in the developer, two minutes in the water, repeated at least ten times.

And suddenly he was interested, really interested, in spite of himself. What she was describing was a technique he'd not tried before. He mentally worked his way through the process. It would require patience in the darkroom, but he saw no reason it wouldn't work.

Meanwhile, she'd gone on to describe exactly how the print would look.

He interrupted. "That's how your father got the look of his last photographs. I could never quite figure out the technique."

Now she seemed embarrassed.

So was he. He'd grown up with the notion that there were few things and almost no women he couldn't have. It had made him too cavalier. He knew a hundred ways to tease. But he had no words for serious sentiments. He couldn't think of a single way to express his amazement at Kate, his sudden fascination for everything from her carrot-colored hair to the ankle he'd held. That included her singular passion for photography.

129

He couldn't help himself. His fortress was down. He was invaded by her, by the tone of her voice, the flutter of her hand, the curve of the top of her ear. She was too close and the moment too full. He reached out and touched her arm. Just brushed it, but at the touch she suddenly stiffened, and just as suddenly they both lost their footing. Their slippage sent a cascade of loose rock tumbling down the hillside. He grabbed her arm, pulled her close, trying to hold her. It was no use. They both sat down hard, riding the cascade downward. He was holding her when they slid to a stop. "Are you all right?" he asked.

She nodded and caught a quick breath. Then there was a moment while they were still entwined when he wished they had continued sliding, spinning downward, deeper.

"I'm fine," she repeated. "You can let go."

He couldn't, and that was his mistake. He felt her wiggle, struggle slightly against him. He held on a second too long, and her voice took an edge. "Must I always remind you to let go?"

"I guess I got carried away," he said, releasing her and scrambling to his feet. He offered her a hand up.

She refused, saying, "I can find my own way back."

He nodded and stepped aside. There was nothing else to do, the magic of the moment was gone. But he couldn't resist calling after her.

"Kate."

She turned.

"If you ever need anything . . ."

She paused long enough studying him that he hoped she might say something. She didn't. Instead she turned and was gone.

When Kate got back to her camp, she found Mary washing clothes in a tub outside the tent. Inside, Bill was awake and seated at the table. He was holding his head between both hands. He raised his chin slightly and gave her a squinty, one-eyed glance. "This is terrible coffee," he complained.

"Better than you deserve," she answered, noting that he'd

been up and rewarmed the pot. Then she drew a quick breath. She didn't want to fight with him. "I'll make fresh coffee," she offered, "but we have to talk about something."

He grunted one of his exasperated noises.

She said, "There are too many photographers taking too many pictures of this trial. Nobody's going to be all that interested in an Indian who shot an army officer. It's not like it's the first time that ever happened."

Bill groaned and pulled a roll of liver pills from his pocket. "Not now, Kate. I'm not up to whatever it is you have on your mind."

She paused. Maybe it wasn't the best moment, but truth was, there weren't many moments when she had his attention. It had been better when they were out on the prairie following the army. Then there had been fewer distractions for either of them. She dumped out the old coffee and put on fresh water.

Bill dreamed of "deals." He talked endlessly of William Henry Jackson's famous photograph, "Mountain of the Holy Cross"—a picture of a peak in the Rockies where the snow that lingered all summer formed a natural crucifix. It was shoddy photography. The cross had been enhanced by some darkroom tricks, but it graced homes, rectories, even chapels all across America, and it had made Jackson a millionaire.

She sat down across from Bill.

"What if we could get pictures of something no one had ever photographed? Wouldn't that be better than this trial?"

He snorted a little laugh. "Don't tell me. Some local liquored-up brave has promised to take you to a secret place where the Indians continue to ghost dance. Those rumors are all over town."

She swallowed. "Actually, I had something else in mind."

"And you're not going to leave me alone about it, are you?"

Kate bit her lip, but went on. "Sioux women have societies, sacred societies like the men. Only nobody has taken any pictures of them."

He cocked his head a little and winced at the motion.

"How do you know that? You haven't been to Indian camp, have you?"

She didn't deny it.

He popped two of the pills into his mouth and swallowed them dry. "And what do they do in these sacred societies? Dance?"

"Mostly they do quillwork."

"Quillwork? You're saying that they sit around and sew?"

"Well, it's not exactly sewing, and there's more to it than stitching. They have to pull the quills and dye the quills. They have special songs. Their designs come from dreams." That sounded weak even to her.

He grunted one of his deeply impatient noises and rubbed his hand over his face. "Oh, hell, Kate, you and your ideas are going to be the death of me." Then grunting another deep, low noise, he stood. Steadying himself with one hand on the table, he slowly crossed to where a trunk was sandwiched between two boxes of photographic plates. He pulled it open and rummaged in the top compartment until he found a small volume stitched without hard covers. He tossed it to her.

It was a guidebook that had been given them as a wedding present: *The Prudent Traveler's Guide to Western America.*

He grunted. "Chapter two, I believe. If you're going to yammer at me anyway, you might as well read it aloud."

She thumbed to the page entitled "Proper Etiquette with Indians." The second paragraph read: "It is not advisable to give Indians anything or show any kindness. This recommendation is not meant to foster cruelty. Rather it has been found that such gifts or attentions are all too often misunderstood. The Indian will become a nuisance,"

"Good advice, Kate. Trust me." He popped another liver pill.

A hollowness opened inside her. Maybe she was naive. Who was Woman-Who-Dreams? Nobody, a stranger, an old Indian. Kate knew absolutely nothing about her except that she made quilled bags, had strange dreams, and even stranger notions taken from the newspapers she'd read. There wasn't much in any of that to recommend her. But deeper, there was a stubbornness in Kate that hated caution. It was the reason she'd never troubled herself to read this guidebook. She hadn't planned to be a particularly prudent traveler.

Kate closed her eyes and tried again. "Imagine traveling across the country lecturing about Sioux quillworkers. I hear there's ever so much money being made on traveling tours these days."

"Oh, that's just like you not to let a thing go. Excuse me, but I think I'll take my hangover to a bar. Less noise." He pulled a jacket out of the same wardrobe trunk and was now working the fastenings with a slow deliberation. "Besides, Kate," he added, "to fill lecture halls, you have to have something people want to hear about."

"Oh, but they would. I have to believe people all over America would find looking at pictures of Indian women interesting, seeing what they really do, how they live. Don't you see? It's just familiar and at the same time exotic enough. It would generate an excitement that might surprise you."

He grunted a nasal noise. "Kate, what if it did? Hell, I'd be known as a 'photographer of squaws.'" He chuckled softly and shook his head slowly. "I, sure as hell, don't want to be known as a 'photographer of squaws.'" With that he crossed the tent, slapped back the flap, and kicked Homer out of his way.

The dog yelped once.

Kate sat on the bottom step and swore quietly. She hadn't even gotten to the part about how it had to be her, not him, who took the pictures. Why? Because men weren't allowed where the sacred quillworkers wove and stitched their dreams. Woman-Who-Dreams had said any man who trespassed risked impotence.

Kate didn't imagine Bill knew that. So what was the fear that sent him scurrying off? Something instinctive?

8

Later that morning, the colonel stopped in the entrance of the Masonic Temple. Kate Burke was on the opposite side of the room, and seeing her was like spotting a she-bear out on the grass prairie. She-bears were the worst. They could turn on you.

His aide continued a couple of steps, then stopped, and gave the colonel a quizzical look. "Anything wrong?"

He had spies everywhere, and he'd just learned that Kate had been to Indian camp, but he didn't share that information with his aide. Instead, he gestured generally at the makeshift courtroom with its spattering of brightly colored bonnets. "Where did all these women come from?" the colonel asked. "When did all this become women's chit-chat?"

"Everybody does seem to be taking an interest," the aide answered.

That wasn't what the colonel wanted to hear. In fact, that was precisely what was keeping him up nights—the extraordinary number of people who were taking an interest in this trial. An Indian shot an army officer. Nobody disputed that fact. Anything else was a wallow of details, repeated testimony, legal mumbo jumbo. When he sent his men to arrest Plenty Horses, he hadn't thought a trial would be more than a formality. The army had hung thirty-eight Indians following the Minnesota uprising, four after the Modoc affair, including one called Captain Jack, the chief. Plenty Horses was nothing but a young hothead. Even many of the Indians didn't like him. More, he couldn't figure Kate's interest. What business did she have in Indian camp?

The colonel was jostled from behind. He turned. The man, a store clerk if his clothes were any indication, muttered, "Excuse me," and then continued to his seat before the colonel could say anything. He hadn't known what to say anyway. He wasn't used to being knocked aside. He was used to soldiers and most everyone else stepping out of the way for him.

His aide was gesturing him forward. He took his seat and turned his gaze again to the ladies, their heads bobbing under their wide hats as they talked. He tried to imagine how those hats might bob if a wild Indian were to suddenly pop up in their midst. He could almost hear how they'd scream. He thought they ought to be pleased Plenty Horses was under guard. Instead, on the way in, he'd heard two of them refer to that murdering savage as "the poor boy." When had a back-shooting renegade become anyone's "poor boy"? He noted the symbols carved into the doors behind the judge's table. The world was not as nice as the female sex pretended. Even the Masons swore blood oaths.

Of course, the ladies had acted quite differently a few months ago when they'd felt threatened by "the Indian menace." Not one wild man but whole tribes feverishly dancing hoodoo. Then many of those same ladies, even the ones living in Sioux Falls, had huddled in their houses and begged the soldiers to protect them. Then he was a hero, his soldiers "the saviors of the peace." Now those same ladies kept themselves and their children off the streets when his soldiers went by, and complained to the authorities if his men got rowdy. They'd turned on him. Worse, he had a sense of the worm turning about this whole thing.

Unconsciously, he took an arrowhead from his pocket

and began rubbing it between his fingers, flipping it over and over, a nervous habit.

His aide nudged him and pointed. The Indian's lawyer had arrived, his pants sagging in back where he'd missed a belt loop. The two of them shared a look of amusement. In private they referred to Powers T. Nock as "the little monkey." That was apt, except that he was a very smart little monkey, and the colonel hated smart monkeys who tried to make field men look foolish.

The colonel had marched men and guns big enough to blow craters in the ground across the plains for the better part of eight months, chasing Indians. He'd ended the uprising, stopped the madness before it spread. Then this little squeak of a man who read books and lived with his mother stood up in this courtroom and suddenly everything changed. The colonel hadn't missed the fact that since the trial began, people on the street looked at him differently, with less adoration, less hero worship. When he'd first arrived in town, they'd mounted a parade in his honor.

He fingered the arrowhead and wished he was out riding, feeling his horse moving under him, feeling the animal's hooves pounding the prairie. Sitting here in this courtroom was making him a little crazy. He woke up in a sweat this morning, cut himself shaving. But he wasn't really worried about Nock. Kate was the real problem.

Wars weren't only fought commanding men and guns. Not since telegraph wires were strung across the country. Not since trains, telephones, reporters, and photographers. That's why he'd taken Bill Burke and a couple of reporters along with his troops. When Bill's pictures and their stories hit the eastern press, it had been like the "glorious Seventh" were the only soldiers on the Indian frontier. In a sense they were. His unit was the only one to see any real action. Who'd even heard of the Ninth Cavalry, for example? That was because he knew those reporters needed things to write about, not "peacemaking." General Miles would have talked the situation to death if the colonel hadn't forced his hand. Once everyone in the country was reading about the "glorious Seventh," General Miles had the choice of approving the colonel's actions or looking weak. Not much choice.

But here in Sioux Falls, the press had turned. They'd become a pack of dogs invading the battlefield, sniffing every corpse. They were asking questions no one wanted asked, much less answered. Nobody made a hero out of a choirboy. A hero was someone with stomach enough to do what most couldn't do but wanted done.

The new atmosphere around Sioux Falls and this trial had emboldened Bill Burke. Except for present investigations connected to the trial, he couldn't imagine that old boy being brave enough to try blackmail. Blackmail! The colonel chuckled to himself. He could handle blackmail. He knew exactly what to do about Bill Burke and his single damning photograph.

In fact, in a way he respected Bill for appreciating the value of his evidence. Deep down, he suspected the two of them were a lot alike. For that reason, he wasn't worried about Bill. He'd never reveal what he knew as long as it was worth something

It was starry-eyed sentimentality that worried him— hearts and flowers stuff. What kept him up nights was people wanting to pretend this could all go away sweetly, wishing for explanations, assurances, some kind of general absolution. Didn't they know war wasn't nice?

Kate was the embodiment of all that wishful starry-eyed foolery. While Bill knew what to do with his incriminating picture, namely, turn a dollar with it, the colonel couldn't guess about Kate. He didn't even know what pictures she had. He'd never paid any attention. He'd assumed her snaps were mere amusements until he caught her taking that picture of the Indian and the buffalo the other day. That had started him wondering. He wouldn't have worried if he'd thought she was capable of blackmail. Problem was, he figured she was capable of worse—misplaced sympathies. Who knew how she might share her photographs, especially if she gave in to some sentimental logic of the heart. The more he thought about Kate, the more she worried him.

His jaw tightened. The incident with the Indian girl and

her ghost shirt wasn't the first time Kate had defied him. Bill Burke, with the sensible logic of a huckster, would have demanded half what the shirt brought. Kate's defiance had been rooted elsewhere in an idealism harder to name, harder to contain. If she were a horse, he'd have insisted she be ridden with a martingale to keep her head down. Too late for that now. She'd already developed the habit of the headstrong.

His finger caught a sharp edge on the arrowhead. He looked down. The arrowhead was old. No one used arrows any more, not even Indians. He'd found this one as a boy. It was his lucky piece, worn smooth from his frequent fingering, except the rough edge. He'd learned to deftly finger around that.

The colonel looked over the roomful of people again, taking in the sheriff's deputies sitting behind Plenty Horses, the ladies under their hats, the local barber wearing a suit. Truth was, everyone wanted the rough edges worn smooth or deftly avoided. Even the reporters with their notebooks in hand didn't really want to know how the U.S. Army took care of things for them. And deep in their hearts, the fine citizens of Sioux Falls knew that wild Indians couldn't be tolerated. Wild women either.

Midway through the morning, it was all Powers T. Nock could do to stifle a yawn. The courtroom was crowded to suffocation, and the testimony had become repetitive enough to put several spectators to sleep. He knew because he made it a point to keep track of everything that went on in that room, not just the court proceedings. Routine cases were determined on merit or courtroom procedures. This was not a routine case, and much as he liked to fancy he could maneuver a courtroom as deftly as anyone, the outcome of this was not going to be left up to the jury. Too many powerful interests had too much riding on this to ever let it come to that.

But as near as he could tell, the prosecution hadn't figured that out yet. They were snowing the jury with too many witnesses telling the same story. It was to the point where

Nock doubted anyone could separate the accounts anymore or even remember how many witnesses had been called. It was all beginning to sound staged, which to Nock's way of thinking scraped closer to the truth than anyone in this courtroom really wanted to admit.

Everyone he'd talked to who'd actually seen any ghost dancing agreed it was peaceful. In a time when every part of the great Sioux Indian nation was in upheaval, the buffalo gone, the sacred Black Mountains mined, their children taken to strange schools and taught strange ways, the Indians had turned to dance the way others might have turned to desperate prayer. Setting up a pine tree decorated with eagle feathers in the middle of the dance ground in some remote location, the participants danced sometimes day and night for days until the dancers fell into hallucinogenic trances and the visions came—visions of buffalo on rolling hills, sweat lodges next to mountain springs, and no white men anyplace. Nostalgia turned to hope. Yet never in that ceremony had anyone suggested fighting for that future. They were simply going to dance that new world into being. Dance and dance, whirl and whirl, hope and hope, because it was unthinkable to them that the unseen world would abandon them completely.

By contrast, Nock had heard soldiers who'd never seen any ghost dancing describe what they thought it was. Those barroom descriptions were always fearsome and false. Same with the ranchers who'd screamed for the army's protection. Their descriptions were terrible both in content and accuracy. Not that it mattered. Ranchers regularly cried "wolf" or even faked uprisings to get the militia called out. Then they sold the army horses, hay, and grain. Even the Indians knew it was largely a game. Usually they disappeared into the hills until everything blew over.

This time things had gotten out of hand.

Faced with "a strange mania," the army had sent too many troops at too much expense with too many reporters following. All that strut with no stuff to report began to make the army look foolish. Even restricting the reporters to nearby towns hadn't helped. They still didn't have anything to write about except the fact that the army was out there chasing ghost dancers they couldn't find. It had begun to sound comical in the eastern press—soldiers with a Hotchkiss cannon chasing dancing ghosts.

Nock shot a glance in the colonel's direction. He was the one who'd decided to make something happen. In that glance, Nock caught him eyeing Kate Burke. That wasn't the first time he'd noticed the colonel taking an interest in Mrs. Burke.

Meanwhile, the prosecution called an Indian army scout named Rock Road to the stand, or at least that's how the interpreter translated his name. He told the exact same story of how Lieutenant Casey had been shot.

By now the telling was almost litany. The lieutenant, a man much beloved by his Indian scouts, to hear them tell it, had ridden out with several of them looking for Red Cloud's camp and found it. Upon being stopped by Red Cloud's guards, the lieutenant had insisted that he must talk to the chief. The guards sent to camp for him. Not Red Cloud, but Red Cloud's son-in-law returned. At the time, Plenty Horses was one of Red Cloud's guards. Mounted, he and three other young Indians had been positioned behind the lieutenant while he was speaking to Red Cloud's son-in-law. No one could say exactly why Plenty Horses suddenly raised his rifle and shot the lieutenant dead. In any case, those facts were not in dispute and, in Nock's opinion, hardly required an additional repetition. But there it was, one more time.

Nock twisted round in his seat and let his gaze wander to the row of reporters. Not one of them was taking notes. He saw the German tailor from down the street take out a pair of pocket shears and begin paring his nails with them. If it was the prosecution's plan to take the excitement out of this case by the sheer excess of collaborating witnesses, they were certainly being successful.

The prosecution finished with Rock Road, who now sat erect in his newly cleaned blue uniform with its polished buttons and white trim. He was waiting for Nock's questions.

Nock made it a point to follow only one line of questioning with each witness and never the same line. It was a strategy that had worked so far. While the prosecution's stories had become boring and blurred, his questions stood out. While the prosecution had established that Casey was killed by Plenty Horses—something no one disputed—Nock had established that Lieutenant Casey had probably been spying, that he had been warned to leave, that Chief Red Cloud, in particular, had warned him that there were a number of young bucks in the vicinity who wanted to kill him. Yet he'd chosen not to go. Those were things most people hadn't known.

Nock stood. He straightened and buttoned his jacket as though he thought such tidiness would improve his appearance. In truth, he looked exactly the way he wanted to look, unforgettable. He moved around the table and surveyed the spectators one more time before he turned his attention to the witness.

In that brief moment, he again caught the colonel watching Kate. She was something to look at. He'd had a fantasy or two about her himself. But he couldn't help wondering if the colonel's interest went beyond that.

Nock faced the witness. He cleared his throat. "What did you do after Lieutenant Casey was shot?"

Nock waited while the question and then the answer was translated. "I went to help him," was the reply.

"But I thought the lieutenant was beyond help, that he died instantly."

Translation, then return translation. "Yes, he was shot through the head. He was dead."

Nock put on a puzzled expression and turned to let everyone in the courtroom see his face all scrunched up. "But what about Plenty Horses?" he asked. "You mean to say that you and all the other army scouts with the lieutenant that day didn't do anything to detain Plenty Horses? You just let him ride off? Is that what army scouts do with a murderer?"

With that, Nock returned to his seat. He didn't need to wait for the translator to render that in the Indian's language. The answer wasn't nearly as important as the question. Everyone in that room had heard the same story over and over again. Now he wanted them to wonder why seven army scouts hadn't done anything to apprehend Plenty Horses if they were so sure they'd just witnessed a murder.

He sneaked another glance at the colonel. In some ways he was fascinated by the man. It seemed to Nock that he, too, was living out of his time. Only, in the colonel's case, that missed timing was likely going to trip him up. Nock wondered if he had any sense of that.

Nock doubted it. The man gave interviews with the stance of an American Napoleon. That was out of sync, wrong. The time had passed when Indians could be thought of as trees and simply cleared off the land.

Nock glanced over his shoulder once more. The colonel was sneaking a swig from his pocket flask and checking Kate Burke again. That was beginning to annoy Nock. Why Kate?

Now the prosecution called Pete Reshaw to the stand. Reshaw was part French and part Indian. He was a big man, swarthy, with a black mustache and bushy eyebrows. His English was tinged with a French accent. It was said he spoke Sioux better than French and French better than English. Nock didn't know about that. He only knew Reshaw was the only Indian army scout not using an interpreter, and so he'd saved a particular set of questions for him.

First, Nock had to wait while the prosecution had him tell his story—same story.

When it was his turn, Nock paced back and forth in front of Reshaw a couple of times, letting the tension in the room mount. Then he asked, "In the last few weeks, you've helped deliver food from the army to the Indians who surrendered, sometimes acting as interpreter, is that not right?"

Reshaw nodded and then said, "Yes."

"Where did those foodstuffs come from?" Nock asked.

The French half-breed looked at Nock blankly. Then he shrugged. "From the train depot in Kearney, Nebraska," he said, and smiled.

Nock let the ripple of ensuing laughter wake up the last of the sleepyheads in the room. This was not a point he wanted anyone to miss. He leaned closer to the witness. "What is printed on the side of the bags and barrels?" he asked.

Puzzlement and then understanding dawned on Reshaw's face. He lost his grin and glanced to where the colonel and his aide sat, but got no help. He shrugged. "I don't read so well, especially the English."

"Oh, I know you read well enough to tell me. What does it say?"

Reshaw glanced over to the judge, then down at the floor. He muttered, "U.S. War Department."

Now it was Nock's turn to smile as he turned and repeated, "U.S. War Department." And he couldn't help noticing how the reporters' pencils were moving again. Then, glancing up, he checked the colonel to see his reaction and was surprised to note his continued interest in Mrs. Burke. That made no sense, unless . . .

With a chill, Nock realized Mrs. Burke must know something—something that had the colonel worried. He glanced in her direction. She was whispering something to Bill Burke and didn't seem to be aware of the colonel's extraordinary attention.

He turned back to Reshaw. "Were you with the men who arrested Plenty Horses?" he asked.

Reshaw said he was.

"Where did you take him?" Nock glanced again at the colonel. If the condition of Nock's front window and door were any indication, it wasn't wise to worry the colonel.

"We took him to Fort Meade," Reshaw answered.

Nock shook his head and said to the French-Indian, "He's a civilian. Why Fort Meade?"

Reshaw shrugged. "That's where we were ordered to take him."

"Because he was a prisoner of war?"

And while that idea rippled across the room, sending the reporters' pencils scribbling, Nock glanced again in Kate's direction and thought she ought to be warned.

* * *

On the first day Kate had found the trial interesting, even exciting. Today it was boring. Bill slept through parts of it, but then Bill had been up all night and was still nursing a hangover. Her own pent-up energy didn't allow such. She fidgeted and squirmed. She didn't get the point. Bill complained when she wasted plates taking more than one picture of the same scene, but that's what this parade of witnesses was—different views of the same scene. At least she knew to print only the best.

That's where she really wanted to be—printing pictures in the dark lab, not sitting here. At the noon recess, she told Bill she had work to do. Then she headed for Tony Amato's studio.

The distance between the front door of Tony's studio and one of his dark labs in back was not great, but Kate had come to think of it as running a gauntlet. First, there was Tony's overzealous greeting. "Mrs. Burke," he'd say, his voice a blossom of surprise and pleasure. Then he'd hurry around the counter and usher her forward, touching her back and arm and shoulder in what she suspected was a practiced rhythm. Once he'd even brushed her breasts. All the while he chatted on incessantly about his nieces, Miss Emmaline and Miss Georgalene.

Once the pair of them had come in while Kate was there and talked to their uncle with such rudeness, Kate was envious. She didn't dare such antics for fear Tony would forbid her access to his labs. But Tony appeared to be completely unaware of his nieces' inelegant behavior. Even as they were mutually whining about not having a two-horse carriage like someone else they knew, he was nudging Kate in a place she thought inappropriate and saying with a wink, "Such spunk. It's more than I can handle. They need men in their lives, don't you think?"

This day, after enduring Tony's hands and the latest gossip about his nieces with what politeness she could muster, Kate at last found herself in one of Amato's dark labs. She pulled the second set of dark curtains shut and turned on the safety light. Then she paused and breathed the close chemical-laden air of the tiny space with something akin to the anticipation she imagined an opium smoker brought to his pipe. This was the place of her solace, her peace, her escape. More than close and familiar, the dark lab was her enchanted forest. This was where images emerged and flowed together. It wasn't until she and her photographs left the lab that she even thought of them as pictures. Before that, they were more like dreams. She drew another deep breath and began setting out the trays and mixing the chemicals. Her dog curled himself under one table, out of the way. Soon she heard him snore softly.

Her reverie was interrupted by Tony. He slipped back through the second set of curtains to ask if she was "all right." It was as if he expected some drain monster to rise up out of the pipes and swallow her whole if he didn't check every few minutes. What's more, asking was never enough. Tony crowded next to her, brushed up against her, looked over her shoulder and down into her developing trays.

The room wasn't five feet square and included an earthenware sink and two small tables that more or less created a continuous counter. There were also shelves above for bottles and a rack to hold trays and other utensils. The rack was remarkably similar to the usual kitchen article used for dishes except that it was clearly labeled as coming from "Abbot's Photography Supply House."

The dark lab, being damp, was used strictly for developing and fixing and washing. No cameras, lenses, or other apparatus were kept there. Kate didn't even keep her extra supplies of platinum paper there. She preferred to get the sheets two or three at a time. Unfortunately Tony figured that out. Every few minutes he popped back into the lab offering to bring her more sheets or whatever else she needed, as if he didn't have anything else to do.

When he left again, Kate checked the thermometer. It was important to keep the temperature above fifty degrees Fahrenheit, a fact that had driven her to near distraction out on the prairie when she was developing Bill's plates under truly primitive conditions. That explained the need for the kerosene stove in their tourist wagon and the one here in Amato's lab. The one in the lab wasn't fired at the moment. She was going to have chilled toes and fingers before she was through, but the gauge read above the fifty mark by eight degrees.

Tony popped back in. Seeing him, Kate made an exaggerated show of inventorying the supplies before starting her work. It was never good to start the developing process and then suddenly need something. There simply wasn't time to get the missing item without the delay having some effect on the print. So, like a schoolgirl singing her alphabet song, she always mentally named off the essentials as she arranged them around her: one developing dish (size of the plate), a lid to cover, a fixing dish (double the size of the plate), a toning dish (also double the size of the plate), a washing dish, measuring cups, a glass jug holding water from which the air had been allowed to settle out, scales and weights for measuring . . .

"My Emmaline and Georgalene should be so careful when they're cooking," Tony interrupted her thoughts. "I'd have fewer stomach problems, I'm sure. They're always forgetting something important. I'll bet you're as good in the kitchen as elsewhere." He chuckled to himself.

"I'm a passable cook," she told him, and continued her show of being busy.

He lifted her skirts with the toe of his boot.

She turned and gave him a solid stare, her only defense. If she complained, she was sure he'd act surprised and then blame the tight quarters. If she mentioned the matter to Bill, she was equally sure he'd forbid her using Amato's labs and in his mind congratulate the man on being macho. A choice between being bumped and ogled and not using the lab was no choice as far as she was concerned.

The sixth time Tony just happened to pop in to see how she was doing, she was ready to throw something at him. That was until she looked up and noted a new expression— tickled. He appeared for all the world like the proverbial cat that swallowed the canary.

With a wry smile, Tony said, "I have nothing against a lady using my labs. She's welcome, I say. That is, until she starts entertaining there like it was a fancy parlor or something."

Kate had no idea what he was talking about.

"You have a guest," he added.

"A guest?"

"Powers T. Nock is the gentleman's name." Tony placed the lawyer's calling card on the bench beside her print frames.

She couldn't have been more startled if he'd told her the president of the United States wanted to see her. But she'd just exposed a couple of prints and couldn't leave them. She'd had enough interruptions for one day, anyway. "Tell him I'm busy. I'll have to return his call at some more convenient . . ."

"It won't wait." Nock pushed his way into the dark lab, his jacket over one arm, a newspaper under the other. "I'm sorry, I know this isn't convenient." He gave a glance to Tony.

Amato tapped his fingers on the end of the bench. Then he excused himself.

Nock looked around. "I've never been in a dark lab before." He came closer, peering into the developing tray. "What exactly are you doing?" he asked.

Kate was in no humor. As if Tony wasn't bad enough, now she had to satisfy the curiosity of this little man. It made her feel like a circus sideshow, the oddity everybody had to see. Wordlessly, she pulled an exposed print from the frame and slid it into the developer. The image sprang up instantly. That was a particular property of platinum paper, that it gave its image immediately.

Nock stepped back. "That's amazing. I had no idea it was all so magical. Now what? You dry it or something?"

"I have to fix it and wash it and dry it. You really don't know anything about photography?"

He shook his head. "Clocks. I know quite a bit about clocks." He patted the front of his vest where he kept his pocket watches. "But I think you know that already. However, I'm going to appreciate photography more after this, I think." He turned around and brushed against her.

She stiffened.

"Sorry," he said, and then continued before she could respond. "My mother likes photographs. She collects them. Not just family portraits but scenes and places she's never been and finds interesting. She has this curio. It's a miniature Ferris wheel, only instead of seats, it has holders for photographs. You spin it around and look at the pictures. She keeps it in the parlor with the Turkish rug and shows it to guests. I don't know. Maybe you're familiar with such a thing." He raised his hands to shape the size of it and nearly knocked over one of Kate's trays. "I'm sorry," he apologized again.

She slid the tray back and another that was precariously positioned.

He stepped back and bumped a shelf. The bottles rattled. "There's a lot of stuff in here," he said. "You know what's in all those bottles?" he asked.

She nodded, but she honestly couldn't say which she found more annoying—Tony bumping her or Nock bumping everything else. "If you're really interested in photography, I'm sure Mr. Amato would be happy to show you . . ."

"Oh, I don't think I'd have any knack for it. That isn't why I came. I'm concerned about something."

"What's that?"

"The way the colonel is always watching you. I couldn't help noting his extraordinary interest in you while we were all in court today."

She laughed.

"Did I say something funny?"

"Excuse me for being blunt, Mr. Nock, but being watched is not exactly a new phenomenon for a woman. It starts with the servants, the housekeeper, the nanny, the maid. From as early as I can remember, I've been followed and watched, too much meaning being laid to every movement, glance, fretted brow. Details magnified to responsibilities. A lady has to be an example to the servants, a credit to her father, an asset to her husband. A lady not only conducts herself by the highest principles, she has to avoid any appearance that might be misconstrued. Such conduct distinguishes her from the lower classes. The layers and layers of such responsibility piled and piled until . . ."

Kate suddenly realized she was breathing too shallow, too quick. No matter how many people warned her, she was not going to let a fear of the colonel make her scared. She couldn't take the kind of pictures she needed to take that way—honest, fearless views. She stopped for more breath. "I'm sorry, Mr. Nock, but I travel, I take pictures, and I don't pretend to be the perfect lady, so I expect to be the object of some notice and probably more comment. I really don't care who may or may not be watching my every move, including you, I might add. I noticed you didn't miss much in that courtroom today, especially me."

There was silence. Nock tucked his elbows closer and gave another glance around the room. "Perhaps this wasn't the right moment."

"Perhaps not."

"Or perhaps you don't understand about the colonel. He can be dangerous and most determined."

"And just how well do you know him?" she asked. "He ate breakfast in my tourist wagon the other morning and tried to arrest my serving girl. She's Indian, a child really. He'd have dragged her off, but for me. I think I understand Colonel George."

"Did he want the girl or was he testing you?"

"I don't know what you mean?"

"Maybe he wanted the girl, and maybe he wanted to know if you'd stick up for an Indian."

Kate didn't know what to say. That had never occurred to her, but now that she thought about it, she thought he might be right. Then she shook her head. "With everything going on around here, why would he care about me?"

"I was hoping you knew the answer to that."

"He doesn't care. There's no reason," she said, shaking her head some more. "You're imagining things."

"No, I'm afraid that's one of my faults, Mrs. Burke. I have

very little imagination." He took the pair of watches from his pockets. "I prefer exactitude."

He looked up from his watches and caught her eye. The dim light muted his look, but there was no mistaking his seriousness.

"Be careful," he added. "A little care shouldn't be too hard to manage." Then, slipping the watches back into his pockets, he slipped himself between the dark curtains and was gone.

Kate leaned against the worktable and tried to sort out the churn of her feelings. She didn't want to believe Nock. She couldn't believe Nock because the care he wanted her to manage wasn't possible. "Taking care" in this case meant one thing—not having anything to do with Indians, not having anything to do with Woman-Who-Dreams.

Her mind rebelled at that. Why did everything have to be needlessly complicated? Why couldn't she use a dark lab without being cornered and fondled? Why couldn't she sit in a courtroom without being an object of attention? And what was wrong with her going to Indian camp to take a few photographs? There was something deep inside her that hated accommodating that kind of "taking care." It was gray. She needed her blacks and whites.

With that thought, she remembered the print. It was ruined, left in the developer too long. She pulled it out of the bath thinking she couldn't remember the last time she'd ruined a print from carelessness. But then that was a different sort of "taking care."

Tony stuck his head back in. "Well, well, what was that all about?" he asked as if he hadn't been listening behind the curtains all the time.

"I'm sure I can't explain it. Maybe you can," she retorted with enough snip to her voice he suddenly had other things to do.

She finished in the lab and washed the smell of the developer from her hands. Then, using a glass held up in the safe light, she checked her hair. But she didn't check her stubborn determination, quite the opposite. She knew now that she was going to do the pictures of the quillworkers.

She had to. Otherwise a part of her would die, the gutsiest part, the part she full well knew the colonel most wanted squelched. He couldn't have it.

Twenty minutes later, she entered the dining room of the Cataract Hotel and immediately spotted Mr. Arrowsmith. He was a government ethnologist who sometimes bought pictures from photographers. In fact, he'd had dealings with both her father and Bill. She'd heard he was in town and expected she might find him here. She signaled a waiter and sent her card to his table.

Thadius Arrowsmith took the card, read it, and looked up with surprise.

Kate offered a smile.

A broad-shouldered Englishman of some girth, he stood and crossed the room to greet her. Then together they recrossed the dining room where fancy chandeliers hung over linen-covered tables surrounded by carved mahogany chairs. He held one of the chairs out for her.

Once they were both seated at his table, Mr. Arrowsmith asked after Kate's health, the health of her husband, and her dog. She had left Homer outside, but everyone always asked after her dog, knowing the two of them were inseparable. He went on to comment on the service at the hotel and the weather before he gave into curiosity.

"May I assume I can be of service to you?" he asked, his words, as always, charmed by his English accent.

Kate sipped her tea. A lady likewise did not plunge right into her business. She set her cup down so gently, there was no hint of a clatter. "I was hoping I might interest you in some rather unusual pictures," she said.

"Unusual in what way, Mrs. Burke?"

"Unusual in that there are none like them," she explained.

He smiled. "I suppose that might be said of every photograph. Might not that be the case?" he asked. "I mean, they are a bit like snowflakes in that regard. Except for prints from the same negative, of course. But that's not the same thing at all, I suppose."

She nodded.

They both sipped their tea.

"But I'm interested. These are pictures your husband has taken?" he asked.

"Not yet. Actually not ever."

"I'm afraid you'll have to explain."

Kate did. Carefully choosing her words, she told him how she had received the quillwork bag and the invitation to photograph the quillworkers.

He listened quietly, like a gentleman, his eyes always on her, his head nodding from time to time. All of that tended to make her talk longer and perhaps freer than she might otherwise. When she finished, she apologized for that but added that she felt sure he would be interested. It wasn't every day that an invitation like this was extended to any photographer.

He took out a cigar and tapped it on the edge of the table. "Do you mind if I smoke," he asked.

She shook her head.

He tapped the cigar again and lit it which took time. When he spoke, his voice was lower, quieter. "I knew your father," he said. "Fine man, excellent photographer, a pioneer in the business. And I dare say I've known your husband longer than you have."

Kate nodded.

He continued, "I don't know if I ever told you how I came over from England to help set up the Bureau of American Ethnology. That was when it was first organized by your Congress in 1879. They asked for me especially."

Kate shook her head. "No, I don't believe I've had the pleasure."

He puffed his cigar. "Well, it's a long story, too long. Let's just say that since then, I've practically become an American. Haven't been back to London in years. I probably know more about the American indigenous races than almost anyone, if I'm allowed to brag."

"Please," she told him.

He puffed some more. "I feel the same urgency as you do. We must get the last of this dying race committed to

152

pasteboard before it's gone. With that in mind, I travel almost constantly, buying pictures from men like your father and now your husband—pictures of the West and Indians, pictures of things nobody has pictured before, as you so aptly put it."

"Exactly," Kate said. "I thought you would understand."

He leaned across the table. "But do you understand how long it took Jackson to get his pictures of the Hopi Snake Dance?"

"Years," he told her, not waiting for her response. "Even then he would never have gotten those pictures if he hadn't tricked some of the chiefs. There are no pictures of ghost dancing. That pseudoreligion, or mania, or whatever it was, came and went before any photographer could build enough rapport with the Indians to get such a picture. In short, Mrs. Burke, uninitiated outsiders are never allowed access to the esoterica of native religion without years of careful confidence-building. So I ask you, doesn't it seem odd that this medicine woman would invite you to take pictures without even knowing you? You did say you never met the woman before this incident, didn't you?"

Kate nodded.

"I'm afraid you're being flattered, Mrs. Burke."

Kate looked into her lap and fussed with her napkin. "I don't think I follow your meaning."

"There are no sacred Indian women's societies," he said.

She looked up. "No women's societies, but . . ."

He held up his hand. "It's nothing to be embarrassed about. I sometimes work with a woman anthropologist. She's a fine, fine person who learned the profession along with her husband and chose to carry on his work after he died. Anyway, she was similarly flattered about a year ago. She came to me with almost the same story. But after I explained what would happen to her professional standing if she continued with such nonsense, she quickly saw her error."

The woman without courage, Kate thought, remembering Woman-Who-Dreams' description. "But what if she wasn't mistaken?"

Arrowsmith shook his head. "I've been in the field a long time, Mrs. Burke, a long time. I'm sure if such existed, I'd have had some notion of it by now."

"You're quite sure?"

"Oh, quite. I haven't heard of such a thing anywhere in any tribe. Don't get me wrong. I think the redemption of the red race lies with its women. Perhaps that's true of all mankind—but more so with the Indian, I'm afraid. Indian women are neither too proud nor too indolent to labor. The squaw accepts work as her destiny while the brave is absolutely disinclined to any steady monotonous exercise of muscle. He would rather drink and lie in the streets of cities like this one than take up farming. No, I absolutely believe what civilizing of the red race is done will be done by Indian women."

"But she gave me a quite remarkable quilled bag." Kate took it out and handed it to him.

He examined it briefly and handed it back. "Nice work. I didn't mean to imply that the women don't sit and sew a little for recreation. They do, but there's no myth, no ritual attached to it. Same with their games. The women play games quite often, but never games of skill. They seem to prefer games of chance—gambling of a crude sort." He shook his head. "I don't advise you to continue your involvement with this Woman-Who-Dances."

"Woman-Who-Dreams," Kate corrected.

"Woman-Who-Dreams," he repeated. "It's obvious she's looking for money. Sooner or later she'll ask you for it. Watch out for that." He chuckled. "Your husband obviously gave you good advice."

"My husband?"

He chuckled again. "I'm sure Bill Burke must have told you not to get involved. That's why you came alone, isn't it?"

He'd guessed right about that. He might even have sounded sensible if he hadn't concluded that Woman-Who-Dreams wanted Kate's money. She didn't have any. If she had, she wouldn't be sitting here trying to get him to sponsor the project.

"But come, come, finish your tea, Mrs. Burke. It's nothing to be embarrassed about. Even the best of my colleagues have been taken in from time to time. I have a friend who once paid a hundred dollars, thinking he was getting a chance to photograph Crazy Horse . . ."

Kate knew the story. She excused herself.

He stood when she stood.

"You've been most kind to hear me," she said softly, but wanted to scream, shout, wake him up. If he was the eyes and ears collecting the last of the Indian culture, most of it was going to be lost. "Please excuse me," she added again. "I really must be going."

"Of course, of course," he said bowing slightly.

As she left the dining room and crossed the hotel lobby, she saw the reporter from the New York *World*. He had evidently just picked up his mail. He tipped his hat to her. "You look nice this evening, Mrs. Burke."

Kate paused and then crossed to where he stood sorting through his messages.

Seeing her approach, he stuffed the envelopes into his breast pocket and tipped his hat again. "Mrs. Burke? How are you?"

"Fine, quite fine," she answered, and thought that enough of pleasantries. "Have you heard of Indian women's sacred societies? Would you be interested in a story about them?"

"A-a-a . . . Ah-h-h, no. A story? What did you say?"

"Indian women's sacred societies," Kate repeated. "Specifically the Sacred Quillworkers of the Sioux."

He raised an eyebrow.

She continued telling him what she'd told Thadius. Only more hurriedly emphasizing the part about the ceremonies, dreams, and songs.

He rubbed his chin. "Well, I don't know," he said. "It doesn't sound like a newspaper story, although it sounds fascinating in its own way. I was fascinated," he assured her. "Maybe if it were written up as a travel piece for a magazine?"

"A travel piece?" Kate repeated. Her friends back in New Jersey sometimes forwarded her letters to the town weekly where they were reprinted. That wasn't what she had in mind. She tried again, "May I be so bold as to ask, what would be exciting enough for your newspaper?"

The reporter smiled. His smile had too much condescension. "Maybe a story on Mrs. Donning. You've heard of Mrs. Donning?"

"The white woman who was living with Sitting Bull when he was killed," Kate said.

"That's the one. Maybe she'll talk to another woman. She won't talk to me."

"That's it?"

"Well, I think that would make a very good story," he told her. "I could guarantee good payment on a story like that."

"I'm sure you could. But that also assumes your readers are far more interested in scandal than news, doesn't it?"

9

Kate clutched the squaw blanket and ran as fast as she could. Not good enough. Her skirts kept getting tangled in the tall grass and tripping her. Once she actually stumbled to her knees. She got up quickly, tried to hold her skirts even higher, and ran harder. Still she couldn't keep up. The quillworkers, five women of varying ages and builds, were all so fleet of feet, it was as though they glided through the grass.

The second time Kate tripped and fell, she gave up. Sitting there in the first light of morning amid a sea of prairie grass, she undid her sash and the neck of her dress so she could breathe better. Then standing, she pulled off her petticoats, one by one, and hung them on a low woody bush.

She was farther down river than she'd ever been. When she and Bill traveled with the army, they'd been upriver—north and west. Didn't matter, the landscape was the same, a broad expanse of green-brown grass broken only by draws and hillocks and an occasional outcropping of stone. The sky was as wide and flat as the land and offered little to arrest the eye beyond a few high wispy clouds, an occasional hawk.

Her dog returned first. Mary showed up next, asking if Kate was all right. Then the other women and their dogs came back, obviously wondering what had happened to her.

"Sorry," Kate muttered as she stooped to tie her skirt into bloomers. "I'll keep up now."

She'd met the women before dawn at a place well past Indian camp and the soldiers. She'd had to trust Mary to know the spot. Woman-Who-Dreams had sent a message, but it was brief. She hadn't come herself. "Too old" one of the other women had grunted when Kate asked about her. "Dreams and stitches, but doesn't hunt," was the only additional explanation.

The five other women had introduced themselves and their dogs to her dog. Then with no more formality than that, they'd started off at a swift walking pace. It was when the dogs began to bay that the women began to run. Now Kate hoped her stopping hadn't lost them their quarry. She finished securing her skirt and looked up.

One of the women, the youngest, was feeling Kate's black taffeta underskirt, rubbing the edge between her fingers. She picked it up and twirled with it, listening to its rustle, laughing at the sound. Kate chuckled, too. The sound struck her as odd out here on the prairie. Back home she knew women who worried about having just the right amount of rustle to their skirts. Enough to draw attention, but not comment, was the rule of thumb.

Now the other women picked up Kate's underskirts. They chattered about them excitedly in words Kate didn't understand. She wasn't sure what this new interest meant.

The other women had pulled up their calico skirts and tucked them into their waistbands, exposing their bare legs to their thighs. But in another sense they were as over-dressed as Kate. Elaborate quilled bags hung from their waists, the shiny hard quillwork contrasting with the velvety soft leather. They wore quilled pieces in their hair and quilled bands around their arms and necks. A quilled star pattern decorated the yoke of one woman's dress and the sleeves of the other women's dresses. Next to them, Kate felt plain.

The older of the sisters, called Blue Crow, undid the tie, and expanding the waist, she pulled one of Kate's underskirts over her own calico dress. Smiling, she began to strut as straight-backed and proper as any church lady. The others thought that funny and immediately used Kate's other underskirts for a similar "dress-up." Pulling them over their own clothes, they assumed the manners of fine ladies, strutting and turning, their chins held high. Kate pulled her sash off and offered it to one of them, the younger of the two women who'd first brought her the quillwork bag. She tied it over her head like a bonnet and then curtsied properly. Kate laughed out loud. The others paused, startled by Kate's merriment. Then they laughed, too.

Now holding up one of Kate's underskirts, the one called Rosy Blue Crow asked, "Why do white women wear so many clothes?"

Kate shook her head. She'd wondered that herself from the time she was a schoolgirl. "I don't know," she answered.

"You might as well wear horse hobbles," her sister added. "You can't run in them."

"I know. I'll do better now," Kate repeated. "Really."

And she did.

A few minutes later, the dogs flushed another porcupine. They'd found it in a shallow draw of tall grass and tansy. Kate came over the rise in time to see the animal whirl and hiss. Too slow to outrun the dogs, the porcupine spun one way and then the other, answering the dogs' snapping with the bristle of its back and sometimes the swipe of its paw.

Kate paused to catch her breath. The other women made no pause. Whooping and hollering, they joined the dogs encircling the porcupine. Chanting something in their Indian language, they teased the animal into a fury of whirling fight, prodding it with sticks.

"What are they doing?" Kate asked Mary.

"They notice it," Mary said. "They let it fight, express itself. Otherwise its dying would be like ambush. Otherwise the quills would be stolen and without beauty."

That was an odd notion, Kate thought, but before she could consider it fully, using her walking stick, the older of the Blue Crow sisters delivered a death blow to the porcupine's head that dropped the animal instantly. One moment it was a swirl of snarl. The next it sank in its tracks without even rolling over.

At almost the same instant, the women dropped to their knees. They bounced and swayed, making rolling motions like a porcupine waddle while one of them chanted something slow and low. Leaning over the dead animal, the women paused for a heartbeat, then they breathed out such a collective sigh, Kate thought she would never forget the sound, never hear its like.

"What was that?" she asked Mary.

"They talk to it. They tell it they are the women of the sacred quillworkers. They will turn its quills into things of beauty. First they must give its spirit to the wind. It must not haunt them. Its tiny eyes must not make their eyes tiny. They need good eyes to do the fine work of braiding and sewing the quills."

Kate moved closer. She squatted just outside the circle of women. One of the dogs sniffed her. She shooed him away. The younger Blue Crow sister looked up. She motioned Kate even closer.

Kate stepped into the women's circle and sat. Then Rosy Blue Crow took her hand and guided it to the long quills on the porcupine's back. They were slick and soft. That surprised her. Kate stroked the porcupine again but miscalculated and suddenly drew back, barbed with a single quill that Rosy plucked so swiftly, Kate didn't know it was gone until she looked down and saw a bright bead of blood where it had been.

At that the women laughed a light, merry noise and bragged, "Even dead our sister porcupine can bite. This one has fierceness and beautiful quills. Is that not so?"

Kate nodded.

Then the women got busy. They pulled sacks from a larger bag and shook them free. The brown burlap bags were stamped U.S. Army and had, no doubt, once contained wheat rations. Now holding the edges of the bag, the women stretched it over the porcupine and worked it back and forth, from the animal's tail to its head, going against the direction of the quills. The largest quills stuck and came off onto the bag. They set that bag aside.

They then pulled a second bag over the porcupine, pausing to roll its body first one way and then the other with their sticks. The next size quills came off. They did that again and again until almost no quills remained. Then Lena Blue Crow rolled the porcupine over, slit its belly, and tossed the entrails to the dogs.

While the dogs ate, the women sat in the tall grass and picked the quills off the burlap bags and bundled them by size.

They laughed and elbowed each other, sharing gossip and sillinesses and bits of dried fruit. Mostly they spoke in their own language. Mary translated for Kate, quietly whispering the words as she sat by Kate's side.

Then the younger one said something and rubbed her belly where a baby was beginning to show. The women laughed and cooed. Mary didn't translate that part. Kate looked over to her. "What's that?" she asked. "What did they say?"

"I don't know." Mary answered.

"You don't know?"

Then suddenly Kate was aware that the other women had gotten quiet and were watching. They started kidding Mary, who snapped something back at them in their Indian language.

"What's wrong?" Kate asked.

The one called Mattie answered. "She has been taught too much at the Christian school. She's become a child of the nuns. Part of her tongue might as well be cut away. She does not talk about certain things."

"What things?" Kate asked.

"You are too harsh on the child. You don't know how to say this thing either." One of the Blue Crow sisters made a gesture at Mattie that was clearly contemptuous.

Mattie straightened. "Whites don't do it."

The Blue Crow sisters laughed in unison. "You think that only because you do not have a white man."

"You brag. You don't know either."

Now Kate was really confused. Mary had gotten up and walked away. The sisters and Mattie had lapsed into Lakota and were almost shouting at each other while the quiet woman, called Sarah Grass Mountain, kept plucking quills, her eyes down. Finally, the young one, a niece to the Blue Crow sisters, leaned closer to Kate. "They speak of a particular pleasure men take with women. If there is an English word for this, they do not teach it at the mission schools. The girls at the dorm of my school always used the Lakota word for it. They bragged that their Indian boyfriends knew how to do it, their white boyfriends didn't. But that was mostly talk. Mostly the girls didn't have boyfriends at all. The nuns watched them too careful."

Now the Blue Crow sisters asked in English if their niece's husband could do it?

"Of course," she answered, and shot a glance at them. Then throwing back her shoulders, she went on the brag how her husband was so full of this, she was sure he'd filled her baby full of it, too. She was going to feel the birth pangs, her woman's pain, as one big jab of that pleasure.

Kate wasn't sure how to take that, but it amused the other women.

The Blue Crow sisters laughed and congratulated her. Mattie, too, acted as though she were pleased. She elbowed the quiet woman, who looked up at the group and offered a couple of bodily movements unmistakably earthy.

Kate nearly blushed.

Then one of the Blue Crow sisters passed Kate a burlap bag and indicated with a gesture that she should pull quills. She did, adding them to the women's piles.

Later when the moment seemed right, Kate said, "I would be honored if you would allow me to photograph how you work. Woman-Who-Dreams thinks pictures might preserve the tradition."

Mattie laughed. "Preserve this? This is stupid work. Anyone can pluck quills."

Kate didn't agree. She was wishing she had her camera and box of plates right now. She had been thinking what an interesting group picture the women would make. She thought Mattie, in particular, would make an interesting portrait.

Now Lena shook her head. "I don't know. Why give the secrets of quillworking to a shadow-catcher? Always before we give them only to our granddaughters."

"No, Woman-Who-Dreams is right," the quiet one, Sarah Grass Mountain, said with enough voice the others straightened and listened. She went on, "The soldiers kill us without seeing us. We are less to them than this porcupine." She kicked the carcass in front of her. "We poke her, we say to our sister that we know her. She snarls and snaps and shows us her life. We honor her fierce fight. The white man will not even look at us when he kills us." She kicked the carcass again. She paused. When she continued, her tones were softer. "No more. The power to catch shadows in a box is Double-Woman touched. It sees. It will honor what is fierce in us, so when we die, we die with soul."

That had an effect on the others. They sat respectful of the moment, listening to the sounds of the prairie, the wind, the hum of insects, and the rustle of mice in the grass.

Then Mattie slowly shook her head. "We will lose it. It will no longer be sacred. It will become like silly beadwork." She spit on the ground.

Lena Blue Crow nodded. "It is a serious matter. We must dream on it."

"What does that mean?" Kate asked.

"It means nothing," Sarah Grass Mountain said. "You can bring your camera where I work. I do not die quietly."

That same morning, Colonel Elliot George looked up from his desk as the reporter from the New York *World* ducked through the door of his tent. He was young and tall, but too squinty-eyed behind his glasses to make a good soldier. The colonel stood and offered his hand.

The reporter returned a firm handshake, but hadn't the courtesy to look at the colonel. Instead, his eyes wandered over the interior of his field office. At that, the colonel bristled and shot a glance at his aide, who had stood when he stood and by his expression now appeared to be equally peeved.

The colonel was glad to see he agreed. This was exactly the trouble that came from being camped at the edge of town. It left too many army affairs to the scrutiny of too many busybodies. In his opinion, that's what reporters were: busybodies—male gossips. He didn't enjoy entertaining their sort, but this one had been particularly insistent.

He cleared his throat. "My aide tells me you have questions."

The newspaperman finally looked at the colonel. His eyes were large behind his glasses. "It's these rumors I keep hearing," he said. Then his big eyes spied some Indian relics piled in one corner of the tent. "You're a collector?" he asked, and paused to finger the fringe on a couple of ghost shirts.

"I've managed to gather a few things," the colonel answered.

"Wish I could afford it. These things have really shot up in price now that everyone thinks we've come to the end of the Indian era. But I keep wondering if we're really going to change every living one of them into farmers, good as Quakers." The reporter was now inspecting a painted parfleche.

"You said you were wondering about some rumors?" the colonel reminded him.

"Yeah." The reporter half turned to face the colonel. "I'm hearing that a great many Indian women and children were killed at Wounded Knee—some of them quite a distance from the actual battle site."

The colonel offered a little laugh. "You've been talking to the Indians in town for the trial, would be my guess."

The reporter nodded.

"Then what did you expect to hear? Ask the defeated about any battle and they'll claim it was unfair."

"Well, I suppose." The reporter flipped over the edge of a buffalo robe and uncovered an oval picture frame. He picked it up and brought it close to his face and his big, spectacled eyes.

The colonel glanced again at his aide, who was now nervously shifting his weight from foot to foot. The colonel didn't share that worry. He was amused to see what this fancy eastern pencil-pusher was going to make of what he was seeing.

It was an Indian woman's beard—the skin tanned, the lips parted in an oval like the frame. A favorite prostitute of the colonel's had curled and twirled the hair and mounted the thing under glass. That had given it the appearance of a hair wreath—the kind of decoration currently in vogue in fine ladies' parlors, but usually made of a beloved's curls. In fact, the prostitute had wanted him to give it her so she could hang it in her parlor. She agreed that it was the only good use of an Indian woman's cunt. More, she laughed and teased the colonel about knowing exactly where to take his "scalps."

The reporter wrinkled his nose. "Is this Indian?" he asked.

The colonel nodded.

"I don't think I've ever seen anything like it."

The colonel shrugged. Lots of his soldiers had similar trophies. But mostly they tanned them and then inserted their saddle horns through the stiffened lips. Sometimes they took the tits, too, but they were too fleshy and usually rotted before they could be tanned properly.

The reporter turned the frame into different light. "I'm not sure I know what it is. Some kind of native embroidery? Horsehair? Moosehair?"

The colonel shot another glance at his aide, who had now discovered the humor of their situation. He was having trouble keeping his face straight.

"I'm sure I don't know," the colonel answered. "I haven't had a chance to show it to a relic hunter yet."

"It's a very odd piece," the reporter said, and shook his head some more. "Mrs. Burke is interested in unusual Indian crafts. She spoke to me about taking pictures of quillworking women or something like that. She seemed quite excited."

The colonel suddenly sobered. "Mrs. Bill Burke?" he asked.

"Yeah. She wanted to sell me a story about it. She had been to Indian Camp and talked to somebody there about a secret society or something. But I didn't think my paper would have any interest."

"Of course not," the colonel agreed, but he considered this revelation more serious than the snoopy reporter. He knew Kate had been to Indian Camp. He didn't know why and still didn't understand what she was doing. Secret quillworkers? He didn't believe that was all of it.

He wasn't worried about this reporter because he didn't think it likely his editor would print a bunch of rumors in preference to the word of a colonel in the U.S. Army. That was, unless the reporter hooked up with Mrs. Burke and came by proof of those rumors. Minus shallow loyalties to her husband, what was to stop a young reporter like this one from turning her head? That was assuming Kate had proof. That was the real rub. He wasn't sure about her in any sense.

"Do you speak to Mrs. Burke very often?" he asked.

"No, just that one time, and sometimes to greet her on the street." The reporter slid the frame back under the buffalo robe. "Getting back to the other matter. Do I understand that you deny killing any women and children at Wounded Knee?"

"No, I don't deny that." The trick with this reporter was to offer something reasonable, he'd decided.

"I beg your pardon?"

The colonel cleared his throat. "The braves fired at us from within their own camp. Naturally, that put their own families in danger."

"So you're saying you couldn't avoid killing women and children?"

"Often that's the case."

"But I understand some bodies were found three miles from the camp."

166

"We're talking about fighting Indians—not neat rows of Continental soldiers."

"No clear battle line."

"That's what I'm saying."

The reporter ran his fingers through his hair. "Seems reasonable."

The colonel smiled. "Reasonable as it gets in a nasty business."

The reporter nodded and then offered the colonel his hand as he was leaving.

When he was gone, the colonel turned to his aide. "I want her watched. Until we get done with this trial and out of this town, I want to know every place she goes, and everyone she sees."

"Who?" the aide asked.

"Mrs. Burke," the colonel snapped.

The aide nodded. "And what about the reporter?"

"Him?" The colonel chuckled. "He can't smell what's in front of his nose."

Powers T. Nock was on his way to visit his client in jail when he spotted Kate Burke. She was coming down the street from the opposite direction, her clothes a bit more disheveled than usual. More, she didn't have her camera. He was under the impression she didn't go anywhere without her camera, but she'd plainly been someplace this morning—someplace more interesting than shopping, he thought from the look of it.

He tucked in his pockets and straightened his vest, anticipating the moment when he would greet her as she came by. That's when, looking up, he noticed that two soldiers who'd been lounging outside Amato's Photography Studio had also spotted Kate and were now hastily putting out their smokes. They'd been waiting for her, he realized.

"Mrs. Burke," he said, and tipped his big hat to her.

She started, as if out of a reverie, then stopped and gave greeting. "Oh yes, Mr. Nock. How are you this morning?"

He again wondered where she'd been. Her dog had cockleburs in his fur. Her serving girl was carrying a pair of army-issue blankets, the kind squaws wore. He gave a glance to the soldiers. They were keeping their distance, but clearly taking in everything.

"Would you care to meet my client?" he asked because he didn't want to let her pass trailing a couple of soldiers and do nothing about it.

"Plenty Horses?"

He nodded. "I'm on my way to see him now. If you'd care to join me."

He watched how she considered the invitation. It was obvious she found the idea intriguing. There was never any question that she'd do it. Still she straightened her dress and mumbled softly, "I'm not sure I'm completely presentable."

"We're going to the county jail, not a social event," he told her and added, "You've been out walking early this morning, I take it."

She agreed without offering any further explanation. She straightened down the front of her dress again and then sent the serving girl off, giving her a brief list of domestic matters to attend. Nock used the time to note that the soldiers were now lounging in a nearby doorway. He also saw that Kate's dog had a slight limp. He bent, turned Homer's paw up, and removed a porcupine quill.

"Unusual," he said handing it to her.

"What's unusual?" she asked.

"A single porcupine quill. Usually a dog's a complete mess with them or has none at all."

She gave him a quick glance. Then she returned a casual comment in a tone too light. "Well, I never know where he finds half the stuff he gets into."

Then he also handed her the button—the smoky gray mother-of-pearl. "I believe this is yours," he said.

"Oh yes," she said. "Or at least I have some like it. Thank you. But where did you find it?"

"I had reason to return to the bandstand after the photography session when the soldiers' horses were spooked." He shrugged. "I happened to see it and thought it might be yours."

"Thank you," she repeated.

Three blocks later, Nock asked, "Do you know the soldiers following you?"

"Soldiers?" Kate asked.

He paused at the street corner and, trying not to be obvious, pointed them out.

Kate looked, then shook her head. "What makes you think they're following us."

"Because they are," he told her. "And they're not following us, they're following you."

He watched as she shot another glance at the pair who were now leaning against a hitching post waiting until she and Nock moved on. He sensed an edge of concern in her, but she wouldn't admit it. "Following me? That's crazy. There are soldiers all over this town. I'm sure they're just strolling up the same street."

"And pausing every time we pause?" he asked.

Kate shook her head. "It's a ridiculous notion. Mr. Nock, I'm sorry to say it, but I think this trial has gotten you a bit overwrought."

He gave her his arm, and they continued without comment. He wasn't a man who managed the usual "sweet nothings" with any aplomb. He thought "sweet nothings" was a complete misnomer. He found that kind of light talk impossible. It was hardly a "sweet nothing" if you hoped your words would lead to a woman giving you her "sweet everything." Not that he was interested in Kate in that way. Yet, sensing some danger connected to those soldiers, he'd had to admit she meant more to him than a casual acquaintance. She was rare. A man was entitled to appreciate the rare wherever he found it.

"A very fine rose-marble pendulum clock," he said.

"I beg your pardon?" Kate asked.

"I'm sorry, it's a bad habit of mine," he said. "I think of people as clocks. And you brought to mind a rose-marble pendulum clock—a very fine instrument, a rare piece. I haven't got one myself."

"I'm afraid I don't understand."

He shook his head, wishing now that he hadn't gotten into this silliness. He didn't imagine it would improve her

169

impression of him. "I know it sounds strange. I collect clocks, as I think I told you, and while one clock might mark the same hours pretty much the same as any other clock, they strike me as having distinct qualities. That has led to my habit of comparing them to people."

"You think of people as clocks?" Kate stated.

He nodded. "I'm afraid so. I shouldn't have brought it up."

"What kind of clock is Colonel George?" she asked him.

"An octagon lever, the kind you see in train stations. Highly functional, not much beloved by anyone."

"Not an iron clock?"

He shrugged. "That would imply too much substance, don't you think?"

"And the photographer Richard Houston?"

He shook his head.

"You don't have a clock opinion of him?" she asked.

"I think you're having fun with me," he answered.

"I think I need more than one example if I'm to appreciate what it means to be a rose-marble pendulum clock. After all, you started the game."

He drew breath. "Richard Houston is a fine inlaid case clock with Seth Thomas works."

She puzzled a moment. "More common than he appears."

Nock held open the jailhouse door. "You should see my clock collection some time, Mrs. Burke. I think you'd be an appreciative audience."

Kate gave a last glance over her shoulder as she stepped inside. The soldiers Nock had pointed out didn't look any different than soldiers she saw all over town. He had to be imagining things, like his clock nonsense, she decided.

The jailhouse attendant, a young deputy with a ruddy face, acted surprised to see her. He didn't say anything, but his look had an unmistakable curiosity. He looked her over again as he walked the two of them to the back. Before he put the key to the door, he asked, "The lady will be going in?"

Nock answered affirmatively.

Kate was having second thoughts. The jail was dim and stonewalled, and she wasn't sure why Nock had invited her. But she returned the deputy's glance without wavering. He shrugged. Then he unlocked the door and pushed it open for her.

Kate stepped into the cell first. Plenty Horses was sitting on the edge of a cot. Seeing them, he stood, but rather than greet his visitors, he turned and paced to the barred window. He took a position there, staring out, keeping his back to them.

Up close, he seemed younger, thinner, and far more tense. What she'd thought was stoic in the courtroom, she now experienced as a tightly controlled rage, that anger evidenced in his every movement, even the tautness of his breathing.

The jailer closed the door.

That sound made Kate start.

"I brought a guest," Nock said. "Hope you don't mind."

"The one with the camera," Plenty Horses said without turning. His tones were flat.

"Yes," Nock said. "Mrs. Burke, may I present the now-famous Mr. Plenty Horses."

"Plenty Horses," the man said, and turned to glare at Nock. "I am Plenty Horses, not Mr. Plenty Horses, not a red-faced white man."

Nock nodded. "Yes, I'm sorry."

Plenty Horses continued to glare in Nock's direction, then he shifted that same look to Kate. "Why did you come? Are you amused to meet an Indian?"

"No," she said. "I've met many Indians."

"Soldier-killing Indians? Or can't you tell them from the regular sort?"

Kate didn't know what to say.

Didn't matter. He bent, picked up a canvas bag, tore it open, and upended it all in the same motion. A pile of letters spilled at Kate's feet.

She jumped back.

He laughed a deep hollow sound. "Maybe you should

have written a letter. Perhaps you could have included a pressed flower or lock of your hair."

The letters were mostly on pastel stationery, many of them perfumed. It was a popular pastime for ladies to send such letters to condemned men, Kate knew. She'd always thought that practice silly but harmless. Now it struck her as more sick than silly.

Nock spoke. "I asked Mrs. Burke to come. It was my idea. I'm sorry if it doesn't please you."

At that Plenty Horses turned and made a stiff bow in Kate's direction. "I do not forget my manners. Pleased to meet you," he added in tones deliberately rounded. "See, it is as the newspapers say. I have been well educated. I have had every advantage and still I'm a savage. But the newspapers do not write about the soldiers who destroy our homes, kill whole families, even the babies. Maybe that's too savage."

Kate nodded.

"You agree?" Nock asked, suddenly turning his attention on her.

She shook her head. She didn't know what she thought except that coming here didn't seem a good idea.

"Were the soldiers killing whole families?" Nock asked her.

Kate shook her head. She hadn't been a witness to anything unless photographs could be memories of events seen but never witnessed. She shook her head again. "I was never allowed near any battlefield."

"You got closer than most reporters," Nock told her.

That was true. Many of them hadn't been allowed closer than Kearney, Nebraska. Not that she thought that made much difference. She truly hadn't seen much more than Bill's pictures. "I don't know what I can tell you. What I saw is for sale everywhere. Anthony's has three representatives who do nothing but sell Bill's pictures, you know."

"I was at Pine Ridge with my father," Plenty Horses interjected. "We were there when the troops brought in the bands who'd surrendered." He ran his hand along the window ledge and continued growing more serious. "Then came the killing of Big Foot and his band at Wounded Knee. I heard the shooting. My father and I and several others from Red Cloud's band rode out to help our brothers. It was an awful sight. The survivors told such a pitiful tale. They had no guns, nothing to defend themselves against field cannon. They thought they had surrendered. They wanted peace. The soldiers murdered them anyway."

Plenty Horses shook his head. "Big Foot was a fool to give up his guns. I know. I am from Red Cloud's band. We do not give up our guns."

There was a quiet moment. Then Kate shook her head. "That's not quite right."

"What?" Nock asked.

She looked at Plenty Horses. His glance had become a glare again. He turned back to the window.

"A great many soldiers were also killed at Wounded Knee. Big Foot's Indians had to have had guns. You know that. You've read the reports."

"Twenty-nine soldiers died," Nock agreed. "But what do you know of them?"

A swirl of images, not pleasant, flooded Kate. She collected her thoughts. "Bill and I went to the agency for the holidays," she told him, remembering how they'd arrived at the cluster of buildings that marked the reservation headquarters called Pine Ridge Agency. That had been the night before Christmas.

She swallowed and continued, "Several days later, December twenty-ninth, I was in the chapel with some of the other wives, white women, whose husbands administered the reservation. We were sitting around the Christmas tree sacking candy for the coming New Year's festivities when we heard guns. We could hear them clearly, coming from the east. We all knew what it meant—a fight in progress."

She paused, swallowed, looked upward, searching for the right words. "All the tribes camped at the agency knew what it meant, too. I guess they got scared. The rest of that day, the other white women and I watched the Indians camped at the agency take flight. Hundreds and hundreds had come in surrendering and seeking protection. But once the gunfire started, they all began to take down their white canvas tepees and pack up. It was like watching the snow melt on a spring day. The hills around the agency were suddenly alive with horses and men and families loaded onto wagons, all of them disappearing into the distance as fast as they could go. Then at nightfall, the wounded from the battlefield began to arrive, soldiers mostly." She glanced up at Plenty Horses. "They'd been shot with guns, some of them badly wounded."

She drew a deep breath. She'd never told this story, she realized. Never included it in any letter home. She wondered why. How was it that she'd decided to be silent on this point.

"We cleared out the chapel and turned it into an infirmary. The wounded kept coming all night, and then it started to snow. We couldn't get any help or medical supplies because of the storm. There was almost nothing we could do to help those soldiers."

Kate walked to the door. "I had seen death before. I had watched my father die in the privacy of his upstairs bedroom almost a year earlier. He drifted off to sleep, and then I saw the pallor of his complexion change slowly becoming ashen gray as his hand grew cold. It was an amazing thing—that change."

She turned to face the cell. "I saw at least twenty soldiers die that night and the next day. It was not the same. For them death was a struggle that rattled in their throats and contorted their faces as they struggled to keep breathing. Some of them moaned even after they'd lost consciousness. I am sorry for the Indians. I know more of them died, but I saw those soldiers die of gunshot wounds, so I don't believe it was an entire massacre as some say."

"Big Foot and his people surrendered their guns the day before," Plenty Horses restated. "They had no guns, none."

"Then how did the soldiers get shot?" Kate asked.

"The soldiers shot the soldiers," he told her through clenched teeth with enough force, enough fierceness, she stepped back and bumped the jail door. It clattered.

This was craziness. She saw what she saw. She knew what

she knew. Plenty Horses hadn't been at Wounded Knee. He was Red Cloud's tribe. By his own admission, he'd arrived after the fight was over. And yet in that moment a sudden swell of feeling came over her for Plenty Horses. She sensed his depth of confusion not as a rage but a shattering. In all existence there was an inner and an outer world. Light on the surface, and the understanding of something underneath. So too with human consciousness. At a certain age we decide to define ourselves. We say we will reflect this image of ourselves, not that one. Others aid the selection: parents, friends, schools. It occurred to Kate that too many contradictory forces had worked on Plenty Horses. He'd lost the connection between what he was expected to reflect and who he really was. There were too many pieces of him. She imagined that felt like looking into a shattered mirror and trying to find a focus.

Nock took Kate's arm. "Well, I think that's enough chitchat." His tones were light, too light.

Both Kate and Plenty Horses gave him a look.

He shrugged. "I don't think we're going to agree on this one. So we might as well call it a visit."

Plenty horses grunted.

Kate bent and picked up a handful of the letters. None had been opened. She set them on the cot. "They mean well," she told Plenty Horses. "They just don't understand."

He turned his back to her and said nothing.

Nock called for the guard.

Outside, Kate turned on him. "You set that up. You invited me to meet Plenty Horses because you wanted to know what I knew about Wounded Knee. That was your way of finding out. But you don't need to be so clever. Next time just ask."

He took her arm and guided her down the street. "Kate, everybody has a blind spot, even photographers. Unfortunately, yours is dangerous. You're right, I wanted to know what you knew, but not about Wounded Knee. I don't care about Wounded Knee half as much as I care about you."

At that, he stopped, his mouth half open as if his own

words had confused him. Then he stuttered. "I . . . I mean only that I had hoped your meeting with Plenty Horses might trigger some explanation." He stopped again and shook his head. "You're right. I was too clever. It didn't work."

"Some explanation of what?" she asked.

"Of why those soldiers are following you."

"Oh, the soldiers again," she said with sarcasm. "You're going to drive us both loony seeing shadows behind shadows. Or maybe you have another fancy clock theory."

Without comment, he guided her forward several more steps, turned, and tipped his hat. "Good day, gentlemen. I assume you've met Mrs. Burke."

Kate looked up. To her astonishment, Nock had greeted the exact same soldiers he'd pointed out before. They were lounging against a barber pole. Now both came to attention, and one dropped his smoke.

10

Next morning Kate paused at the entrance to the Minnehaha Natural Hot Springs and Baths. Homer barked impatience, but she needed to catch her breath. She'd taken the hill faster than her usual pace, thinking that would force anyone following her to show himself trying to keep up. She really didn't expect to see anyone. She hadn't seen anything suspicious since Nock surprised those soldiers yesterday.

They couldn't have been more surprised than she was. They'd mumbled "good day" and "how are you" and touched their hats. She hadn't managed any response. Then the pair of them had practically tripped over each other, excusing themselves and hurrying off down a side street. She hadn't seen them or their like again. Not the rest of that day. Not this morning. She'd turned unexpectedly, kept a watch over her shoulder. No one was following her that she could tell. She'd decided Nock was wrong, after all. Whatever coincidence had caused those soldiers to be outside the jail when she and Nock emerged hadn't had anything to do with her.

She heard footsteps on the gravel behind her and turned with a start. It was an older lady walking her dog through the park at the entrance to the springs. She didn't even look in Kate's direction as she and her little fluffy friend passed a nearby gazebo, stirring up a flock of sparrows that noisily fluttered in and around until she was gone.

Kate drew several deep breaths. She couldn't exactly explain why she was so jumpy. She read the sign announcing the spring because her mind required the concentration.

> **Heynshon Brothers**
> Proprietors and manufacturers of
> ginger ale
> champagne cider
> soda water
> all manner of mineral waters.
> Also health baths

She wasn't interested in fancy bottled drinks. She'd come for the baths. But reading those words kept her from repeating the phrases that had become almost litany: "This is stupid," "This is impossible." She hated how Powers T. Nock had gotten her upset like this, her mind all a jumble.

It didn't make sense. No one had any reason to pay her much mind. As a child, she'd imagined all kinds of fantasies in which her father somehow turned his full attention on her. Even for a moment. If he'd never noticed anything she did with more than a casual nod, she had no reason to believe anyone else should. Certainly not the colonel. He had to have lots of other things on his mind.

Nock, of course, had been very sure of himself. She found the man alternately charming and annoying. There was something unmistakably engaging about his wit and his warmth. She'd been impressed at how respectfully he'd talked to Plenty Horses, even when the Indian was being rude. Then again, he could turn around and be absolutely impossible, embarrassingly so. She could swear he'd bumped into those soldiers the way he'd bumped into everything in her dark lab just to get on her nerves.

With that, she pushed through the door of the bathhouse. The lady's attendant, a large woman named Fran, greeted

Kate. "Nice to see a decent woman," she said in hushed almost conspiratorial tones, even though there was no one near to hear. Kate glanced into the mirror behind the woman and wondered what it was about her that appeared visibly "decent." She would have thought her thick, curly, always unruly red hair would have been enough to make that questionable.

The first time she'd come in, Fran had whispered close to Kate's ear that she didn't care where a woman went as long as it was with her husband, an obvious reference to some gossip circulating about Kate and how she'd spent her winter. That was the first Kate had known anyone cared about that, either. It had startled her enough that she hadn't known what to say.

But Fran never needed encouragement. Without waiting for words from Kate, she gently touched the cross at her neck and went on in those same conspiratorial tones. "We got lots of them divorsays that come in here," she said. "Ask me they ought to use the hotel baths. Keep this place for decent folks. I mean, I don't even know if I can continue my employment here if this place should get a reputation. You know what I mean. A woman has to keep up appearances."

If the woman was keeping up "appearances," it wasn't obvious to Kate. She was wearing a frumpy dress, out of style. Her hair was pinned up in a harsh, old-fashioned way. The overall impression was more scrubbed and common than proper. Kate thought the woman could have taken a lesson from Kate's grandmother to whom "appearances" had been paramount. She'd spend hours mending and restyling her fancy stage dresses because she refused to appear "dowdy," no matter her circumstances. More, Fran was wrong about the "divorsays." Easy divorces had become something of an industry in Sioux Falls. But the women Fran was referring to were still married and staying in town only long enough to meet the short residency before obtaining a dissolution of their marriages, impossible to effect in many eastern states. Technically, that meant they were not "divorsays" until they left town. But clearly that didn't matter to Fran. Opinions were cheap; she had lots.

"They all come in for the fancy stuff," she confided to Kate, adding a little implied intimacy with a nudge of her elbow. "Not hard to figure how they drove their husbands away, spending money like it was theirs."

Some of it probably was, Kate thought. The only women who could really afford a divorce came from upper-crust eastern families with money of their own. But Kate didn't argue. She nodded to Fran like she knew, like she understood. She did understand that by "fancy stuff" Fran meant the "spring water baths," "electric baths," "tonic baths," and "salt rubs." Kate was content with hot water and perfumed soap. It was the one luxury she allowed herself. A hot bath made anything bearable, including lawyers with too-active imaginations.

Fran handed Kate fresh towels. Homer knew the routine, he entered the bath cubicle ahead of Kate and sat next to the tub. Fran had objected the first time Kate brought him with her. Now she cooed over how well behaved he was, "a real gentleman in a doggy fur coat," she said with a chuckle as she opened the pipe, letting hot water into the enameled tub. Then leaving Kate and Homer, she returned to her cash box and towel stack.

Kate shut the door. That closed space smelled faintly of mildew and mineral salts. The walls were wood, unpainted. A wide bench stood along one side, a tub in the middle. The floor consisted of closely spaced wooden slats between which the water could drain. She and Bill had a portable bathtub, a rubber-lined sling that hung over a folding wooden frame. Not deep, it was worse than a tin tub for losing heat. One was never tempted to linger in it. Here she could while away most of the morning except that Fran, like Tony Amato, would be in and out checking on her.

Kate undressed and slipped into the bath, letting its fluid warmth ride up her body to her chin. The sensation of it drifted her into mindlessness or, at least, a floating feeling of nothing but physical sensation. She noted in particular the slightly sulfur scent of the water, the gentle rippling ebb of the fluid against her shoulders. A little later, she let her thoughts dreamily focus on the power of the ordinary—a simple bath in this case. As far as she was concerned, the spectacular was unnerving while the ordinary was to be enjoyed, repeated. She seriously believed if there were more hot baths, there would be fewer hot tempers. As a child, whenever she needed anything from her mother, she'd always waited until after her bath to ask.

Fran's first knock came a few minutes later. "You be needing anything?" she asked.

"No, I'm fine," Kate answered. Then she sat up and began to suds herself.

As usual, Homer had rested his head on the side of the tub. He raised it for that interruption, then put it back down, the water wetting the bottom of his chin, giving him little wet whisks of whiskers that Kate found amusing. She rubbed them and cooed to him.

Kate could remember exactly when she'd discovered the ordinary. She was sixteen years old one fall when her father and Bill Burke came home from a photographic junket they'd taken jointly to Japan. Her father brought her a roll of silk to take to the dressmaker. It was very fine silk, and she was pleased that he'd remembered her. Then Bill gave her a book. He was her father's oldest friend, but he'd never given her anything before. He'd only recently stopped tussling her hair when he saw her. Typical for Bill, he hadn't made much of the gift. Seeing her, he'd simply tossed her the book wordlessly, as though it were nothing.

The book was a collection of Japanese woodcuts—page after page of pictures. But what pictures! Ordinary people doing ordinary things, but drawn with such simple clarity, she'd found herself completely absorbed. Looking back, she supposed that was an odd sort of thing to give a young girl, but for her it had been pure serendipity. Bill could have flashes like that, yet to this day she had no idea if he had any sense of that part of himself. She'd tried to tell him once how much that book meant to her, but he'd been in no mood to listen. Odd, she thought, how lives could become entangled like that without embracing.

For a while that book had become the center of her life. She'd studied it for hours, for days. She'd studied it until she began to see the things around her the same way, as sharply focused bits of simplicity. It was as if a veil had been lifted from her eyes. She began to think of the "ordinary" as a mask of familiarity that had been slipped over the face of the everyday. It could be stripped away to reveal surprising beauty. That's when she started letting those kinds of shapes and subjects fill her frames. That's when she began to feel that if she did nothing else with her life but elevate the ordinary, she'd be full. It would be like giving her eyes to the world.

That's what she'd been doing out on the prairie with Bill and the soldiers, taking "pretties"—pictures of simple things, nothing that anyone would care about, she thought, remembering the nagging worry Nock had planted. She let herself groan softly at that returning anxiety and slid deep to rinse the suds.

She wasn't ignorant of the enormity of what had happened out there between the Sioux and the soldiers. She knew. But she had no images, no new understandings to offer. She'd turned to other things, taking photographs of ferrets and foxes and falcons.

Same with her father. He knew. He knew of her mother's alcoholism and endless whirl of anger that filled their house. He knew what it meant for Kate to be left there with no escape. Still, every summer he packed without speaking, closed up the photography studio without comment, and left. Kate had never thought his actions heartless. They simply reflected his own distance. He'd absented himself from their house for so many years, a part of him was unrecoverable. Even when he was home, there was an emptiness. He was, in a sense, always gone. She supposed that's why she tolerated Bill. She knew too well how to live with a man who would never let her completely love or hate him.

Fran was knocking at the door again. "You need more soap, maybe?"

"No," Kate told her through the door. "I'm nearly finished."

About this time, Fran usually kidded Kate about "getting her money's worth," as if soaking long was somehow thrifty, but today she offered another observation. "Too much of anything isn't healthy, you know."

Thrifty, but not too healthy, Kate thought with some amusement. Nevertheless, the water was getting cold.

An hour later, Kate entered the local office of the Indian Reform Movement and was startled at the activity. Kate stated her business to a young, round-faced secretary at the first desk, then sat and looked around while she waited. There were three desks, all occupied, all piled high with papers, but there was no decorations. Everything was functional even to the window covering, which Kate recognized as a parade banner. It was no doubt taken down and used every Fourth of July and then returned to the window. That was truly thrifty, she thought.

Kate's gaze came back to the round-faced secretary. Between answering the phone and greeting visitors, she worked a spindle, about six inches high, designed for hairwork, a popular drawing room occupation that turned a beloved's locks into bracelets or chains to be worn as mementos or wrapped into shapes resembling flowers, hearts, or crosses and framed under glass. Kate noted a certain surprising deftness to the woman's hands as though she did this often, as though she had an endless supply of tresses needing such treatment.

A couple of minutes later, Amy Farnsworth came forward from where she'd been occupied at one of the back desks. She greeted Kate. She was the Indian Reform Movement's national leader, a Bostonian of some celebrity who'd come to town for the trial.

"I had no idea you were kept so busy," Kate said as she followed the woman back to her desk.

"Well, things don't change on their own," she told Kate with enough curtness Kate wondered if she'd offended.

In an effort to make sure they were understanding each other, Kate asked, "What things don't change on their own?"

The older woman looked over her glasses. "My dear girl, surely you realize how far we've come as a nation since women kept liquor laced with morphine as their only means of taming the wild Indian who came to their door."

That, Kate suspected, was a practiced bit of dialogue meant to shock—meant to establish Mrs. Farnsworth as a woman not to be ignored or underestimated, in short, formidable.

Kate gave what she supposed was the expected response, "Thank goodness," even as she questioned the sense of what Mrs. Farnsworth had just said. Then Kate sat across from the other woman and wondered what she was going to say next when she noticed a Kodak sitting on top of one pile of papers. A brown rectangular box, not even as big as a loaf of bread, it had been introduced three years earlier with the promise of perfect picture-taking ease. "You press the button, we do the rest," was the slogan.

"Do you take pictures?" Kate asked, indicating the Kodak.

"Oh, Mrs. Burke, you embarrass me. I imagine to you that is hardly a camera at all."

Bill thought of it that way. He could hardly say the word *Kodak* without a sneer. He considered the Kodak a toy of the rich and a passing fancy. Kate didn't know what she thought of the camera, but she knew she didn't think much of flexible film. She preferred the tonal quality and clarity of large negatives. Besides, glass was cheaper.

"I've never actually taken a photograph with a Kodak," Kate told Mrs. Farnsworth. "Is it really as easy as they say?"

"Aim and shoot," the woman said.

Kate picked up the box. Supposedly, it held film enough for forty pictures. When the forty pictures were taken, it had to be returned to the factory where the film was developed and the camera reloaded. Kate's hands felt along the sides and fingered the mechanism. The Kodak dispensed with ground glass and plateholders, which intrigued her. On the other hand, she didn't sense that this was a camera to be loved, its idiosyncrasies learned, its every mechanism memorized. No matter which way she turned it, it was a basic brown box.

"Do you take a great many pictures?" Kate asked, returning the camera to the top of the same pile of papers.

"Oh, I suppose one could say that," Mrs. Farnsworth answered. "I'm enough of a progressive woman to enjoy a novelty."

"Ever thought of taking pictures of Indian women?"

"Documentary pictures? Oh heavens, no, you flatter me."

"I wasn't thinking of documentary pictures, exactly. Just pictures of what the women do, where they live, their sacred societies."

"I'm not sure what you mean, but I can assure you no one has more Indian friends than I do. I've had my image put to pasteboard with more than one of them. Sarah Winnamucca and I testified before Congress together. Our pictures were in the newspaper together, side by side."

"Oh yes," Kate hastened to add. "I've heard of your work. Everyone has. I can't imagine anyone else doing even half so much. It's just that I had something a bit different in mind. The ordinary. I was wondering if you'd ever had occasion to take a picture or two of ordinary women on the reservations. I should think their way of life might be quite curious. The sacred quillworkers, for example."

"You mean the women who decorate things with porcupine quills?" Mrs. Farnsworth asked.

Kate nodded.

"I prefer beadwork myself." She opened a desk drawer and pulled out a bag. It had been stitched with a tapestry of beads forming a bold flowered pattern.

It was the kind of work that made Woman-Who-Dreams spit. She called it "tourist trash." But Kate could imagine the bag being admired in parlors back East. In fact, Woman-Who-Dreams was not being fair. Beadwork was hardly to be scoffed at. Manhattan island, as any school child knew, had been purchased by the Dutch for twenty-four dollars worth of "wampum"—mostly beads. An incredible bargain accomplished not because the Indians were gullible but because they had immediately recognized the value and labor-saving possibilities of glass beads over quills as a new medium for their most revered art. But Kate saw no point in trying to explain that. In fact, she felt quite sure she couldn't make any of it sensible to Mrs. Farnsworth.

Instead, she simply said, "It's beautiful," and then added, "But you must realize how few Indian women do quillwork anymore. The symbols mean things from dreams. That's interesting, isn't it?"

"Dreams? I don't know that I've ever heard anything like that before. Where did you learn it?"

"From an old Indian woman . . ."

"Who was selling quillwork," Mrs. Farnsworth added with a smile. "You know they become quite crafty at making one interested in what they want us to buy."

"She gave it to me, a pocket bag, a quite remarkable one." Kate pulled it out from the folds in her skirt and showed it to Mrs. Farnsworth.

"She gave you this?"

Kate nodded.

"What did she want? She must have wanted something."

"She wanted me to take pictures of the quillworkers so they wouldn't be forgotten. But I'm afraid I won't be staying in Sioux Falls long enough unless I can interest someone in the project. I was hoping your organization . . ."

Mrs. Farnsworth shook her head and gave a dismissing wave of her hand. "As I told you, I'm a progressive woman, Mrs. Burke. I sincerely believe in progress. I believe in the future, and I don't see any Indians in the future. I see Americans, all of us dressed modern and adapted to Christian behaviors. In short, Mrs. Burke, you might say the sole purpose of the Indian Reform Movement is to make the Indian feel at home in America. That doesn't include encouraging quaint customs and crafts."

"I see," Kate said, glancing over her shoulder at the secretary working her hair spindle.

The woman went on. "If this ancient Indian women's society exists, I'm sure it only impedes progress. I hope you don't think I'm rude to speak so bluntly, Mrs. Burke. I'm sure this Indian woman and her stitching is quite a curiosity, but we can't let ourselves get caught up in curiosities, now can we? There's ever so much more important work to be done."

Kate returned as small a smile as she could and still be thought respectfully sociable. "Perhaps you're right," Kate muttered, and then standing, she turned to the secretary who'd just twisted another strand of hair into her braided pattern, and said, "I couldn't help noticing. That's a most interesting curiosity. Just what are you making?"

From the look the pair exchanged, Kate knew her use of the word "curiosity" hadn't been lost on them. But politeness dictated their taking no notice.

The secretary replied, "It'll be a love chain, a bracelet."

Mrs. Farnsworth simply added, "Well, yes, but really I'm quite sure we're right. We've had some experience with Indian reform, you know."

Powers T. Nock was the first to enter the men's room at the back of the Masonic Temple. He didn't like the closeness of the place. He preferred space, lots of it when he needed to make an argument, pacing room, thinking room. Confined like this, his hands and arms turned gestures into accidents. He poked his hands into his pockets and hoped that would keep them from knocking over the soap dish or something.

Meanwhile, the others crowded the room, the two prosecuting attorneys and their military observer, the colonel, his aide, a fair-haired young officer Nock had never heard called anything but Baldwin but who commanded respect, even from the colonel, inasmuch as he'd been sent by General Miles to observe the trial. Lastly, Judge Sherman pushed into the room. It wasn't that big. It had two toilets with a single stall wall between, a sink, a trash receptacle, a heat register, a window. The floor and lower half of the walls were covered in small hexagonal tiles, white with black borders in a busy pattern. A single bare lightbulb hung from the ceiling. Hardly an appropriate space for anything but its intended purpose, nevertheless, the judge was using it as chambers, the lodge not offering any more suitable place unless one went down a floor.

When everyone was crowded in, he ordered the door closed. Then he parted his robe, unbuttoned, and made water into one of the toilets at the same time as he said, "All right, Nock, what's the problem?"

"My witnesses haven't arrived from the reservation."

The judge grunted, finished, buttoned. He was a stocky, big-nosed man who might have been mistaken for an Irish boxer if it weren't for his robes and his perfectly trimmed gray hair. He grunted again. "This whole goddamned town is full of Indians. You been down to the Stevenson Hotel lately?"

Nock shook his head.

"It's a beehive of Indians, all of them sleeping in fancy beds because of this trial."

"Those are all army scouts, the prosecution's witnesses," Nock told him. "Believe me, the defense can't afford such. Our witnesses will be staying in Indian camp when they arrive. But they haven't arrived."

"Why not?"

"They left the reservation four days ago," Nock told him. "They should have gotten here by now, but they haven't. I'm only asking for a short delay."

Besides the judge, he watched how the man called Baldwin was taking this in. He couldn't tell. He wasn't sure why Baldwin had shown up this many days into the trial.

The judge turned to the colonel. "How long does it take to get here from Pine Ridge?"

The colonel shrugged. "Depends. Half day by train. Two days by horseback."

"Where are they, then?" He shot the question back at Nock.

He couldn't keep his hands in his pockets any longer. Pulling them out, he gestured as he spoke. "I'm sure they've only encountered some unexpected difficulty. It's spring. The rivers are swollen."

"They don't have to cross the river."

"I know, I was speaking figuratively. There are other similar possibilities." He wasn't sounding convincing, he knew. That's because he'd never been able to argue anything he didn't believe. What he believed was that the colonel had detained his witnesses. Outside Sioux Falls, he was the law. He was practically the law inside Sioux Falls. If he didn't want those witnesses to arrive on time, he could make that happen.

"We have any reason to think those Indians will show up at all?" the judge asked.

"Well, I don't know that we have any reason to think they won't," Nock countered.

"They're savages," the judge returned. "Don't understand courts, do they? Don't respect the law much, do they?"

"But we know they left the reservation," Nock tried again. "One day's delay won't matter that much, will it?"

He was hoping that wherever they were, the colonel couldn't keep them detained indefinitely. He was hoping that sending Baldwin to observe meant that General Miles had taken an interest in Nock's defense and might even decide it was to the army's advantage to admit they were at war.

"Problem is, we got all those other witnesses sleeping between sheets at the Stevenson," the judge returned, "at government expense. A day means a lot of somebody's tax dollars are being wasted making redskins comfortable."

Nock shook his head. "But I can hardly be expected to mount a defense without witnesses." He shot another quick glance at Baldwin. The man showed no indication he intended to enter the fray.

"You're defending an Indian," the judge told him. "If his own kind won't show up to help, what's the court supposed to do? We're going forward with this. I'm not going to wait around for some redskins to show up in their own good time."

With that, the judge pulled his robes closed and elbowed his way around the others, who respectfully let him be the first one out.

Nock hung back. He'd stirred things, surprised some, angered others including the judge, who obviously had been expecting only a token defense. He'd honestly expected his efforts would be noticed. And once noticed, he'd thought people would begin to ask questions not just about the trial but about this whole "Indian uprising." He didn't usually miscalculate this badly. But somehow all his efforts were out of sync. Nothing seemed to connect, carry through. He'd even wound the wrong clocks this morning. That wasn't like him. He was orderly about his clocks and which ones he wound on which days; all the ones with cathedral gongs on Sunday, all the ones with half-hour bells on Monday, the cuckoos on Tuesday . . . He shook himself. This kind of thinking wasn't helping anything.

Outside the washroom, Baldwin stopped the colonel. "Sir," he said. "General Miles asked me to convey a message."

The colonel stiffened. Baldwin had shown up at the trial yesterday without prior notice. He was staying in a hotel room, not army camp, like he was too good to bunk with field men.

"What message might that be?"

"The general sincerely hopes you've not interfered with this trial."

"What? Does he think I've had something to do with those witnesses not appearing?"

"I don't know, sir. That's the entire message."

The colonel considered that. He wanted to believe this message was the only reason for Baldwin being there. But he wasn't sure. What he knew for sure was that Baldwin was a junior officer, an academy man with family connections. He was expected to rise quickly. But at the moment he was General Miles's toady. The colonel didn't like other men's toadies. He pushed his face close to Baldwin's. "I thought you were Lieutenant Casey's friend. I mean, surely you can see that I'm just trying to get the man some justice."

"I was more than the lieutenant's friend," Baldwin returned. "I was his best friend. But he died like a soldier.

And I honestly believe if he could, he'd appear as a witness for the defense himself. He'd not desire the punishment of that poor savage."

The colonel swore. "Hell, when did a back-shooting renegade become a poor savage? You seriously want me to believe you want that stubby weasel of a lawyer to win, to prove this was war same as some battle with the Confederates? Or maybe it's that you aren't old enough to know what it was like to have fought in a real war."

"Permission to speak freely, sir."

"I thought you were speaking freely. Yes. Of course."

"I believe it was you who proved it was war."

"I beg your pardon."

"Sir, I think you underestimate the depth of General Miles's anger. He had this whole affair nearly settled. Talked out. No bloodshed. It was you who turned it into the 'end of Indian wars' and got yourself into all the newspapers."

"General Miles got his share of that attention, didn't he?"

"That's just it. You made him a war hero. Now you want to reduce his campaign to a dress parade affair in order to hang this Indian. Once a war hero, the general would just as soon remain a war hero."

"He'd let the Indian go?"

"Sir, he never wanted him arrested in the first place. This trial opens too much of the recent military campaign to public scrutiny. Nobody needs that. You could have let the Indian go. He's only one Indian."

The colonel couldn't believe what he was hearing.

Let one Indian get away with murder and then what? he asked himself.

But he didn't say anything. Nobody did. Nock was coming down the hall. They all quietly stepped aside and let the lawyer pass. Meanwhile, the colonel continued to seethe. A field officer who marched his men for months in the cold of winter was not supposed to be mocked by a junior grade officer, who thought he could speak for the general, and a bookworm lawyer in a checkered suit. The bookworm lawyer and the junior grade officer were sup-

posed to be grateful that somebody was standing guard—
keeping the savages in their place. Every last one of them.

But, of course, the colonel gave no voice to those
thoughts. Instead, he lied. He told Baldwin to assure the
general that he had no thought of interfering with the trial,
and that he had absolutely no idea where the missing
witnesses could be.

"There is one good use for Indians," the colonel told his
aide when Baldwin left.

"What's that?"

"Fear. Nothing like a good dose of Indian fear. Works
better than a spring tonic—shuts the mouths and opens the
bowels."

"You thinking to stir up a little Indian excitement?" his
aide asked. "Get everybody to figuring they need the army
again?"

"And just how in hell am I supposed to do that?" the
colonel returned. He paused. When he spoke again, it was
softer. "Maybe we whipped them too good this time. But I
can tell you one thing—I don't intend to do a nation's dirty
work and not get my due respect."

When the trial resumed, Nock called his only witness,
Plenty Horses. The young man went to the witness stand,
stood where he was told to stand, raised his right hand when
he was told to raise his hand, listened while the bailiff read
the oath, and then didn't answer. Nothing.

After an awkward moment, the bailiff read the oath again.
"Do you swear to tell the truth, the whole truth . . ."

When he finished, there still was no response.

Nock stood and asked the judge for permission to consult
with his client. That being granted, he approached Plenty
Horses where he stood with his arm still raised and whispered in the man's ear, "What's the matter?"

"Where's the translator?" Plenty Horses whispered back,
without turning his head, without lowering his arm.

"The translator?" Nock glanced in the jury's direction. It
wasn't going to help to have them think his client was
uncooperative. "But you speak very good English."

"I am Tsunka Waka Otta," Plenty Horses returned, and this time he did lower his arm.

Nock hadn't anticpated this, but he should have. All the other Indian witnesses had spoken through a translator. Why wouldn't Plenty Horse have expected the same, especially as he wanted to be Indian, wanted to forget everything he'd ever been taught by the white man, including English. But that was a notion he was sure the judge would never understand. He doubted there was a man on the jury who could imagine *wanting* to be Indian. Worse, Plenty Horses' sudden obstinacy, his show-stopping antics would make the jury think him arrogant, stubborn, unworthy of mercy. This might well be the final straw, the tip in the balance, the thing that finally sent him to the gallows.

With a pang of feeling he hadn't known he harbored, Nock looked at this bronze-faced young man with his straight-backed stiffness and felt for his rage, his confusion. He really didn't want him to die. He wanted him to find his peace some other way.

He also knew better than to try to reason with him.

Nock turned back to the court. "We need a translator," he said to the judge.

"A translator?" the judge replied. "He speaks English at least as well as I do. If I'm not mistaken, your client just gave an interview to a New York reporter that appeared in every newspaper in the country. He did that in English, didn't he?"

Nock nodded. "But in front of all these people, he'd be more comfortable with a translator. I'm sure one could be gotten quite easily."

The judge motioned Nock to his table. He leaned close. "If you think you can use some cheap trick like this to delay the trial, you better think again. I'm not stupid. Now get on with this."

Nock stepped away from the judge's bench. He glanced around the courtroom wondering why he'd ever thought he could save an Indian who'd shot an army officer in the back. Had he thought he could sandbag inevitability? Time devours us all. Only in the case of the Sioux, time had opened a wide maw, large enough to swallow their whole nation, and all they'd been able to do in the face of that was dance like they thought they could dam the flow of time with a ritual—warp events into some strange Messianic end with buffalo.

Nock paced back to his table. He didn't want to give up. He couldn't think of another time or place when his wits had failed him. He couldn't think of a single thing to do here. Time ticked. The tension grew. And then it came to him. Plenty Horses had had his day in court. He had stood up, and without speaking a word, he had said to the judge, the jury, this room full of spectators, and all history that he was Sioux. The United States of America with its soldiers and its schools and its courts could strip him of everything but that stubborn pride, that sure knowledge that he came from good stock, a proud nation. All Nock had to do was let him have his moment, small as it was.

Nock turned and faced the judge. "The defense rests."

Stunned silence.

The judge screwed up his face. He leaned across the table. "I beg your pardon," he said.

Nock repeated, "The defense rests. My client is unable to testify. I have no other witnesses. The defense rests."

The judge gave him a long stare. There was a moment when Nock thought he might back down, might reconsider, and call a translator. But then a hardening took over his face and the gavel came down.

That evening Bill took Kate for a stroll through Picnic Island, a favorite local spot. The park was full of townspeople and soldiers and visitors all out for a walk in the pleasant spring air. There were baby carriages, bicycles, scooters, and skates. Homer sniffed the other dogs and trotted in circles. A banjo band played near the waterfront. To Kate it was almost as if Nock's surprise move at the trial that day had rippled through the whole town leaving a relaxed, settled, finished feeling. It was spring. The winter was now behind them.

Bill was in a good mood. Wearing his best hat and silk

vest, he strode along humming a tune Kate couldn't quite make out. His mood had improved the moment he thought that the trial was over. All that remained was the summation and jury deliberation. Word around town was that it was all over but the hanging. Bill was already talking about California and maybe places beyond. Going to Japan was a possibility he'd raised. Her own feelings were mixed. But she'd understood the problem, understood instantly why Nock did what he did.

Bill said, "You know if we settled down in a town like this, you could stroll every evening and have a regular house with plumbing and closets."

"No, thanks," she replied. He knew her thoughts on that subject.

"Lord, I've lived my life backward," he replied, giving his voice a bass roll. "In my youth I had a wife who nagged me all the time about settling down. Now in my older years I've a wife who can't abide the notion. What did I do to deserve such a fate?"

"Think of me as easier to please," Kate answered.

He grunted a low disbelief. "If only that were true." Then he chuckled deep and long. "Thadius Arrowsmith found your ambitions amusing."

Kate stiffened. She'd known her conversation with Mr. Arrowsmith would likely be repeated back to Bill, but she hadn't counted on it happening so quickly or with such shared male amusement.

"Thadius painted quite a picture of me trotting from town to town lecturing about Sioux squaws before Temperance groups, ladies' book clubs, and church supper socials. That's who would come to something like that you know. Lord, he had me wearing a top hat and fancy cravat—the better to impress the womenfolk." He jabbed Kate in the ribs playfully. "But he thought you had spunk. He envied me a wife with spunk."

They met two couples, also out for a stroll. Kate smiled. Her husband spoke greeting and exchanged a comment on the weather. In a contrary way typical of Bill, she realized he was both annoyed with her and pleased. He liked that she'd

aroused a bit of envy from Thadius even if he'd had to take
a ribbing for it.

When the others had passed, he returned to their conversation. "Thadius said he'd never met a woman who preferred travel. He asked if you had a sister. I told him you
had a dog, and that was worse than any relative." He
chuckled at his own wit.

She started to say something in her dog's defense when
she spotted two soldiers. The words caught in her throat.
There were lots of soldiers in the park. She couldn't say why
that particular pair attracted her attention. No reason, she
told herself and shrugged them off. She thought she'd
forgotten Nock's silliness.

Her husband asked, "You were saying?"

"Sorry," Kate answered returning her attention to Bill. "I
merely asked Mr. Arrowsmith for an opinion. I didn't know
he would make so much of it."

"Were you asking that reporter for an opinion as well?"
he asked.

"What reporter?" she replied. She couldn't believe that
bit of conversation had been repeated back to him as well.

"The one who suggested I might buy you a lady's camera
for your lady's pictures."

"I suppose he thought I had spunk, too."

"Guts. He called you a gutsy lady."

"Is that meant to be a compliment?"

"I thought you might enjoy it," he answered. "Myself, it's
a toss-up as to which is worse—a wife who nags me to stay
home, or one who tattles to the men I do business with. At
least, you should be satisfied now. Obviously, I'm not the
only one who thinks these squaw pictures are a fool idea."
He chuckled.

A fool idea, Kate thought. That was close to the words
Woman-Who-Dreams had used. *A fool idea to fool the
fools—to trap their lies.* Kate had never thought of her
husband with the kind of amusement he was expressing at
the moment toward her. Did that make her silly or him?

They started across the bridge, leaving the park, and were
confronted by an old Indian woman wrapped in rags. She

thrust a beggar's bowl at them. "Go away," Bill told her. But the woman stepped closer, still pushing her bowl forward. She was all but blocking the way until, with a sudden exclamation, she drew her bowl close to her chest.

"What is it?" Bill asked.

"I don't know," Kate answered.

"Woman-Who-Dreams' design," the Indian woman said, and pointed to Kate, to the quilled pouch that hung from her waist.

Bill saw it then, too. "What's this?" he asked. He reached for the bag, tugged it loose from Kate's belt, and held it up for closer examination. "Where'd you get this?"

Kate shrugged. "From that old woman I told you about, the quillworker."

"You spent good money on this?"

The beggar woman shook her head. "No buy. Woman-Who-Dreams no sell that."

Bill grunted. "Oh, I get it. This is how you came by that cockamamy story about sacred Indian women's societies. You believed someone like this?" he asked and pointed at the beggar woman. "Then you tried to sell that story to Thadius Arrowsmith?"

Kate shook her head. That was entirely wrong. She started to explain, but before she got her thoughts pulled together, the older woman began to chant a string of Indian gibberish, and then switched to English. Her voice was low, but strong. It silenced Bill and captured Kate from her thoughts, which was all the more remarkable as the woman's words were not so much directed at them as at the air.

"The power not to be seen was a good gift we women once had," she intoned, her voice climbing a note higher. Her eye caught Kate's. "Now it is not a good gift. Now we are hungry, and the white man cannot see us. Does not want to see us. Except when we ghost dance." The Indian woman chuckled. "Then he imagines us everywhere. And he is afraid."

"Come on," Bill said, grabbing Kate's arm with enough force it surprised them both.

Kate followed him a couple of steps.

"I will tell you of Woman-Who-Dreams," the Indian woman called after them.

Kate pulled away, turned back. "What of Woman-Who-Dreams?"

The Indian woman's look took distance as if she were seeing the story rather than her surroundings. "One time we walked. And the soldiers came. Our men had taken the horses and gone to look for the buffalo. The soldiers had horses. They hollered. They fired their rifles into the air when they saw us. We had small children and old men, no longer hunters—no guns, no horses, no place to run. The land is flat all around us. And the sun is high. There is not even shadow to hide us."

Her arm defined the arc of the sky. "What are we to do? Our children cry. Our old men begin their death chants. A hundred horses' hooves pound the ground, coming down upon us. I pick up a stone. I stand there with a stone in my hand and my children by my side, and my feet touching my grave."

The old woman paused.

Kate felt her husband's tug again, but she didn't move.

Then the Indian woman threw back her head and cackled a wild noise that found Kate's spine. "Then it was that Woman-Who-Dreams touched the grass with fire. She called the wind. It came. It whipped across the prairie as if all the dead had been given breath, and we disappeared. The soldiers cannot see us. We have even left their minds. They can only think to run. But there is nowhere to run. It is the same wide prairie with no place to hide. Their bullets will not stop the flames. Their swords cannot cut the fire. They can only hope their horses run fast and far enough to carry them ahead of the wildfire."

The woman cackled, softer this time. "It is a power we once had, we women, the power to be invisible when we wished it. It was a good gift once. Now, no more."

There was a brief silence.

Then Bill threw back his head as he rolled out a deep, long laugh. "This gets better and better." He chuckled more. "Maybe I could see taking pictures of squaws sitting around smoking and sewing, but women with the power to disappear? You want to take pictures of that?"

Kate said nothing. The beggar woman had picked up a handful of earth and was giving it to the wind, twirling herself into the dust, her own form blending into earth and air. Beyond that, two soldiers lounged at the opposite end of the bridge. Same soldiers. No question. She could no longer deny it. For some reason she couldn't imagine, the colonel had decided to take notice of her—obviously quite a bit of notice.

But Bill had clearly decided not to take any of this seriously. "Hogwash," he answered her silence. "Pure hogwash." He shoved the quillwork bag at Kate. "And I don't want to see you wearing that thing anymore. It's too Indian."

That night near midnight, Kate was sitting next to the stove in her wagon. She was wrapped in a blanket, a lantern hanging overhead, a book on her lap. Bill was out, his usual routine. Homer had been restless, jumping at noises, pacing. She'd put him out thinking if he ran around for a few minutes he'd come back more contented. She checked her watch. He'd been gone a long time. She closed the book.

She was having trouble concentrating anyway. There were too many things going on that she didn't understand: Bill's reaction that afternoon, the soldiers she'd spotted, where her dog had gone. She felt like a child again caught up in a sea of events, all of which seemed frightening, none of which made sense.

Putting the blanket aside, she stoked the fire and stepped down from the wagon to the tent area. She straightened a few things. If there was anything she'd learned living in a traveling wagon, it was neatness. She couldn't have things scattered about when the sweep of her own skirts required space, and she had a big dog. Where was that dog?

Her ears alert, she expected any moment to hear the pad of his feet, his snort and shake before whining to come in. She checked her watch again.

A few minutes later, she pulled a cloak around her shoulders and, taking the lantern, she stepped outside. She paused, listening to the darkness. Nothing. "Homer," she called. "Homer, where are you? Come here, boy." Nothing. Then a muffled whimper she thought she recognized. He was hurt. She moved quickly in the direction of the sound, calling again. At the edge of the river, she was unsure but took the path upward calling, pausing to listen, calling again.

As she rounded a rock outcropping, she was suddenly confronted by the colonel. He was sitting on a tree stump holding her dog too tightly by the neck. The only sounds Homer could make were muffled whimpers as he strained toward her, his eyes big.

The colonel's lantern hung on a low branch about shoulder height. It lit his face from one side, brightening his cheeks and nose unnaturally while it cast the rest of his face into deep black hollows. His eyes were almost invisible. She was so surprised, she took a step backward and didn't know what to say. The obvious came to her lips, "Let go my dog. You're hurting him."

He twisted his hold, cutting Homer's whimpers to a rasping gasp.

She took a step forward. "What do you want?" she asked. "Bill's not here, and I don't know anything about anything."

He smiled. His teeth glistened. "I had me a fine pup once like this one. That was when I was a boy. Took him on a spring bear hunt with my uncles, my pa, and my cousins. It was an annual event, that spring bear hunt."

Kate shivered, more from the fear overtaking her confusion than a chill. The colonel meant her no good. Her eyes wandered left and right. If she had to run . . .

"Usually we found the bears in the open and treed them," he went on. "The dogs enjoyed that. But this day my dog got the scent and followed it right into a den. An older dog probably would have known better. My pup just didn't know where not to put his nose. Time we caught up with him, there wasn't much left. It's dangerous, Mrs. Burke, to put your nose where it doesn't belong."

She swallowed. "If my dog has bothered you . . ."

"It's not your dog who needs to learn its place."

"I'm sure I don't know what you mean. I'm sure I don't think this is the proper way to discuss . . ."

He laughed. "Don't talk to me about 'proper' this and 'proper' that. Truly proper women don't have any use for Indians." He smiled and patted the top of her dog's head in a way she knew was meant to annoy her. "You know, I can't figure you out. You're not a missionary. You're not a schoolteacher. You don't seem to be an Indian lover like those fancy lady reformers you went to visit today, so all I can figure is that you must be a born meddler. But you don't know what you're meddling in."

"Bill and I will be leaving soon. We're going to California," Kate told him.

"I'm not interested in where you're going. I'm interested in where you've been. What have you been doing in Indian camp?"

"Oh, that." She tried a little laugh. "Nothing, just talking to an old woman about quillwork, about taking pictures of the women doing their stitching and such. Nothing that matters."

The colonel felt the quiver of her voice like ice against warm skin. He hadn't known he could enjoy a white woman's fear like that. With the hand not holding the dog, he reached inside his jacket and pulled out a photograph. He turned it into the light and watched her eyes widen. It was the one of the Indian hugging the buffalo. She thought she'd gotten away with that. She needed to learn. He had spies everywhere.

"Doesn't much look like stitchery to me," he told her, and watched how she swallowed.

She was small, her neck was delicate. He wondered if she had any idea how easy it would snap.

"What do you want?" she asked.

201

That was the rub. What he wanted was hard to explain. He wanted her scared enough to close her eyes, the way most people's eyes were closed because they didn't want trouble, wanted to pretend trouble wasn't even there.

"Ever wonder how an Indian takes a scalp?" he asked, and pulled back her dog's head as if to demonstrate.

He enjoyed the little gasp that got.

He chuckled. "Oh, I'm not going to hurt your mutt, Mrs. Burke. I'm the one who protects the likes of you from being scalped, remember? Or has it been that long since you were out there on the prairie with my soldiers?"

He watched her nod, but he didn't feel she meant it, not really. That was the problem with this woman. The respect wasn't there.

He continued. "The Indian grabs the head and makes two cuts. Then he sits on the ground, places his feet against the subject's shoulders to get leverage and holding the hair with both hands, he pulls off the spoils of war with a sound not unlike slop hitting a trough." And for effect, he made just such a slopping, slurping sound. He watched her shudder. For a brief moment, he felt he had her, that one more squeeze and her fire would have snuffed.

But her dog broke free, jumped the space between them, whirled and snapped with such ferocity, he was forced to leap to his feet and reach for his gun.

"Don't shoot," Kate shouted, and threw herself on the dog, holding him. "Please, don't shoot."

He grunted a little laugh and put his gun away. "Mrs. Burke, I'll be brief. A fondness for Indians is trouble, more trouble than you want. Stay out of Indian camp. Better yet, stay close to your own camp. Terrible things can happen to those who don't know their place."

202

11

She was running through a field looking for something—her dog. He'd gotten too far ahead. And she'd been gone too long. Someone would be looking for her. She wanted to turn back. Sometimes she glanced over her shoulder. But mostly she kept running.

She was out of breath. She couldn't call out. When she tried, her mouth made no sound.

Now she was stumbling. The field had changed to railroad tracks. She was still running, but she had to watch her feet. She had to make sure she stepped on the wooden ties. In between was nothing but empty space.

The empty space frightened her. She hadn't realized she was so high. It was a bridge, a railroad trestle so far above the river, she could barely hear the water rushing over the rocks beneath.

Now she couldn't move. Her legs had become paralyzed by the emptiness between the trestle ties. It made no sense. She could see the firm cross ties, like wooden steps, stretching ahead. But she couldn't move. The bridge couldn't be trusted. It might twist and toss her down, down . . .

Something else was going down, down . . .
Her dog! He hung in the air beautifully suspended—legs,
tail, head, and ears catching the wind. Then he became a bird
and mounted the sky. His screech split the air . . .

She woke, her legs twitching, her throat dry. She felt for
Homer where he lay next to her bed. His nose nuzzled her
arm. He licked her hand. She sat up.

Bill, sleeping beside her, had thrown his leg over hers. She
pulled free, careful not to disturb him. Then, grabbing a
wrap, she got up and padded barefoot to the tent door.

She remembered kittens being thrown from a bridge. She
was thirteen. She liked wandering along the Delaware River
behind her house. She had her own paths and hideouts
under the bank. One day as she climbed along some rocks, a
kitten splashed into the water in front of her. Then another.
Some boys were on the bridge above throwing them off.

She recognized them. They were from her school, only
older. She yelled for them to stop. Laughter. Another kitten
hit the water. She scrambled up the embankment and onto
the trestle. She was too late. She screamed at them, "Killers.
Murderers. Fiends."

The boys surrounded her. The oldest and biggest wanted
to see her tits. He knew she was growing tits, he said. All the
girls her age were growing tits. Now he wanted to see hers.
He wanted to know if she was really a girl because girls
weren't supposed to be out by the river climbing on the
trestle. Girls were supposed to stay home.

Kate rubbed her hand across her forehead and voiced a
little ditty:

> "Mary had a little lamb,
> She tied it to a heater.
> And every time it turned around,
> It burned its little peter."

Her grandmother had taught her that verse when she was
too young to know what it meant. Reciting it for her father,
he'd grabbed her by the shoulders and asked her to promise

she'd be a "good girl"—always a "good girl." She hadn't understood, especially when her grandmother laughed and told her to sing it louder. It was shortly after that when her father began taking her to the studio with him.

But good old Granny, the actress and one-time singer, had taught her one other useful thing—a certain gesture she sometimes used when she talked about men. It was something girls *really* never did. Kate had no idea if her grandmother had ever actually done it. But Kate did. She slammed her fist, thumb pointed up, between the legs of the oldest of those boys. That crumpled and so surprised him and the others that Kate managed to run away.

She hadn't thought of that in a long time. And she'd never, never told anyone. What she'd done hadn't been nice, and even though she'd won the day, so to speak, she was never able to hang around the railroad tracks after that or along the river frequenting the haunts she loved.

She hadn't told Bill about the colonel's visit last night, either.

Giving a glance over her shoulder at her sleeping husband, she stepped outside. She heard the excited twitter of birds and noted the pink dawn. She breathed in the early morning air and then dipped some water from the bucket. That's when she saw the soldiers, two of them, sitting on the bank of the river nearby. They had fishing poles. She wanted to laugh. Did the colonel think she needed to be fooled by some pretended ruse? Or was it that he expected her to play along?

She took a drink and then, dipping her hand in the water, she bathed her throat. Meanwhile, Homer circled in anxious anticipation of their usual morning walk. He didn't understand her hesitancy.

"I know," she told him. "I know."

She knew what the colonel expected. He wanted her to add her own acquiescence to all the lies and silence. But she knew too much, not just about the affairs of the Seventh Cavalry and ghost dancing, but she knew too much about lies and silence in general.

It was odd, considering the amount of time she spent with

him, but that's what she remembered most about her father—his silence. He spoke little and almost never of anything of consequence. Surface talk, courtesies, only the necessary voicings one needed to get through the day. A child shut out learned to find answers in other ways. She began to think of her family as photographs, the silences giving form like the blank spaces around an image. But unlike the picture that could be grasped at once, the silences of her family had to be understood over time, the missing pieces surfacing bit by bit like flotsam. But the truth always surfaced, Kate believed, like an object lighter than water and meant to float.

She drew a deep breath of morning air, which nearly always had the effect of making her feel fresh and brave. Then stepping back inside, she got dressed. The sane thing was to do nothing. Soon the trial would be over, and she would leave Sioux Falls, leave the colonel, leave the soldiers. . . . But it was Sunday. Nothing would happen with the trial today. Besides, she hadn't escaped her mother and grandmother to find herself ensnared in some other fashion. The colonel be damned.

She pulled on her shoes and slipped a cloak around her shoulders. When she reemerged from the tent, Homer trotted away, turned, and waited. He crouched and then jumped playfully. His tail beat the air, back and forth, back and forth. Morning was their time together.

Twenty minutes later Kate got off the trolley next to the stockyards arena. The soldiers got off as well. They were still carrying their fishing poles, which looked a little odd this far from the river. That made them almost comically conspicuous. She didn't care.

She passed the Wild West exhibition's big top now standing in the middle of the fairgrounds and circled the corral where the seventeen buffalo were standing swatting flies. The novelty had worn off. Only a few bystanders and no Indians hung over the fence watching the animals. Her destination was a smaller tent on the far side of the grounds that had been pointed out to her once as belonging to Mrs. Donning—the notorious "white squaw of Sitting Bull." She thought she might take that reporter's suggestion and interview the woman.

But when she came to the entrance to Mrs. Donning's tent, Kate hesitated, then walked on by. She had seen Mrs. Donning on the streets of Sioux Falls once. She was dressed like a man in cowboy clothes. Kate had heard of other women who dressed like that, pretending to be men. Only Liz Donning hadn't bothered to tuck her hair under her hat. The sight was enough to cause wagon drivers in the middle of the street to rein in for a better look. She wasn't sure she knew what to say to a woman like that. Did one start the conversation with the usual niceties—"Good morning," and "I hope you're feeling well?"

And what was she supposed to believe? That Mrs. Donning was Sitting Bull's white squaw? That she had traveled to England with Buffalo Bill? That she was stolen by the Indians when she was baby and made a white Indian princess? That she had ridden with an Indian renegade until he was killed? All those stories couldn't be true.

Kate turned around. What became of such? Where did women like that go to grow old? Kate wondered. She got to the tent, and her courage failed her again. Coming had been an impetuous thought. Now she wasn't feeling quite so cocky.

She made it all the way to the trolley stop but couldn't make herself leave. Turning, she suddenly found herself face to face with the soldiers. There was a moment of confusion. Then they tipped their hats and acted like they were strolling by. She wanted to laugh. She wondered if they were as confused as she was at her aimless wandering.

The next time she found herself back in front of Mrs. Donning's dressing tent, she took a deep breath. Now or never, she thought and scooted her dog in ahead of her. In that instant she came face-to-face with a broad-shouldered, sturdy-looking woman wrapped in a dressing robe, smoking a cigarette.

"I'm sorry," Kate said turning to make sure the tent flap was closed behind her. "I don't normally barge in like this unannounced. It's just that . . . ."

"You wanted to meet me," the woman said in a deep voice. She was seated at a dressing table, her chair pushed back, her feet propped on a wooden box with enough bare leg showing to make Kate embarrassed at her immodesty.

The woman chuckled and then coughed. "Actually, I've been wondering for some time when you'd make it inside."

"Beg your pardon."

"You paced by the place three times." She motioned back and forth with the hand that held her cigarette.

"How did you . . .?" Then Kate saw the way the sun lit that side of the tent. Her shadow had given her away.

"You scared of me? Or you just like walking your dog by my tent?"

Kate shook her head. Liz Donning was a middle-aged woman, her face sun-darkened and creased near her eyes. There was a lingering beauty to her face, but her hair was so full and free, it gave her a look of wildness befitting her reputation. "I—I don't know."

"You don't know," the woman repeated. "Well, then, sweetie pie, let's start with an easier question. Who the hell are you?"

Kate stiffened, then said her name. She also introduced her dog. He was trying to wag the tail he was sitting on.

Mrs. Donning took a long drag on her cigarette. "I don't believe I've ever been formally introduced to a dog before."

Kate shrugged. "I didn't mean it that way, exactly."

"You want to meet my horse?"

Kate nodded.

"No, you don't."

"I beg your pardon."

"You haven't the slightest interest in meeting my horse," Liz Donning said. A smile that Kate found unsettling spread across her face.

"But I've heard your horse can do such wonderful tricks."

"I do the tricks. My horse runs round and round the ring."

208

"Oh, yes, of course, I meant to say that."

"I'm sure you did. You're certainly smooth with the chit-chat. Can you pour a proper tea?"

"I suppose so. Why do you ask?"

"Because we both know you didn't come here to compliment me on my riding or to meet my horse. You're too old and too married to want to run away with the show. So maybe you've come to share a cup of tea with me. Only I never could handle proper tea etiquette. So I'm very sorry, but you're going to have to take your dog and run along now."

"But I want to ask about Indians," Kate said.

"That would have been my second guess."

"What would have been your first?"

"That you wanted to ask about men."

Kate hated it when she suddenly felt hot all over.

Mrs. Donning laughed a hoarse, deep cackle. "Maybe you better ask me about men if you can still blush like that."

Kate shook her head. She looked around, taking in the feathered costume draped over one travel trunk, a saddle, a twist of rope, and then the shotgun leaning against the far end of the dressing table within Mrs. Donning's easy reach.

"May I sit down?" Kate asked.

Mrs. Donning pulled her feet off the wooden box.

Kate stepped forward and started to wipe the top with a handkerchief until she became aware of the other woman's bemused observance of her little ritual. She shoved the hanky back in her pocket and plopped herself down.

Mrs. Donning put out her cigarette. "I'm afraid I don't have much use for the finer ladylike politenesses, so if you have something on your mind, let's get to it."

"Ladylike politenesses serve only to flatter the lady," Kate repeated. It was a saying she'd learned as a child.

Mrs. Donning laughed. "Nobody can *be* a lady. That's impossible. We all just learn to act like one. But surely you have that much figured out."

Kate cleared her throat. She didn't know what to think of Mrs. Donning. She had come to interview the woman but didn't know how to ask. She had to say something, so she

209

plunged forward with the matter most on her mind: Woman-Who-Dreams and the quillworkers and why taking those photographs was important but impossible because her husband wanted to go to California and there were soldiers everywhere. That part came out awkwardly because she didn't think she wanted to actually mention the two soldiers she knew were just outside the tent. When she finished, she realized she'd done it all backward. She'd told her story instead of asking for the other woman's. This wasn't going to work at all, she suspected.

But Mrs. Donning's face softened, her voice took a different tone. "I know. I know what you mean. Go on."

Kate did. She didn't know why, but she let it all spill out. She told about the attempts she'd made to interest Thadius Arrowsmith and the reporter and Amy Farnsworth at the Indian Rightser's office. Now she didn't know what she would do. She even let it be known that she'd come for an interview because that's what the reporter had suggested, and she'd thought, why not?

When she finished, Mrs. Donning sat for a long moment rubbing her hand over her knee and not looking up. She was so deeply withdrawn, Kate was afraid she'd offended, probably because the woman didn't want to do an interview with anyone. Kate was about to excuse herself and leave when the other woman stood. She crossed to one of her travel trunks, opened it, and pulled out a bundle wrapped in a lace shawl. She returned and sat with the bundle in her lap, carefully unwrapping it to reveal a pair of moccasins decorated with rows and rows of braided quillwork—a yellow cross on each toe.

"They're beautiful," Kate said, leaning forward to admire them.

"I lost my baby," Mrs. Donning said. She cleared her throat and looked up at Kate. "I don't know what you've heard about me. Most of it is true, I suppose, but really it's not as scandalous as you might think. I was a missionary once, all pretty and proper and fired up with the word of God. I was going to save the heathens. Instead, I fell in love with a Pawnee brave—Man-Who-Hates-His-Horses. That was his teasing name. He really loved his horses. I never knew anyone who could ride better. He taught me."

Mrs. Donning drew a deep breath and shook her head. "But that was unthinkable. White missionary women don't fall in love with Pawnee braves. What was I supposed to do? Go live in a tepee on government rations? I went back to Boston. I became engaged to a lawyer, but I couldn't do it. I couldn't marry him. The night before our wedding, I caught a train going West only to discover my Pawnee brave was dead. He'd been killed in a skirmish with the army four months earlier."

She paused. When she continued, her voice was quieter. "I didn't much care if I lived or died, but I had to keep on eating, if you know what I mean. So I started doing laundry in a mining camp up in the Black Hills. Then I took up with one of the miners, Benjamin Donning. That's how I got my 'Mrs.' I didn't really love him, but he understood. He was a rough, uneducated man, but he respected me, even that part of me I couldn't share with him. That's rare, you know. Then I had my baby, a little girl so pretty and perfect, I almost believed my luck had changed. I was blessed again. I loved again.

"Six months later, she died. Then I knew I couldn't live. But the sun kept coming up and the sun kept going down. I don't know how much later it was. Time then is all a blur to me. But one morning when I got up, the sister and second mother of my Pawnee brave were waiting for me outside my cabin door.

"They said they had heard my spirit calling in their dreams, and they had come to bring me a gift, these moccasins. They apologized for not knowing any of the dream symbols of my people except the one I'd talked about as a missionary. They hoped their gift would give me my dreams back."

Mrs. Donning fingered along the design. Then in a near whisper she said, "It did." Then she gave herself a little shake and added, "I've never worn these. But I regularly tell folks I want to be buried in them. I suppose that sounds strange."

"Not at all," Kate said, but she wasn't sure.

"Well, strange or not, that's my story. Let's just say I've got a lot of respect for good quillwork. It's not parlor fancy, if you know what I mean."

"That's your story? But . . ." Kate stopped.

"Oh, I know. That's not the story your reporter is going to want. That's why I never talk to reporters. They don't want the truth. They want stories that will sell newspapers."

"The rest of it's not true?" Kate asked.

"The rest of what? Oh, you heard I was Sitting Bull's white squaw?"

Kate nodded.

"I was. Not officially, but I was in the other way. I thought he was going to make changes, get things improved with all this ghost dancing."

"You believed in that?"

"What? That all the buffalo were coming back? No. But neither did Sitting Bull. The dancing brought his people together, gave them courage—gave them a dream. I think he saw it as a chance, a last chance to hold his people together. It didn't work. He's dead, and I'm riding my horse in a Wild West show—not even a very good Wild West show."

She laughed softly. "Wild West shows are about as out of fashion as Indians these days. Westerners have developed a taste for opera. Can you imagine? They're set to open three new opera houses in this town alone. They already got two."

Mrs. Donning folded the covering over her moccasins again. "Do you have any idea the honor you've been given? For quillworkers, true women of the sacred society to share their work, their dreams . . . It's unthinkable unless . . ." Her face took a new expression. "Woman-Who-Dreams must think you're a visionary—Double-Woman touched. That has to be it."

"But I don't see how I can do it," Kate said. She was thinking again of the soldiers outside and Bill and how even this visit was going to complicate things. When he found out, Bill was going to accuse her of "consorting with the worst type." Not that he didn't feel free to consort with some of the worst types. He'd brought that woman, Edith, home, but she'd turned out to be rather nice. Mrs. Donning had turned out to be different than Kate expected. Still, he'd want to know why she had to do things like this.

"If you don't take those pictures, you'll always regret it," Mrs. Donning continued.

Kate's head swirled. The woman had no idea of the impossibility. She hadn't told her about the colonel. Besides, before a week ago she hadn't cared about quillwork. What had changed? An old woman had given her a pocket bag. That's all.

"Honey, I saw it before you came in," Mrs. Donning went on. "It's in the way you carry yourself. You walk on the edge. You flirt with adventure, but you haven't really embraced it. Believe me, it's easier to just step over the edge, let go, plunge in."

"I'm sure I don't know what you mean," Kate retorted. She stood to leave.

"I mean I never regret catching that train going west. Go take those pictures. What are you afraid of?"

Kate closed her eyes. She knew what she was afraid of. It wasn't the soldiers outside. It was her own wild, defiant nature, the willfulness that had brought her here. She was a child of too much passion. All the women in her family had been conceived out of wedlock in moments of wild love. It had cursed them with a wildness that had brought them all ruin. She'd thought she could channel hers into taking photographs and travel with a man she only partly loved. But deep down, she knew different. Deep down, she knew it was going to get the better of her.

It was also the thing her father had feared most, telling her over and over to "be a good girl," sometimes pleadingly, "be a good girl, Kate." He knew because he wasn't really her father. That man had been dangerous enough to love and leave her mother all in a week's time, and yet cast such a shadow over all their lives that none of them had ever found sunlight again. And without much effort, she could close her eyes like this and feel that same danger creeping closer, waiting for the moment when she'd give in to it. Meanwhile,

Mrs. Donning was right, she flirted with it. Her being here was flirting with it—daring ruination to pounce on her.

She heard singing—a lullaby so soft as to be barely audible.

She opened her eyes.

Mrs. Donning had cradled the moccasins in her arms and was rocking them gently, back and forth, singing:

> "Hush little baby, don't be a'feared
> Mama's going to buy you a mockingbird
> And if that mockingbird don't sing
> Mama's going to buy you a golden ring
> And if that golden ring don't shine . . ."

Bill Burke also saw the soldiers that morning. He'd gotten up in time to see Kate leave, the pair of them trailing her. Immediately his anger flared. They were like spit in Bill's face. He knew what was going on. The colonel was trying to unnerve him. But he'd gone too far. Gentlemen didn't let their business involve their wives. Bill dressed and pulled his boots on. Half an hour later, he was standing on the corner of Phillips and Eighth Streets trying to guess where he might find the colonel. He wasn't going to let the man get away with this.

Bill looked up and down both streets as he pulled out his roll of liver pills. Sioux Falls was a city that was trying hard to take itself seriously, a fact that was obvious in the cobblestone paving and ornate false storefronts covering cheap boxy buildings. The web of electrical wires that sagged between poles running down one side of the street suggested prosperity, but what the scene lacked was a sense of permanence. For all its bustle and bravado, nothing about Sioux Falls belied the fact that it wasn't much different than any other ramshackle western town grown up too quickly. It was an outpost, a stopover. The only people who stayed in places like these were those who got stuck there. He popped three liver pills in his mouth and worked them down his throat with a dry swallow. A gaudy red and gold sign announced "home cooking" and "fresh-baked pies" at Mama Rose's Restaurant halfway down the next block. He decided to try there.

Inside the restaurant, he was greeted by the greasy smell of fried eggs and potatoes with an overlay of an aroma of coffee and bacon. His luck was good. The colonel and his aide were sitting in a booth near the back. Bill sauntered over and slid in beside the aide, who was making notes on a small notepad but ceased as soon as he saw Bill.

Besides whatever business they were doing, the colonel was finishing up a stack of flapjacks. The aide was sopping up runny eggs with a biscuit. Bill ordered coffee, then plunged right in. "Couldn't help noticing the soldiers following my wife."

The aide stopped stirring cream into a fresh cup of coffee. He removed his spoon.

The colonel leaned back, eyed Bill.

In a war of nerves, the spoils went to the bold, and that's what this was, a battle of nerves, Bill had decided. The colonel had complained before that Bill had no control over Kate, knowing the way a snake smells living warmth that Bill was a little sore on that point. Now to needle, he was having Kate tailed, watched, controlled. He was demonstrating that he could do what Bill couldn't. It was exactly the kind of nasty he enjoyed—this blend of blunt force tinged with psychological terror, no actual harm, but the hint that something might happen. He probably expected Bill to beg him to leave Kate alone, but he didn't. Looking the man eyeball to eyeball, he said, "Call them off."

The colonel didn't flinch. "I hear your wife has been going all over town trying to interest all sorts of folks in what she calls 'some most interesting pictures.'"

"Oh, that," Bill said with relief and put his liver pills back in his pocket. "That's nothing, just some silly pictures of Indian women Kate wants to take. I'm not going to let her, mind you. She gets crazy notions like that. Something to do with Indian stitchery—quillwork."

The colonel didn't soften. His aide was sitting in perfect stillness.

"She's young, headstrong," Bill added, trying to treat the

215

whole matter lightly, now that he understood it was all a misunderstanding.

The colonel tapped the edge of the table with his fingers. "I used to think she was nothing but your bauble. I'm not fooled anymore. If she's not up to blackmail, which we both know is more your forte, then it must be worse."

"I don't think you understand." Bill started, and then paused. "What do you mean worse?"

"Do-gooder meddling, and that after I allowed her to come along with us last winter and everything."

Bill's heart nearly stopped. He knew the colonel. He was more likely to tolerate a back-shooting Indian than a back-shooting do-gooder who ungratefully detracted from the man's glory, his "end of Indian wars heroism." Bill swallowed and controlled himself the way a man who has stumbled at the edge of a precipice controls his balance. It had never occurred to him that the colonel might seriously consider Kate some kind of threat. And he knew too well what the colonel was capable of doing when he felt threatened.

"You're wrong." Bill breathed and pulled his liver pills out again. "Kate's too much involved in her picture-taking, photographing birds and animals and other nonsense to take up causes. Never enters her mind, believe me." He meant it. He popped a couple more pills. He couldn't imagine how the colonel had formed some other notion of her.

The colonel slapped the table. "It's the ones who stir up sympathy for the Indians that are the worst. You know how I feel about that. It was those savages or it was us out there. Anyone who says different is a goddamned traitor of one stripe or another."

But clearly the colonel had formed some other notion of Kate, and it didn't look as though he could persuade him otherwise, Bill realized. He fingered his roll of liver pills. It was empty. They'd crossed into dangerous territory here. He swallowed again. "You can have the plate."

The colonel lifted an eyebrow.

All three of them knew what Bill was talking about, the glass plate Bill had been using to blackmail the colonel—nothing too greedy, but nothing too cheap either because they both knew the colonel didn't want that particular picture to come to light.

This was like folding a straight flush. Bill stood to make a good amount of money over time from that picture, more than if he sold it to Anthony's, and he was giving it away. Bill's father's words about "expensive women" echoed through his head again. He'd shake some sense into Kate for this one, he promised himself. Or maybe not. The other thing his father told him was that "expensive women" were the only ones worthwhile.

"You can have the plate," Bill repeated. "Just leave Kate alone. Call off your soldiers. Stay away from her."

Later that day, Kate presented her calling card to the owner of the rooming house where Richard Houston was staying. She asked if the gentleman was in.

Mrs. Hartnett took a pair of glasses from a pocket and studied the card. She rubbed the photograph with one thumb as if she hadn't seen one before. *Cartes de Visite* with pictures on them had been in vogue for at least ten years. But then, as near as Kate could tell, nothing in the woman's house appeared newer than twenty years. The rug was so worn, one could only guess at its original color. Same with the wallpaper.

"You may wait for him in the sitting room," Mrs. Hartnett muttered, and then led the way to her parlor. She opened the draperies and folded back one dustcover exposing a rather tall straight-backed chair. "Make yourself comfortable," she said and left.

Ignoring the chair, Kate went to the window. The drapery had been turned, carefully taken down, and reconstructed to keep the faded side from showing. Kate ran her hand along one reworked seam. Delicate make-do. Mrs. Hartnett had known better times, but they had been a long time ago. Kate realized that in a sense she was as trapped in her house as Kate's mother and grandmother were in theirs. That was the thing she didn't intend to let happen to her. It was what she'd been trying to escape, even in her dreams.

Mrs. Donning had brought that into focus. She'd decided . . .

"Mrs. Burke, this is a surprise."

His voice caught her still fingering the drapery. She turned and realized she didn't know what to say—hadn't planned how to lead up to this.

She was saved by Mrs. Hartnett fussing about the room, pulling back the cover on a second chair and saying, "There now. Shall you be staying long enough to need tea?"

Kate shook her head, still wordless.

He crossed to stand beside her at the window. "It's a lovely view," he said. "If I were Mrs. Hartnett, I'd leave the draperies open all the time, wouldn't you?"

She shook her head.

"Why not?" he asked.

"It would fade so."

"What? The view?"

"No. No." She brought her hand to her mouth. The notion of the view fading! Her nervousness had made her almost silly.

"I'm serious," he continued. "Why cover up the most beautiful part of the room just because everything next to it fades? It doesn't make good sense, does it?"

No, it didn't, she thought. That's what she'd finally figured out—that everything in her mother's and grandmother's lives had faded the moment they'd stopped following their passions.

"Of course, the view is not the most beautiful part of the room at this moment," he continued. "You are looking lovely, Mrs. Burke."

Good, she thought. He was pushing the bounds. If she was going to do this, she wanted his full complicity. "You have a way with the ladies."

He shrugged. "Hardly. If I had a way with the ladies, Mrs. Hartnett would have uncovered the couch and set out a few dainties. I have absolutely failed to charm that woman."

"Shhh," Kate said. "She's probably listening."

"Oh, no doubt. Not much exciting happens in this boardinghouse, I'm quite sure."

Exciting, she thought. And she ralized it was. Her life had taken new verve, like the shift in vibrations when a train begins to climb. That had happened the moment she decided there was nothing wrong with coming from a line of passionate women. Unless she denied it. Mrs. Donning was right; she flirted with her desires, which wasn't exactly the same as denying them, nor the same as embracing them. She was going to embrace them, all of them, starting with a determination to take those pictures of the quillworkers and whatever it was this man aroused in her. The notion that the women in her family couldn't control themselves was such a huge piece of her life, she had to know.

She faced him. "I suppose it must seem quite out of the ordinary for me to be here, but I've come to make you a business proposition. You see, I've been offered an extraordinary opportunity, but I need a partner to finance it."

Instantly, she could tell that he didn't like that. And just as quickly she guessed the reason. His family. She imagined lots of people made him all kinds of offers, hoping to come by some of his family money. She'd honestly not thought of it. She'd simply assumed he had ways of raising what was needed, and thought he would agree if she was willing to throw herself into the bargain.

She paced to the middle of the room, then turned and faced him again. "It shouldn't require a great deal of money."

"That's good because I don't have a great deal of money. Daddy cut off my allowance."

"Oh, I didn't know."

"Doesn't matter."

She thought, how true. Mrs. Donning was right. Once you stepped off the edge, a lot of things didn't matter.

Since their trip to the red pipestone outcropping, Richard Houston had been smitten with this woman such that he could hardly imagine anything she might want that he'd not

219

be willing to do. He listened carefully. It took him a bit to catch the drift of what she was proposing, it came in such a flood of words.

Then the scope of it nearly took his breath away. What she was suggesting wasn't exactly going to be cheap. More, he doubted there would be any return. He couldn't imagine who would buy pictures of squaws sitting around in the Indian equivalent of sewing circles, even if he was willing to concede that any pictures Kate took would be damned fine.

All of a sudden he found himself embracing a new respect for Bill Burke and the depth of difficulty he must experience almost daily being married to this most original and ambitious woman. He stopped her. "Am I to understand this is to be a partnership between you and me?" he asked, watching her closely. "I mean, it makes a difference. I've already tried partnering with Bill. That didn't work."

"I know," she said and paused, suddenly out of words. "My husband doesn't know I'm here," she added a moment later.

He knew then he ought to say something. He thought he ought to agree to her business proposition because the last thing he wanted was to let this woman get away. But he was suddenly paralyzed. Usually he played the game of love as he played poker—never betting anything he couldn't afford to lose. This felt different. He was afraid of making a mistake here. And there was another fear. If even half the rumors going around were true, the colonel had serious reasons not to want anyone stirring up anything having to do with Indians, not that he imagined fear ever factored into Kate's reasoning. She was the most fearless person he'd ever met, but this wasn't like climbing out on a ledge to photograph a pair of birds.

"I—I'd be most pleased to be your partner," he said, and couldn't believe he was hearing himself say it without qualification.

"Oh, thank you," she returned as if they'd agreed to the most ordinary of arrangements. "I thought you'd understand the opportunity of this." Then, just like that, she began to list what supplies she would need. But there was a nervousness to her words that he recognized. Her agitation gave her away.

He played along. He handed her a pad and pencil and suggested she write down what she needed. Then he suggested they ought to check his equipment wagon parked behind the boardinghouse and see what materials he might already have. He kept waiting for Kate's pretext to crumble. When she insisted they leave by the back, not the front, door so as "not to be seen by anyone who might be watching," he knew what this "partnership" was really about. It didn't startle him. He'd sensed the potential for abandon in her even before that morning on the ledge.

"You're a surprising woman, Mrs. Burke," he told her as they crossed Mrs. Hartnett's backyard, ducking past the laundry she'd hung out that morning. "But I'm curious. What brought you to this?"

Kate gave him a glance. "Is there anything wrong with wanting to take pictures of Indian women?"

"No, absolutely not," he told her, and chided himself for moving too quickly. He thought they'd moved past that. He held the door of his tourist wagon open for her. Unlike hers, his wagon was set up more for working than living. He'd never tried entertaining there.

"I have to take those pictures," Kate went on. "I can't explain it well, but sometimes a woman's space gets terribly constricted. Like this wagon," she made a gesture at his quarters. "I don't mean any criticism of your place," she said. "I mean that a woman is supposed to keep her hair contained, her walk constrained. That's why I made Bill take me with him last winter. Space. Travel gives me a sense of breadth even when I'm keeping all my things in a wagon like this. Does that make any sense?"

Kate stopped herself. She was talking too much and making too little sense. She knew because she'd watched him nod, shake his head, furrow his brow, and sometimes try to smile. That was masculine camouflage for complete confusion. "I didn't expect that you'd understand that part," she added.

221

He raised an eyebrow. "Well, I'm not sure, but . . ." Then he cleared his throat. "I don't mean to be indelicate, Mrs. Burke, but what are you going to tell your husband about our partnership?"

She didn't know the answer to that one. Those boys on the railroad bridge had never spoken of their encounter with her. Not once. Not in teasing. Not in anger. It was as though no one wanted to believe it had happened. And yet they all knew it did. In a way she expected Bill wouldn't be surprised.

"I don't know," she answered.

"You don't love your husband?" he said.

She started. What did that have to do with anything, she wondered. More, why did Richard care. He was a ladies' man. Everyone said so. He loved them and left them just like the man who'd loved and left her mother. The moment she decided she would take those pictures of the quill-workers, no matter what, she'd also decided to stop trying to be her father's "good girl."

Richard had the means and the equipment to help her with the pictures. He also possessed the secret to her childhood, the missing piece, the passion that overwhelmed all good sense. Why not? What good was good sense? Was not this desiring the very thing that kept the world alive? Mrs. Donning took her train West so she could live large, not die by inches as some proper wife of a lawyer.

Kate said, "I think I might have loved him if he'd let me. Bill repels people rather effectively."

At that, Richard pulled her close. When she didn't resist, he kissed her. She was confused. What next? It was almost as if she'd never done this before.

He, too, hesitated.

Then he began working at her clothes. Richard Houston was a ladies' man. Everyone said so. Now she knew the truth of it. He knew how to do this. Softly. Soft voice, trailing off. Soft touches from soft hands. She helped with her petticoats. That was easy. She'd been taking those off for lots of reasons. Beyond that, she was all fumble. Fine, she was more than willing to surrender to his hands. He was discovering her, peeling through the layers of her clothing looking for her. She wished him success.

When they got past the clothes, he laid her on the narrow wooden bench where he usually kept his developing trays. The smells the wood had absorbed from his processing chemicals tickled her nose with a pleasant familiarity. That amused her—the notion of making love amid the developing trays. He stroked her, feeling her all over. He moved her hands helping her stroke him. Together they rubbed and rode their passions higher and higher. Near the peak, he reached off the bench, fumbled in his pile of clothing, and found a "French secret," a rubber so naughty the printing of it's name was illegal. But she wanted such naughtiness. What could be better than a man prepared for love's union, she thought, and then also wondered how many others he'd initiated like this. The skill and preparation suggested many. That was fine as long as she had her moment. She even thought she liked the idea of his being a man of reputation.

As if reading her mind, he whispered, "You're the only woman I could be faithful to."

Sweet lies, she thought dreamily. Good. Too much truth would be binding. Falsehoods. She wanted to hear only falsehoods—how he would get her the moon and the stars. Later they would escape through the lies. But for now she would play the whore, faithless except to pleasure. She opened her legs. He and his "French secret" found her center.

Suddenly there was a noise and voices outside. Close by. Footsteps and a rustling. Richard paused. His breathing quickened. He got up and peeked out the door.

"What is it?" Kate asked.

"A couple of soldiers, looking around," he said.

They'd lost her, she thought. That struck her as funny. If they only knew!

She started to giggle, quietly so the soldiers wouldn't hear. He didn't know what was funny but caught the infectiousness of her mirth. He laughed, too, holding it in with pursed lips and puffed cheeks. All they had to do was look at each other, and they could hardly contain their merriment.

Finally, they heard the footsteps of the soldiers leaving. Homer came to his feet and went to the door. He sniffed around its edges. There was nothing funny about that. But they both fell into a fit of renewed laughter such that Richard slid down and bumped to the floor.

Sitting on the floor, he leaned his shoulders against the bench. Drawing a deep breath, he whispered, "Ah, Kate," and it was as if the sound of his breath were enough to split her open.

What a thought! She'd never entertained a thought like that before! She sat up.

"What's the matter?"

"Nothing," she said.

And it was true. She was in a state of bliss such as she'd never known. And it was pure, no raw edges of desperation such as she'd seen in her mother and her grandmother. She breathed in the exhilaration, and then let go a deep sigh. "It's for the best. I mean, after this, I don't imagine I'll be the sort of woman who needs to worry much about her reputation."

"If I'm supposed to be sorry for that . . ."

"No," she told him. "It's perfect." She meant that, but not in a way she thought he'd appreciate. She knew now that passion didn't have to damage a woman and leave her clinging to a particular man or a lost past. She could love and let go, and that was the most freeing feeling she'd ever experienced.

She rolled up on one arm and looked at him. "You should see your face. It's picture perfect." She framed him with her hands. "It's so dark, I swear, you'd have to sit like that for about an eternity before a plate could be exposed, but if it could be captured, that little shaft of sunlight on your shoulder flatters your cheek and lightens one eye—just the left."

She paused. "But it would never work. The tonal qualities are pleasing, but I'd never be able to print through the blank sunlit area without getting a flat textureless value." She shook her head. "I can't tell you how many times I've failed chiefly because I accept the visual without anticipating the film's response."

"It was you."

"I beg your pardon."

"Those pictures I saw in New York—your father's last exhibition. They weren't your fathers, they were yours. You took them."

"I don't know what you're talking about."

He fumbled in his clothes and pulled out the photograph she'd taken of the birds. He leaned into the shaft of light coming through a crack in the door. "I should have seen it. I just never imagined."

She slid back and pulled her knees up under her chin. She had to do it. Her father needed her to do it. Neither of them wanted to give up the studio if it meant spending all their hours at home.

"He was ill," she said. "He could hardly work. I mean, I had no idea it would mean his winning falsely."

Richard propped the photograph against the bench. "Amazing," he breathed.

"Please," she went on. "If they took the prize from him . . ." She caught her breath. "He's dead, but I can't, I won't have him defamed. Besides there was the prize money accepted falsely. That's fraud, you know. I could go to jail over that part of it."

He reached up and touched his hand to her mouth. "Don't worry. All your secrets are safe with me."

Bill was on his way to Amato's photography studio to retrieve the plate when it hit him. He'd played the colonel exactly wrong. Offering to give him the negative for nothing more than a promise had probably served only to confirm the man's suspicions of Kate. In fact Bill was sure of it. The colonel would assume Kate was up to something—something bigger than Bill's blackmail. He wouldn't consider any other reason for Bill's sudden capitulation. That's how the man's mind worked.

Almost mid-stride, Bill turned. Three blocks later he was

at a dead run. He hoped Kate was in camp. Lord, how he hoped Kate was in camp because they had to get out of there now!

But she wasn't. Even the Indian girl was gone. In fact, it was so quiet, he paused and approached warily. He called to Kate, once quietly, then louder. He tried calling her dog. Nothing. Something about the eerie quietness didn't feel right. But he didn't see anything out of the ordinary. He entered the tent, looked around. Still nothing seemed out of place except that he thought the Indian girl ought to have been there. But he knew Kate sometimes took her with her. Where was Kate? he wondered. He looked around one more time, shrugged, and then blaming his unease on his general agitated state of mind, he started throwing things into a trunk.

He ought to send Kate away on the next train. That would be faster, easier. Only he didn't think she'd go. Not that she wouldn't leave him. He expected she'd leave him sooner or later. Not with any malice. Kate never did anything with malice. She just followed her instincts, and he'd always known her instincts would lead her away from him. He was too old and too world-weary for her. He imagined that Kate at eighty would still be younger than he could ever remember being. No, she wouldn't leave because of her plates. Her work from the last eight months was stored in that wagon.

He slammed one trunk shut and started throwing things into another.

Kate was completely attached to her "pretties," those odd pictures of hers. Odd and compelling, like the woman herself. He sent his work East regularly. Sold it. A few of her plates had been sold as well, but most of her work had been packed away. He wondered now if she'd had any plans for it. That was a large piece of her for him not to know.

But there was a lot of Kate that escaped him. His first wife had parts of her he never knew, little secrets, an interest in opera he never shared, but Kate was like a stranger in many ways. He paused. He knew why he never asked. She was so unfathomable, the very act of asking made him feel small, stupid. He held himself back because mostly he wanted to

226

shake some sense into her. Yet he appreciated that it was the unsensible in her that mattered.

He slammed the second trunk shut.

Where is that Indian girl? he wondered again as he climbed into the wagon. She'd even left the stove door open. With annoyance, he slammed it shut.

Too late he saw how it had been rigged to explode. There was time for one last breath. "Oh, Kate," he sighed, "you are an expensive woman."

12

On the way back to camp that afternoon, Homer become agitated. It was not his usual bounding impatience but a nervous alertness Kate had never seen in him before. He circled her, whimpering, until the hair on the back of her neck came alive. "What's the matter?" she'd asked, bending close. Then she smelled the smoke. Her heart started to pound even before she picked up her skirts and started to run.

At the edge of the clearing, she was greeted by a scene she could never have imagined. Volunteer firefighters with handkerchiefs pulled over their mouths and noses were handing buckets back and forth, drawing water from the river to douse the last charred remains of Kate and Bill's wagon. It was still hot enough that the water splashed into steam, hissing into the air. Other men stood around watching, talking. She began to sort them out. She recognized the local sheriff and the deputy she'd seen at the jail when she stopped there with Powers Nock. She also noted one of the two brothers who kept the makeshift livery down river and several soldiers. A couple of photographers were taking pictures. She wondered what they saw worth picturing.

Everything of importance to her was gone, including her camera. She swallowed. Losing that old Scofield was like losing part of her father, the last tangible piece of him.

With that thought, she gave in to a sinking numbness. She didn't even have other clothes, just what she was wearing. All that remained were a few smoldering pieces of the wagon's wooden frame and a scattering of blackened metal, the developing trays, the frame of what had once been her lantern.

Homer rushed forward, barking. He snapped at the firefighters and drove the photographers back with his lunging fierceness. Kate thought she should stop him, call him, make him behave, but she didn't. Her numbness was such that she not only couldn't raise voice, she couldn't move forward or turn away.

Then the sheriff was at her side, taking her arm, talking to her with the sort of voice one uses on children or frightened horses. "Mrs. Burke," he said. "I'm sorry I didn't see you arrive. I didn't mean for you to see this without some warning. I tried to send for you, but we didn't know where you were. There's been a terrible accident."

She could see that.

He continued, using too many words, explaining too much that was obvious. He was a man of middle age who carried a gun, but she suspected he used this calming voice more often than he used his firearm. It was clearly practiced, but she found it grating. She wished he'd shut up and let her absorb this, get used to this.

The deputy grabbed her dog. He slipped some kind of leather strap over Homer's head and around his muzzle. She didn't appreciate that. She wished everyone would leave her dog alone. Everyone was looking at her, she realized.

The sheriff was talking again. "I'm afraid your husband didn't fare well in this accident."

He'd fared better than she did, she thought. At least his pictures hadn't been stored in that wagon, destroyed there.

"It must have been the kerosene stove," the sheriff was going on. "They have a bad reputation for this sort of thing, you must know. It blew up with enough force to singe some of the nearby trees."

She looked around into his face. One tooth was chipped inside the mouth talking to her. What did she care about singed trees. He paused. She watched him swallow; his Adam's apple bobbed.

"I'm afraid your husband's dead," he told her.

She drew air with an audible gasp. She hadn't thought. Never imagined. Bill hardly ever came to camp in the middle of the day. He had important things to do, people to see. If not that, he preferred to hang around the local saloon and card game. Suddenly her eye saw what it had refused to see before—the mound wrapped in a blanket that had been pulled away from the rest of the charred remains.

"I'm afraid there's not much to see," the sheriff told her. "He was burned rather badly."

Her knees got weak, but that weakness was only momentary. She was not the fainting type. She wished that deputy would leave her dog alone. Homer was struggling, whining. She thought he ought to be allowed to bark, whine, growl, all the things that, as a lady, she was expected to contain. This was not an event that ought to pass quietly.

Worse, the photographers were getting on her nerves. Why would anyone want to see a charred wagon where a man had died? She closed her eyes. Bill would have done the same if this had been someone else's misfortune. In fact, photographs of battlefields with the bodies still in place were popular enough to be highly profitable. For that reason, photographers outdid each other trying to curry the favor of the appropriate military contacts. That's why Bill had considered his connection to the colonel a "fine piece of luck." Maybe his last luck, she thought, letting a little of this new reality settle in.

She opened her eyes again and wondered how she should be feeling. Her numbness was complete enough to allow that degree of detachment. She thought she ought to feel some kind of teary tenderness, and searched herself to see if she could find any such feelings.

If she'd never loved Bill completely, he'd certainly become a big part of her life. As her father's oldest friend, she couldn't remember a time when she hadn't known him. He'd married her. They'd shared bed and board and a cold winter of adventure chasing ghost dancers and their own uneven relations. In ways hard to enumerate, he'd bored into her making a space for himself she knew she'd never close. If nothing else, he'd worn her tender with repeated irritations: his card playing, deal making, whore loving. He'd rubbed her raw with his flashes of deeper possibilities never realized. He'd never really given himself a chance, but he'd given her one. She could overlook a lot because of that.

In the midst of those thoughts, which would have loosed her tears, the colonel appeared flanked by his aide and the two soldiers who'd been following her. For some reason, he went directly to the deputy holding her dog and took Homer by the leather strap. Why was he here? she wondered. She did not want him touching her dog. She started in the colonel's direction, intending to get her dog from him. But the sheriff stopped her, holding her arm.

"There's nothing for you to do. Nothing to see," he repeated.

"My dog," she managed to say. "I want my dog." She shook free of his grasp and confronted the colonel, "Let go of my dog."

He glanced around. It mattered to him how all this looked, she realized. Then he smiled and handed her the strap holding Homer. "I'm really very sorry, Mrs. Burke," he said as Homer snuggled close to her skirts, the fight gone out of him.

The colonel continued, "Terrible things happen when one isn't careful."

A flush rose in her. She'd heard those words before. She knew what he meant. He'd warned her last night with exactly those words, telling her what happened to women who didn't know their place. Then it hit her like a slap in the face. She'd been in Richard's arms when this happened. For a brief moment she entertained the notion that her passion, her infidelity had sparked this fire consuming her former life.

Maybe it was worse than that. She'd been to lectures where phrenologists displayed their charts and talked at length about how criminals could be identified by the bumps on their heads. Why not unfaithful wives or women with desires too strong for their own good? It fit her facts. For at least three generations the women in her family had destroyed their lives and the lives of the people around them. Was there any reason to think that destruction had to be slow? Why not spontaneous like combustion? But she knew better. If she'd wanted to embrace that dark dance of unrelieved guilt, she could have done it as a child. She was the product of her mother's fatal alliance, the daily reminder of it. There was a kind of reasoning that might have assumed everything would have been different, but for her. There was a truth in that, the same truth that knew things would have been different if any number of life-defining junctures had somehow resulted in different choices. But how was anyone to know? She had no eyes, no way to frame pictures of what might have been. She'd long ago refused to take responsibility for what she couldn't help.

Her thoughts needed to focus on where to go from here. Not home. Not back to her mother and grandmother. She vowed when she married that she'd never return there. But, she suspected, that might not be an easy vow to live. She didn't know half of her husband's affairs, but she knew without doubt his assets would not cover his bills. From the first day of her marriage, she and Bill had been avoiding his creditors. That was one of the reasons Bill had decided to join the colonel and his soldiers in their pursuit of ghost dancers. South Dakota was a long way from the people he owed money.

"I'll have my aide take you to the hotel," the colonel offered.

He was looking around at the others again. Any kindness implied in his offer was meant to impress them not her, she realized.

"And I'll see that Bill is taken care of. You'll want to take him East for burial, I assume. I'll check the train schedule for you."

Details, details. How did something this large get reduced to worrying about train schedules, she wondered. Only she wasn't going East—no matter what. *I'm not going home,* she vowed silently once more.

Besides, if she had been killed by that stove, not Bill, she'd have wanted to be buried right here. That's when it hit her. If anyone was going to be killed by a faulty kerosene stove, it should have been Kate or Mary. They were the only ones who ever did anything with that stove, not Bill.

"Where's Mary?" Kate asked.

The sheriff had moved up beside her. "Mary?"

"My serving girl. She's an Indian child. She should have been here." With a sickening, sinking feeling, Kate thought Mary must have been killed as well.

"She wasn't here," the sheriff told her. "I haven't seen her."

"She was here," Kate insisted. "I left her with instructions, things to do. She was a good girl."

"She wasn't here," the sheriff said again.

"You know Indians," the colonel was telling her. "They run away at the first sign of trouble. She'll show up later."

Kate looked around at him. She took in the landscape of his face like a strange foreign vista, never before glimpsed: nose, cheeks, brow, and eyes that were too deep, too dark. He was lying. If things were as he said, there would have been no hint of trouble, no warning, no reason for Mary to have become frightened and run away.

All of a sudden Kate wanted out of there, away from the colonel, these men, that sheriff, those photographers, all of whom were staring at this tragedy without really seeing it.

"I don't need your help. I can take myself to the hotel," she told him, stepping back. "I don't need your soldiers following me, either. And I don't want you touching my dog."

The sheriff felt he had to quiet her. "You're upset," he said as if that wasn't obvious, as if she didn't have more reason than he knew to be upset.

"I'll not play your charade," she continued. "I'll not let you act the gentleman when you aren't." Her voice had taken on a pitch of hysteria, but she didn't care, she wasn't going to let this go unsaid. "Bill thought you were his friend. I never understood why. I knew better. But he thought the two of you understood each other."

The sheriff was making excuses for her. "She's upset," he was now saying to the others. "Shock of it. The smoke and all." She couldn't figure out why he thought he had to explain her. She was being more polite than he knew. She ought to scream, "Murder," at the top of her lungs.

The colonel put on a puzzled look and repeated the sheriff's words, "You're understandably upset, Mrs. Burke."

Indeed, she thought.

Then, shaking off the sheriff's last attempt to take her arm, she bent and pulled the strap off her dog. Holding it in front of her as though she might use it, she backed away, then turned, and fled.

The Cataract Hotel was the oldest, most stately of a fleet of such establishments clustered near the center of Sioux Falls. It sported a striped awning rolled out over the boardwalk by day and enough brass and glass on its double front doors to suggest a class of clientele a cut above the plainer Stevenson across the street or the Prairie Pioneer in the next block. Kate didn't know how long she could afford to stay at the best hotel in town, but her grandmother, the actress, believed a woman should never give in to reduced circumstances. At the moment Kate couldn't think why that wasn't good advice. She stepped up to that fancy front door.

"You alone?" The voice was nasal. The man who was blocking her way into the hotel was ruddy-faced and portly.

She made no answer.

"I'd like to be of service," he said, and offered his card. His coat was rumpled; his mustache needed a trim.

"Do I know you?" Kate asked. Then the situation came together like a shot of whiskey hitting the back of her throat. He was a divorce lawyer working the hotel. Seeing her arrive alone, he'd assumed she needed one. She pushed the card back at him. "You don't understand."

"Oh, but I assure you I understand too well. You need a

little time to gather yourself. That's understandable. When you're ready to talk about it, my office is on the second floor across the street." He gestured with enough force that Kate turned and looked.

She was amazed. This man knew nothing about Bill and what had happened. She would have thought the size of this shatter in her life would have been obvious, even to strangers.

"You're mistaken," she told him again, and pushed past.

She'd no sooner stepped into the lobby of the hotel than a second lawyer thrust his card at her. Younger, better dressed, he was handsome enough to feel he could take the liberty of leaning close to her ear. "I can handle everything, every little unpleasantness, including checking you into this hotel," he offered. With that he nodded in the direction of three matronly women dressed in church primness. They were softly singing a hymn about "the joys of home and hearth." One marked time with the bounce of a placard. It read:

What God Has Joined, Let No Man Put Asunder.

Kate drew breath. She hadn't anticipated this. But looking at those women brought another bit of her grandmother's advice to mind: Flaunt your faults. Granny had firmly believed a woman who flaunted what should shame her was all the better for it. For proof she liked to list all the exciting places an actress could go compared to what was allowed "upstanding wives." If Kate's mother had only figured that out. But it was that fundamental philosophical difference that kept her mother and grandmother scratching at each other.

The second lawyer, misreading Kate's momentary confusion, touched her arm. "A woman in your position needs a friend."

"A woman in my position needs guts," she told him, knowing that last word would shock. With that she returned his card and crossed the foyer, passing the potted ferns, fancy fringed lobby chairs, and singing church women.

As she and Homer approached the hotel desk, the church women's voices grew stronger, loud enough so Kate had to speak up when she asked for a room. The desk clerk, a young man with an angular nose, hemmed. "The customary stay?"

He meant the residency period—six weeks.

"A week," she answered, her voice now louder than she'd intended.

"And the dog?"

"He stays with me."

"There will be an extra charge for that."

"Fine," she answered.

"And if he should disturb any of the other guests . . ."

"I understand."

"Baggage?" he asked.

She hesitated.

"Your baggage?" he asked again.

"I don't have any," she told him.

The clerk studied her briefly. His nose twitched. "Coming later, I suppose."

She didn't say anything. She didn't want to explain.

He shrugged and continued. "If you should decide to extend your stay, we'll need notice."

She nodded. The clerk, those lawyers, everyone would treat her differently when they found out. And they would. News of her tragedy was bound to become a part of the talk in town. She was merely a little ahead of it. She didn't imagine she would enjoy a widow's deference any more than this.

"Eddie will show you to your room," the desk clerk told her, and handed her key to an older man in striped pants and a jacket with the hotel's name stitched across the pocket. Eddie was thin and bald and more than a little stooped. He moved slow enough for Kate to hear a whole chorus of "Home, Oh, Bring Me Home" from the church women before he managed the length of the lobby and got to the electric lift.

"First time in Sioux Falls?" Eddie asked as he held the lift door open.

She didn't want any conversation. She simply answered, "Yes."

"Sioux Falls is a godforsaken place," he told her as he fastened the door and pulled the lever. "But at least that keeps us honest."

She didn't understand. "Godforsaken?" she returned.

"You ever been to Florida?"

"No," she answered, realizing Eddie was going to get his conversation regardless.

"California?"

"No."

"South America?"

"No."

"Me, neither." He slowed the lift. "Always dissatisfied. That's human nature for you. Sometimes there ain't no better place than the one you're in, but we cain't accept that. Nope. We got to be always dissatisfied. But, now, if you're in Sioux Falls, you can be pretty sure there must be better places—lots of them. All that dissatisfaction ain't misplaced here. Keeps us honest, thank God."

Kate chuckled in spite of herself. "I think I see what you mean."

"A person should travel. I never got around to doing much traveling myself, but I still say a person should travel. Where've you been?"

"I grew up back East."

"Where you going?"

"Not back East," she said with conviction. She knew that much of what lay ahead.

He laughed a raspy wheeze. "Well, I guess that's what would be called going someplace else."

"I thought I was going to the third floor," Kate said.

"Nope, you got there." He opened the lift and started down the narrow hallway ahead of her.

The walls and doors and floors were framed with wide woodwork, all if it under coats of dark varnish. Between the woodwork was a mauve wallpaper and a row of brass lighting fixtures. Underfoot was a padded carpet of matching hue, if the dim light could be trusted.

"I like your dog, too," Eddie added as he turned the key in the door and pushed it open for her. "A dog is a good traveling companion. I suppose you'll be writing about your travels with your dog the way some ladies do?"

Kate laughed lightly. "You're a flatterer." She pulled two coins from the cloth bag dangling from her left wrist. "I'll bet you make lots of tips."

He touched his hat. "The ladies like my con-ver-sa-tion," he drawled. "You can put that in your writings, if you like."

"I'll keep it in mind," she returned.

He sniffed. "From the smell of it, you must have been near an awful big fire or a real smoky train."

She stiffened and didn't know what to say.

He touched his hat again. "I suppose that's the adventure part. Got to have some adventures along the way. Something to write about, I say."

When Eddie was gone, Kate shut the door behind her and flipped on the electric lights. A brightness that startled her washed across the room She'd been camped too long with only dim, old-fashioned kerosene lanterns.

Kerosene, she thought and shivered.

That wasn't like her. As far back as she could remember, others had tried to discourage her wanderings, the chances she took to get the pictures she liked. Being afraid all the time was such a handicap when precaution couldn't be counted on. Bad things happened anyway. With that thought, she stepped to the window and, looking past the narrow ledge and straight down three stories, opened it, letting fresh air push back the curtains and sweep through the room.

She did smell of smoke, she realized, but there wasn't much she could do about that, either.

She turned and tossed her handbag on the bed, removed her cape and made a slow survey of the room. It was blue wallpaper, lace curtains, and old-fashioned furniture—frillier than she liked. She sat on the edge of the bed, which seemed overly soft for the same reason the room seemed overly bright. She wasn't used to common luxuries any more. She hadn't known she'd even missed them. She bounced on the edge of the bed a couple of times and then went to the mirror. The reflection was familiar, but she was hardly the same woman who'd checked her hair in another mirror this morning before defiantly leading those soldiers to Mrs. Donning's tent. How could she have known?

She remembered a time when she and her best school friend had spent hours spinning nasty-sweet fantasies about what would happen if they were kissed in a certain way or touched in certain places. They believed that if a man touched a woman just so, she would faint or feel on fire. Supposedly there was nothing she could do if she was touched like that. It was out of her control. That's why ladies had to be so careful. But, of course, they had never been sure where those places were. So mostly they got silly and giggled until their sides ached. What they hadn't known was that it was all out of control. Life was a wild careening. Anyone who didn't know that had never really tried to touch its pulse.

Homer whined. Kate shushed him and paced to the window again. Somehow she couldn't shake a growing sense of foreboding. It felt like she'd neglected something. It was more than her usual impatience with inactivity. It was a feeling that somehow the wrong things were occupying her mind, that she ought to be worrying about something else, but she couldn't think what.

There was a knock on the door.

She paused, glanced at the mirror once more, and wondered who it could be. She straightened down the front of her dress and then opened.

It was Richard.

He obviously didn't know what to say.

Neither did she. After a brief awkward pause, she blurted out, "What are you doing here?"

He worked a hand into a pocket and pulled out a single waist pin, one of a set of six that held her belt in place.

Seeing the piece, she quickly felt and found the spot near the small of her back where the pin was missing.

"You left this. I went out to your camp to return it, and . . ." He stopped.

She looked up, but he was right. What more was there to say? She took the pin and stepped away from the door, letting him in.

While she worked the waist pin into her dress, he went to the window and closed it, remarking on the chill of the coming evening. That almost reduced her to tears. If he'd made excuses about what had happened between them this afternoon or offered some elaborate condolence, she would have resisted. But that simple concern for her immediate circumstances was unexpected. More, as he turned from the window, he nearly stumbled over her dog. That awkwardness in a man usually smooth pricked her.

But she refused to cry. In her mind letting her tears flow equated with letting the colonel get away with this. She would not let him reduce her to tearful timidity when she considered rage a more appropriate response to what he'd done.

Now Richard was handing her the list, the one where she'd itemized the equipment she would need for the quillworker pictures. He said, "It was a nice idea. Sorry it won't work out. Sorry about all this." He made an odd gesture, clearly meant to take in the whole of the room, maybe the whole of life.

"Sorry it didn't work out?" she asked. She took the list and glanced down it. She would need the use of a camera. That wasn't noted on the list because she'd thought she could get by with her old Scofield. Other than that, she didn't think anything had changed. What was he saying? Then it hit her. He'd called it a "nice idea."

"Did you ever think I was serious about this?" She waved the list at him.

He was visibly taken aback, and his denial came too quickly. "Of course, I knew you were serious. But, I mean, you can't intend to continue with it."

"Why not?" she asked, wondering if he'd only humored her in order to get her to allow him liberties.

"Why not?" he repeated. "Well, because of Bill and . . ."

"Because Bill was killed, I'm supposed to fold up my life

240

and forget everything I ever wanted to do? I think you underestimate me. I'm sorry about Bill, but not sorry enough to pass up what might be the opportunity of a lifetime."

She meant it. All she'd ever wanted to do was take photographs of ordinary things such that people might notice the unnoticed. But Richard was like all the rest. He thought Indian quillworkers were nothing more than silly squaws stitching pretties. He'd never looked, never thought them worth his time. Obviously they weren't the kind of "ladies" that interested him.

"If it means that much to you," he said. "Really, I had no idea." But he was lying to her, lying to himself. His hands knew. His hands insisted too much, shaping the air with too much motion. Then came unbidden the memory of those hands caressing her, and she remembered having enjoyed the lie of their stolen love. How could she be hard on him just because she hadn't caught the fact that it was all lies this afternoon.

Mary, she thought.

"Mary," she said out loud as the nagging worry that had been circling her suddenly took a focus.

"I have to find Mary," she said, and grabbed her handbag and her cape thinking she must be muddled not to have realized before.

"Mary? What about Mary?" he asked.

She fumbled the cape around herself and started for the door.

He grabbed her by the shoulders. "What is this? Where are you going?" He gave her a little shake.

She looked up and didn't know what to say. She didn't think she had time to explain. She might be too late already. But she couldn't break free of his grasp, even though she struggled. Then pausing, she drew breath and let a flood of words loose, hoping some of them would hit the mark.

"I tipped him off. I put her in danger. The colonel didn't know she was there. Now he knows she must have seen. She's a witness—a witness to murder."

* * *

Murder, Richard thought. *Whose murder? Bill's?*

He was having trouble understanding. What he knew for sure was that he cared about Kate in a way he'd never cared about any woman. In fact, he'd never been nervous about a woman before. Now here he was stumbling and stammering and trying too hard to please, so that he suspected she doubted his sincerity. He could see it in how she eyed the way his hands stroked gestures too large. But he'd had no idea she was serious about taking those quillworking pictures, and what was this about finding the Indian girl? And Bill was dead.

After she left him this afternoon, he'd stopped by the hotel bar where Bill Burke usually hung around. He'd fully expected to see the old boy sitting at a table in the back cheating at cards. He'd meant to hail him like an old friend and offer to buy him a drink while secretly gloating. But Bill wasn't there, and as he hung his foot over the bar rail and ordered the drink he was going to have to drink alone, he realized no satisfaction in having had Bill Burke's wife. He wanted Kate. He wanted her with an ache that touched deeper than the dull of the whiskey he was putting back.

That was new to him. He'd been cavalier about matters of the heart, thinking it was all a game. Now the stakes seemed high, his skills inadequate. Standing there, drinking alone, he'd fingered the waist pin he'd found. Returning it was an excuse to see her again, he knew. But he resisted the idea. It was a frivolous excuse, even if the pin was one of a matching set and would be missed. He had a hard time imagining Kate being impressed with a common chivalry, even if she had been impressed when he gave her the gear knob. But what else did he have to offer? That struck him as ironic, given his reputation as a ladies' man, a reputation he'd enjoyed until that moment.

Now, as she wrenched herself free of his grasp and opened the door, he felt a flush of the same uselessness he'd felt out on that bluff when she'd been photographing the birds. She didn't have a thought for him, he knew, except maybe as a nuisance or an obstacle in her way. She had more important things to do. He hadn't liked that feeling then, he didn't like it now. The real measure of his affection was his knowing she'd seduced him this afternoon, not the other way around. And it only bothered him a little that he'd discovered she was a better photographer. He'd always thought of himself as being inspired by a woman, not taught by one. But he could adjust to that idea. He followed her out into the hall, nearly tripping over her dog again as Homer also pushed through the door, keeping close to her heel.

"I don't have time to explain," Kate was telling him. "I only hope I'm not too late."

"Too late for what?" he asked.

"To warn her. I didn't think what I was saying. I only wanted to know where she was."

Halfway down the hall to the lift, he sorted things out. "You think the colonel killed Bill?"

He asked it as a question because he couldn't imagine it being true. Other times, he'd seen the colonel and Bill drinking together in that same hotel bar where he'd stopped this afternoon. Now he considered the possibility that Kate was experiencing a hysteria grown out of the shock of recent events. That seemed quite likely. That was also all the more reason not to let her go off by herself—not in her current state of mind.

"I'll rent horses," he offered.

As the lift opened, she looked at him, and he felt her taking him in this time. Together they stepped inside. As the lift door closed, she said, "Is there any part of this you really believe?"

"I'm trying, Kate," he returned. "I'm trying."

Half an hour later Richard watched Kate push her horse to a gallop and lean into the ride. At the stable, she'd picked a roan mare with enough spirit to be impatient at the congestion of wagons, people, and other riders that clogged the main streets of town. Once clear of that, Kate gave the mare her head and rode the way she did everything—pell-mell, straight ahead, caution to the wind. It gave him second thoughts about her mental state. No one rode like that without having her wits focused.

Arriving at Indian camp gave him more pause. The whole place was a fever of activity. Women were packing, pulling down tepees. Men were rounding up horses. Kate dismounted in the midst of that activity and started asking for Mary. She stopped everyone she met. No one would talk to her. She got shrugs, head shakes, and feigned confusion as if her English weren't understood.

He kept his eye on the soldiers scattered around the perimeter of the camp. They appeared only mildly interested in the wagons that were leaving with such haste, but they had noted his and Kate's arrival with enough interest to make him nervous. He wished Kate would find that girl, and they could get the hell out of there.

He dismounted and started asking Kate's same question. He interrupted a man hitching a pair of horses to a wagon. He stared at Richard, and then let his eyes slide to where some of the soldiers stood, rifles at their sides. Next Richard tried a man who was unhobbling a horse. He wouldn't even look up. Coming on a couple of boys, elbowing each other as they carried parfleches, he asked again. The youths got sullen and silent and stepped around him as they carried their bags to a waiting wagon.

Looking around, he saw Kate standing at the entrance to the only tepee that wasn't collapsed or being taken down. He stepped to her side. "What is it?" he asked.

"It belongs to Woman-Who-Dreams," she told him. "Something's wrong."

"We need to leave," he told Kate.

She wasn't listening. She circled around the tepee.

He followed. "Kate, it's dangerous here."

She didn't give him any more response than he'd gotten from anyone else in this camp. Still he didn't give up. "Kate, this isn't like hanging off a cliff to photograph birds. At least when you're hanging off a cliff you know where the danger is."

Then Kate grabbed the arm of a young girl with a birthmark on her face and stooped to her level. "Where is she? What's happened to Woman-Who-Dreams?"

Before the girl could answer, the three of them were

surrounded by women and dogs. Richard stepped closer to Kate. He didn't understand any of this. First no one paid them any mind; now they were the center of attention.

Homer growled.

A couple of the other women's dogs answered.

Oh, great, Richard thought. Things weren't bad enough. Now they were going to be in the middle of a dogfight.

"Let her go," one of the women commanded.

Kate released the girl and straightened.

"You caused enough trouble here," the same woman said, now catching the frightened child into her arms.

Another of the Indian women disputed that. There was a lively exchange in their language.

"I don't know what you mean," Kate told the women when they seemed to be finished. "I only wanted . . ."

"Woman-Who-Dreams is down by the river. Talk to her."

"She's all right?" Kate asked.

"She's old and ignores trouble," the other one said.

With that, the women and their dogs disappeared about as quickly as they'd appeared. Richard swung around, trying to figure out where they'd all gone. "Who is Woman-Who-Dreams?" he asked.

"The woman who gave me the bag and the invitation to photograph the quillworkers," she answered with enough curtness he expected he should have remembered. He'd truly underestimated her passion for that project. And she was right, he should have known better. Kate's only real passion was photography, which put him at some disadvantage concerning his own feelings. That was the one thing that did bother him. That and the fact that they were attracting the attention of more and more soldiers.

"I think it's a good idea to go and find Woman-Who-Dreams," he said, feeling for any excuse to get her away from there.

"First I have to find Mary," she told him. "Mary's the one who is in danger."

"She's not the only one," he reminded her.

But Kate was beyond being rational. She shook her head. "They all know. Doesn't that strike you as strange? The sheriff ought to know, his deputy, those photographers taking pictures of the scene, but they couldn't see—didn't want to know. But everyone here knows what really happened to Bill."

Richard wished he could be sure that's what this meant. It was possible they figured the trial was over, and it was time to leave. Although he had to admit, that didn't explain the haste. He needed more time to truly figure it all out. "Kate," he suggested again. "I'd like for us to go and find Woman-Who-Dreams."

She hesitated.

He tried again. "No doubt she knows where Mary is. You're not going to find her here. Nobody will even talk to us here."

An hour later, Kate nearly gave up looking for Woman-Who-Dreams. There was too much prairie to search. Then, riding up over a rise next to the river, she spotted her as a dark figure contrasted against a lavender background, the prairie grasses having been turned rose-gray in the setting sun. Riding closer, she saw that the older woman wandered this way and that, poking plants with her walking stick as if she hadn't a care in the world. When she was still several yards away, Kate dismounted, and leaving her horse with Richard, she approached on foot, alone.

"Everyone in Indian Camp is leaving," Kate said when Woman-Who-Dreams looked up.

"I know. They are afraid. The colonel blames the girl. He say she do something wrong. That she make the stove to blow up."

Kate hadn't heard that but didn't doubt that the colonel might try to explain things that way.

"That's not what happened," she said.

"Doesn't matter. Indians afraid anyway. They think soldiers come and kill them all because of it. Happened before."

Kate couldn't deny that.

Woman-Who-Dreams squatted to the ground. She dug

around a certain plant, shook her head, then pushed the dirt back into place.

"Where's Mary?" Kate asked. "No one would tell me at the camp."

Woman-Who-Dreams grunted and straightened. She continued her walk. "I am sorry for what happened to your husband. It is a bad thing."

"Yes, but what about Mary?"

Woman-Who-Dreams rested on her stick. "She saw him come. She ran away and hid in the trees immediately. From there, she watched him searching the wagon."

"Who? The colonel?"

"Yes. The colonel. He was by himself, and he was looking for something, Mary says."

"What?"

Woman-Who-Dreams shrugged. "When he goes, Mary is still scared. She doesn't go back to the wagon. She comes here. Then when we hear of the explosion and what happened to your husband, we know there is big trouble for Mary. And maybe not just for Mary."

"Where is she now?"

"She's safe. The little rabbit hides, and no one finds what we don't want them to find."

"Thank goodness for that," Kate breathed. "But why aren't you going with the others?"

"I was with Sitting Bull when he ran all the way to Canada. It didn't help." Then she walked on as if that was explanation enough. She had her gathering sack flung over her shoulder, her walking stick in one hand, a shorter stick with strange marks in her other hand.

Kate glanced back to where Richard was holding the horses, but followed Woman-Who-Dreams. She was bent slightly, but her pace was brisk. Kate had to work to keep up, mostly because her skirts tangled in the grass, and she had to kick them out of her way.

Homer scared up a rabbit and chased it, barking loudly. The sound carried across the prairie evening like whip-cracks. Woman-Who-Dreams paused to watch. Then with a backhanded gesture she said, "He chases the rabbit away from you. An enemy does that. I don't know how your people survive. You should have starved long ago."

Kate didn't know what to say to that. She called Homer. He left off the chase and trotted back to her side, wagging his tail.

"I still want to do the photographs," Kate told the other woman. "I'm not sure just how I'll manage it, but you were right. I'll find a way."

Woman-Who-Dreams shook her head. "We must all follow a different path now."

Kate wasn't sure she'd heard right. "You're saying you've changed your mind?"

The older woman nodded.

"I don't believe that. What about the dream? The one where you saw a red-haired woman with a red dog?"

"All has changed," Woman-Who-Dreams said.

Kate stood as if stunned, trying to absorb this new development. Her hope of taking those pictures was the last thing left to her. No husband, no camera, no clothes, and now this disappointment. It wasn't as though she required much, just a chance to work.

She kicked her tangled skirts and caught up with Woman-Who-Dreams. "You have no idea the trouble this has caused me. You can't expect me to just give up now."

The older woman shook her head slowly. "An impossible thing is a thing that is out of its time. Buffalo Woman teaches us this. Buffalo Woman and Double-Woman . . ."

"Oh, quit." Kate stopped her. "You're very clever at making up fancy stories for simple things. Truth is, the quillworkers are afraid like everyone else. That's why they don't want me to take the pictures, especially since it's my husband that got killed. And I don't imagine they've much patience for your wise tales right now either. They know when to pack it up."

Kate and the older woman's eyes met.

Woman-Who-Dreams looked away first. "You were born in the regular way, no twin, no caul?"

248

"You asked me that once before."

Woman-Who-Dreams shook her head. "But you *do* see to the heart of things. That is a gift. But still, it has all changed. They are afraid and there will be no pictures because they are afraid."

Kate kicked her tangled skirts again and then a clump of grass. She paused until she was calmer and then caught up again with the older woman. "Take care of Mary," she breathed. "Her spirit is not all rabbit."

Woman-Who-Dreams looked up. "I know. I have hope for her."

Woman-Who-Dreams watched Kate and the man with her ride away. Their horses pounded the prairie, shaking the ground, stirring up the dust. "The white man moves like thunder" she remembered her father saying. "We will always know where he is." Woman-Who-Dreams shook her head. That was a long time ago, and her father could not have known that the white man would be everywhere.

She squatted to the ground and set her walking stick beside her. She cradled the shorter plant stick in her lap letting her thumb rub down the markings along its edge. It was both map and inventory. The spacing and number of symbols told her where she was likely to find certain plants and how much of a medicinal herb or edible plant was in any known area of her tribe's territory. It had never failed her before. But now the buffalo were gone, the prairie was changing. New grasses. New plants. She wondered if anyone but old Indian women like her knew that. It was a large thing not to notice.

She poked the stick upright into the ground in front of her. Good for nothing. She would give it back to the prairie.

Coyote was in the world.

There was no other way to explain the strange upside-downness of things. Woman-Who-Dreams folded her arms across her chest and began to sing softly to herself. She swayed as she sang. It was not a medicine song. It was a story-song about the beginning time when Coyote made the

249

Indians and scattered them over the land. It was about when he killed the monsters and outsmarted the evil spirits, when he taught the people how to hunt buffalo, dig roots, and catch eagles. But mostly it was about how Coyote loved to play tricks.

Sometimes he went too far with his tricks and got someone killed. Sometimes he got himself killed. This happened so often Fox got tired of bringing him back to life. Coyote had to learn to jump over his own droppings three times and bring himself back to life. Problem was, he had to find the right droppings. Some were magical. Some were just shit.

The story-song explained that Coyote was no longer in the world. The story-song said that Sky-Grandfather knew that Coyote's work was done and came down disguised as an old man. He greeted Coyote and told him it was time to go, time to leave the world alone. But Coyote was having fun in the world and didn't want to believe the old man was Sky-Grandfather. They had a contest.

Coyote said to the old man, "Move that mountain."

Sky-Grandfather said, "No, you move that mountain."

Coyote did.

Then Sky-Grandfather said, "Move it back."

Coyote tried. He couldn't. He thought that strange. He tried again. Nothing.

Sky-Grandfather moved the mountain back.

After that, Coyote believed he was Sky-Grandfather and went with him, disappearing from the world, no one knew where. But before the Sky-Grandfather took Coyote, he promised the Indian that when the Earth Mother was old, he would send Coyote back. "When you see him, you will know I am coming. When I return, I will bring all the dead with me. There will be no more two worlds—the seen and the unseen. All the people will live together, and Earth Mother will once again be among her children."

Woman-Who-Dreams rubbed her knees where they ached. That was an old, old story-song much told, but not to missionaries. The ghost dancers had thought they could hasten the time when Sky-Grandfather returned, dancing it into being. But that was not to be. The dancers had been deceived. Sky-Grandfather was not returning with the dead. It was Coyote. Coyote had come into the world again, turning everything upside down. She was sure of that. Hadn't everything become Coyote droppings? Hard to tell the life-giving from the stink piles?

White women lived in webs of fear. It was her oldest and best observation of them. They confined themselves to the insides of houses, schools, and churches. They hid under layers and layers of clothing. They held their teacups a certain way, tied their hats just so, and never laughed too loudly. Such fears made their spirits small. Such women organized classes in the "female arts" for their "Sioux sisters."

Woman-Who-Dreams spit.

But the red-haired woman with the red dog dared wander the hillside and greet the day. Generations of holy women native to these hills had done the same. Had she been wrong to hope on her?

Woman-Who-Dreams shook herself. A chill had penetrated her bones from the ground up. She pulled two more plant sticks from her gathering bag. She poked them into the ground on either side of her own. One had been her mother's. The other belonged to her grandmother. Her granddaughters and great-granddaughters would not need them. They had been tricked at the mission schools. They no longer learned to quill or chant the generations or hunt the plants of the prairie. They were jumping over the wrong Coyote droppings—the ones that didn't give life. And they would become like white people—motherless.

White people had mothers, of course, but no sense of belonging. They moved through the world so fast it was as though they thought they could stay ahead of their own chaos. They were a meteoric people, brilliant, and just as fast gone. They were bigger fools than Coyote. There was no escaping the circling of cycles, the repeating of pattern.

But her granddaughters and great-granddaughters could

not live if they had no pride. If she could not leave them plant sticks and photographs, she would leave them legend—a doing large enough to become story.

That was why she had decided this was not a time for running. She would not run. This was a time for bravery.

With that, she stood and raised her hands to the sky. She waited. At the exact moment when the last ray of the setting sun pierced the horizon as a single flash of green, Woman-Who-Dreams began her chant, calling out the names of her generations in a long chain of thankful being. She sang loud and strong, expecting this was the last time she would give the wind her names.

13

Earlier that same afternoon, Powers T. Nock stopped at home for a cup of coffee. His mother was peeling potatoes in the kitchen and humming a popular ditty. He poured the coffee and leaned against the sink to drink it. She nudged him aside, complaining that he was in her way.

"Everybody's expecting a big dish of my spicy potatoes at the church social tonight. I haven't got time to be bothered right now."

He nudged her back. "Don't know what you're worried about. You could make those spicy potatoes in your sleep. You could make those spicy potatoes while standing on your head."

She straightened. "You saying I've made them too many times? You think folks are tired of my spicy potatoes?"

He shook his head and chuckled softly. "You ever bring any of those spicy potatoes home from a church social? Nobody's tired of them until they stop eating them."

She didn't say anything to that, but he could tell by the little wiggle in her shoulders that he'd pleased her with that comment. He sipped his coffee and then got to the real reason he'd come home in the middle of the day. He asked her about the latest Gilbert and Sullivan opera. A traveling company had brought it to Sioux Falls, and his mother had attended the week before with some of her women friends. It was a polite thing to ask about, but he had more on his mind. He was on his way to see General Miles's aide, the man everyone called simply Baldwin, and he'd thought a bit of opening banter concerning Gilbert and Sullivan might be in order, especially as the man had made it clear he had no time to discuss anything with Nock unless he was willing to come to his hotel room while he was dressing for the opera tonight.

Nock's mother set down a half-pared potato, wiped her hands on her apron, and sighed. "Oh, I don't know. It's quite complicated, and sometimes the characters pretend to be one thing when they're really something else." She clicked her tongue several times, an unconscious mannerism that accompanied her trying to remember things.

He'd already regretted asking. He'd wanted a sentence or two. That's all. Nothing she needed to wipe her hands for. Nothing she needed to cluck her tongue over. "Never mind," he said, hoping to forestall a major discussion.

Too late. "If you had an interest, you might have come," she started in. "I'm sure you'd have understood all the complications far better than I do."

He doubted that. He preferred a good game of chess. At least with chess one could count on a certain logic behind the moves, unless one was playing with an idiot. He didn't know that he could say the same for opera, where the plots made twists no one could anticipate much less believe. Of course, he wasn't about to tell his mother that. She was terribly fond of "light English opera," which she considered the epitome of sophistication.

"Nanki-Poo, the disguised son of the Mikado, falls in love with Yum-Yum, who is betrothed to a tailor named Ko-Ko," she began telling him.

Nock nodded, but he'd decided this was a truly bad idea. He couldn't hear himself repeating names like "Yum-Yum" in any serious conversation—never mind the fact that *The Mikado* had swept across the country with such a wave of popularity, it had created a national fetish with everything Japanese.

"But no execution had taken place in the town for almost a year, and the rule was that unless someone got beheaded at least once a year, the town would be reduced to the status of a village," his mother continued.

"There's a rule like that?" Nock interrupted. "Who makes rules like that?"

"Do you want to hear the story? Or do you want to argue it like a case?"

He shrugged and made a gesture for her to continue. In a sense he suspected that "rules" like that were more universal than anyone wanted to believe. Sioux Falls needed a hanging—some ritual to end this Indian uprising. In a way, it was the only sense he could make of his client's fate, even if a hanging didn't quite fit the town's image of an up-and-coming modern city.

That's what really bothered him. This whole affair ought to have played like a chess game, not an opera. In fact, he'd been counting on the forces behind the scenes, namely General Miles, stepping forward to put a stop to all this before it went too far. With that in mind, he'd given the man the right opening, offered him the perfect way out. All he had to do was agree that they were at war with the Sioux, and everyone would walk away from this trial and this hanging none the worse.

"Of course the Mikado is happy at first to learn of the execution," Nock's mother was going on. "That is until he realizes it was his own son who was executed. Then that makes him most unhappy. He orders everyone executed. Only it turns out that his son wasn't really executed. The people in the town had faked everything. Of course, the Mikado is happy when he learns that his son is alive, but that doesn't change anything. It's still a capital offense to disobey the Mikado's orders, so he still has to execute everyone. It's the law, you see. But then Ko-Ko and the others figure out a way to explain things. Only I didn't quite understand that part. But it all ended happily. I know that much."

Nock shook his head and poured the last of his coffee into the sink. He'd missed something in his mother's explanation. He suspected he'd missed something in the larger context of what was going on here in Sioux Falls, as well.

Half an hour later, he was trying to remember who Yum-Yum was in love with, figuring he still might need that as opening chitchat. He knocked on Baldwin's hotel door and shifted his weight back and forth, wondering how he was going to manage this. Baldwin certainly hadn't indicated any eagerness to see him.

Baldwin opened. He was a young man of medium height with a full dark head of hair and a slight scar above one eye—the mark of a fighting man. In fact, the mark so distinguished his looks, Nock sincerely hoped it wasn't the result of a barroom brawl. A scar like that needed a story.

He was half dressed—stocking feet, pants pulled over his underwear, no shirt. With only the briefest of greetings, he let Nock into the room while he went to the mirror and began combing a part into his hair. With his other hand he waved toward a pair of newly pressed uniforms spread over the bed. One was a dress uniform, the other standard issue. "Which do you think I should wear?" he asked. "I mean, I never know about western towns like this. Sometimes they take themselves so damned seriously, folks dress as if for a grand ball. Other places if you so much as polish your shoes, you get looks like maybe you're trying to put on eastern airs." Suddenly he paused. He'd caught Nock's reflection in the mirror. He half turned and gave a sidelong look at Nock's gray- and blue-checkered suit and shook his head. "Sorry, I forgot. You're not much into dressing for any occasion."

Nock tugged his vest down and shrugged.

"You probably don't like opera, either."

Nock sighed and wondered why he'd cluttered up his head with convoluted love affairs and characters with baby-sounding names. It never worked for him to try and be something he wasn't. "I'm afraid I've never developed much of a taste for singing," he admitted. "I like clocks and chess. Things with some precision."

Baldwin finished the part in his hair. "Then why don't you get precisely to your point?"

Nock hesitated. Word around town was that Baldwin, like the general, was a fair man, willing to consider most things. On the other hand, Nock had a great deal riding on this, and while he wasn't usually given to sweating, he could feel a moisture building around his neck. This was his client's last chance. If General Miles chose not to intervene day after tomorrow when the court reconvened, the rest was going to be formality. This was important. At the very least, he wished he had Baldwin's complete attention. The man was now waxing his mustache.

Nock cast one glance at the ceiling and decided to go for broke. "I think we all know Lieutenant Casey died like a soldier while performing his duty as a spy. Ask me, he ought to be remembered with a medal, not a hanging."

Baldwin left off with his mustache and turned to face Nock. There was a moment of silence, then he raised an eyebrow and gave Nock a respectful nod. "Well, I guess that does get precisely to the point. Only he wasn't spying."

"What else could he have been doing?" Nock asked. "Besides there's actual testimony . . ."

"Reconnoitering," Baldwin interrupted. "We call it reconnoitering."

Nock swallowed the rest of his argument.

Baldwin gave Nock another respectful nod. "You got it all right, all of it. But sometimes being right isn't enough."

Not enough, Nock thought. What did that mean? General Miles was a peacemaker who'd gotten forced into a war. Baldwin was known as a "cool head." What wasn't enough to make them want to set the record straight?

"All the general has to do is release a few documents, make it clear a state of war existed. That way Judge Sherman has no choice but to rule that his court has no jurisdiction. It's not like you're exonerating Plenty Horses.

Nobody's going to accuse you of being soft on the lieutenant's killer or of being an Indian lover."

Baldwin shook his head. "You want to know the worst of this? Lieutenant Casey was a close friend of mine, and you're right, he died like a soldier, but unfortunately, he died as part of something nobody wants to remember."

Nock toyed with that a moment, trying to put together the idea behind Baldwin's comment. Did he and the general think that if they didn't stir in this, it would all fade into history unnoticed? "This is not going to go away," he told Baldwin.

"If it weren't for this trial, who'd even care anymore?" Baldwin countered. "That's the real reason the general didn't want to go to court. Hell, I hear even the photographs of this 'last Indian uprising' aren't selling like they once did. People have lost interest already, which shouldn't surprise anyone. No one wants to remember what's unpleasant. Or if they never knew, they really don't want to know."

Nock paced to the window and poked his hands in his pockets. He didn't know what to say. He could see the appeal, but it was wishful thinking. The secrets behind this were too enormous to disappear into time. The soul, whether it was the soul of an individual or the soul of a nation, had a natural, undeniable movement toward knowledge. That's why the truth will always out—because not knowing was blank and anchorless, the equivalent of despair. No one willingly embraced emptiness. That was the trouble with censorship of any kind, even censorship intended to spare the ugliness of reality. Ultimately, it wasn't benign. It was another kind of warfare, in this case another kind of massacre, as destructive as the first because it truncated stories, removed lives.

He turned back to Baldwin. "Knowing it's not right, are you going to let Plenty Horses hang?"

Baldwin obviously wasn't comfortable having it stated so baldly. He shifted his shoulders, looked away. "We're soldiers. Soldiers make sacrifices for the greater good. In fact, that's what we mainly do."

The greater good, Nock thought. And he wondered who

was the judge of that? The sweat about his neck had moved to the palms of his hands and his mouth was dry. He didn't know what to say, but he wasn't going to accept some false notion of a "greater good." This was more like trying to ignore consequences. It was believing that one more death didn't matter beside all the other deaths. But it did matter. Real events simply couldn't be fragmented into pieces that mattered and pieces that didn't.

Nock shook his head. "It won't work. None of this is going to go away. What you'll buy with your silence is one more thing added to the list of improprieties that will be investigated when all this bursts into public view. And let me give you a personal word of advice. Last time I checked, the law didn't accept 'the greater good' as a defense for anything."

Nock expected a heated response, but Baldwin showed himself true to his reputation as a "cool head." He ran a hand across his forehead and sighed. "I really wish I could help you. But there are truly larger concerns here."

"Yeah, I know," Nock replied. "You already told me about the greater good, whatever the hell that means." But then he thanked the man and extended his hand. Unlike the colonel, he had some respect for Baldwin and General Miles, even though he'd never met the general. From all indications, they were good men caught in a bad situation, and in a way, he couldn't blame them for trying to find an easy out. At the door Nock paused. "Wear the dress uniform. Sioux Falls is definitely the dress-ball sort of western town. People around here actually imagine this place might become the next Chicago, which is why nobody's going to thank you for a public hanging. It's not exactly the same sort of spectacle as a Gilbert and Sullivan."

Nor was a public hanging quite like a church social, Nock mused later that evening, and then chided himself for that thought. A hanging was no laughing matter. But then neither was carrying his mother's large and very heavy dish of spicy potatoes all the way down to the social hall in the church basement. If they didn't hurry, he felt sure his arms were going to be stretched to apelike proportions, but hurrying was not on his mother's agenda. She stopped to greet everybody.

"I brought my spicy potatoes," she said again and again, stopping to greet everyone they passed. "You remember my potato dish?"

At last arriving in the hall, Nock set her dish down on a long table amid the other hot dishes. Then, leaving her to fuss over how it ought to be arranged, he made his way across the room to where the men stood. Like country dances, church socials divided into the men's side and the women's side and included a certain amount of nervous eyeing of each other. As Nock joined the group, a pocket flask was being passed behind the men's backs where the women couldn't see it. It was the sort of activity that created a naughty schoolboy club. When the flask came to Nock, he pulled a swig and wiped the neck for the next guy. He wasn't much of a drinker, preferring a clear head, but a little booze was probably the best this evening had to offer.

He didn't have much use for church or church socials. He went mostly to humor his mother and because he'd made a mental game of noting the logical fallacies in the preacher's Sunday sermons. Not out of disrespect. Deep down he knew the wonder of the world ought not to be dismissed lightly. He frankly enjoyed the inexplicable in life. But preachers for some reason seemed to think they had to argue religion rather than celebrating its awe.

He took another swig of the offered whiskey and passed the flask with a single comment, "Looks like a nice spread tonight, good as any Thanksgiving."

He meant nothing by that comment, but George Hendricks, a foreman at the mill, grunted and said, "Yeah, maybe if we invited your Indian friend, we could pretend it was a right regular Thanksgiving. Only I heard them Indians at that first Thanksgiving were friendly, not back-shooting murderers."

Nock shrugged. George had the reputation of being an oaf—the kind of man who used his fists, instead of his head, even on his wife. In fact, he had a fresh bruise on the side of his face. Nock indicated it and said, "Ask me you ought to be picking a fight with whoever did that to you, not me."

The man raised his hand to his bruise. "Yeah, well, I got this doing my civic duty as a volunteer firefighter. Slipped on a rock down by the river. Landed on the side of my face. I might have gone into the water except for Henry grabbing me." He was referring to a quieter man who also worked at the mill, Henry Barlow.

"Sorry to hear it," Nock added, intending to move on.

"Leastwise it weren't as bad an accident as what killed that photographer."

"What photographer?" Nock asked, his blood taking a chill.

"Sheriff said his name was Bill Burke, I believe."

Several others nodded. At least half the men were volunteer firefighters and proud of it.

"And he was killed, you say?" Nock repeated trying to take in this information. "How?"

"Kerosene stove in his tourist wagon blew up. Made a real mess. Time we got there, only thing left was burned embers."

"And his wife, was she hurt?"

"No, she came along later. Her and her dog. That damned dog went after some of the firefighters. That animal got real upset. The woman was like she was in a daze. Guess it was hard for her to absorb. Sheriff wouldn't even let her look at the body. Just as well, it was burned pretty bad."

The others nodded to that, and then several of them started comparing the details of what they remembered. There was some disagreement as to how far the stove door had been blown in the explosion.

Nock stepped back. He'd been so absorbed in the trial and his own affairs, he hadn't heard any local news. That wasn't unusual. Most of the time, he preferred to keep to himself. Even now, a part of him heard what the others were saying, but in another sense, his mind had taken an even greater distance. It was as if the news had dazed him, as well. For a moment he couldn't think. Then he concentrated on the fact that Kate was all right, but didn't take much comfort in that fact because he didn't think she was going to be all right for long.

He didn't believe it was an accident. What's more, he didn't believe Bill Burke was the intended victim. If somebody had wanted to kill Bill Burke, they'd have staged something in the bar where he played cards. Almost everyone knew the man cheated. If he got himself killed over cards, no one would think anything of it. Blowing up a kerosene stove was how you killed a woman.

Nock excused himself. He found his mother discussing the same news. She was agreeing as another woman said, "I hate kerosene stoves."

"Did you hear about the woman over in Nebraska who lost an arm when one of those stoves blew up?" someone else said.

Nock pulled his mother aside. "You'll have to find someone to take you home. I have to leave."

"Why? What's the matter?"

"It's business," he said, an excuse that usually served. But not this evening.

"Oh, Powers, don't you tell me that," his mother started in. "What kind of business can you possibly have at this hour?" Then sucking a little gasp, she added, "You look positively pale." She pulled him by his arm into better light. "If I didn't know better, I'd say you'd just received bad news—a shock."

"Your imagination is running away again," he said.

"It's that photographer who got himself blown up, isn't it? And it has something to do with your case, doesn't it?"

He started to shake his head, but didn't. She was right. He suspected it did have something to do with his case. It was all tangled up together—everything—if he only understood how. But that really wasn't his main concern. He had to make sure Kate was safe.

"It's a right terrible shame," his mother was saying. "It's cast such a pall over this whole social. You should hear the women talk. Half of them have kerosene stoves and are

262

scared to death. They've all heard stories of how some woman was blinded or maimed by one of those stoves. But they never heard of a man getting himself killed with one. That's new."

"I know, I know," Nock said and pulled away from her. "But really I have to go."

Suddenly she gripped his arm harder. "She's the button lady, isn't she?"

"I don't know what you mean."

"The button lady—the one whose smoky colored mother-of-pearl you found and brought home. You met her when Plenty Horses was having his picture taken."

Nock paused. He'd never been in the habit of lying to his mother, even as a child. He didn't have to. Careful omissions had always been enough to throw her off. But he was tempted in this instance simply because he didn't need the complication of his mother's interest in a situation he hadn't figured out. He just knew Kate was in danger, and he needed to warn her.

As it turned out, he didn't have to say anything. His mother leaned close and whispered, "The woman hasn't been a widow twenty-four hours, but no doubt she needs a helping hand. And no doubt she'll remember those who helped her in her time of need. It never hurts to make a good impression, no matter the circumstances, I say. But I want you to know right now that I don't like dogs. Never have. And I don't intend to spend my later years of life stumbling over that woman's big dog."

Nock couldn't believe what he was hearing. It certainly wasn't worth comment. He shook his head, patted her arm a couple of times, pulled free, and left.

Kate returned to the hotel feeling thoroughly worn out and thoroughly bedraggled. If her clothes smelled of the fire before, she felt sure they now also smelled of the horse she'd ridden. Richard left her at the front door of the hotel. They agreed he would return the horses to the stable, and she would get some rest. That's exactly what she intended to do until she entered the hotel lobby and was confronted by

Powers Nock. For a moment she thought maybe he'd joined his colleagues in working the divorce trade, but then she realized he was too agitated to be soliciting business. He was almost frantic.

"Where have you been?" he asked in tones that reminded her of her father. "I've been worried sick. You shouldn't be wandering around alone. Not after dark, leastwise, not here and now."

She had no idea what he was talking about. She had no patience for any of his notions. She wanted him to leave her alone so she could get her rest.

"I'm sorry, but when I found you'd checked into this hotel, but no one knew where you were, I got worried." He caught his breath and added, "I'm truly sorry about Bill."

"Thank you," she said, not knowing how else to respond. She didn't know why he was here. She was too tired to do more than wonder.

When she didn't say anything more, Nock said again that he was sorry and added, "I've been waiting here for almost an hour. I'm not good at waiting under the best of circumstances. My mother says I've never learned to put my mind at rest. It's true. If I have to sit around too long with nothing to do, I get a little crazy. But you don't want to hear about that. What am I thinking? I'm not thinking very well at all. But you don't know how relieved I am that you're all right." He gestured her to one of the lobby chairs.

The last thing she wanted was to sit and chat. "It's kind of you to be concerned," she told him. "But . . ."

"It was no accident," he told her.

"What?"

"The stove blowing up. It was no accident," he repeated.

She glanced around as if expecting someone might have overheard. The clerk at the hotel counter had changed. The singing church ladies were gone. She drew a deep breath. "How do you know that?"

"I just know."

She nodded and found that somewhat refreshing. She wasn't sure Richard believed even now. Not that she faulted him. It was a common reaction to not want to believe difficult or ugly truths, as if choosing not to know could insulate.

"But where are my manners. You must be hungry. I'm sure you haven't eaten in a long time. I mean with all the excitement and all. Would you have dinner with me?"

She shook herself free of her thoughts long enough to wonder if she'd heard right. Having dinner with a gentleman was the last thing she'd had on her mind.

She brushed across her dress which was soiled around the hem.

Evidently he noticed. "You look fine," he told her.

She felt for some other excuse. "They won't let my dog in the dining room. There's a rule about that and . . ."

"If I arrange for your dog to join us, will you share a meal with me?"

She brushed at her dress again. She didn't think getting her dog into the fanciest dining room in Sioux Falls was likely, but then she'd witnessed Nock's persuasive powers and expected he wasn't going to leave her alone until she agreed. And having thought about it, she realized she was hungry. "I'd have to freshen up a bit."

Half an hour later, after having brushed the worst of the dirt from her dress and washed up, Kate and her dog were escorted into the fanciest dining room in Sioux Falls. The waiter even made a show of bringing a cushion for Homer to sit on right next to the table. Feeling somewhat revived, Kate laughed lightly at that and marveled, "I can't imagine how you accomplished this. Is there anything you don't succeed at?"

He was pouring wine and stopped. "I don't seem to be doing too well for my client."

That sobered her. "Oh, yes, I know. I'm sorry."

He finished pouring the wine and watched how she glanced around the room, taking in the curious looks of the other diners. He straightened his jacket and said, "I apologize. We seem to be attracting some attention."

"It's the dog," she returned.

"And me," he added. "It takes an uncommonly kind woman to not mind being seen with a man dressed in a blue- and gray-checkered suit."

Her gaze came around to his. "So why do you dress that way? I mean, I know you know better. You managed to dress Plenty Horses quite nattily for his photograph."

"It saves time."

Her look turned quizzical, and he realized he liked that scrunch in her expression. He liked having her attention. He sipped his wine. "I know a person instantly by how they react to my appearance. That's useful, especially in my business, and since I'm not likely ever to be mistaken for 'tall, dark, and handsome,' I don't see any reason not to wear blue-and-gray checks."

He watched how she mulled that, avoiding the easy responses. A moment later, she raised her glass to him. "You are remarkably clever. I applaud all your checkered suits. But you really might consider whether the bottle green suit isn't a bit too garish for even a costumed effect."

"You don't like that one?"

She shook her head.

He nodded. "I'll be rid of it first thing in the morning."

"Oh, but it's just a suggestion. You don't have to do that for me."

He paused. He wanted to tell her he'd be willing to do most anything for her, but the banter was light, the moment wrong. Time, he swore under his breath. Always, it was not quite the right time—story of his life.

"In that case, I think I'll do it for the sake of all the ladies," he answered airily.

Perhaps she had been more hungry than she knew or in need of company. It was hard to explain, but Kate found herself feeling better, more relaxed, as the evening wore on. Nock surprised her with his sophistication ordering the wine and food and entertaining her with just the right blend of shared stories and quiet listening. Near the end of the main course, she caught herself talking about her father. She didn't do that often and never in situations where she didn't feel completely at ease. She hadn't been sure what to expect having dinner with Nock, certainly nothing this engaging.

The waiter returned. While Nock ordered a little sweet to end the meal, she glanced around at the polished chandeliers and rows of tables covered in pressed white linens. It was quiet, most of the other diners had gone, and it was getting late. The atmosphere was pleasant and yet not particularly remarkable. Still, there was no denying the warmth of feeling she felt toward Nock. She was sitting across the table from a man whose kindness and wit had cut through and found her.

She didn't know why that amazed her. She knew there was a secret, almost erotic edge to all of life that could be discovered almost anywhere if one wasn't satisfied with surface, and she never was. She lived to expose glimpses at the core of being when a person or a situation truly revealed itself. That's where the real picture was. But to her knowledge, she'd never been the subject of that kind of examination, never had her own self similarly stripped. Until now. This strange little man had a soul capable of completely encompassing her. What startled her most was the knowledge that unlike the passion she'd shared with Richard, there was no sense of falsehood in the feeling here. No easy escape.

She wondered if it was possible that for every event there was a double, an inverse that mocked or gave depth. Clearly the world turned on opposites—man and woman, night and day. But more than simple mirrors, the opposing forces of the world danced such a delicate dance, it was as though events brushed by one another, circling and defining each other in ways barely ponderable for the mystery of it. She'd certainly ridden through this day on a waltz of highs and lows. It was almost more than she could imagine. How could it all have swirled together into a single day—the passion she'd shared with Richard, the horror of Bill's dying, now this warm discovery of Nock's finer qualities.

Then over dessert, Nock broke the spell. He set his fork down and said, "Kate, there's something we have to discuss."

She nodded. She'd known the conversation would turn serious. It was asking too much to believe he'd dined with her simply to cheer her. Same as when he took her to meet Plenty Horses in jail, he was expecting her to know things. She didn't. Kate stirred the last of a too-sweet bread pudding.

"Do you know why the colonel would want Bill dead?" he asked.

She looked up and then away. She didn't know how to answer that exactly. Bill had never been Sunday School honest. She suspected he had been cheating the colonel or something. That didn't deserve to get him killed, but then she didn't know what could possibly be important enough to get anyone killed.

"Don't you think it was sort of chancy using a stove to do the job?" Nock continued.

She brought her gaze back to his and nodded. "It could have killed me."

"Precisely."

She stirred the pudding some more.

"Kate, he meant to kill you."

She'd considered that. In some ways it made more sense. After all, Bill had been the colonel's best ally. The Seventh Cavalry's great victory over Sitting Bull and the ghost dancers existed more in Bill's pictures than in fact because Bill always staged—recreated—his shots, old style, putting only what he and the colonel wanted in them. He was the one who'd made the colonel a hero in the eastern press.

On the other hand, she'd seen through that charade and consciously made a different photographic record. She knew there had been nothing brave or glorious about how the colonel and his men hunted down cold, hungry, defenseless bands of Indians whose only crime was a strange sort of dancing. And that's how she'd pictured it, slyly, when no one was watching. But the colonel didn't know that. Hadn't even noticed what she was doing. She wasn't sure why he'd begun to pay attention to her of late, but she didn't think it was because of her pictures. Even the night when he came to her camp to threaten her, he'd been worried about some vague fear that she was "out of control" rather than what pictures she might have. He'd never mentioned her photographs, never seen them. Ironically, he probably had nothing to fear from her. The only time anyone had ever taken an interest in her "snaps" was when she put her father's name to them. No, she thought, her pictures threatened her with a slow death of neglect, not murder. And besides, they'd all been destroyed in the explosion that killed Bill.

She set her fork down and looked up at Nock. "You're mistaken. Something was going on between the colonel and Bill. It had to do with money, I'm sure. One day the two of them were beer-drinking, back-slapping buddies and then, all of a sudden, they were wary of each other. But the problem was between them."

"That doesn't explain why he would have his men follow you."

"It does if you understand him. He does things like that. He seems to enjoy harassing the weak. It's more than being the bully. He enjoys creating fear, and the best way to do that is to threaten for no reason at all, like having me followed."

She drew a deep breath. "I don't know how to explain it exactly. One day, one of his Indian scouts mistook the trail of some wild horses for a party of renegades. He led the colonel and his men on a half-day chase into the badlands all for nothing. Everyone else thought it was an honest mistake and maybe even laughable. Not the colonel. He took to shooting at that scout randomly, anytime he felt like it. He always missed deliberately. But the poor man never knew. That went on for days until the colonel got tired of the game. I annoyed him the other morning when he wanted to arrest my serving girl. He was simply letting me know he was annoyed."

"No, Kate, you're avoiding the truth. There's more to it than that. And sooner or later you're going to have to admit it. But for now, you have to take care. If not for your sake, for mine."

"Yours?" she asked.

Suddenly there was an increased nervousness to Nock's

mannerisms—more than his usual boyish, and somewhat
endearing, awkwardness. He was speechless, feeling for
words. It was enough to make her wonder: Did he fancy
himself in love with her?

This was not the time or the place, and yet the idea
captured her fancy. Powers T. Nock dressed funny and
couldn't keep his hands from fumbling everything around
him, and yet she had to admit there was a real power of
persuasion in him; it amounted to an unmistakable magnetism. She could do worse than to be the object of his
affection because he could never be fickle. Unlike Richard,
Powers T. Nock had staying power. In fact she imagined he
might descend into Hades and talk his way out again if
that's what it took to win the object of his intentions. In a
sense, that was exactly what he was attempting with this
trial, and it was unmistakably flattering to think he might
find her worth the same kind of attention.

She stood. "It's all been very fine. I appreciate the dinner,
but I'm afraid I really have had too much happen to me
today. I don't have the energy for anything else."

No argument. He stood and signaled the waiter. He
settled the bill and accompanied her. All the time it took to
leave the dining room, cross the lobby, and take the elevator
to her room, she kept expecting him to lecture her about
being careful, not taking unnecessary chances—all the
things she'd heard over and over all her life and never
heeded. But he didn't. She almost thought he'd abandoned
the idea of her being in danger until at the door of her room
when he grabbed her arm.

"Here, take this," he said and pulled a gun from the waist
of his pants.

She stepped back, speechless.

Undeterred, Nock pressed the revolver into her hand
saying, "You really don't have to know how to use it. At
close range, just point it in the general direction and pull the
trigger. It'll do the rest."

"But I hate guns," Kate said.

"So, do I," he answered.

Looking up, she caught his gaze and she knew, right or

wrong, he believed what he'd been telling her. With that thought came a shiver of fear. She took the gun. For an anxious moment she fingered it awkwardly having no idea what to do with it.

She could shoot, not that she'd had much reason to use a gun. Besides, camera work had taught her to sight clearly and keep a steady hand. But Nock's revolver was old and rather large. It was too big for her pocket or her bag. Holding it close to her side, she folded her skirt around it and said, "I hope you're wrong about this."

"But I'm not," he answered.

14

In the darkness before moonrise, Woman-Who-Dreams darted from one shadow to the next working her way, building to building, along the edge of Sioux Falls. Stealth was her object, not hard to accomplish in a town, even a town full of soldiers. The patches of black were more complex and varied than on the prairie. Here the alleys, the angular gray castings of tall buildings, the dark lines and corners behind railings and porches aided the deception. Sneaking across the prairie was harder. There the flat sameness accentuated movement, and eyes, accustomed to the dark, noted anything out of the ordinary. But people who lived in towns had eyes dulled with pools of light from windows and street lamps that kept them from ever growing used to the darkness. Slipping past them was easy.

Her only real concern was the two soldiers, armed and on duty, at the entrance to army camp. The camp itself occupied an old public fairgrounds complete with a grandstand and perimeter fence that the soldiers patrolled. Drawing close to the entrance, Woman-Who-Dreams ducked behind a watering trough where a pair of horses stood at the ready. She paused behind the trough, then moved quietly around it, keeping the horses between her and the soldiers. As she moved, she spoke quietly to the horses and rubbed their necks. She had a way with animals. They knew her. These horses pricked their ears and flicked their tails but didn't give her away. A little later as she still peered around the horses, watching the sentries, one nickered gently. She rubbed that animal's ear. It liked the attention and settled again to calmly flicking its tail.

The soldiers never looked in her direction, not even to note the nicker. They had eyes for only one thing—the girls who came to camp at this time of night.

Woman-Who-Dreams watched as two girls arrived, swishing their skirts with the sway of their walk. The soldiers were of such similar height and weight she could only distinguish them in that dim light by the fact that one was bowlegged. When he stood still, she could see light between his knees, coming from the lantern hanging on the fence behind him. Only he didn't stand still much. He possessed a nervous energy. He paced and frequently fingered his belt where his gun holster hung. More peculiar was the way he had of shaking his legs whenever any of the girls appeared. He ogled them as they lifted their skirts and then shook his legs, first one and then the other, as if he'd sat on them too long, lost the feeling, and was trying to get it back. Woman-Who-Dreams figured it was more likely he'd lost feeling in the appendage between his legs and was trying to shake some life into it. Whatever the case, he was the one to be wary of, she decided, the one to watch.

And watch she did from behind the horses, carefully observing over and over as more and more girls arrived, sometimes alone, more often in groups of two or three. She noted every subtle nuance of how they held their blankets or shawls over their heads and how they walked. Each time, at just the right moment, the girls, whether Indian or Irish or Mexican, lifted their skirts and stuck a bare leg out for the sentries. And each time the bowlegged one shook his own legs and made some jocular ribald comment before he let them pass.

Woman-Who-Dreams saw all of that with the keenness of

a lifetime of observation. As a young girl, she'd been taught by her mother and her grandmother how to watch the sky. Always aware of the weather's mood, her mother and grandmother were never surprised by rain or wind. They noticed other things, as well, the animals, the birds, the insects. They marked the way the grasses grew and how the dust devils turned. It all meant something.

There were three parts to landscape: home, wilderness, and the magical places touched by legend, where one got dreams. It was the same with all knowing. There was language, inner voice, and that silence beyond language where experience could be understood only by myth, story, and symbol. One needed only to observe to know how everything fit into the overall pattern. At least that had been the case until the white man came.

As more and more white men came, Woman-Who-Dreams watched how her people observed this new feature in their landscape and tried to make sense of it. And failed. Unlike the sky, which could manifest itself in endless variations, all of them observable, the white man's ways remained hidden, a mystery, and her people suffered for it. That's why Woman-Who-Dreams began to read newspapers. She was determined she would understand the white man from his own words.

She read, seeking something solid in a world where nothing was safe, not buffalo herds, not even the endless grasses of the prairie itself. Overnight they both disappeared, replaced by the white man's plow and fences. How could her people not be surprised by that, no matter how carefully they observed?

But these soldiers on sentry duty were not hard to understand. She stroked the horses' necks and watched another group of three young women approach, Indian girls, this time, wearing squaw blankets over their heads. Same as the others, they lifted their skirts, giving the sentries an eyeful. Then they entered the camp. Simple. Woman-Who-Dreams knew what she had to do. But could she do it? The girls were young, and they walked with a certain sprightliness that worried her. She didn't know if her old bones had that much bounce left in them.

Again stroking the horses to keep them calm, Woman-Who-Dreams stepped back and sought the shadow behind the nearest building. She practiced. She lengthened her stride, swinging her whole body to give emphasis to her hips. It felt awkward at first, and then a little airy, as if she'd dropped the weight of half her years. She threw back her shoulders and lifted her fanny. By the time she'd paced back and forth a dozen times, working on that walk, she almost hoped those soldiers noticed. Taking one more strut through the darkness, Woman-Who-Dreams pulled a blanket over her head and emerged swinging herself along as jauntily as anyone, she thought.

The horses noticed first. One stomped a foot. The other nickered. That pleased her. Then she got so concentrated on her young walk, she almost forgot to lift her skirts. The bowlegged soldier shouted, "Where do you think you're going?" She remembered and wordlessly pulled up her dress.

She'd walked all her life. She imagined her legs weren't all that bad, especially given the poor light. Besides, she expected those soldiers imagined more than what they could actually see. Still there was a moment of hesitation. It stretched until she almost despaired of her disguise. Then the bowlegged one shook his right leg, as he had with all the girls. He also shook his head. "Hell, I hope your beau ain't expecting much," he called out.

Woman-Who-Dreams dropped her skirt quickly, as if offended, and continued her bouncy, hip-swinging walk. She wasn't going to be stopped now.

"That's all right, honey," the bowlegged one called after her, shaking his left leg. "I'm sure the rest of it is just fine."

By that time, she figured he wasn't going to stop her and so had the nerve to spit in his direction. He liked that. He laughed and whistled. "A little sass is good sauce," he called.

The last laugh was going to be on him, she knew.

Once past the sentries and safely into the shadows of the

camp, Woman-Who-Dreams allowed herself a bit of euphoria, a little thrill that gave a different sort of bounce to her walk. Sitting Bull, who had fancied himself the leader of her people, had been a lot of places, traveling with Buffalo Bill's Wild West Show. She remembered how he bragged to her about all he'd done, including visiting the queen of England. But Sitting Bull had never walked into the heart of his enemy's camp unchallenged the way she just had. She wished he wasn't dead. Then, maybe, she could have bragged to him.

But that was only the beginning. She had work yet to do if she was going to accomplish her purpose. Staying alert and keeping to the shadows, Woman-Who-Dreams made her way to the heart of army camp. Pausing near the mess tent, she looked around once, taking in the rows and rows of white tents, the livestock enclosure, wagons, and hastily anchored stockade all outlined in the newly risen moon. It was quiet, except for the usual night noises, and still. She saw little movement anywhere. A couple of the girls who'd slipped into camp earlier now slipped between tents. A soldier stumbled on his way to the latrine.

Feeling sure she hadn't been seen, Woman-Who-Dreams stooped and scooted under the wagon closest to the mess tent. There, sitting in the darkness, she opened her knapsack and pulled out seven carefully twisted bundles of grass. Untying them, she spread the grasses around her: needle grass, bluegrass, cheat grass, creeping salt grass, buffalo grass, yellow bunch, and short grass. She noted from the feel which was which and arranged them in a preplanned order.

Sitting Bull had liked to tease her about her newspaper reading. He used to brag that he could shoot and ride and lead men into battle—important things no one learned from newspapers. Shooting and riding and leading warriors had gotten him killed. But he was right. Most of what was important never got written down. What she knew about fires, for example.

She had a lifetime knowledge of fires, having built and tended one or more almost every day of her adult life. One kind of fire for smoking buffalo, another for cooking deer, or fish, or the fat tail of a beaver so it would crisp just right. One kind of fire for warming in winter, another for displacing the chill of spring. There were fires that drew spirits and fires that portended a change in the weather. Woman-Who-Dreams moved her hands over her grasses, selecting first a handful of one and then a handful of another. Blending them together, she wove them into little bundles capable of holding a smoldering fire and then letting it flare.

On the other side of town, Kate slept fitfully, waking often, startled by the last vivid images of her dreams.

She was climbing stairs, not many, only six wooden stairs to a hangman's noose. It swayed gently in the breeze like a child's tree swing. Children were singing:
Ring around the rosy,
Pocket full of posy . . .
They circled, dancing around the gallows, spreading spring flowers that turned to ashes as they hit the ground.
Ashes, ashes,
They all fall down.
The children's cheery voices finished the verse. They sang as if they couldn't see what was happening. Kate tried to scream at them to stop singing and look, but she had no voice.

She woke. She listened to the church bells mark the hour, then the half hour. She worried that Nock might be right. Then exhaustion overtook and she slept again.

She was wearing a ghost shirt and leather leggings. A quilled pouch dangled at her waist. She'd become Indian. Hadn't she been warned about becoming too Indian?
She began tearing at the ghost shirt. It wouldn't come off. She pulled at the painted birds on the shirt. They fell at her feet like blue leaves. The painted moon and stars fell to the ground and lay there like a young girl's game of ball and jacks. But the shirt wouldn't come off.
She heard Homer barking. He was barking and barking. She spun around, looking for her dog. Some soldiers were

277

holding him, but he got bigger and bigger, growing a hump where his hair was thickest across his shoulders until he couldn't be held anymore.

He charged her like a red buffalo, snorting and stomping and barking . . .

She started awake again. Homer was barking. She sat bolt upright. For a moment, she couldn't remember where she was. A breeze was blowing over her from an open window. The curtains rippled in the dim light making strange shadows. She remembered where she was the same instant she knew she hadn't left the window open, and someone was in the room with her.

Now someone else pounded on the wall behind her and yelled, "Shut up that racket in there."

Kate felt in the dark for Nock's gun. She couldn't find it. Then she knocked it off the nightstand. It hit the floor with a thud. The someone who was in the room with her whimpered a surprised noise. Now what? Kate wondered, as she freed her feet from the bedcovers and slid out, reaching for the gun, feeling along the floor for it fruitlessly.

She flashed to her dreams, the noose, the stairs, the children singing. She wanted to believe she was dreaming again and that the shadow near the window that was moving slowly forward would shift to some other form. She wanted to wake up to the sound of church bells, nothing more.

"Who's there?" she asked.

From the other side of the wall the voice shouted again, "Shut up your damned dog."

She wasn't dreaming. Now Homer jumped onto the bed beside her and crouched between her and the shadow. If she could just find the gun . . .

Then someone pounded on the door. "What's going on in there?"

The shadow, now at the end of her bed, jumped and whimpered again. Only this time there was something about the whimper that seemed familiar.

"Mary?" Kate whispered, her hand no longer feeling for the gun. Straightening, she felt instead for Homer, holding him. "What are you doing here?" she asked.

The person at the door was pounding again. She could hear him trying the door. It was locked. Kate glanced toward the open window. Her room was three stories up. How had Mary gotten in? Homer was still barking. He was making enough noise so she was having trouble thinking. This didn't make sense. Again she half expected everything to shift as in a dream. Mary would become her mother sneaking through the house late at night. The barking would become her mother's drunken laughter. Instinctively, Kate drew back as if to make herself small and invisible. She didn't want to be jerked out of her sleep and swung by her arms, her mother twirling her round and round the room singing, "Ring around the rosy."

Kate shook herself. That hadn't been a dream, either.

"Mary?" she whispered again, and jerking Homer's collar, she finally quieted him. At that the girl, still no more than a shadow, stepped forward and thrust something into Kate's arms. Her camera.

"You nice Christian lady. You save me. I save your camera."

With no more explanation than that, she slipped away moving toward the window. Kate followed. "Wait," she called. She had questions, lots more that she wanted to know. Too late. Kate made it to the window only in time to see the girl skinny along the narrow ledge and out of reach.

More pounding on the door behind her. "What's going on in there?"

Then a new voice, "I'm the hotel manager. Let me in, or I'll use my key." She knew who he was. He'd been working the desk when she checked in. As manager, he occupied living quarters on the first floor. No doubt, somebody had awakened him.

Kate found her voice. "Everything's fine." But then Homer started barking again, and there was more noise at the door, someone fumbling with a key. "Wait," Kate called again to Mary. A moment later the door flew open, and the lights came on. "Wait," Kate called one more time only to see the girl jump to a nearby rooftop and disappear.

Kate turned to find that five men had burst into her room. They were now standing around staring at the ceiling and the floor, embarrassed at her state of undress. She grabbed the bed covering and wrapped it around herself. At that, Homer jumped off the bed and went to the window. The hotel manager came forward, and grabbing her dog by his collar, he started dragging him out. Clutching the bed covering to her shoulders, Kate protested, "Let him go. He'll be quiet now."

"I told you if he caused trouble, he'd be out."

"But there was someone in my room. My serving girl. She left out the window."

She could see disbelief in his face, and she had to admit it didn't sound likely. "There's a ledge or something out there," Kate tried to explain, and beckoned him to the open window to look.

The hotel manager glanced at the other men. "I'm sorry, but this hotel can't tolerate this kind of disturbance."

Kate shook her head. "She brought me my camera. I didn't have it when I checked in. Don't you remember? I didn't have anything." She went to the bed and picked up her beloved Scoville. That's when the reality of having her camera once more in her hands hit her with such a flood of feeling, she was left speechless. She glanced toward the window, marveling that Mary would have risked life and limb to return it—little Mary, who was normally so fearful, she jumped at her own shadow.

Meanwhile, a smile had crept across the hotel manager's face. All the men were amused, Kate could see. She imagined how it must sound, the idea of an Indian girl climbing in a three-story window to return a lady's camera. A child could make up a better tale.

The hotel manager sobered and said, "The dog has to go."

"No," Kate said. "You can't expect me to stay here alone. Who knows what else might come through that window."

"You mean, fly through that window?" one of the other

men said with jest in his voice. Then they all laughed, the situation having gotten the best of their politeness. She'd embarrassed them, she realized. They were grown-up men who didn't want to have to entertain her crazy story or anything like it, not in each others' company.

On her wedding night, Homer had crashed through a closed window, breaking the glass and tearing his shoulder open in a long gash just to be with her. To her new husband's chagrin, he'd had to fetch the doctor and wake the pharmacist, both of whom had been at the wedding and found Bill's situation amusing. That story, at least, had made good barroom talk. Not this.

"I'm sorry, Mrs. Burke," the hotel manager was saying again. "I can understand your agitated state, but this has gone too far." He again pulled her dog in the direction of the door. The other men bobbed their heads in obvious agreement.

That's when Richard suddenly pushed past the others and, entering the room, asked if Kate was all right.

She was so startled, she couldn't answer.

The hotel manager laughed. "The lady had a bad dream, that's all."

Next instant, Richard had the manager shoved against a wall. "And that made her dog bark?" he asked. "Since when does a nightmare set a dog to barking?"

In that excitement, Homer got free. He bounded onto the bed next to Kate. Licking her face made it hard for her to keep the bed covering wrapped about her, but she didn't care.

"What kind of a hotel are you running where a lady isn't safe in her own room without a dog?" Richard wanted to know.

The hotel manager didn't answer that. Instead, he got his footing and shoved Richard off. Then, taking a fighting stance, he raised his fists. Richard took his own wide stance, bringing his arms up. They were going to slug each other, Kate thought with alarm.

At that moment, someone else came running down the hall, shouting and pounding on doors. "Indians, Indians,

Indians," went the alarm. "Indians have attacked the city. The whole army camp is on fire."

Hearing that, the hotel manager disengaged from Richard and went to the window. He pushed it open wider, and at that instant, the whole city erupted in sound. A fire wagon clanged. Church bells stopped marking the hour and started marking the emergency. There were shouts and confusion.

Far more interested in this new diversion than her domestic drama, the men shoved each other trying to be the first out the door, all except for the hotel manager and Richard. They eyed one another for a long moment. Then the hotel manager pointed his finger at Homer. "I want that dog and both of you out of this hotel first thing in the morning."

"You didn't need to ask," Richard returned.

When the hotel manager was gone, Richard went to the window and shut it, muffling the outside sounds. Not that it helped. The hotel had erupted in a pandemonium of its own—doors slamming, people running up and down the halls, shouting the news, repeating it.

Kate dropped the bed covering and started putting on her clothes. "What are you doing here?" she asked. "You get kicked out of your boardinghouse or something?"

"That's gratitude. I took a room so I could be nearby. Only that damned hotel manager wouldn't give me a room on the same floor. If your dog had any less bark . . ."

"You took a room to be nearby?" Kate asked turning to face him. "Why?" With a little shiver, she wondered if, like Nock, he thought she was in real danger. She noted the gun on the floor just under the edge of the bed.

"I was worried about you."

"Why?"

"Why?" he echoed. "In case you hadn't noticed, there's a lot going on—Indians, a murder."

She stooped and pulled on the last of her petticoats, picking up the gun at the same time and secreting it under her skirt at her waist. "You're right. Thank you," she said. "But as you can see, I'm fine." She tucked her shirtwaist in and tied her sash over the bulge the gun made. She ran her fingers through her hair and checked it in the mirror.

"You really don't get it, do you?"

"Get what?"

"Where I come from women scheme to find a man who'll worry about them. Their mothers help them scheme for that. When it happens, it's thought to be romantic."

She paused and looked at him. He was a little disheveled, having obviously dressed in haste. A part of her wanted to tuck his shirt and straighten his collar, maybe fold herself into his arms and feel safe. Another part of her knew better. Even if he loved her, his arms were false security. Real safety was in figuring out what was going on. "I said, 'thank you,'" she told him. Picking up her cape, she pulled it around her shoulders.

"Where are you going?" he asked.

"There are no Indians," she told him. "You saw. They were packing and leaving as fast as they could. Whatever is going on around here is not an Indian attack, and I intend to find out what it is."

"Kate, that's stupid and probably dangerous."

She called for Homer and opened the door.

He grabbed her arm. "Is it so terrible that I care about you and want you safe?"

She groaned. "I'm truly sorry, but I won't be caged by your concern."

With that, she shook off his arm and continued into the hall with such a determined stride, she bumped into another gentleman and sent him reeling back two steps. He was an older man with a full head of hair and matching beard. He glanced from Kate to Richard as she mumbled, "I'm sorry." However, he chose to comment only on the dog. "That the source of all the barking?" he asked.

"Sorry if he disturbed you," Kate answered.

"Doesn't matter. We were destined to be disturbed tonight anyway. You going to the excitement?"

"On my way."

"That a girl," he said, and poked out his arm for her.

283

"Most of this hotel has emptied already. People enjoy going to a fire. I know, I do."

She shot a glance back at Richard.

So did the older man. "Your friend can come, too," he said.

Kate made no comment. She curtsied and took the man's arm as if she were going to nothing more out of the ordinary than a country dance.

Richard caught up at the elevator saying, "I think I will tag along, if no one minds."

"My pleasure," the older gentleman said.

Kate merely nodded.

Fortunately, the older gentleman liked to talk. His name was Peter Cottle; Musical Pete to his friends, he told Kate, and laughed. "I can't play a note. Can't sing, either." He laughed some more. His laugh was infectious. She smiled in spite of herself. Richard didn't.

"I sell parlor organs and pianos," Musical Pete continued. "Done it for forty-five years. I've personally sold more fine musical instruments for home entertainment than Sears and Roebuck's catalog." He dropped his voice to a hush. "Although I'm thinking of retiring soon, or I may not be able to continue that brag." He winked at her, then held open the front door of the hotel.

"You play a little parlor piano?" he asked when they were outside.

She shook her head. Then she mentioned her grandmother's stage career as a singer. His eyes widened. "You're from a theatrical family," he said with such enthusiasm, it was as if he equated that with royalty.

She shrugged, having never thought it worth any brag before now.

The three of them caught the trolley. It was full of curiosity seekers. She and Musical Pete and Richard had to catch the outside and hang on like schoolboys. Homer ran along beside.

As they rode, Musical Pete told her about several fires he'd seen. He had a deep, mellow voice and laughed so easily, she couldn't help being amused. "I never miss a fire," he concluded. "I wouldn't miss a fire even if I was in the middle of a lover's quarrel." At that he gave her the elbow.

Kate imagined that was how it looked between her and Richard. But was it? Musical Pete paused. It was the only silence he'd allowed. He was expecting some kind of response, some explanation, she realized, but she didn't know what to say. She had no idea what Richard expected of her. He was the "love and leave" type. That's why she'd picked him for her fling, her taste of passion. She didn't really want an entanglement any more than she thought he did.

"I'll bet they used to fight over your grandmother," Pete told her.

She nodded. She had heard stories of that sort, exaggerated by booze and thrown up to her mother who had "settled" for her father, or so her grandmother liked to claim. A photographer was not an English lord or rich business tycoon—the kind of men her grandmother was supposed to have entertained before she "came down in the world."

Musical Pete laughed and nudged her elbow again. "I'll bet you take after your grandmother. I'll bet beauty runs in your family. Am I right? Huh?"

Kate shrugged again and looked over at Richard. He returned her look and rolled his eyes. She had to agree. Jolly as he was, Musical Pete could be annoying.

The end of the trolley line was chaos. Shouts. Confusion. The smell of smoke everywhere. People were running in every direction. Yet nobody knew where the fire was. Some said it was on the west side of army camp. Others said the east side. Some were running toward the army camp, wanting to see the excitement. Others were running away, yelling for everyone to "take cover," it was an Indian attack, and there was no telling when the "murdering savages" might strike again. As if to confirm the worst of that rumor, mounted soldiers were taking up positions on many of the main street corners, their guns drawn.

Undaunted, Kate made her way through the crowd always moving in the direction of the army camp. She and Richard got separated from Musical Pete. Then she almost lost

Richard in the general hubbub. He caught up, and taking her arm, he insisted that she let him shoulder his way through the crowd for her. She did. In that fashion, they continued to the broad flat area just outside the fairgrounds where the army had set up camp.

By that time, the landscape had begun to be brightened with the coming dawn. Coming upon an abandoned wagon with a broken wheel, Richard helped Kate up onto it. From that heightened vantage point, she looked out over rows of white army tents and saw five columns of smoke rising to the sky. Five fires, she thought. No wonder there was such an excitement. How did five fires get started all at once, all across an army camp full of soldiers? She certainly didn't think a bunch of renegade Indians could have ridden in and done anything like that. She'd seen renegade Indians. No match for well-armed army men, they'd have been cut down in a minute.

Richard climbed up beside her. His only reaction was a soft whistle. "This is more than some soldier being careless with his smokes."

"But it's not an Indian attack," she repeated, and climbed off the wagon to see what Homer had brought her. He'd come from the direction of the camp dragging something.

"Good boy," she cooed. "What have you got?" She stooped to take a blanket from him, government issue. A lump caught in her throat. But then she reminded herself that one squaw blanket looked pretty much like every other squaw blanket. She had no reason to suspect . . .

Before she could finish that thought, Musical Pete found her and Richard. He slapped Richard on the back and elbowed Kate. "You won't believe the rumors going round," he said, shaking his head in an exaggerated motion.

"What rumors?" Kate asked.

"Oh, I'm not sure I want to repeat them. They're just too unbelievable." But then he didn't need any prompting. Shaking his head more, he started in. "Well there's some who want to believe this is the mischief of some soldiers who are owed back pay. Congress hasn't voted enough funds for this uprising business, you know."

"That does make a certain sense, doesn't it?" Kate asked, looking around at Richard.

Musical Pete laughed. "No, ma'am, if you ask me, it makes no sense at all. What soldier would burn down the mess tent? Maybe he'd think about leveling the officers' quarters, but not the source of his next meal. No siree."

He chuckled at his own observation and then elbowed Kate again.

"Of course, there's the rumor that this is an Indian attack. There's even some talk of folks who claim they know folks who say they saw a bunch of Indians dressed up in their finery and wearing war paint. They're supposed to have seen them riding through the streets of town carrying torches. But I haven't found anybody who's actually seen anything like that, just folks who think they know other folks who've seen it."

"It wasn't an Indian attack," Kate answered, and gave another glance to Richard.

This time Musical Pete shrugged. "Maybe, maybe not. I've heard stranger things tonight."

"What?" Richard prompted.

Musical Pete slapped his side. "The wildest rumor would have a person believe this is all the work of one Indian—a tall old squaw that some say they saw the colonel arrest. According to this story, she set all five fires by herself with some kind of slow-burning material. The fires flared up, one right after another, but not until she'd gotten clear of the area. They say she almost got completely away. Supposedly, they caught her right over there." He pointed in the direction Homer had just come.

Kate pulled the squaw blanket to her chest. It was as if she'd been plunged back into her nightmare, tearing at the ghost shirt that wouldn't come off. What was to be believed? Children dancing and singing around a wooden gallows? An old woman who quilled dreams, read newspapers, and set fire to an entire army camp? Unfortunately she knew the answer. She steadied herself on Richard's arm.

"Are you all right?" he asked.

No, she thought, and then *yes.* "It's coup," she said.

287

Musical Pete stopped laughing. "It's what?"

"I know the old woman," Kate said. "She was taking coup, embarrassing an enemy in the heart of his own camp. It's an old Indian tradition."

"You mean you believe some old woman did this?" Richard asked.

Kate bristled. Why not? Half of Crazy Horse's exploits had been turned to jokes. Schoolchildren played games. One pretended to be Crazy Horse and scared the others. They laughed and screamed and ran away. A sudden strength rose up in her. Of course one tall old woman could set a whole army camp into an uproar if that old Indian was Woman-Who-Dreams.

Musical Pete was back to laughing and slapping his side.

Kate didn't have time to explain such that he'd believe. She picked up her skirts and took off in the direction of the army camp.

Richard took off after her. He didn't know what to make of any of this. The briefest hint of Indian trouble was enough to make most women bolt their doors, themselves inside. Not Kate.

He caught up with her. "Now where are you going?"

"The colonel doesn't understand coup," she told him. She was moving with enough stride her skirts slapped. "He only understands killing. He'll kill her."

Richard grabbed her arm, swung her around, and stopped her momentarily. "Even if that's true, what can you do?"

He watched her draw a deep breath. "I don't know. But I have to do something." And with that, she turned and continued on her way.

This was what really exasperated him about her. Whether it was climbing out on a ledge or stomping into an army camp, she never gave a thought to the danger or whether what she was doing worried someone else. Worried him.

Fortunately, she was stopped at the entrance. The soldiers weren't letting anyone through except firefighters and other soldiers. He was relieved and expected that would be the end of it. He'd just gotten a job with a survey team mapping the Colorado River. In a more relaxed moment, he wanted to ask her to go with him.

But she wouldn't give up. She demanded that the sentry take a message to the colonel. "Tell him Kate Burke is waiting to see him. He'll want to see me," she said. Richard didn't understand. Neither did the sentry. He looked her over, shrugged, and decided to deliver the message.

"Just tell me you know what you're doing," Richard demanded.

She only shrugged.

Then before he could get a real answer from her, the sentry returned and announced that the colonel would see her. Richard couldn't believe it. In the middle of a crisis that had enveloped his entire camp and most of the city, Colonel Elliot George was going to take the time to see Kate Burke. Suddenly Richard wanted to know why. And another part of him chilled at the possibilities.

Then there was some confusion. The sentry had orders to admit Kate, not Richard. He wasn't going to allow that. He wasn't going to let her go in there alone. Musical Pete had caught up with them. He protested even more loudly, saying he was the "lady's oldest and dearest friend." It didn't do either of them any good. Richard even tried shoving the sentry aside only to have himself grabbed by two other soldiers. His last appeal was to Kate. "Don't go."

But Kate didn't even look back. He watched as she disappeared into the colonel's tent with her dog. Then the soldiers pushed Richard back several steps until he shook them off.

Inside the colonel's tent, Kate blinked several times trying to adjust to the strange, dim light. The combination of the dawn filtering through the white canvas and the lanterns, still lit, hanging from the tent supports, gave the interior a hazy, unshadowed look such that it was hard for her eyes to define anything but the larger features, the slope of the walls, the slanted roof, the field desk, and folding chairs. The colonel was standing behind that desk dressed in shirtsleeves, his suspenders hanging at his sides. It appeared that, like Richard, he'd dressed in some haste. Unlike Richard, she had no urge to tidy him.

"The mayor and the sheriff are also waiting to see you," his aide said.

"They can wait," the colonel barked.

His aide gave Kate a glance and left.

By that time, Kate had taken in the pile of Indian relics rather haphazardly stacked in one corner. In particular she'd noted Mary's ghost shirt rolled up and thrown on top.

The colonel brought one hand to his hip. "I must say, Mrs. Burke, you do keep surprising me. A proper widow ought to have her mind on her duties to the newly deceased, I should think. Is it too much to ask if you've made any arrangements to leave? Or is Bill expected to bury himself?"

At that, she felt a pang of guilt. It wasn't that she meant to be disrespectful in the handling of her husband's final arrangements. It was just that there was so much going on. Then, before she could find some way to answer, Homer started to whine. She looked around. She couldn't see him at first in that odd dim light. Then she saw that he'd gone around the side of the desk. He was clawing at something— boxes of photographic plates. She recognized them. They were her photographic plates, the ones she thought had been destroyed when her wagon burned.

She looked up at the colonel. He offered no excuse, no explanation. She'd never needed proof, but if she had, this was it: The colonel had murdered Bill. There was no other way to explain his having those boxes. They both knew it. She would have thought a revelation of that enormity would be worth some comment. An anger flared in her. And to think he'd tried to suggest some fault in her for neglecting Bill's burial.

"Did you mean to kill him? Or were you after me?" she asked, because somebody needed to state the obvious.

He actually chuckled.

"Do you think I'd kill Bill with a stove?"

Nock had been right, she thought. Nock was always right.

"Why?" she asked.

The colonel chuckled again. "Guess the local paranoia

got to me or something. I thought you'd seen too much, taken too many pictures." He thumbed in the direction of her photographic boxes. "But there's nothing in there," he said. "A stranger lot of negatives I've never tried to decipher." He shook his head. "Pictures of photographers taking pictures of soldiers, empty ghost dance grounds, abandoned Indian camps. I can't imagine the good of any of them. Who wants to look at stuff like that? Bill was a far more indulgent husband than I ever imagined."

Kate marveled at the man's blindness. In a sense, she'd been taking "coup." She'd followed Bill into the heart of the Seventh Cavalry and taken pictures she expected would more than embarrass some day. But clearly the colonel hadn't understood her "coup" any more than he understood Woman-Who-Dreams'.

"Can I have them back?" she asked.

He gave her one of his not-nice smiles. "Maybe if you give me what I want."

"What do you want?"

"Bill's negative."

Bill's negative, she thought as she struggled to grasp all that was going on here.

"I don't know what you mean."

The colonel shook his head. "I didn't worry about Bill having that picture, even if he was blackmailing me with it. I figured Bill understood how the game was played. But now with him dead, I think I better know where that plate is."

What plate? she wondered. She'd seen all of Bill's pictures, processed them. Or had she?

"Do I understand Bill was blackmailing you?"

"That's what I said."

Kate drew a deep breath. She was having trouble believing this. She could believe Bill had been cheating on the colonel's cut of the photographs sold, but she'd given him credit for a petty thief's sense of what he could get away with and what he couldn't. The colonel was a crook of a whole other league. During her months of traipsing across the prairie following the Seventh Cavalry, she'd seen him divert whole shipments of Indian annuities to his own use, and that was only the thievery that was obvious. She wanted to find Bill and shake him. He had no business blackmailing the likes of the colonel. With that thought came a pang of regret. There was never going to be a way to shake sense into Bill.

Meanwhile another part of her was trying to get a clear focus on how Bill might have been blackmailing the colonel. She knew it was with a plate, a photograph that he must have hidden even from her. But where was it? She didn't know, and not knowing limited her options.

She looked around again, taking in the tent's closeness and the colonel's closeness. She was standing there with nothing but raw courage, and the gun poked into her petticoats. Only the gun was laughable. How was she supposed to get that gun? Reach up under her skirt and sort through her petticoats until she found it? Undo her sash? In the time it took her to do either of those things, he could wrestle her to the ground.

"I want my plates returned and Woman-Who-Dreams released," Kate told him because she'd decided the only bluff worth trying in this situation was a big one. "And I think I'd like Mary's ghost shirt thrown into the bargain." She turned and indicated the pile of relics with the back of her hand.

He came round the desk and grabbed her. The color in his face was like no shade she'd ever seen. That's when she knew he could kill her. Right there. Right then. Interestingly, that knowledge came with no fear, just an expectant anticipation. And her mind, still trying to sort this, suddenly fixed on Bill's mysterious photograph. If she died, her regret was going to be not knowing what was in Bill's picture that was worth blackmail. It had to show more than dead Indians, she decided. She didn't imagine the colonel worried all that much about dead Indians. Meanwhile, her hand groped in the direction of the gun. If she got it twisted around, she could fire it through her skirts.

But before she managed that, her dog grabbed the colonel's leg, sinking his teeth in. The colonel swore, jumped back, and kicked Homer with enough force he almost lost his own balance. Homer rolled across the ground, righted himself, and then crouched, growling.

She moved her hand away from the gun as the colonel's aide returned. He took a moment to size up the situation. Homer had actually drawn blood. The colonel had lifted his foot to the top of the desk and applied a handkerchief to the bite.

The aide cleared this throat. "The mayor and the sheriff insist that their business is urgent." He paused. "Are you all right?"

"Do I look all right?" the colonel snapped back. Then he waved the back of his hand at Kate and her dog. "Get them out of here," he said. "Lock them up until some of this excitement blows over."

The aide nodded. He beckoned for Kate to follow him. She was only too glad.

"But I'm not through with you," the colonel called after her. "Just remember, I'm not through with you."

She had no doubt of that.

The colonel wiped the blood from the cut, swearing under his breath. He wasn't going to forget this. He was never going to forget this.

After stopping the bleeding, he pushed his pant leg down and told his aide to bring in his newest visitors. He was going to be pleased to see them. Even his anger at Kate didn't dampen a certain satisfaction he had in the fact that the mayor, the deputy mayor, and the sheriff had all found it necessary to leave their warm beds at this odd hour and come to him. It proved his point that there was nothing like the fear of Indians to get the army some respect.

The colonel greeted his visitors. He offered them a seat as if their business were no more extraordinary than discussing a couple of rowdy soldiers on a Saturday night. The mayor, a balding dentist who'd turned politician, couldn't take the time to sit down. He started talking immediately, his hands flailing the air, giving emphasis to his words. "I always knew it would lead to trouble. I mean, what did anyone expect bringing Indians right into town for that trial? Of course, there was going to be trouble. But an attack? Right in town?"

"Have you caught them?" the sheriff asked. He was a paunchy man, wearing only his pants and a plaid mackinaw pulled over the top.

The colonel gave a glance to his aide and shook his head. "We were more concerned about securing the citizens of Sioux Falls," he answered. "But you don't need to worry. They've got no place to run except back to the reservation. We'll get them."

The mayor made a broad gesture. "Oh, you're right. Yes, indeed."

The sheriff also nodded to that.

The colonel could hardly keep from smiling. He was truly enjoying these sissified city officials.

Then the deputy mayor, a young lawyer, looked around the tent taking in the pile of relics, and said, "I didn't think the army could order troops into a town unless . . ."

"Unless what?" the colonel cut him off. "Would you have preferred full-scale Indian warfare on Phillips Street before I moved my troops in?"

That got a quick shake of the mayor's head. The sheriff set his jaw.

The deputy mayor ignored the question. He continued, "I was merely suggesting that an official declaration of martial law is usually required before such action."

"This isn't the usual situation," the mayor answered.

"And such a declaration has already been requested from the governor," the colonel added. "Things are in order, I assure you."

Actually to the colonel's way of thinking, things were more than in order. Getting martial law declared was going to be his crowning demonstration of General Miles's softness on Indians. If he and Baldwin, his aide, had ever had any plans for interfering with the trial, they'd have to forget them now or look weak.

As if picking up on his thoughts, the mayor sliced the air with a gesture and declared, "We should stop making treaties, cease putting those redskins on a par with ourselves. We know they are not our equals. What's more, we know we have a God-given right to the soil, as we've proved ourselves capable of the land's improvement. Let's act openly and directly on that faith, I say."

Quite a campaign speech, the colonel thought and then said, "I'm glad we're in agreement."

The sheriff nodded, "Yes, and we're encouraging people to keep off the streets."

This was getting better and better, the colonel thought. City folk peering out windows at empty streets were likely to let their imaginations run wild—wilder than any real Indians.

And surprisingly, that satisfied the city officials. That was their urgent business. When the three of them had taken their leave, the colonel gave his aide a knowing look. Together they chuckled and repeated out loud, "Nothing like the fear of Indians to put the army back in control."

15

Richard Houston pounded on Powers T. Nock's front door. It had been scrubbed, but it still showed signs of red paint and the words *Indian lover* splashed across it. That didn't surprise Richard. He wondered if the layers of paint beneath that graffiti might not harbor other such epitaphs. Nock was a man who generated considerable animosity among the local citizenry, he knew. He'd heard him described in worse terms than Indian lover at some of the local bars. But to his credit, the man knew the law, which was what brought Richard to his door at this early hour.

He pounded again, hard enough to rattle the window. Nock had to be up. Given the general excitement, the whole town was up. Richard pounded again, and the door opened slowly about six inches. An older woman peered through the crack. "What do you want?"

"I need to see Mr. Nock on business, legal business," Richard told her.

"This is a strange time of day to need lawyering," she returned.

"This won't wait. A woman is in trouble. Maybe you know her—Mrs. Burke."

The door swung wide to reveal a short, matronly woman wearing a dressing coat clutched tightly to her neck. "That newly widowed Mrs. Burke? The one who takes pictures and has a big dog?"

Richard nodded.

"Wipe your feet first," she told him pointing to the mat just outside the door. "The carpet is genuine Turkish. My husband, God rest him, bought it special for me."

"Oh," Richard said, and then made an exaggerated show of rubbing his shoes across the mat.

Traversing the parlor, the woman turned friendly. "I never met Mrs. Burke myself," she volunteered. "It's my son. He's taken quite a real fancy to her. But I already told him that I'm not going to live with her big dog."

Richard was so taken aback by that, he stopped in his tracks. He glanced around the woman's parlor, taking in not only the richly patterned Turkish rug but the dark wooden cabinets, overstuffed divan, fancy French pier mirror, and ornamental wall pockets. These were not the sort of surroundings that fit Kate, he thought.

"This way," Mrs. Nock prompted, having noted his hesitation.

"Oh yes, of course," Richard said, coming to himself. He followed her down a short hall and into a room lined with clocks, all of them ticking.

"You can see why he didn't hear you pounding on the front door. He doesn't hear anyone, no matter how loud they are," Mrs. Nock chatted on as her son, the lawyer, looked up from the papers he was working on. "You got a guest," she announced. "Says he needs a lawyer. You're going to find the reason real interesting."

Nock stood and nearly knocked over his chair. Then it was as if he didn't know what to do with his hands until leaning across the desk, he extended one to Richard.

Richard took it and shook it and then, looking around at all the clocks, he couldn't help asking, "How do you work with all this noise?"

"Oh, it's good noise, steady, rhythmical. It keeps me from

hearing much else that might distract. I almost missed the fire bells last night."

Richard made a complete turn checking all four walls. There had to be upwards of thirty clocks in the room. There were some citizens of Sioux Falls who considered Nock a little crazy. He could see why.

"My mother says you need a lawyer," Nock began.

Richard turned his attention back to Nock. "Yes, in fact it has to do with last night's excitement. You see a friend of mine got locked up in the army's stockade, and I'm thinking the colonel can't do that to an ordinary citizen, can he?"

"Not unless he gets martial law declared. What did your friend do?"

"Nothing. Nothing that I know of. She's a bit impetuous is all. She marched into his tent looking for that squaw they say set those fires. Next thing I saw two soldiers marching her off to the stockade."

"She? Who is your friend?"

"Kate Burke."

Richard had played this coyly hoping to get the maximum reaction. He wasn't disappointed. He gave a glance over his shoulder. Nock's mother was gone, but his mother was right. Richard couldn't believe it. Never would it have occurred to him that this clever little manipulator of courtroom facts might entertain a fancy for Kate Burke.

But by that time, Nock had already pulled a jacket off the back of his chair and was putting it on. "You were with her when this happened?"

"Yes, I took a room at the same hotel. I've been looking after her since her husband's accident," Richard added because he couldn't resist adding that information.

Nock gave him an assessing look. "If you don't mind my saying so, you didn't do a very good job of it."

"I suppose you think you could have done better."

"I might."

Richard couldn't believe the audacity of Nock. If the clocks weren't crazy, this was. There was no way he could seriously think he had a chance with a woman like Kate.

"I think you should know I'm asking her to go with me on a survey job down the Colorado River."

Nock picked up his hat and laughed out loud. "You're going to have to be more imaginative than that."

"What do you mean? That's exactly the kind of adventure she loves."

"Yes, but how is it better than the deal she struck with Bill?"

"I'm not Bill."

"Oh, yeah, that's right. I hear the ladies are supposed to find you handsome and charming. But Kate's no ordinary lady. You're going to need more than a pretty face and a river trip."

Richard felt himself flush. "Yeah, well, maybe you're familiar with the expression 'a face only a mother could love.'"

Nock took on some warmth at that comment. The two of them were suddenly eyeball to eyeball, breathing heavily. They stood like that for a moment, the clocks ticking while they took each other's measure.

Nothing to fear, Richard thought as he considered Nock's size and book-worn reflexes. He could have the man down and pinned in two moves. But he needed him. Straightening, Richard apologized. "Sorry. I think we should think of Kate."

"I always do," Nock said.

"Oh, me too," Richard had to add.

Meanwhile the colonel was entertaining another guest, Baldwin. The general's aide, wearing a uniform so clean and pressed it couldn't have seen more action than the gentle horse ride out of town, ducked through the entrance to the colonel's tent. Then, noting the pile of relics, he stopped to finger a buffalo hide, but offered no comment on it.

The colonel was pleased to see him. He thought it was about time the quiet, aloof aide to General Miles deigned to come out to army camp. From all appearances, the man had more interest in opera than soldiers.

The colonel outranked Baldwin, but little in the man's demeanor indicated more than a passing acknowledgment of that fact, something that was more than clear as they dispensed with the customary greetings and preliminary military niceties. Baldwin took a seat and crossed his legs, an action the colonel considered prissy in a man. But he didn't let that bother. He was feeling too self-satisfied.

Nothing like a little fear of Indians to get everyone's attention, he thought, even General Miles's attention.

He sat back. He couldn't wait to hear what Baldwin had to say.

Baldwin scratched behind his ear, looked around again, and asked, "Where are the Indians?"

"The Indians?"

"Yeah, the ones who supposedly caused all this havoc. I haven't seen any."

"That's the point. I've secured the town."

"No, that's the problem," Baldwin told him. "You have soldiers on every main street, but you don't have a declaration of martial law."

"I've requested it."

"And you're not going to get it. Upon getting your request, the governor checked with the general, who checked with me. I told him I hadn't seen any Indians on the warpath since this whole thing began."

The colonel gave a glance to his own aide. He couldn't believe what he was hearing. Maybe the general thought he could go soft on Indians, but that stance was political suicide for any governor in this state.

"I'm afraid you've overstepped yourself this time," Baldwin continued. "You can manufacture war parties and invent battles all you want while you're out on the prairie. Who's going to know the difference? But in town? Let's face it, in town you might be able to throw people into a momentary panic, but if nobody sees any Indians, pretty soon someone is bound to ask why. That's likely to be followed by some other interesting questions. The general and the governor have decided they'd just as soon not have to answer some of those other questions."

Jerrie Hurd

"You can't be serious," the colonel said, leaning across the desk. "I had the mayor himself in here earlier. He was clamoring for protection. The sheriff was with him."

"Protection from what?" Baldwin asked, and stood. "They're going to figure it out. Better for you to pull your soldiers back now and admit it was all a false alarm."

Turning to leave, he again fingered the buffalo hide. "I assume you came by all this honestly."

"Of course," the colonel responded, thinking Baldwin ought not to be so smug. If he wanted Indians, the colonel knew more than a few white ranchers who'd be more than happy to dress the part, especially if it discredited the tribes and served to get the reservation broken up and sold off.

"And what's with the boxes of photographic plates?" Baldwin asked.

"Documentary shots."

"Yours also?"

"Yes."

Nock took in the scene outside army camp with bewildered amazement. He'd never been one to chase fires, even as a boy. In fact he didn't willingly engage in any event that involved more human bustle than his mother's church suppers. This was distinctly different. *Uproar* was the word that came to his mind. It left him wondering at the chaos that must have marked the actual fires. Fortunately, Richard took over and cut through all that activity with a directness Nock noted with some appreciation.

During the excitement last night, he'd gone downtown and stood around sampling the rumors. Then, having pieced together most of what was going on and figuring it wouldn't affect the trial, at least not in any positive sense, he'd retired to his study and his books. He hadn't known Kate was in danger. He thought he'd warned her.

Now the lingering smoke was enough to make his eyes water. He stumbled on the uneven ground. Looking up, his attention took a focus. He'd spotted Baldwin. He was on his way out of the camp mounted on a gray gelding with a combed tail. Nock paused while his mind played with the

301

possibilities. What did Baldwin's coming to army camp mean?

He had to have seen the colonel. Nock couldn't think of any other reason for him to be here at this particular moment. But what had the colonel and Baldwin talked about? He wished he could have been a fly on the wall during that conversation. But, in a sense, he thought he knew. Deep in his being the clock of the universe ticked one almost audible tock. Something had changed. Nock was sure of it. Some shift in the balance. That was good, he sensed, but not necessarily good for Kate. It could be extraordinarily dangerous to be in the way when fortune took a cartwheel.

Noting Nock's hesitation, Richard turned and gave him a look of perturbed impatience. They hadn't exchanged much more than looks of varying irritation since leaving the house. Nock trotted a few steps and caught up.

Ten minutes later, the two of them were face-to-face with the colonel. Up to that point, Nock had been under the impression that Richard had come to him so he could do the talking. That's what lawyers did—they spoke for their clients. That wasn't how it happened.

Dispensing with any niceties, Richard squared himself across the desk from the colonel and immediately blurted out, "You can't hold Kate Burke. It's illegal, and I've brought her lawyer to prove it." Then he shoved Nock forward.

Nock had no idea how to follow that up. He'd planned to try something a little less direct, like exploring why the colonel had arrested Kate in the first place. Then he was going to ease around to the idea that arresting her might not be a judicious action, suggesting that it might not be legal, and that if it wasn't legal, keeping her locked up might mean more trouble than it was worth. It was Nock's experience that nobody really wanted trouble, and winding around to the truth allowed for a gracious shift in the other person's position. It was a strategy that almost never failed. But Richard had ruined it in his first sentence.

The colonel spoke two words: "Posse Comitatus." Then

he chuckled and added, "I've read a couple of law books myself."

"What's Posse Coma—whatever," Richard asked.

"Posse Comitatus," the colonel repeated. "Ask your lawyer."

Nock cleared his throat and tried to think of some way out of this. "I'm not sure the law will recognize a temporary camp as being the same as a bona fide military base," he offered, knowing Posse Comitatus applied only to military bases. That was weak, he knew, but it was all he could come up with.

The colonel shrugged. "Challenge it in court."

That would take far too long. The colonel and Nock both knew that. It's what made the colonel so smug. In a game of chess, this would be check. Not checkmate, necessarily, but definitely check. That hardly mattered. Time was on the colonel's side, as Nock had already figured out that there was no quick legal way out of this.

"What's Posse Comitatus?" Richard asked again.

Nock drew breath. "It's Latin for 'power of the country.' More technically, it's Section 1385 of Title Eighteen of the United States Code. Briefly stated, it allows military personnel to detain, question, and even charge civilians who commit crimes on a military base."

"But Kate didn't do anything. What crime did she commit?"

Reckless endangerment was what came to Nock's mind. Her own endangerment. Kate never knew when to hold back. The Shakespearean expression "The better part of valor is discretion" obviously hadn't been included in her education. Or her personality.

Trespassing was the fault the colonel named. "She was arrested for trespassing," he reiterated.

"Trespassing?" Richard returned with incredulity. "When does trespassing get you thrown in the stockade?"

This wasn't getting anywhere, Nock knew. He elbowed Richard trying to get him to shut up. Richard didn't take the hint. "I don't think you understand who you're dealing with. My father—"

"What my friend means," Nock interrupted, "is that we expect Mrs. Burke will be well treated while in your custody." The last thing Nock wanted was to make the colonel more nervous, especially if he was already feeling pressure from Baldwin. If the man got desperate enough, there was no telling what he might do.

The colonel pounded the desktop. "I dare say I know more about taking care of Mrs. Burke than either of you. I spent all winter looking after that woman."

"Oh yes," Nock said, nodding vigorously. "I've heard Mrs. Burke speak highly of her adventures out on the prairie chasing Indians with the brave men of the Seventh Cavalry."

The colonel was taken back by that.

Good time to go, Nock decided. He thanked the colonel and practically shoved Richard backward out the entrance.

Once outside, Richard turned on Nock. "That was a fine piece of bootlicking. But it didn't get us anywhere, did it?"

"Yeah, and bringing Daddy in was going to be better?" Nock returned.

"My father happens to know everybody who is anybody. A couple of telegrams, and I'll have Kate out of this. You watch. You just have to know who to talk to."

"Fine. Send your telegrams," Nock told him. They both knew that if Richard really believed that would work, he'd have done it instead of rousing Nock for this bit of early morning exercise.

But Richard wouldn't admit it. He huffed, "I suppose you have something else in mind?"

Nock shrugged. "We could break her out of the stockade."

"Break her out of the stockade?" Richard repeated.

Nock nodded.

Richard exploded a laugh. "Oh, that's rich. You're going to stage a jailbreak in broad daylight in the middle of an army camp. Then what? You and Kate off on the lam? This whole thing with you and Kate is such a fantasy."

When Richard was gone, Nock paused to survey the camp and its continuing hubbub. Normally he would have been only to happy to let someone else solve the problem by bringing influence to bear. But there wasn't time. He sensed the pendulum had already swung, and he needed to get Kate out of the colonel's clutches now because he had no idea what was coming next. Fortunately, he was pretty sure he knew how to do it.

16

Kate paced the stockade she shared with her dog and Woman-Who-Dreams. For the umpteenth time, she turned and marked the same five steps, running her hand along the bars, feeling the metallic coolness across her fingers. The army's stockade, like everything else in their temporary camp, was mobile, essentially a cage mounted on a wagon with canvas stretched over the top and sides that could be rolled up or down depending on the weather. At present, two sides had been rolled up letting in the morning sunshine and a slight breeze. The breeze flapped the canvas. It snapped against the bars, punctuating the creak of the wagon as it rocked under Kate's nervous energy.

By contrast, Woman-Who-Dreams sat almost trancelike on a couple of rolled-up mattresses next to the chamber pot. Homer lay next to her, his head in her lap, his eyes following Kate, back and forth, back and forth. Kate paused, thinking Homer's eyeballs needed a rest. But standing still drove her crazy. She couldn't imagine trying to sit still. Woman-Who-Dreams had barely moved in the last hour. Kate had paused once just to check whether or not she was breathing. At least she was keeping Homer calm, Kate thought. The woman had a way with animals. That was sure.

When Kate was first thrown into this barred box, Woman-Who-Dreams had jumped to her feet and exclaimed, "No, this is wrong." Then she'd followed Kate's explanation of how she'd gotten herself into this situation with obvious interest, but offered little comment except to repeat like a refrain, "No, this is wrong," at every pause in Kate's narrative.

"I know this is wrong," Kate had responded with exasperation at one juncture. "That's why I wasn't going to let him arrest you."

Woman-Who-Dreams thought about that. Then she said, "I had to find good grasses, not too dry, not too wet. And just the right kind of grasses. I worked carefully and . . ."

Kate started pacing. She got the point without having to listen to the whole story. Woman-Who-Dreams thought she'd acted rashly. Maybe she had, but she wasn't going to admit that.

"Yeah, and what did you and your grasses accomplish," Kate returned when the older woman paused. "The colonel has everybody believing Indians attacked Sioux Falls. He's got his soldiers on every street corner."

Woman-Who-Dreams hadn't responded to that. She'd simply sat on the mattresses and let her gaze take a far-off look. Now Kate was to the point where she couldn't take that quiet anymore. What if she was rash? If she hadn't learned fearlessness, she might never have survived her mother's rage. Or her family's muffled response. Kate had felt as though she were caught in a silent scream, forced to watch the disintegration of her family, without words to express what she was seeing, and with no one who would speak of it anyway. As a result, she'd come to hate being in the presence of anyone who wouldn't talk to her.

Kate paced one more time, turned, and stomped her foot with enough force to rattle the stockade door. "Taking coup was stupid. Did you really think you'd get satisfaction from setting a few fires? You had to know you'd be caught."

Woman-Who-Dreams roused herself slowly. "Understanding sleeps deep," she said. "We think we know something from what we see. It looks close and clear. We think we have it. But then things shift. That's how it is in Coyote's world. Sometimes the change is slow. We hardly notice. Sometimes it is swift. We are swept up, helpless against it."

"What's that supposed to mean?" Kate asked with a tone of exasperation.

"It means my fires stirred things. I was Coyote for a while."

Kate thought a moment. That much was true. Woman-Who-Dreams had stirred things. Kate turned and looking out over the army camp. She thought of the porcupine hunt and how the quillworkers had poked the animal, letting it show its life, letting it rage against the inevitable. Woman-Who-Dreams had shown her spirit last night. Kate would give her that.

"I expected to be caught," Woman-Who-Dreams continued. "I didn't expect you would be caught. That's what's wrong. I didn't speak the truth earlier when you found me out on the prairie. I still believe the dream, the one about the red-haired woman with the red dog. You must get away from here. For me, it does not matter. I am old."

"I have a gun hidden under my skirt," Kate told her.

At that, the older woman glanced around.

Kate had made the same assessment. There was one guard, a young, round-faced soldier who sat with his rifle across his knees while he played Lonesome with a deck of dog-eared cards. He'd spread his game across an upended supply box and was so intent upon it, he rarely looked up. But beyond him, there was a whole camp of soldiers. One gun wasn't going to get her or Woman-Who-Dreams out of their present predicament.

Woman-Who-Dreams obviously came to the same conclusion. She shook her head. "There's really nothing to this life but a beautiful, strange foolishness," she said. "It's Coyote's world—the trickster's world. He made it, and nothing in it can be trusted, especially a gun."

She was right about that, Kate decided.

* * *

Later when the sun got high, the stockade got warm. The canvas covering offered only partial shade. Kate opened the neck of her dress and leaned her back against the bars. She'd about worn herself out pacing that cage. She felt the weariness in her knees. Woman-Who-Dreams and Homer had gone to sleep. She wished she could do the same, but sleep never came easily to her. Then out the corner of her eye, she caught something and straightened.

Mrs. Donning, sitting atop her horse, had just jumped the fence. She was riding across the compound at a full gallop. More, she'd worked herself up and was now standing on the back of her horse. Then, as she swooped past the stockade, she swung herself down, her feet touching the ground briefly as she flipped herself over the back of the horse and came down on the opposite side, her feet again touching the ground as she pushed off into another flip over the horse. The amazing thing was that while flipping from side to side like that, she'd also managed to snatch the guard's hat as she rode by.

He jumped to his feet and grabbed his rifle. Obviously confused, he was unable to take aim. Instead he stood there, rubbing the back of his head as he watched Mrs. Donning ride round and round. Kate nudged Woman-Who-Dreams awake. Homer came to attention.

Mrs. Donning, now wearing the guard's hat, was drawing a crowd. The guard shouted at her. He advanced several more steps, approaching the open space she was circling as if it were an arena. No one paid him any mind.

In the midst of that excitement, Powers Nock suddenly popped up from under the stockade wagon and slid the keys across the floor. They came to rest at Kate's feet. Then he ducked out of sight again. Kate had been watching Mrs. Donning and was so startled to see Nock and the keys, she had to think a moment about what to do. Then, watching the guard who was watching Mrs. Donning, Kate bent and picked up the keys. She moved to the door and carefully worked the lock. Woman-Who-Dreams got to her feet. Kate grabbed Homer's collar. Giving a quick glance all around, she was about to open the door when the guard remembered his game. He returned to the upended box and gathered his cards. He stuffed them in one of his pockets and glanced in the direction of the stockade. Kate dropped to one knee and petted her dog, hardly drawing a breath. The keys still dangled from the stockade door.

A soldier called to the guard. "What is going on?"

"Damned if I know," the guard answered, "but that's my hat that woman trick rider's wearing." Then, giving one more glance in the direction of the stockade, he joined his friend at the edge of the crowd. Mrs. Donning was giving quite a show.

Kate waited. When the moment was right, she gently pushed the door open and guided her dog out. Woman-Who-Dreams followed. Mrs. Donning was getting cheers and applause.

Outside, Nock soundlessly directed them to a milk wagon, the kind that made door-to-door deliveries. It was boxy and white with the name of the dairy stenciled on the side panels. Two horses, a black and a gray, stood in the harness.

Inside the wagon, Nock spoke his first whispered words. "Meet Harry," he said, and indicated the driver, a kindly looking man with rounded cheeks and jowly chins.

Harry nodded to his passengers and then flicked the reins over his horses. The wagon jerked into motion. Kate had to brace herself between a couple of milk cans to keep her balance. Woman-Who-Dreams sat down hard on a block of ice. Nock helped her to a better seat while he explained, "Harry's my mother's friend. He regularly delivers milk to the camp." With that, he braced himself against the wagon's motion and looked away, as if that were all the explanation his rather extraordinary stunt required.

Kate didn't know what to say either. She'd never been rescued like this before. She'd decided to grovel if she had to. Next time she was face-to-face with the colonel, she'd planned to beg him to let her take Bill East for burial, promising him anything. She liked this better, even if a somewhat sour-smelling milk wagon wasn't exactly her notion of being carried off on the proverbial white horse by the fairy-tale prince. In fact, she couldn't think of a less likely crew of jailbreakers than Nock and Harry and Mrs. Donning. But they were wonderful.

Then she remembered her plates. "The colonel has my pictures, all the photographs I took when I was out on the prairie with Bill following the Indians," she tried to explain all in one breath. "They're in his tent. I can't leave without them."

Nock gave her an odd look. "We need to get you to safety," he told her. "Photographic plates can be replaced."

"Not these photographic plates." She stood and started working her way to the front of the wagon intending to tell the driver to stop.

Nock grabbed her and turned her. The wagon lurched. They both lost their balance and were slammed against the side, him pressed on top of her, and suddenly there was no mistaking the physical magnetism. It was enough to take her breath away. On second thought, she didn't know why that surprised her. She'd observed the personal magnetism of Powers T. Nock as he charmed a whole courtroom. He was truly not a man to be underestimated.

Then their eyes met, and what she saw reflected there was beyond surprising. In that instant she knew the way she knew she breathed that she could crumble him with a word. The loquacious, witty, and very intelligent Powers T. Nock was completely unstrung by her. That amazed her. She'd turned heads before, she knew. But the effect she was having on Nock was more akin to turning blood.

Regaining his footing, he stood away from her, and his obvious confusion cleared. He shook his head. "Kate, don't be silly. We can't go back for the plates. You're endangering everyone with this foolishness."

But he picked the wrong word if he hoped to engage her sanity. "That's what the colonel called my pictures—'foolishness.' Bill called them 'foolishness.' Why does everyone think my work can be dismissed as foolishness, nothing more?" She kicked the milk can closest to her, then continued in low, steady tones. "Some things are larger than individual lives. Far from being foolish, the images on those plates document a truth that will outlast everyone in this wagon, in this camp, maybe even in this town."

"She's right," Woman-Who-Dreams said.

Nock looked around at the Indian woman with more incredulity than he'd shown Kate. He'd thought she was seasoned enough to be sensible. "Stop the wagon," he called softly to Harry.

"What? You sure? That's going to look mighty suspicious."

"Act like you're checking one of the horses or something."

Harry grunted an obvious disapproval. Then he stopped and climbed off the driver's seat, causing the wagon to rock.

When Harry was gone, Nock ran his hand through his hair and caught Kate's eye. "Would you mind telling me what's on those plates that makes them so damned important?"

He watched her hesitate and then draw breath.

"They're not documentary pictures, if that's what you mean," she said speaking softly. "They're just pictures of what I really saw. Your courtroom strategy was clever, but it's not the truth. It wasn't a war out there. There were no glorious battles, no great dangers to be faced from savages or their dancing."

This wasn't what he'd expected. He was anticipating new information, some startling revelation, maybe something he could use as he summed up the trial. Instead, Kate babbled on in vagaries. Didn't matter. He couldn't deny her anything. Nevertheless, he let her continue.

"I don't know that anyone will appreciate what my pictures show until some time from now, maybe a long time from now. The colonel didn't think they meant anything." She paused and rubbed her hands together. "But maybe you're right. This isn't worth risking lives."

Then, God help him, he thought he understood what she was talking about, because it had to do with time, and he'd thought a lot about time. Absentmindedly, he pulled his dual pocket watches from his two vest pockets and fingered them as he thought how the Greeks had two names for time: *Chronos,* the word for clock time, and *Kairos,* the word for organic time. Sometimes *Kairos* and *Chronos* got out of sync. That's what had happened here, he knew. The army had overreacted to this so-called Sioux uprising because the national *Kairos* was thirty years behind the national *Chronos.* And it occurred to him that Kate's pictures might be the national salvation—the eventual means of getting the collective time back together again.

Harry climbed back on the driver's seat. "The prisoners have been missed," he said. "If we don't go now, none of us is going to get out of here, except that trick rider. She's already jumped her horse over the fence. Whew, that woman can ride." With that, he picked up the harness reins.

"No," Nock told him. "We can't go yet."

Harry wrapped the reins again and turned to give Nock a quizzical look. Nock was aware of Kate's look as well. Hers expressed a startled hopefulness. He hoped she didn't get too hopeful. This wasn't going to be easy.

"This is crazy," Harry complained. "We've got to get going. They're going to be turning this camp upside down looking for her."

"That's exactly why we can't go," Nock told him. "They're probably already searching every wagon."

"But they'll catch us for sure if we stay."

"Not necessarily," Nock returned. "See how close you can get to the colonel's tent. Then stop and knock a wheel off."

"Knock a wheel off?"

"Right. Nobody's going to check a wagon that's broken down and obviously not going anyplace."

Nock watched a slow recognition cross Harry's face. It was really the only plan that had any chance of working. Harry figured it that way, too. A moment later, he shrugged

313

and started the wagon moving. "I don't know how I got myself into this," he said, tossing the comment as a whisper over his shoulder.

"You love how my mother feeds you chocolate cake every time you deliver milk," Nock told him. "You thought helping me would impress her," he added with a quiet chuckle. "And it probably will impress her."

"I'm not that fond of her chocolate cake," Harry returned.

Nock turned his attention back to Kate. She breathed, "Thanks." That's all. She didn't need to say more. Their eyes met, and the understanding was deeper. "Thanks," she breathed again, and that was enough to make him a little embarrassed. "Well, hell, if those plates mean that much," he told her.

A moment later he added, "Do I remember you saying those plates were right inside the colonel's tent?"

Kate nodded.

"Good thing I like a challenge."

A few minutes later, the wagon jerked to a halt. "I'm a couple of tents away from the colonel's. Around in the back," Harry told Nock. "It's the best I can do."

"Can you see who's going in and out of the colonel's tent?" Nock asked him.

"The colonel left with the first excitement, if that's what you're wondering," Harry answered, tossing his words over his shoulder. "No one's around that I can see, except the colonel's aide. He's watching the front."

"Thanks," Nock returned. Then turning back to Kate, he started to say that now was as good a time as any, but she was busy shedding her petticoats.

"What are you doing?"

"Getting ready," she answered. She slid her third petticoat off and pulled the gun free with the same motion. She held it out to him.

He didn't want it. He figured a gun was always the last resort, and in his opinion, using a gun in this situation was sure to get them killed. On the other hand, he didn't know what good a gun was tucked in Kate's petticoats. He took it and said, "Thanks, but you're not going anywhere."

"Yes, I am," she returned as she bent to tie her skirt into bloomers.

"In case you forgot, you're the one everybody's looking for." Then before he could say more, there was a thud and his corner of the wagon sagged. He reeled backward. The wheel was off, he realized. He righted himself and repeated. "You're not going anywhere."

She tied a scarf over her head, milkmaid style. As she tucked her loose curls under the edges, she explained, "The job requires two. One to go inside and get the boxes, one to stand outside and keep a lookout. Harry has to stay with the wagon. I mean, it would look pretty strange for him not to be fussing over that wheel. He's got a wagonload of milk sitting in the sun, spoiling. And there's no chance an Indian woman can move about without attracting attention, so that leaves you and me."

Kate watched as Nock shook his head in obvious frustration. He was a man used to winning arguments. Her forwardness tested his mettle, she knew, but this was not a time to play coy. Not if she meant to retrieve her plates. She watched him draw a deep breath.

"You going to work the inside or the outside?" he asked.

"Inside," she told him. "I can roll under the canvas easier than you."

With that, he slipped out the back of the wagon, checked all around, and then motioned for her to follow. Together they darted to the first tent, paused, checked, then darted to the next tent. Two soldiers were coming along the opposite side. Nock and Kate slipped around the tent, keeping themselves out of view as the soldiers passed. Then together they crossed the short space to the back of the colonel's tent. Easy. The colonel's aide had his attention focused on the two soldiers who'd just passed by. One more quick glance all around, then Kate dropped to the ground and rolled under.

She smelled the colonel's boots. Her stomach tightened.

She rolled up onto her knees and quickly stood expecting to see him. He wasn't there. But that lingering odor had been enough to start her heart pounding. She drew a deep breath and looked all around. The scene was too familiar. It held more than enough memory to make the colonel's presence almost palpable. She shivered.

Then she got to work. There were seven boxes of plates, each containing ten photographic negatives. The boxes weren't heavy, but they could be awkward and required some care in the handling, even though the plates had been packed individually in padded upright slots. Kate grabbed the first two boxes and shoved them under the canvas to Nock. She got the next two and did the same. When she shoved numbers five and six under, Nock whispered, "Get out of there. He's coming."

Kate gave a glance to the last box. It was on the opposite side of the tent. She thought about leaving it, especially as she could hear the colonel's voice. But she knew her plates the way a mother knows her children. That last box held the negative for the photograph of the Indian hugging the buffalo and the one of the birds suspended wing tip to wing tip. With the colonel's voice booming closer and closer, she darted the distance, grabbed the last box, and shoved it out. By then, the colonel was right outside the door. Kate crouched, ready to roll herself out, when she realized he'd stopped to speak with his aide. She took that last opportunity to once more cross the width of the tent and snatch Mary's ghost shirt. Clutching it to her chest, she dropped and rolled.

She was still on the ground outside when she heard the colonel enter the tent with his aide and another soldier. She'd heard him refer to the other soldier as "Lieutenant Smith" as they were speaking earlier. She froze. The colonel and the lieutenant were discussing her escape.

"I tell you it's impossible," the colonel bellowed. "How can a woman with red hair, a red dog, and an Indian squaw disappear without anybody seeing them?"

"I don't know, sir. But as I told you, we checked thoroughly," the lieutenant answered.

"Maybe if we could find that trick rider," the aide suggested.

The colonel slapped his desk with enough force, Kate started. "They're headed for the reservation," the colonel said, and slapped the desk again. "Won't do them any good. They can't hide there. I'll find them. I'll never give up until I find that Burke woman."

Kate shivered and glanced up at Nock. He hadn't moved since she rolled out, but they couldn't stay like that. Any moment she expected the colonel would notice that the boxes were missing and start bellowing about that as well. Worse, he'd know then that she'd been there. She quietly got to her feet. Nock slipped the carrying straps from two of the plate boxes over his shoulders. He gathered two more of the plate boxes in his arms. Kate tucked the ghost shirt under her arm and picked up the remaining three.

Meanwhile the colonel's rant had become less coherent. He was going on and on about how he was going to show everyone. He'd show this town and General Miles. He'd show the mayor, the sheriff, and even that squeaky little complainer of a deputy mayor, he continued. She didn't understand that part, but she was glad he had other things on his mind. She and Nock edged slowly and quietly out of earshot, carrying the boxes the colonel still hadn't missed.

They got to the wagon without incident. She pushed her boxes in ahead of herself. Nock did the same. Harry closed the door behind them, saying, "If I get that wheel back on, can we get out of here now?"

Nock nodded.

It took Kate's eyes a moment to adjust to the dim interior. She couldn't see Woman-Who-Dreams or Homer. At that her heart skipped a beat. It skipped two beats when she heard someone outside hail Harry.

She listened without breathing as Harry return the greeting. From what she could hear, a couple of soldiers passing by had taken an interest in Harry's wheel problem. She relaxed and turned back to worrying about Woman-Who-Dreams and Homer.

"What seems to be the trouble?" another voice outside

asked. Kate stiffened with recognition. That was the colonel's voice. She turned to warn Nock, but he'd already drawn the gun. He was leaning close to the wagon's back doors, listening.

"Oh, this damned wheel came off," she heard Harry reply to the colonel. "And my ice is melting. If I don't get this wheel back on and get going soon, everything is going to sour on me," Harry continued in a complaining voice. His act was so convincing, she thought he ought to try the stage. At the same time, she heard a little whimper of recognition from Homer, and looking behind a stack of cheese boxes, she found him and Woman-Who-Dreams tucked into a neatly arranged hiding space. The older woman motioned for Kate to join her.

She glanced to Nock.

He encouraged her with a little wave. He also cocked the gun.

Kate wriggled into the space and looked around. It was womblike close and about as damp, but lacked warmth. The space around one of the melting ice blocks had been cleverly camouflaged with an arrangement of cheese boxes and milk cans. It was tight, which was good; without the body heat of Homer and the other woman, Kate would have chilled.

"From the time I was a child, I learned to making hiding holes out of anything," Woman-Who-Dreams told Kate in a low whisper. "Unfortunately, I was never given a chance to outgrow that game. Been hiding from soldiers all my life in places less pleasant than this one."

Kate understood that. As a child, she'd also had secret places, a corner of the attic, a place in the undergrowth behind the orchard, a box inside the toolshed. When things got bad, she hid and sang to herself, humming the world away. She'd had to sing to keep from being afraid of those dark, dank holes, but her singing gave her away. Her mother followed that sound, drawn to the music, bottle in hand. She made Kate promise things. She had to promise she hadn't seen things—the men who came to the house and visited in her mother's upstairs bedroom. She had to be "good" and not tell. She had to rehearse the words like humming a tune over and over. Still, sometimes she forgot her lines. She wasn't as good as her grandmother, the actress.

Kate shook her head. There were no hiding places. If the soldiers thought to look inside the wagon, they'd find them. Fortunately, the soldiers outside had other things on their minds. They were discussing how to lift the wagon to fit the wheel. Kate couldn't believe it. They were so distracted, they were actually going to help them get away. Even the colonel was offering helpful suggestions. Suddenly the wagon pitched. Kate could hear the wheel being worked on. One of the voices complained, "God Almighty, this wagon's heavy."

"Milk and milk cans aren't light," Harry answered with a grunt. "Lots and lots of milk in there."

There were more noises as the wheel was attached. Then the wagon settled and leveled. The men outside uttered satisfied remarks, and she heard Harry slap backs and give appropriate thanks.

"Glad to help," Kate heard the colonel respond to Harry's enthusiasm. "It's nothing compared to what I've done for the citizens of this town," he went on. "And I've never been thanked for that, I can tell you."

A minute later, Harry climbed on the driver's seat and whispered without turning round, "He's waving us through the gate."

Nock uncocked the gun.

"Can you beat that?" Harry asked, and dared flash a grin over his shoulder at his passengers.

A few minutes later, outside the camp, Mrs. Donning reappeared. She rode up beside the wagon and asked Harry "Where have you been? I thought for sure the army had caught the lot of you by now."

Harry turned the wagon into an alley and stopped. He came around to the back and opened. Nock stepped out. Kate and Woman-Who-Dreams emerged. It was late afternoon. The shadows had lengthened such that in the alley it was almost dusky and completely deserted except for a couple of cats that took off as soon as Homer jumped down from the wagon. Harry quickly checked one direction, Nock the other. Satisfied that they were safe for the moment, the group allowed themselves a quiet round of congratulations and a retelling of events for Mrs. Donning.

"He actually sent you through the gate?" she asked, repeating the last of the story.

"Harry was wonderfully convincing," Nock answered, and clapped the older, rounder man on the back.

Harry practically beamed.

Mrs. Donning shook her head more and then added, "But we can't stand around here. I've got the horses. Let's get moving."

Kate had noted Mrs. Donning's three horses and already decided she wouldn't be riding away on one of them. The colonel might let an old Indian and a crazy trick rider escape, but he'd come after Kate. He'd never rest until he found her. He'd said as much in the conversation she and Nock had overheard. And she knew him well enough to know that was no idle threat. Now speaking up, she said, "I can't go with you. I'd endanger everyone on the reservation."

"It is a small matter. My people live with danger all the time," Woman-Who-Dreams told her.

Kate shook her head. "He'll send soldiers, lots of soldiers. You know that," she added, appealing to Nock.

He took her side. "Kate goes with me," he said. "If the colonel expects her to hide on the reservation, then better to do the unexpected."

There was an exchange of looks amongst the others, but no real disagreement. Mrs. Donning mounted her horse. Harry helped Woman-Who-Dreams onto one of the other horses.

"My sisters, the quillworkers, will wait for you. Don't forget us," Woman-Who-Dreams said to Kate. "They won't be afraid forever."

She nodded and squeezed the older woman's arm.

By that time Nock had gone to the end of the alley and checked the street. He gave an "all clear" sign. Trailing the third horse, Mrs. Donning started off, but not before leaning down and plopping the guard's hat atop Kate's head and then giving her a little salute.

On the other side of town, Richard Houston hung over the counter at the telegraph office. "That for me?" he asked, referring to the tapping signal that had just begun to sound.

Any noise from any of the telegraph keys was enough to bring Richard to the counter in anxious anticipation.

"That for me?" he asked again.

The head telegraph operator, a slight man, raised a hand to silence Richard while he leaned into his work, concentrating on the incoming message.

With his back turned to Richard, the man's thinning hair and the ears that stuck out from his head were his most noticeable features. But by now, Richard had hung over that counter so often, even the stain on the back of the man's collar was familiar.

Richard shifted his weight. Impatient. He chewed the side of his mouth and hoped this time for news—good news. Then, unconsciously, he began drumming the counter with his fingers almost in unison with the sounds of the incoming message.

The operator shot him an annoyed over-the-top-of-his-glasses glance. He'd been giving Richard a variety of annoyed looks lately.

Richard stopped the finger drumming.

When he wasn't inquiring about incoming messages, Richard paced while his mind continually replayed scenes with Kate. It amazed him the details he could remember of how she smiled and walked and talked and used her hands. The woman had literally taken over his consciousness, and all his thoughts eventually circled back to her present danger. He had to do something. He had to get her out of the colonel's clutches and away from here.

He shoved his hands in his pockets and once again castigated himself for not completely believing her when she told him the colonel had killed Bill or that the old Indian woman had started the fires in army camp. He'd wanted to believe and pretended to go along with her ideas.

But he should have believed, really believed. He might have acted with more conviction if he'd trusted her more. He might have tried to think of something to do before she took it on herself to stomp into the colonel's camp. Why hadn't he stopped her?

Not that he thought stopping her was easy. Kate hadn't ever acted demure, acquiescing to him, listening to him, or waiting for him. That was the real problem, he decided. Kate didn't understand what a man from a family such as his could do for her. He could have helped her find out about the old Indian woman. He knew people who could make other people take notice of situations. That's how it was done—knowing people who know people who can do things.

The operator finished taking the message, and turning around, he slid it across the counter to Richard.

"Thank you," Richard said, and opened the folded paper.

The wired message was from a U.S. senator, an old friend of Richard's father, who had dined often at the house when Richard was growing up. Richard remembered him as barrel-chested and hairy-armed. Those were the kind of features a kid catalogued before his assessment of people was clouded by an awareness of fine tailoring and fancy titles. The senator was now over at the War Department. But like all the other messages Richard had gotten today, this reply was cordial and noncommittal.

Richard crumpled the paper. Then, picking up the blank pad on the counter, he began to compose yet another message. Richard had spent the whole day sending and waiting for telegrams, lots of telegrams.

"Why not give it up for today?" the head telegraph operator said. It was a suggestion spoken almost as an aside. The power of his voice didn't even have enough command in it to make Richard look up into his face. Richard noticed the man's frayed cuffs instead.

Seeing that shabbiness, Richard suddenly missed the privacy of those stuffy clubs where his father conducted business of this sort. That gave him pause. He'd told himself that he didn't like his father's clubs and the way business was conducted in them. But it was an undeniable fact that if a member of his father's club wanted something as much as he wanted to free Kate, it could be done. Usually. That was understood. They were all gentlemen. There was raw power in that. There was also comfort. Get jammed up and someone would slap you on the back and fix it for you.

"I never had a customer send thirty telegrams in one day. Most don't send thirty a year," the head telegraph operator continued.

Richard only grunted and handed across his new message. However, this time, he also included a generous tip. After all, he was a gentleman, and he'd just remembered why that was important.

In short, there was more than one key to Kate's prison. And as a gentleman, he had only to find the right one. And he would, if he had to send telegrams to every other gentleman in the whole United States.

It was after dark when Nock opened the back door to his house. Homer pushed ahead entering first, his claws clicking against the linoleum as he circled the kitchen and sniffed near the icebox. Kate and Nock followed, struggling with the seven boxes of photographic plates. Nock had no idea how his mother was going to react to this unexpected intrusion, not that he thought preparing her for something like this would have helped.

His first glimpse was of her poised over the stove, a spoon held midair as she watched Kate's dog make his rounds. He was now sniffing next to the sink. Nock stacked the boxes next to the pantry and waited to see what his mother would say.

Nothing.

Kate voiced the first words. She apologized. "I'm sorry. My dog's usually better behaved. It's just that we've had a bit of excitement lately, and he is more agitated than usual."

"He's a very big dog," Nock's mother said. She glanced at

the boxes, but offered no comment on them. She put the spoon down, and wiping her hands, she said, "And you must be Mrs. Burke."

Kate nodded and then dropped a curtsy like a schoolgirl, an action Nock found startlingly charming. Evidently so did his mother. She smiled.

He was exceedingly glad for that. He'd been worried that his mother might insist on putting the dog outside, something they couldn't do without advertising Kate's whereabouts. At the same time, he wasn't keen on trying to explain that difficulty to his mother. Likely she would understand only the danger and begin to imagine things, perhaps worry too much. He wasn't particularly eager to tell her what had happened this afternoon for the same reason. That's why he'd been glad when Harry excused himself without coming in, saying he really did have milk to deliver.

But his mother smiled, and more, she was at a loss for words. "Well, well," she said as she wiped her hands on her apron again. "Well, well."

He didn't know what to say either.

Kate got Homer settled on the rug next to the woodbox.

Nock's mother went back to stirring whatever it was she was cooking.

Nock looked round the kitchen. It had been a long time since he'd really noticed the room. Now he thought it homey, maybe too homey. A wet dish towel hung from one of the stove handles. The curtains were faded and didn't match the skirt round the bottom of the sink. The oilcloth on the table was worn white in spots. Three pears sat on the windowsill ripening. He wondered what Kate thought. He suspected she came from finer folk, eastern society.

"I really hope you don't mind us showing up like this with no warning," Kate said.

"No, no, not at all," his mother responded. "Powers doesn't bring near enough guests home. I'm always telling him that." Then, seeming to find herself, she started chatting. "You must be hungry. Oh, but all I've got is a pot of oatmeal—plain old oatmeal, nothing fancy. I was just stirring it up. But I can put something else on. It won't take me but a minute."

"Oatmeal," Kate said. "But I love oatmeal."

And with that, Nock sat back and listened as the two women wove a whole conversation around the latest health craze—oatmeal, a food he frankly found fit only for horses and maybe the toothless. His was a minority opinion, however. Oatmeal had been popularized recently by a cold-water doctor in Minnesota. The demand was so great, Sioux Falls had opened its own oatmeal mill, which Nock's mother was now describing in detail, as if knowing where to get freshly rolled oats ranked in importance with knowing the Bible.

"Want some?" Nock's mother asked him, remembering him for the first time in several minutes. He shook his head and took black coffee instead.

Meanwhile, Kate and his mother continued to fuss, stirring up the oatmeal and putting it into bowls. The domesticity of that scene warmed him. Following the excitement of the afternoon, this was like *joie de vivre*, if not the reason for living itself.

He should have known it couldn't last.

Just as the women sat down with their bowls of oatmeal, and a jar of brown sugar to sprinkle on the top, someone pounded on Nock's front door. Loudly. The three of them exchanged looks. The pounding repeated. Nock set his coffee down and pushed his chair back.

Kate caught her breath. It was trouble, she knew, and she wished Nock didn't have to find out what it was. But, of course, he had to go to the door.

The moment he was gone, his mother leaned across the table and, taking Kate's hand in hers, she asked, "What is it?"

Kate pulled her hand back and shook her head. She didn't know what to say. She had no idea how to explain even a part of what was happening to her, how Bill had been murdered and her life had become entangled in dreams and lies and soldiers and Indian women, not to mention Richard Houston and this woman's son. Fortunately, Nock returned before Kate had to find an answer. But, as she suspected, the news wasn't good.

"Indians have attacked the south side of town. Someone was actually killed this time," he said.

"But there are no Indians," Kate said, standing up from the table and pacing to the stove. "They fled back to Pine Ridge Agency."

"I know. I know," he said. "I don't believe it was Indians. But somebody's making trouble, and some of the citizens are up in arms. I have to go see about it."

"Go where?" his mother now demanded.

He thumbed in the direction of the front door. "That was one of the guards from the jail. They're concerned about Plenty Horses."

"They want to lynch him," Kate said, guessing this new difficulty.

Nock's mother audibly sucked air. "Oh, Powers," she said. "But what can you do?"

"Be the voice of reason," he told her. "Even mobs can be persuaded." At that he tweaked her arm playfully, as if going out to face a mob of vigilantes was nothing.

Kate wasn't that optimistic. Suddenly she felt as though she hadn't really escaped, as though no one would ever escape the present confusion of death and soldiers and Indian uprisings. Except maybe the colonel. She had no doubt he was going to get away with murdering Bill and everything else he'd done, including stirring up this trouble. She suspected he was behind this, as well.

Nock was busy putting on a warm jacket. Then he paused and handed his mother the gun. He told her to be careful because it was "fully loaded." He explained that meant it had six bullets in it. Kate didn't understand why the other woman wouldn't know that, but Nock was clearly concerned that his mother understand that particular detail. Then Nock made his mother promise not to let anyone in until he got back. Done with that, he turned and squeezed Kate's arm once, warmly, before he went.

When he was gone, his mother invited Kate back to the table. "Might as well finish your oatmeal," she said. "Keep your strength up."

Kate sat down more out of politeness than any concern for her strength. She stirred the oatmeal; her appetite was gone. Meanwhile, Nock's mother chatted on and on about the value of wholesome food, no matter the circumstances. She offered an anecdote about her sister and another about a favorite cousin as proof of her point, but Kate couldn't quite make any of that chatter seem important enough to follow it.

At the same time, Nock's mother continued to fuss over everything. She arranged and rearranged the salt shaker and other table condiments. Once she got Kate water. Another time she got Kate a fresh napkin. When she ran out of that kind of busyness, she paused and with great seriousness asked, "What are you going to do?"

Kate hesitated. She wasn't sure she understood the question. Do when? Now? Next week? With the rest of her life? "I don't know," she answered.

"Surely you must have thought about settling down."

Kate really hadn't. Settling down was the last thing she'd ever thought about.

"Maybe raise a family," Nock's mother continued as she fussed with the edge of the tablecloth. "You already had your fling. Last winter out with the soldiers and the Indians must have been exciting. I had a fling myself before I was married."

"What kind of fling?" Kate asked.

"I hired on with the railroad as a cook. I was fourteen years old. There were ten of us cooking for over two hundred men. Not the Chinese. They ate somewhere else."

"When was this?" Kate asked.

"Oh, more years ago than I want to think about. And it was a real job, hard work. We would cook dinner and breakfast in one place and then, while the men were laying track, we would pack up our cook tent, load it onto a mule-drawn wagon, and move it six, eight, ten miles down the roadbed, depending on how much track the men were expected to lay that day. Then we'd unload, set up the tent, and have dinner ready by the time the men caught up with us. All that, and we didn't even have running water."

"It does sound like hard work."

"Oh, it was. It was also the most fun I ever had. Every day was something new." She shook her head. "Then I married. I loved my husband, and Powers was a beautiful baby. Powers was always a good boy." She reached over and twisted the lid tight on the sugar jar. "He's not much good with a gun. I'm glad he didn't take this one with him. He's very clever, though. He'll be all right. He'll talk his way out of this. I swear that boy can talk his way out of anything."

Kate looked up, but she couldn't catch the other woman's eye. She was fussing with the edge of the tablecloth, worrying a loose thread. "He's all I got left," Nock's mother added. "My husband died three years ago."

"I know, I'm sorry," Kate told her. Then she tried a little more oatmeal as she searched for words to comfort, to assure Nock's mother that everything would be fine. But she wasn't sure she believed everything would be fine. The trouble that had engulfed the Sioux and the soldiers was now threatening to engulf the whole town. It seemed as if they were all caught in some widening ripple. Shaking her head and not knowing what else to say, Kate asked, "Ever wish you could cook for that railroad crew again?"

"Oh yes," Nock's mother answered. Then after a slight pause, she added, "Oh, you're going to think I'm awful, but I wish that all the time. I know that's silly sounding. I mean if a person's going to wish for something, it ought to be something grand, like wanting to live in a palace or something, not wanting to slave over a wood-burning stove in a hot tent." She shook her head. "That's just me being an old woman with long-remembered regrets. My husband took good care of me. I'm not saying he didn't, you understand."

"I know," Kate told her. And with that, she suddenly flashed to that moment in the colonel's tent when she thought he might kill her. Her only wish at the moment was that she might know what secret silvered image was on Bill's mysterious plate. That wasn't a particularly grand desire either. Thing was: she still wanted to know. She suspected she would always want to know. But unlike Nock's mother's wish to return to an earlier time, it wasn't too late for her. Kate could reverse her regret.

"Yes, I know exactly what you mean," Kate told her. "It's the little things we leave unfinished that nag us. That's why I hope you'll understand. I have to go now. I have something I have to do." With that, she stood up from the table.

"Go? Right now? In the dark?" Nock's mother asked. "Powers will be back. He made me promise not to let anyone in. If you wait until he comes . . ."

"I can't wait," Kate told her. "I have to find a photographic plate that my husband hid. I think it might be at Amato's studio. I think whatever's on that plate might change everything."

Nock's mother got to her feet so fast, Kate thought she meant to prevent her going, using the gun, if necessary. Instead, she fumbled the gun into a large pocket in her apron and pulled a shawl around her shoulders. "You're not going alone," she said. "No, indeed. This is one time when I'm not going to miss all the excitement."

When Kate didn't respond because she didn't know what to say, Nock's mother added, "I promised Powers not to let anyone in. I didn't promise not to let anyone out."

17

When Mrs. Nock said she wasn't going to be left out of the excitement, she meant it, Kate discovered. The two of them had no sooner left by the back door than she took the lead, directing Kate down one side street and another, then through an alley and across a churchyard weaving her way through the tombstones. Kate marveled at how well she knew the neighborhood. They almost never passed a house without her making a comment on the woman living there.

"Got the gout real bad."

"Teaches piano."

"Can't read. Grew up on the prairie with no schools."

Kate was carrying a lantern Nock's mother had found on her back porch and dusted off, saying she almost never had a reason to go out after dark. No one would have guessed. The woman found her way through the back streets of Sioux Falls as if she might have been a night watchman, never pausing in her commentary.

"Sings hymns like an angel."

"Has a foul temper."

"Lost a baby last spring."

Three times they had to backtrack to avoid soldiers. Once

they encountered a group of men milling around the livery stable and had to duck behind one of the wagons-for-hire. There was tension in the air—not the slaphappy excitement that had drawn folk out of their houses to see the fires, but an edgier urgency. If Nock's mother felt it, she didn't let on.

"Drinks and thinks nobody knows."

"Loves her hollyhocks."

Kate couldn't imagine being so much a part of a place that she might have anything like Mrs. Nock's inventory of people's lives. She wondered how the woman kept up with it all.

"Spoils his nieces something awful," was her comment as they arrived in back of Amato's studio.

"Emmaline and Georgalene," Kate said.

"That's the pair," Mrs. Nock said and added, "They can't help being ugly, but that uncle of theirs has turned them bratty."

Kate chuckled softly. This was the first of Mrs. Nock's epithetical summaries she could check against her own experience. In her opinion, the woman was right. And at that, Kate recalled the way Nock had described people in terms of clocks. He'd been uncannily keen as well. Now she wondered if he came by that skill naturally.

Amato's studio was dark and locked up for the night. With Mrs. Nock continuing to comment on the grocer's wife up the street and the milliner who was "too uppity to wear her own hats," Kate rounded the building, checking all sides for a cellar window that might be pried open or kicked in. No luck. Coming around to the back again, she paused, and puzzled. Then Mrs. Nock touched Kate's arm and directed her attention upward. There was a window over the back door. It was narrow, but Kate thought she could fit through. Better yet, it was slightly ajar.

"I need something to stand on," Kate said looking around, searching the alley's darkness. Again Nock's mother directed her attention. An empty rain barrel stood next to the corner of the building. Working together, Kate and Mrs. Nock rolled the barrel up to Amato's back step. They lifted it to the landing and upended it. Then Nock's mother steadied the barrel while Kate climbed on top. She was stretching, reaching for the window, when she smelled cigarette smoke.

Kate leaned against the side of Amato's studio where the shadow was darkest. Mrs. Nock squatted down next to the barrel and held Kate's dog. A man strolled down the alley, the glow of a cigarette dangling from his mouth. Not twenty feet from the women, he paused and took a leak against the side of the building. He hunched his shoulders as he worked the buttons on his pants. His business taken care of, he rolled the cigarette from one side of his mouth to the other, and then he sauntered off the same direction he'd come.

"He's got eight kids at home needing him," Mrs. Nock said when he was gone. "That's where he ought to be."

"You know him?"

"He's a ne'er-do-well. Always has been."

Kate couldn't believe it. Nock's mother had an opinion on everyone in Sioux Falls. Still shaking her head at that, Kate reached up and pulled the window open. She boosted herself up to the sill. Then she wiggled around and got herself turned feet first. Pausing to catch her courage, she dropped inside. It was pitch black. Not being able to see anything, she had to hope the space below was clear. It wasn't. Her left foot caught the edge of something hard like a table. That pitched her out of control. She landed with enough hurt that when she got to her feet she was dizzy and found herself favoring the leg that had gotten twisted. She gave herself a moment to regain her sense of balance. Then limping a couple of steps, she opened the back door.

"You all right?" Mrs. Nock wanted to know immediately.

Kate said she was. Already her head had cleared. The twist of her leg was the kind of hurt that worked itself out. She just needed to walk a little.

"You might have broken something. You wouldn't know until it started to swell," Mrs. Nock told her.

Kate didn't want to think about that. "I'm fine," she repeated.

A note of irritation must have crept into her voice. Nock's

mother took umbrage. "Well, I'm only asking because it seemed important," she said.

"I'm sorry," Kate said. "You've been a big help. I don't think I'd have gotten this far without you. I wouldn't have known which streets to take."

At that, Kate saw the woman resort to the same modest mannerism her son had demonstrated inside the milk wagon just after breaking her out of the stockade. She looked away and shrugged one shoulder as if to indicate that what she'd done was nothing. Then, without further comment, she helped Kate roll the barrel away from the door.

Inside Amato's studio, Kate checked the window shades to make sure they were shut. Then she uncovered the lantern. Immediately the shadows danced up the walls, and then settled around the lantern's dim glow. That illumination made the room seem larger than it was, the corners retaining a darkness that might have stretched into the night for all the eye could tell. Those undefined dark recesses gave the room an odd eeriness that reminded Kate of childhood fears, but she didn't think she dared risk the electric lights. They'd be bright enough to be noticed, even with the shades pulled, she thought.

Meanwhile, Mrs. Nock turned slowly in that dim light, taking in Amato's clutter, on the shelves, in the corners, under the counter. Her jaw dropped. "I don't know how anybody could find anything in this mess."

Kate, too, felt overwhelmed. Where would she start? She wasn't even sure what she wanted was here. It was just a hunch based on her not knowing where else Bill might have hidden something from her as well as the colonel. "Look for anything that might have my husband's name on it," she told Nock's mother. With that, they got to work. The other woman picked a corner and started sorting through the boxes. Kate started rummaging through the shelves.

Nock's mother was methodical. She not only checked Amato's boxes, she arranged them. When she'd finished the first corner, it looked almost tidy. Kate was the opposite. The shelves she went through looked searched. She didn't care. All the while, Mrs. Nock kept up a running commentary on Amato's housekeeping.

"Never seen such dust."

"His spoiled nieces probably think they're too grand to dust."

"There's dusting that gets the dirt and dusting that stirs the dirt. Neither has been done here in years," she added, and sneezed.

On one of the shelves Kate came across a stack of pocket flyers advertising the local hot springs. One side read, "The famed Minnehaha Springs, known to the red man for thousands of years, has now been discovered to be curative. It's waters have cured twenty cases of the worst forms of epilepsy within the last year. For information and testimonials, see Trayer and Ford in Sioux Falls." The other side was a souvenir photograph of "Chief Sitting Bull," only it wasn't Sitting Bull. It was another somber-looking Indian's portrait done in sepia tones.

Mrs. Nock was still going on about the dust. "You have to dust down. Start at the top. Dirt settles."

A little later, "Those nieces of his could have this place looking fine if they'd only apply themselves."

Still later, "What's this?"

Kate was used to the banter about dust that didn't require a response. She was slow saying, "What's what?"

"It's locked," Mrs. Nock said, and indicated a portion of the counter that was closed and wouldn't open. She rattled the door a couple of times to demonstrate.

Kate hadn't bothered with the counter. That's where Amato stacked the prints that were ready to return to his customers. Prints. Not plates. She was looking for a plate. Now she turned and tried the cupboard door. Definitely locked. Kate looked around. Seeing a screwdriver, she used it to pry the lock away from the frame.

As the wood along the edge splintered and gave way, Mrs. Nock sucked air. "Should you do that?"

Kate shrugged. She'd never intended a polite search.

Mrs. Nock sucked air again when the cupboard door

finally swung open, spilling a tray of Stanhopes across the floor.

Mrs. Nock dropped to her knees. She started picking up the various items—tie tacks, cuff links, letter openers. Then all of a sudden, she froze with a man's hat pin in the palm of her hand. She stared at it as if it were a large and distasteful bug. "What's this?" she asked, her voice taking a new pitch.

Kate knew. She'd seen Stanhopes before and was disappointed to find the locked cupboard held nothing more than Amato's dirty pictures. She brought her hands to her hips and surveyed the room, trying to think where else she might look for Bill's plate.

Meanwhile, Nock's mother, seated on the floor, continued to gather up the Stanhopes, but slowly, examining them one by one, turning each into the lantern's light, catching the secrets under the little lenses. She shook her head more and more as she worked her way through the collection. "All this comes of too much passion, if you ask me," she commented. "Too much passion ruins lives."

Kate paused in her survey and wondered how many times she'd heard that same sentiment. Too much passion supposedly had ruined the women in her family. Everyone said so. Her father. Her father's friends. It was whispered in her neighborhood. Yet even as a child, Kate had known better. Not too much passion but too little courage had ruined her mother's life. She'd known what she wanted. She'd wanted to run away with a younger man, but she'd lacked the nerve to do it.

"Now, what's this?" Mrs. Nock asked.

Kate looked round. Nock's mother was trying to slide the tray of Stanhopes back into the cupboard, but it kept catching on something. She set the tray down and felt along the shelf to see what was causing that hang-up. When she pulled her hand back, she was holding a plate—a single plate wrapped in a handkerchief that Kate instantly recognized as belonging to Bill. Her heart almost stopped.

She crouched and took the plate from Mrs. Nock. With a little tremble, she untied the handkerchief. In professional archive style, the plate had been developed and slipped into a paper sleeve with a single contact print. As the handker-chief came undone, the print fluttered to the floor. Mrs. Nock picked it up and looked at it first.

Kate held her breath, waiting for some reaction. But the other woman merely shrugged and handed the print back.

Taking it, Kate turned it into the light. She didn't know what she expected. There was nothing startling in the image. It showed the colonel and several soldiers posed with Big Foot and several of his men. They were standing next to a pile of rifles. Kate was taken back by the ordinariness of the image. It looked very much the same as dozens of Bill's posed pictures. She shrugged and almost handed it back, thinking it was of no consequence after all.

Then all of a sudden Kate was flooded with a memory. She was in Woman-Who-Dreams' tepee. The memory was so vivid, she could almost smell the squirrel stew. She could almost feel the lumpy stacks of old newspapers under the floor robes. In the memory, Woman-Who-Dreams was holding a magnifying glass while she examined a photo-graph. Her eye was huge behind it. Then the older woman pushed the photograph into Kate's hands. It was curled. Kate smoothed it. Now Woman-Who-Dreams told her to look. Kate was looking. She saw nothing unusual. The picture was nothing but a portrait of Woman-Who-Dreams dressed in her Indian finery. "Look," the older woman kept saying. "Look. Look." She gave Kate the magnifying glass. "Count the rows. How many rows?"

She meant the quillwork on the dress in the picture, Kate realized, and brought the magnifying glass into position. She looked and named the number. "Yes, yes," the older woman had sighed.

Then turning, Woman-Who-Dreams had pointed and said again, "Look. How many horses?" This time she meant the figures painted on a buffalo robe. Kate said what she saw.

"No," the older woman said. She was leaning so close, Kate remembered smelling her breath. "My father, may we not call his ghost, was a great warrior. He captured many, many horses, but not so many as that." Then Woman-Who-

Dreams had laughed. "My father did Coyote work. Too much bragging. But this." She took the photograph from Kate. "The truth is deep in this."

Now holding Bill's picture, Kate's hand trembled. The truth that rose out of that photograph was deep and dangerous. Deep and dangerous enough, she wondered why Bill hadn't simply destroyed it. No reason, she thought, except his own character flaw—the streak of larceny that had tempted him to blackmail. But if Bill had concocted one too many cheap schemes, the colonel had similarly become caught in his own web of interlaced lies. The result was he'd begun to imagine ghost dancing in places where there was none. That's why he hadn't been able to leave Kate alone and ended up killing Bill.

She handed the print back to Mrs. Nock.

"What is it?" she asked.

"Look closely," Kate told her, and then watched as Nock's mother studied the picture again. She watched how it affected her. First puzzlement. Then it was as if the light changed. Her whole countenance took on a recognition. Her eyes, dark and intense, came up to find Kate's face, and neither of them needed to say anything.

To understand the picture, one had to know something about the affairs of the last few months, enough to know that the photograph could only have been taken at one time and in one place, just before what happened at Wounded Knee Creek. It showed Big Foot and his men surrendering their guns.

It was a matter of some dispute, but some believed as many as three hundred women, children, and Sioux men had been killed near that creek in what Colonel George was calling a battle and a victory. Kate set the plate down and paced to the edge of the light. Plenty Horses was right. The Indians of Big Foot's band had no guns.

What happened, she wondered, when a nation rehearsed its history the way her husband and the colonel posed pictures?

No battle. It had been a massacre. But, as Kate had suspected, the colonel wasn't worried about dead Indians—

337

even hundreds of dead Indians. What worried the colonel was the twenty-nine soldiers who died that same day—the young men Kate and the other white women in the chapel at Pine Ridge hadn't been able to help because they had no medicine. They had to have been shot by other soldiers— "friendly fire." No other explanation made sense. The Indians had no guns. That was the truth the colonel couldn't have known because it meant he'd deployed his men so poorly, they'd gotten caught in their own crossfire. Knowledge of that would ruin him, ruin his career as a military officer.

"Oh, dearie, what are you going to do?" Mrs. Nock now asked.

At first Kate had no idea. She said nothing.

"We have to find Powers," Mrs. Nock said, scrambling to her feet. "That's what. He'll know what to do. He'll have an idea about this."

Kate shook her head. The temptation was great and the responsibility so large, she didn't imagine anyone expected her to shoulder it. But unlike her mother, Kate was determined she would never lose her nerve. She knew what to do. It was the same thing Woman-Who-Dreams had done. Woman-Who-Dreams had had the right idea—setting lots of little fires. Only she'd had the wrong incendiary. Kate figured she had the right one.

Hours later near dawn, Nock's mother sat stiffly upright on a chair she'd brought from the back and placed directly inside Amato's front door. The gun rested on her lap. She fingered it and chewed her bottom lip, actions that had occupied her most of the night. She wished Powers were here. That was the thought that had occupied her most of the night. She kept telling herself over and over, "If only Powers were here. If only . . ." It had racked her conscience as she wavered between wanting to go and find him and not being able to abandon Kate, even if her scheme was wildly impractical.

Now with the coming of morning, things were going to get

complicated. Soon Mr. Amato would show up to open his studio. When he did, he was going to find two women occupying his establishment. He was going to be surprised at that. The shock of the surprise would hold him for a moment. But not long. Then she didn't know what she'd do.

Her present predicament was the result of her liking Kate. It was as if she couldn't help herself. The woman was like a kitten raised wild and gone feral; she'd never be chatty and warm like most women, Mrs. Nock knew. She was too much in need of mothering to allow herself to be mothered. And even though she knew Kate wouldn't know how to appreciate it, Mrs. Nock found herself instinctively wanting to help and protect her. That's the only reason she'd agreed to guard the door. She was supposed to stop anyone from coming in until Kate finished. She was to use the gun if she had to.

That had sounded fine in the middle of the night when no one was likely to come. Now with the dawn, she couldn't help wondering if anyone would seriously believe her capable of pulling the trigger. That meant she might actually have to pull the trigger. What other way could she prove her determination? With that in mind, she'd picked her target, the bell at the top of the door, the one that announced whenever a customer came in. She'd practiced sighting that target all night, carefully lining it up, the way her dead husband had taught her. No question, she knew she could drill that bell. She was equally sure she didn't want to. She wished Kate would hurry up and finish before it came to that.

She'd never imagined it would take so long to make the prints. All night, while she sat in that chair and guarded that door, she'd listened to the pop and sometimes saw the flash of the magnesium strips. Because it was dark, Kate had to use flash strips to expose the prints, one at a time. Normally, she would have used sunlight. Kate had explained that, even demonstrated it earlier in the night.

Then, after she exposed the prints, she had to develop them, one at a time. It was a slow process, which was fine, even interesting, Mrs. Nock remembered thinking. The problem was, like her son's clocks, one wasn't enough. Kate was making lots and lots of prints. Enough that the acrid smell from the flash strips had become overpowering. Mrs. Nock found herself rubbing her nose often just to keep from sneezing.

Between the pops and flashes, Kate emerged from the dark lab holding dripping wet prints by their corners. She rolled the prints onto the electric drying drum and returned to the back. All night Mrs. Nock had watched how those prints turned slowly over the cylinder, wet and sticky at the beginning, dry and slightly curled at the end when they dropped into a box. There were dozens of finished prints in the box now. Mrs. Nock thought that ought to be enough, but Kate kept printing, printing.

And Mrs. Nock kept worrying. What if Mr. Amato called the sheriff when he arrived? She imagined he would be within his rights to have her and Kate thrown into jail. They'd broken into the place like thieves. If that happened, she wondered if Powers would be clever enough to get them out. She wondered if Powers had managed to keep the mob from hanging the Indian. On second thought, she felt quite sure he had. Powers seemed to manage whatever he set his mind on. He would win Mrs. Burke if he wanted her badly enough.

Then she wondered if he'd gone home yet and missed them. Mr. Amato had a telephone. She didn't. But the neighbor next door did. She thought about ringing her neighbor and having her check and see if Powers might have come home. But that meant the operator at the telephone switchboard would know where she was. The operator would surely wonder why Mrs. Nock was at Mr. Amato's studio at this early hour.

Then it happened. There was the sound of a key in the lock. Then there was the twisting of the doorknob. Mrs. Nock sat up straight and raised her weapon. When Tony Amato pushed the door open, he was staring straight at the gun held in her outstretched arms.

His expression was a mix of shock and recognition. He worked his jaw several times before he managed to say, "Mrs. Nock? What are you doing here?"

"Close the door," she told him in her sternest voice. "And don't make trouble."

He raised both eyebrows. Then Kate came out of the back, carrying more fresh wet prints. Amato turned his attention to her. "Mrs. Burke?" Then, ignoring the gun, Amato moved toward Kate. "What's going on here?" he asked, his voice taking on more tones of irritation and authority.

Being ignored like that angered Nock's mother enough, so that she knew she had to make good on her practiced intention. She'd known all along Mr. Amato wouldn't take her and her gun seriously. Now sighting the doorbell, Nock's mother pulled the trigger. She temporarily deafened herself, but the bullet was on target. It split the bell and brought it down.

Her ears ringing, she watched Amato take two steps back and bump into the drying drum. It was hot. He jumped away from the drum and nearly tripped over a box of plates. She thought that served him right for keeping the place such a clutter. She was beginning to enjoy this. She looked around quickly, trying to figure what else she might shoot if she needed to get someone else's attention.

Fortunately or unfortunately, her gunfire got more attention than she'd counted on. In the space of less than a minute, half a dozen men came through the front door, asking what was going on. She knew them: the grocer with the club foot; his clerk, who was courting the boss's daughter; the butcher, who was a little less than honest; a pair of livestock buyers who regularly came to town from Chicago; and the assistant from the hardware store, who'd never been bright. A moment later, two of Amato's assistants showed up. All of them took in the shot-off bell with obvious amazement, but not one of them thought to disarm her. They just shook their heads collectively and started talking about what was "going on," meaning Kate and her prints.

Mrs. Nock gave up and slipped the gun into her apron pocket.

Kate had thought anyone catching her making prints of Bill's plate would try to stop her, urging her to think twice about something so sure to upset the established order. It was her experience that even if it was wrong, most people preferred the known, especially if the unknown was ugly. When she finished printing, she'd planned to gather her prints and distribute them herself, selecting the recipients the way Woman-Who-Dreams had selected her grasses. But with Mrs. Nock's gunshot, things took a different course.

It started when Amato noticed the prints rolling off his drying drum. He was obviously startled to see them. He reached into the holding box and pulled out a stack of the prints. He flipped through them quickly and, with a puzzled expression, noted their sameness—dozens of the same picture. At that, he glanced up and gave Kate an odd look, followed by a moment of indecision. She watched the way his eyes darted the room as if considering possibilities. Meanwhile, more and more people were crowding his studio, asking about the gunshot, wanting to know what was going on.

Amato gave Kate one more look and then a nod. Then he began passing her prints around. However, he didn't wait for anyone to figure it out. He told them what the photograph meant.

In a matter of minutes, the place was abuzz with talk.

"That man, Baldwin, ought to see this," one of the men said, and took a print to show him. "And those reporters," another suggested. At that, Amato gave one of his assistants five prints and told him where he was likely to find the newspapermen in town for the trial. He sent his other assistant to wake the judge. Meanwhile, the sheriff arrived, saying he'd heard there was a gunshot. Amato showed him the picture. He decided the mayor had to know. Then Mrs. Nock went out on the street and began inviting people in, telling them to come look at a "most interesting photograph." And just like that, Kate's little flames of truth ignited and spread.

Half an hour later, when there was a lull in the excitement, Amato sidled up to Kate and touched the middle of her back in a way that always made her stiffen. As usual, he didn't notice. "I warned Bill about that picture. I told him it was trouble when he asked me to hide it for him."

"And when he was dead and you knew you still had that plate, what did you think then?"

"I wasn't going to keep it, if that's what you mean. I was scared. I didn't know what to do. Bill offered me a cut of the blackmail money, but I didn't take it. I told him I didn't want trouble."

Kate nodded, but she thought Amato should have taken the money. Bill, no doubt, lost it on cards as soon as he got it. Bill had been a lousy gambler even when he cheated, she knew.

"I have my nieces to worry about," Tony added.

"Emmaline and Georgalene," Kate said.

Hearing their names was enough to make Amato beam. A grin spread across his face. "They're my girls," he said. "Good girls." Then he lowered his voice. "If they knew . . ." He hesitated. He couldn't finish the sentence. "If they knew . . . Oh, they can't know."

"Know what?" she asked, enjoying his embarrassment.

"Oh, you know. They can't, they just can't know where that plate was hidden."

"Mrs. Nock found the plate," Kate told him, knowing that would add to his discomfort.

"Mrs. Nock? Oh, Lord help me," he suddenly exclaimed. "She found the plate?" he asked again.

Kate nodded.

Amato couldn't seem to accept that. He groaned. "I'm done for. She's the worst gossip in town. There's nothing about anyone that she doesn't know. And tell. Embellishing freely. She'll ruin me."

"That sweet motherly lady?" Kate asked, rubbing it in.

Amato clapped his face in both his hands and groaned again.

On the other side of town, Richard was still in the telegraph office, sending wires and waiting for responses. He'd been there all night, sharing the space with the night operator, sleeping only briefly on the wooden bench in the waiting area. He refused to give up, even though he'd found that this so-called Indian uprising had already become so controversial back East, no one with any political aptitude wanted to associate himself with it. But Richard kept trying. He thought there had to be a someone willing to exert a little influence on Kate's behalf. Besides, he really didn't know what else to try.

He was standing at the counter, writing out yet another message, when a reporter from a Nebraska newspaper walked in and told the telegraph clerk he had to wire his home office and fast. Then, because he was a chatty fellow, he showed Richard the photograph and told him the whole story of Kate and her prints. He managed all that while he wrote out his wire and counted his words.

At first, Richard was stunned. Then he flashed with anger and stomped out of the telegraph office thinking this was the most foolhardy thing he'd known Kate to do yet. He had to get her away from here, he told himself, or she was going to get herself killed. Only he didn't know if she'd go anywhere with him.

As he strode down the boardwalk on his way to Amato's, it hit him—the missing piece. How had Kate gotten out of the stockade to print those pictures? His first thought was to wonder if Nock had made good. Richard dismissed that idea as ridiculous. That is, until he slammed through the front door of Amato's studio and saw Mrs. Nock. That gave him pause.

Then he spotted Kate. She was standing beside Amato, one elbow resting on the sales counter as she talked to a reporter from the New York *World*. Flushed, her hair disheveled, her dress rumpled, she'd splashed fixer on her clothes. It had crusted in spots. In short, she was a mess,

344

and she was radiant, and he'd never experienced Kate without a similar mix of impressions that always left him raw and confused and unsure of what to do.

All around Kate, there were people coming and going. Amato was now shouting at his assistant, telling him to hurry, they needed more prints, still more prints. Richard couldn't believe the party atmosphere. Hadn't anyone given a thought to how the army was going to react?

The colonel was not going to take this without a fight. If he'd killed Kate's husband, there was no telling what he might do to Kate, and Richard couldn't stand that thought. He'd wrestled all night with the idea of Kate's being in danger and his not being able to do anything about it. He'd made himself near crazy with all those telegrams because he wouldn't give up, wouldn't accept the notion that he was powerless. He hadn't slept but for a few minutes, or eaten.

He needed to get Kate away from here. The colonel would be coming. But more than wanting her away and safe, he wanted her.

But she hadn't even noticed him. He'd come through the door and stood there, puzzling over the situation for the better part of two minutes, and she hadn't even looked up. To her, his arrival was just part of the general hubbub filling the studio. Not being the center of Kate's attention was the chief source of his exasperation and never failed to ignite him with an overwhelming desire to grab her, possess her.

With that on his mind, Richard rounded the end of the counter, and taking Kate's arm, he turned her until she was facing him. Grabbing her shoulders, he shook her gently, as if that were the shortest way to sense, and said, "You have to get out of here. Don't you know that?"

But there was no way he could be angry with her. One look at her face, and he stopped the shaking and pulled her to his chest in an embrace of relief at finding her safe for the moment, at least.

The smell of her was tinged with the odor of burnt magnesium and photographic chemicals. That suddenly flooded Richard with the memory of their stolen passion in his wagon lab. That, too, had smelled of developer and fixer.

Fine. He'd already surrendered to the idea that loving Kate meant loving her other passion. He was even fine with the fact that she'd probably always be a better photographer than he was. He just wanted a moment now and then when he had her—all of her. He didn't think that was asking too much.

She was surprised. That was obvious in her expression. But then she struggled, pushing with both arms against him, twisting her shoulders away.

"What are you doing?" she asked.

The force of her resistance surprised him. He let go and looked around.

The others were enjoying his rebuff. Amato was grinning, practically ear to ear. Richard didn't care. He'd have Kate. If she didn't understand his embrace, he'd think of something else that would win her affection, but he would have her.

Then Nock's mother suddenly pushed herself between him and Kate. She forced Richard back a step, pointed a finger at him, and said, "What is this? Do you think Mrs. Burke hasn't a thing on her mind more important than to be swooning in some man's arms?"

Kate thought she couldn't have said it better. But then, God help her, she saw the look on Richard's face and knew he was genuinely hurt. For the first time, she was willing to believe he might be serious rather than flirtatious. She searched for something appropriate to say, but before she could come up with anything, three soldiers burst through the front door and demanded her whereabouts.

Amato stepped forward, wanting to know what gave the soldiers the authority to demand anyone's whereabouts. At the same time, Richard grabbed Kate and practically shoved her through the curtained doorway behind them.

"I'm telling you, Kate, you have to get away from Sioux Falls," he said. Taking her by the arm, he led the way to Amato's back door.

She didn't disagree or resist. She was ready to go now that she'd done what she needed to do.

Earlier, if she'd taken the plate to Nock, as his mother wanted, or Baldwin, or Richard, or the sheriff, the reaction would have been the same—caution. They'd have wanted her to get out of Sioux Falls and let them take care of it. That's why she'd chosen to print lots and lots of the pictures instead. She didn't trust caution, and, in this case, this picture needed to be exposed, fully exposed.

Richard opened the back door and peered out, checking each direction. She took that moment to glance upward to the open window above. Her eye moved to the bench that had complicated her fall. Her leg was still sore, but she was whole and satisfied.

Richard beckoned her out and down the back stairs. She followed him, moving swiftly to match his pace, but it wasn't fast enough. They'd not gone far when they were confronted by four soldiers on horseback. They turned in the other direction, more soldiers, more horses, stirring up more dust. Richard turned and tried to get back to Amato's, pulling Kate along by her arm. The soldiers cut them off.

Surrounded, Kate broke free of Richard's grasp and faced the colonel. He had his gun drawn.

"You and your pictures are coming with me," he barked.

"I don't think so," she answered. "My pictures are everywhere. All over town."

He already knew that, she thought, or he wouldn't be here. Their eyes met. Kate didn't flinch. What was he going to do? His dirty little secret was out. There was no changing that, ever.

The colonel broke their gaze. She saw his gun move sideways. The movement was so slight, it was more a knowing than a seeing: he was going to shoot her dog! Without thinking, she stepped in the same direction. The bullet hit with such force, she thought one of the horses had kicked her. She looked down, saw blood.

No pain; sounds faded. Then the taste and smell of the dust grew, filling her with an earthy sensation even as everything blackened, and she spun into her own shadow.

18

Kate was climbing stairs. Someone was following her. She looked. Saw nothing. She climbed again, listening, her whole body strained for sound, any scraping or footfall. Nothing.

She turned quickly. Nothing.

She knew this dream. She ran in this dream and the harder she ran, the closer it got—whatever it was that kept following her. She looked again, staring into the void all around. Nothing came to her, but the skin-crawling sensation that she was not alone. But she would not run. Not this time, she told herself. And with that, Kate whirled and plopped herself down on one of the steps.

She didn't know what she was afraid of. She knew shadows. She'd captured shadows on glass plates and pressed them onto photographic paper the way some ladies pressed wildflowers between pages of a favorite book of verse. She would catch this one. All she had to do was wait.

Sooner or later the shadow would take substance or the substance would become sheer. Then she'd know where she was and how to find her way.

But sitting didn't help.

*The dream turned on her, tilting and twisting the whole
staircase under her. She clung to the banister, then lost her
grip and spun into space—into sky and earth, seed and bone,
water and wind. Not falling, but flying. She soared, looping
through the air.*

*That had never happened before in this dream. It was
startling and fun. She was Double-Woman spinning the
world upside down and laughing, laughing, laughing.*

Kate woke with a start. She'd fallen asleep in the heat of
the afternoon and slipped once more into the fevered
images that had accompanied her those two weeks, when
she hovered between life and death. Then the healing had
begun, and she remembered long stretches of dreamless
sleep wrapping itself around her until her strength rallied.
All that had happened the first part of May. It was now late
August, nearly four months later, but it seemed like half a
lifetime and a world away. The reservation was nothing like
Sioux Falls. Kate straightened her stiff leg, wincing at the
effort.

She was sitting on the ground, her back against one pole
that supported a rough lean-to made of dried pine boughs.
The lean-to created shade where the wide prairie provided
none. The shade and the way the lean-to had been built to
funnel any breeze made the afternoon almost bearable. The
heat was so intense, nothing moved with any speed except
the jaws and the fingers of the other five women.

Quillworkers, the women's mouths were full of porcupine
quills, the ends protruding from their lips like spines on a
cactus. Their cheeks rippled as they chewed. The quills had
to be softened and flattened by that chewing before they
could be tucked and stitched. Each woman worked her own
geometric design, a pattern she'd gotten from a dream
quest. No two women ever worked the same pattern or
someone else's pattern. Working someone else's pattern was
as unthinkable as "going native" was to most white women.
Whenever Kate visited the agency headquarters, the agent's
wife called her little girl from swinging on the picket fence
or playing with her brother. It was as if "going native" was a

disease the woman thought her daughter might catch from Kate.

Kate stretched her other leg. The quillworking women were too busy to pay her any attention. They chatted and stitched while Kate lazily watched.

Most Sioux women were tall. Sitting on robes spread over the ground, their lower limbs made wide laps where they held whatever they were decorating—a dance shirt, a robe, a pipe bag, a cradleboard. Their fingers were long. They worked the quills with a graceful flow of practiced motions.

Woman-Who-Dreams' great-granddaughter sat in the center of the circle. She sorted the quills by color and size, readying them for the others. Besides Woman-Who-Dreams, the group included two sisters from the Blue Crow family, their niece with a new baby, and another older woman simply called by her missionary name, Hazel. Kate had hunted with some of these women. Others she'd met more recently. They all knew each other like sisters.

Last week these same women and a bunch of others from all across the reservation had gathered to dye their quills. Bringing their dogs and their kids and food to share, they'd started arriving at Woman-Who-Dreams' reservation house early in the morning. Each carried a big iron pot and a load of wood. One by one they built fires, filled their pots with water, and added various dye stuff—red trade blanket for crimson, bark and berry pits for black, other ingredients for blue and yellow. While they stirred their pots, the kids chased each other, played hiding games and sneaked bits of food. And all the male dogs, including Homer, mounted one bitch in heat. Later the women spread the piles of newly colored quills in the sun to dry. Then they sat and ate and smoked and told jokes.

The present chatter was loud and animated, the women sometimes leaning their heads together to share some intimacy. Kate understood none of it. When they forgot she was around, the women used Lakota, their language. That was fine with Kate. Often she didn't understand what they talked about, even when they used English. The women shared such long histories, they spoke in cryptic phrases, a single word being enough to remind them of an event or a person. Kate envied that.

She let them talk while she studied camera angles, waiting and watching the light. Right now the light was too flat for her to chance exposing a plate, even though she thought a photograph of the women bent and intent on their work, as they were, might prove interesting even without much contrast. In fact, she thought that sameness might suggest the peace and inclusion of the group. She felt for her camera. It was folded and tucked under the edge of her skirt. Then she changed her mind again and decided against taking the picture. The light was just too chancy. She had only a few plates and limited means of getting more. That meant she had to choose her pictures carefully. Because of that, she worried that her work lacked its usual spontaneity. She had no way of knowing. Without means of developing and printing her pictures, she could only expose her plates and then pack them carefully in crates, hoping the images stayed stable long enough for her to arrange to get them someplace where they could be developed. She wasn't complaining. The conditions were better than some her father had encountered in the earliest days of photography. But they were far from ideal.

She picked up her cane and stood.

Woman-Who-Dreams looked up from her work. Their eyes met. Kate indicated with a gesture that she was all right. Woman-Who-Dreams constantly fretted about Kate. Her arrival on the reservation had been occasioned by what Kate thought was a welcoming party. Only later did she realize it was also a healing ceremony. But Kate was fine, growing stronger every day. She just needed to go inside and get a little water from the bucket.

She watched as Woman-Who-Dreams returned to her work. She was adding a quilled border to Mary's ghost shirt. She'd offered to do that before Kate returned the shirt to the girl. She and her family would be coming to a festival next week. Kate hoped Mary would be pleased.

At the door of the house, Kate stomped the dust off her shoes. Not that it helped. She thought of her time on the reservation as a continual battle against grit. One day of wind and it was embedded in everything—clothes, bedding, food. Woman-Who-Dreams liked to brag that only houses collected dust. Tepees never did. Kate didn't know about that. What she did know was that dust did no good to her camera and plates.

Inside, Kate paused to look around. Woman-Who-Dreams' reservation home consisted of a single room with a stove in the middle. An army-issue iron bed stood in one corner covered with a star quilt. Two photographs and a medicine bundle hung directly over the bed. Next to that was a row of clothes hung on hooks. On the far wall was an out-of-date calendar and an out-of-date U.S. flag. There was a table, two chairs, a few cooking things. Some army blankets on a makeshift bed marked the corner Kate had claimed for herself. She had created privacy by arranging her trunks upended like a screen.

No stairs. Nothing fancy.

But newspapers everywhere. Stacks of newspapers. Piles of newspapers. When she had guests, Woman-Who-Dreams used the stacks of newspapers for stools. Layers and layers of newspapers, wetted with a little flour paste, had been applied to the walls as well. Woman-Who-Dreams continued to apply them almost daily whenever she detected a draft where the dust drifted in or noticed the print had faded. That was how she housecleaned.

Yet despite its quirky unkemptness, Kate felt more at home here than in any house she'd ever known. The place smelled wonderfully from the herbs Woman-Who-Dreams collected and dried near the ceiling. It was frequently full of people. They came to quill, to visit, to ask advice. Sometimes her guests brought eggs, a sage hen, or some other delicacy to add to Woman-Who-Dreams' soup pot. But even those who came empty-handed never left that way. Woman-Who-Dreams filled their bellies with her soup and their hands with her herbs or other things they needed. She was a superior scrounge. Anything anyone needed, she found or wrangled from the reservation officials. Except photographic supplies. That was a little outside her usual fare.

Kate got her drink and gave some water to Homer. He lapped and shook himself. Then Kate returned to the doorway and leaned against the frame as she looked out. A double-track dirt road crossed in front of Woman-Who-Dreams' house and continued along a row of similarly unpainted wooden frame houses, regularly spaced. Around the houses was a jumble of tepees, sweat lodges, wagons, and woodpiles. Beyond that, and far enough away to waver in the heat waves, she saw a church and a cluster of eight other buildings. That was Pine Ridge Agency, the administrative center of the reservation. In every other direction, there was nothing but prairie, flat to the horizon.

Kate heard a meadowlark sing. Another answered. She caught her breath at the sound. Sometimes the sheer beauty of simple things was almost more than she could bear. Nearly dying had left her with that much sense of life's fragile beauty.

She was lucky!

How many times had her doctor told her that? She was lucky she was alive. She was lucky she hadn't lost her leg. The bullet had traveled almost the entire length of her thigh and broken the bone just above her knee without shattering it. That was lucky. In time she would walk without the cane or much of a limp. In time all things changed, scarred, or healed. Fortunately, she'd healed.

The colonel had been lucky, too. General Miles had instigated an investigation that found the colonel "negligent and incompetent." The general had recommended loss of rank and punishment, but his recommendation was ignored by his higher-ups. Bill's murder was only one of many the colonel got away with. Even his shooting of Kate was dismissed as an "accident." Yet despite his good fortune, the colonel had left Sioux Falls complaining loudly to reporters about how he'd done a nation's dirty work and then been blamed for it. Or at least that was what was reported to Kate. In the end, the colonel suffered no consequences except his own bitterness. He'd scarred.

Richard had changed. While she was fighting for her life, he'd taken care of Bill's burial and then visited her every day, lingering by her bedside. When she was too weak to say much, he talked for her. He spun plans. He'd gotten a job with a survey team mapping the Colorado River. He'd already delayed his departure, waiting for her to be strong enough to go with him.

She was amused at such elaborate plans from a man who'd spent his life not wanting to be tied down—not to a woman, not to his family's business. As her strength returned, she reminded him about the quillworkers. That wasn't a part of his plans. They would come back later, he promised. She could take pictures of the Indian women then, if she still had an interest. The survey job was important, paid well, his chance to become known as a photographer. It would lead to other equally important work, he assured her, talking on and on. She tried to understand, but from where she hovered on the edge of life, she couldn't imagine what was so urgent about taking photographs of hills and valleys. They weren't likely to change in an eon. But the quillworkers and their traditions were dying even as she struggled not to die. When he finally understood that she meant to take those pictures and wouldn't be going with him, he'd complained of her "unreasonable stubbornness" and then left without even saying good-bye.

Homer now turned a circle, his toenails scraping against the bare wooden floor, his tail brushing against her skirts. He whined. He wanted to go walking, romping across the prairie the way they used to every morning. He missed that and was losing patience with her. He didn't understand she was still healing, still working and reworking the events of the last little while, trying to give them a satisfactory order. She bent and patted him.

Plenty Horses had gone free. She was told the courtroom had exploded in cheers at the news, public sympathy having swung to the side of that sad, lonely young man. Nock credited Kate with saving his client's life. Her prints had changed everything. General Miles had ordered Baldwin to release documents proving the army was at war. That should have meant Judge Sherman had no choice but to rule that his court had no jurisdiction. He didn't see it that way. Judge Sherman took matters one step further. He ordered the jury to return a directed verdict of "not guilty," saying the evidence indicated Lieutenant Casey had been "reconnoitering" when he was shot. That meant Plenty Horses could not be tried again on those same charges. He was truly a free man.

She was glad for that, but it struck her as ironic that Bill's photograph, not hers, had made that difference. She was the one who'd consciously recorded the truth, hoping to expose someday the uprising for what it really was. Mrs. Nock was now in charge of taking care of those plates for Kate. She'd agreed to that even though she didn't approve of Kate's going to the reservation. Sometimes Kate wondered herself if coming here was such a good idea. Even Mrs. Donning had only stayed a few weeks before joining another Wild West show and moving on.

Nock was the only person who hadn't tried to stop her. He'd even wanted to help, and apologized for the fact that he couldn't buy her the plates she needed for her project. His passion was "lost causes," meaning he rarely took a case that paid. The result was that he didn't have much money. The house was his mother's. But he wrote Kate regularly, telling her about his adventures trying to teach himself photography from a book, sometimes explaining the points of a case he was working on, always asking how she was doing. His letters were witty and as unconventional as the man himself. She'd gotten into the habit of reading them over and over like a schoolgirl with a crush. He was, after all, the man who'd cared enough to go back for her box of plates. She would always be grateful for that. But every letter ended with his expressing the hope that she'd come back to Sioux Falls when she finished. She knew he meant more than returning for a visit. She never answered that part. She didn't know what she was going to do the rest of the afternoon, much less the rest of her life.

Something caught Kate's eye. She straightened. It was far away where the road met the horizon.

Someone was coming.

Anyone coming to the reservation was an event. Still standing in the doorway, Kate watched in an interested but detached way. Reservation kids gathered in the dusty street also watching and waiting to see who was coming. The quillworkers left their work and joined the growing crowd. Men, too, other women. Everyone waited and watched as the wagon drew closer and closer.

Kate's recognition was slow. But when it came, her mouth went dry. It was Richard's wagon. That initial flush of surprise was followed by a surge of feeling, strong and mixed. She was excited to see him, but worried. Was he coming to join her? Or was he coming to get her? Maybe he expected that she'd learned her lesson now and would come away with him. Would she?

Working her cane, she managed the two steps off the porch and made her way to the middle of the dusty road. Homer followed. Then wagging his tail, he trotted ahead, trailing half a dozen other dogs as he went to greet the newcomer.

Kate's second recognition was even slower coming. Richard wasn't driving the wagon. Not his height. Not his way of sitting. Not his kind of hat. An emptiness washed through her. What did that mean?

She imagined the worst. What if something had happened to him?

The wagon came closer and closer. It rolled up clouds of dust under its wheels. Homer had caught up and was now trotting along beside. An extra horse trailed behind.

At last the wagon pulled up beside her. "Mrs. Burke?" the driver asked.

His shoulders were square. His jaw was clean-shaven and firm. She couldn't see his eyes. They were lost in the shade of his hat.

"Mrs. Burke?" he asked again. "You have to be Mrs.

Burke. How many red-haired ladies with a red dog am I going to find in these parts?"

She nodded, yes.

Homer sniffed around one wagon wheel.

"This here is your wagon. A gentleman asked me to deliver it to you."

"My wagon?"

"Yes, ma'am. That's what he said. And everything in it. He was right concerned that I drive careful. Didn't want nothing broke. So I guess I'd be obliged if you was to inspect it." With that, he eyed the crowd of bystanders and then climbed down right there in the middle of the road.

"Where is he?" Kate asked.

"You mean Mr. Houston?"

She nodded.

"Last I seen, he was in Chadron, Nebraska."

"What was he doing there?" she asked, wondering what had happened with the survey job.

"Passing through would be my guess. I don't rightly know for sure. He came to town three days ago asking around for an honest man. He said he had a job for an honest man. Guess that turned out to be me."

Kate followed the driver around the wagon to the back.

He opened it and pulled down the steps.

She climbed in.

"I drove as careful as can be, ma'am, but I never drove no wagon filled with so much glass. Hope it's all right."

She unlatched and opened the cabinets, drawers, storage compartments. Everything was filled with fresh chemicals, print paper, glass plates. All of it was in good order. Even Richard's cameras were stored in their places. The bedding had been cleaned and folded. There were cooking things and food—fresh supplies of flour, cornmeal, coffee, sugar, and fresh bacon. The only thing missing was Richard's clothes.

"Hope it's all right, ma'am," the driver repeated, poking his head inside. "I drove as gentle as the road would allow."

"It's fine. Everything is fine." Kate stepped outside again. "What message did Mr. Houston send?"

"No message, ma'am."

"No message?"

"No, ma'am." He folded up the steps again.

Kate backed out of the way. She wiped her brow with her handkerchief and tried to understand. Richard was a man given to flamboyance, but this?

"I'm afraid I don't know how to pay you," she said. "But if you'll come to the agency, perhaps I can make some arrangement."

"I was paid in advance, ma'am."

"Oh."

He closed up the back of the wagon.

"But I should like to pay you for the trouble of taking a message back."

The driver shook his head. "Can't do that. The gentleman left the same day I did."

"Left?"

"Yes, ma'am. On the train."

"To where?"

"Don't know."

"East? West?"

He shook his head.

"How will he know I got the wagon?"

"That's why he needed an honest man, ma'am."

"Oh, I see. Well, I dare say you are that, Mr. . . .?"

"Judson, ma'am. Benjamin Judson." And he tipped his hat, giving her a look at his eyes, soft brown, the skin wrinkled a little at the corners.

"Well, I appreciate making your acquaintance, Mr. Judson," Kate added.

"Thank you, ma'am." Then he cleared his throat and looked around at the crowd of Indians. "You're living with them?" he asked in hushed tones.

She nodded, knowing there was no easy way to explain. But she not only lived here, she considered it enormously better than sharing stairs with her mother and grandmother. She'd finally escaped them even in her dreams.

"I take photographs of them," she added.

He obviously liked that better than thinking she'd "gone

358

native." He nodded and looked the group over once more. Then giving a little shrug, he added, "But now I was a-wondering if you got someone here who can help with the horses?" he asked. "You see I have been driving so slow and careful with all that glass and everything, it's taken me longer than I expected. My farm needs me. This dry, hot weather is real hard on things. If you can understand."

Kate nodded. "I understand. I can handle the horses fine."

He tipped his hat once more to her. Then he took one more quick look all around. With that, he unhooked his horse from the back.

"You married?" she asked.

"Yes, ma'am. I got a fine wife."

"Then I suppose your wife needs you, too."

He ducked his head.

She'd made him bashful.

He swung up onto the horse.

Kate extended her hand.

He leaned down and took it. His was warm and rough. Then he paused. "I asked Mr. Houston what was so important about delivering this here wagon and he answered. It weren't no message, but . . ."

"Yes," she prompted.

"He said this wagon was what you needed most from him. That's all."

Kate nodded. "Thanks."

Then he tipped his hat, and she stood in the middle of the road and watched him ride away. The dust his horse raised rolled windward along with him.

Meanwhile, the Indian kids were poking around the wagon, curiously checking it. One of the men was holding the horses while the women had burst into excited chatter—quite a different scene than they'd presented Mr. Judson. Then they'd all stood silent as statues, watching intently but keeping their distance.

And Richard, she thought with amazement. What was she to think of Richard?

He was a gentleman whose reputation preceded him.

Even before she met him, she'd been warned to "watch out." He was a man who knew how to please the ladies—knew just exactly what they wanted.

Indeed, she thought.

Then turning, she found Homer had already jumped up onto the driver's seat. He was waiting, his head cocked to one side, his eyes wide. Kate handed her cane to one of the women and pulled herself up beside him. Lately, when she dreamed, she flew. It was a wonderful weightless kind of dreaming that gave energy to her days. She would need energy. She had work to do.

And with that thought came a rush of excited anticipation. She could hardly stand it. She looked around. She needed a place to park her wagon where she could get fresh water. She couldn't wait a minute longer before arranging her trays and mixing her chemicals.

Epilogue

April 1933
Denver, Colorado

The house was a gray brick two-story on a tree-lined street. Nice, but not pretentious. The front door was oak with an oval of beveled glass. The doorbell was to the right side. John Wincher stood in front of that door, drew breath, and quietly rehearsed what he wanted to say. Then he shifted his weight, tugged his jacket into place, and rang the bell.

A Negro woman opened the door. She had her hair tied in a handkerchief. She cast an appraising eye over him, then grunted once. "You must be the new one the Smithsonian done sent."

"I wasn't sent," he told her, the words coming too quickly. He drew another breath. "I came on my own, at my own expense."

She shrugged. "Don't matter none to me. You still look the same as all the others."

"Will she see me?" he asked.

"Sure, she see you," the maid went on, "for all the good that's going to do you." She stepped back.

He took off his hat and entered. There were stairs straight

ahead and, just to the left of that, a hallway to the kitchen. He noticed a hat rack and put his hat on it. Then he fumbled in his pocket, found a calling card, and handed it to the maid.

She took it, looked at it, grunted once more, then handed it back. "She's on the sun porch. Through the parlor, then straight back. You found yourself this far, I imagine you can find yourself the rest of the way." With that, she pulled a dish towel from her shoulder and marched off toward the kitchen.

He was astounded. His mother would never have tolerated such an attitude from "the help." Having no choice, he did a slow turn, checking things, and found his own way into the parlor.

It was neat and nicely furnished, though a bit spare given the current vogue for the overstuffed and overfilled. He paused to check some of the photographs on one wall. He recognized them. There was no mistaking the distinctive quality of a "Kate." Then, stepping away from the wall, he sized up the rest of the room. The rug underfoot was Turkish. The writing desk was Chinese. He noted a weaving from Africa and a mask from Siam. Souvenirs from her travels, he guessed. He saw nothing quilled. He'd heard that she objected to displaying quilled items. She had rather bluntly told a colleague of his that quillwork was "not parlor art." Three colleagues had come before him, older men, more experienced. None had managed an interview longer than ten minutes.

From the doorway to the sun porch, he saw her. She was stretched on a chaise lounge, her feet up, her head back, her eyes closed. She looked tiny and frail. The profusion of hair encircling her head appeared twice the size of her face. The face was pleasantly lined and surprisingly serene, given her reputation for being "a regular spitfire."

Her dog noticed him first, a large black Labrador. He rose to his feet, shook himself, and trotted over.

John bent to greet the animal, letting him sniff his hand first.

That roused her. She drew herself up, swung her legs

around, and stood with agility. "I'm afraid you caught me napping," she said, and straightened her skirt.

"Sorry, I'm the one who called yesterday," he said while still on one knee, petting the dog. "I know you said I need not come, but I wanted to meet you." He stood. "I've got something I'd like you to see." With that, he pulled a quilled bag from his pocket.

She looked him over, then took the bag to the wicker chair near the brightest window and put on her glasses. Her dog settled next to her.

He stood while she examined the piece, studying the design, fingering the work, checking the back where nothing showed. "This is fine quillwork. Not many better. Where did you get it?"

"A Blackfoot woman gave it to my mother. That would be more than twenty years ago. I grew up on a ranch in Wyoming. The Blackfoot woman kept house for my mother when I was small. I'm sorry, I don't remember her name."

"And you're a curator with the Smithsonian?"

"Yes, ma'am," he answered. He was beginning to feel awkward, standing there like a schoolboy called before the mistress.

"And you're hoping I'll give my quillwork collection to your museum?"

He hesitated. "That's what my superiors want. The directors of America's finest museum understand that you have a really fine collection of quillwork and photographs of Sioux quillworkers, some so rare nobody has the like. I'm personally more interested in the photographs you took during the Ghost Dance Uprising."

She shot him a startled look. Then her eyes narrowed as she did another assessment, looking him over more carefully than before. "Sit down," she said. It was more an order than a polite nicety.

He didn't care. He was glad for the invitation. For a moment, he'd been afraid he wasn't going to last ten minutes. He sat in the wicker chair across from her.

"You're a mighty young curator, from the looks of it. They send you because they thought I'd be polite to a boy?"

"No, ma'am. I wasn't sent at all. I came on my own."

"All the way from Washington?"

"Yes, ma'am."

"Because you want to see my ghost dance photographs?"

"Yes, ma'am."

She considered that a moment, her fingers drumming the arm of her chair. "How do you know about my ghost dance photographs?"

He cleared his throat. "My colleagues consider me bookish. I read a lot. I've read everything ever written about you, every interview, every critique of your work, every narrative of your travel adventures. It's common knowledge that you spent the winter of 1890 with the Seventh Cavalry, but you never talk of it, and no one has seen the pictures. I couldn't help wondering why. And the more I thought about it, the more curious I got."

"Maybe I don't care to remember."

This was his chance. He drew breath and gave his practiced spiel. "I imagine that was an unpleasant time. But I think there's more to it than that. I think it's all wrapped up together, the ghost dancing and the sacred quillworking. When one was lost, so was the other. People need to know that. If you'd allow the Smithsonian to display both the photographs and the quillwork together, I think we could make a bolder statement. I think it could be a groundbreaking exhibition. And I'd like very much to work with you on it. I've read a great deal, I admire your work, I think together we could do justice to the photographs and the quillwork and your reputation."

She drummed her fingers on the chair some more. "That was quite a speech."

He shook his head. "It came out like a speech, didn't it? I'm sorry. But I believe what I said."

She shrugged. "You can believe in whatever you want, but there's a depression going on. People are out of work. Some are hungry. Lots are just surviving. In these times, a lot of people think whole museums are a waste. They aren't going to care about quillwork and old photographs. Besides, Mr.

Houston shows all my work. I've never exhibited with anyone else."

"I know," he told her. "I spoke with him at his gallery in New York. He considers you his most famous discovery."

"His first discovery, you mean. By now he's gotten famous himself for spotting young photographic talent. But I have the distinction of still being his most troublesome discovery. My last show caused quite a stir. My subject matter was 'trivial,' the critics said. They called it 'a misguided attempt to raise ladies' Sunday snapshots to the level of art.' "

"Not everyone agreed with that," he told her.

"No, I suppose not."

"More than a few thought you should have been given the Gutzmann-Heinz prize," he added.

"Oh, you are a flatterer," Kate said, and then reflected a moment. "My father won the Gutzmann-Heinz prize once. But that was a long time ago."

"Mr. Houston says that prize was really yours."

"You and Richard must have had an interesting chat."

"Helps to get him a little drunk," he returned.

"My, my," Kate continued. "I had no idea you were so determined. You wanted to know about me and my photographs that badly?"

"Yes, ma'am," he said, and raised his gaze to hers, thinking she had no idea how badly he wanted to know. It was almost an obsession with him.

He'd first seen a "Kate" photograph five years ago. From then on, he'd searched them out wherever they were being shown. He'd been known to stand in front of one of her pictures for as long as half an hour. He thought of them as windows into his mother's world. Not that the subject matter was always domestic, it wasn't. Nevertheless whenever he looked at a "Kate" photograph, he had the sensation that if he stared long enough, he might understand.

"You remind me of my mother," he added.

At that, Kate cocked her head and again fingered the quilled bag he'd shown her. "In that case, I think I'd like to know more about this."

365

But before he could say anything more, the maid came with tea and a tray of tarts.

"Will you look at this?" Kate said to the other woman and held up the quillwork.

The maid made a waving motion with the back of her hand. "You know I don't like that voodoo stuff. You can pack the whole lot of it off to a museum, if you ask me."

Kate chuckled. "Mattie won't sleep in the same room with quillwork, even if it's locked in a chest. Says it gives her nightmares. She said that even before she knew what it was. Mattie keeps a dream journal. Her mother before her kept a dream journal, only she never learned to write. She sketched the images. Some of the designs don't look much different than this." She pointed to the quillwork in her lap. "Astonishing, don't you think?"

John nodded and took the tea Kate offered.

She'd had a remarkable career, he knew. Besides showing her work in Richard Houston's gallery, she'd written about photography for *Leslie's Weekly* and been the editor of *American Amateur Photography*. It was said that when she traveled, she never used a porter. She carried her own eight-by-ten camera and all its accompanying paraphernalia—lenses, tripod, plateholders. And for years she had her own studio with as many as sixteen assistants. Now she mostly did calendar work and taught classes.

Still talking to her maid, she said, "Would you bring me that square box that sits atop my cedar chest?"

"Yes, ma'am."

Then when the maid was gone, Kate fingered the bag again. "This is an odd piece, Mr. Wincher. I can't figure what it is. Not a pipe bag. Not a medicine bag. The shape is wrong."

"It was made special for my mother's favorite book of poetry." He took the volume from his other pocket and handed it over.

She tried how it fit into the bag, nodded, and then examined the book, running her finger down one worn edge. "This is well used."

"My mother's favorite thing. She had a secret spot, away

from the house, down near the river where a few trees grew. She went there to read poetry. She wrote a little poetry too. See on the inside flyleaf?"

Kate found the poem. She read. She looked up. "That's really quite good."

"I know. Funny thing is, she never shared any of her poems with anyone, at least, not so far as I know."

"Why do you suppose that was?"

He shook his head. "I can't say."

"But you have an idea?"

"It sounds odd, but I think she liked having a secret self. I think it was the only thing that kept her going. Our ranch was terribly isolated, and my father didn't talk a lot. Does that make sense?"

"She was Double-Woman touched."

"I beg your pardon?"

She shook her head. "You've never heard of Double-Woman?"

"No, I don't believe I have."

She turned and gazed out the window into the garden. When she spoke, her voice was softer. "It's said that long, long ago Double-Woman taught the quillworkers to quill. More than that, she taught them the importance of beauty." She shook her head and turned her gaze back to him. "Fine quillwork to the Sioux is as precious as anything we keep in a museum, but they used their art to decorate everyday things—cradleboards, shirts, pipestems, bags. How else did one get the power of beauty into one's daily life? That's why quillwork deserves better than to be turned into parlor art or a museum piece. But I digress. From the look of this book, I think your mother must have known that same sacredness of beauty. It would seem that poetry was part of her everyday life. I'm sure that's why your Blackfoot house-keeper made this pouch for her. She recognized another who had been touched by Double-Woman. They shared something deep."

Then she slipped the book of poems into the bag and gave it to him. "I wish I could have met your mother."

He swallowed and nodded. One day his mother had put

367

on her best Sunday dress, walked to the river, and drowned herself. He was eleven at the time and still ached to know why. He couldn't tell that to Kate, but he was about to say something else when there was a sudden clamor of gong and chime. It was loud enough to startle him up from his seat. He looked around.

Kate chuckled. "It's the hour and that's my husband's timepiece collection. Believe me, you want to be glad you're not in the same room with all those clocks." She shook her head. "On the bright side, they keep us punctual. My husband will be joining us shortly. He always takes his tea precisely at the top of this hour."

John sat again. He'd also read about the eccentric Judge Nock. But somehow that didn't prepare him for the short, gray-haired, tweed-suited man who came through the door a moment later. John jumped to his feet again and shook the judge's hand. His tie was purple and his cuff links had palm trees on them. But Judge Nock was highly respected, John knew. It was said that he'd decided more cases that were now written up in law school textbooks than any other living federal magistrate.

After shaking John's hand, Judge Nock bussed Kate's cheek and poured himself some of the tea. Then he asked, "Another visitor from the Smithsonian?" There was a playful tone to his voice. "They must think you lack for interesting conversation."

"Never lacked for that since I married you," she returned, her voice also light.

This was oft repeated banter, John realized. He sipped his tea and watched how the two of them touched and patted and passed each other tarts with an obvious comfortable familiarity. His own parents had never reached that kind of accommodation.

Then Judge Nock brought them back to the subject at hand. "Well, what about it? You going to give in and let the Smithsonian show your quillwork? You know, it might be that the right time has come."

John stiffened. He would never have dared put the question so directly. It practically invited her to say, "No."

But Kate didn't say, no.

"Mr. Wincher and I were discussing the possibility of displaying both my quillwork and my photographs from the Ghost Dance Uprising," she told the judge. "I asked Mattie to bring the photographs down."

The square box from atop the cedar chest, John remembered hearing the request. He hadn't understood the significance. Now that he did, he couldn't help glancing toward the door, wondering what was taking that maid so long.

Judge Nock set his teacup down. "I don't believe it's been forty minutes since I heard the doorbell. You mean to tell me Mr. Wincher has talked you into displaying both the quillwork and the photographs in less than forty minutes?"

No one answered that. Kate shrugged. John didn't know what to say. He couldn't believe his good fortune. He was almost afraid to breathe for fear of upsetting it.

The judge didn't seem to notice. He chuckled and addressed himself to John. "Took me forty months to talk her into marrying me."

"Truth is, I never really had a chance. The judge has such a power of persuasion, he never fails to win whatever he determines to go after," she put in.

"Well, not exactly," the judge said. "I had to make considerable compromise. I had to promise to let Kate travel. She's been all over the world. Worse, I had to promise not to be jealous when she showed her work at Mr. Houston's gallery. I'm not sure I managed that one. I tried. Actually I don't mind Richard Houston as long as he stays in New York."

At that Kate punched him playfully and told him to behave himself. Then turning to John, she added, "Mr. Houston and I share a passion for photography, but not much else. I could never go East again, for example, and he could never stay West. Beyond temperaments, we were different territories."

At that the judge harumphed. "The man runs a fine gallery, but running a fine gallery doesn't make him any less bourgeois."

"Oh, quit it," she was saying. "You know you like Richard as much as I do."

While the two of them bantered back and forth like that, Mattie arrived with the box of prints. She unceremoniously plopped them down in front of John and left again. He pushed the tea aside and began spreading the photographs across the table.

The distinguishing characteristic of a "Kate" was the way her photographic images mingled the public with the private. In these pictures she'd taken a time of stunning national violence and framed it with the personal: a soldier casually cleaning his gun after a battle, an Indian woman cutting her own braid as a sign of mourning, snow drifting over an abandoned moccasin, an Indian hugging a buffalo.

He looked up. He had no photographs of his mother, not even a portrait. Like so much of the world, she'd come and gone unseen. But there were hundreds of pictures of the Ghost Dance Uprising.

It was as if every photographer in the country at that time had gone West to record that "last Indian war." And almost every one of those photographs had come to be cataloged at the Smithsonian. He knew. He'd been through those catalogs. Yet until this moment, he hadn't seen a real record of that event.

He knew why she'd not shown these photographs to anyone until now. It would have been a mistake for her pictures to have been mixed in and cataloged with the others. Her pictures needed the distance of time to be appreciated. With a camera and a few glass plates, Kate had exposed the old myths. And now, from the perspective of forty years, he expected that no one seeing her photographs would ever view the Ghost Dance Uprising, or any Indian war, in quite the same way. No small achievement.

He thought he'd call the exhibition:

Kate Burke Shoots the Old West

Meanwhile, she and the judge chatted on. She was now reminding him to find matching socks before he went to court and not to forget his umbrella. She sounded so grandmotherly, John listened with amazement, wondering if his mother might have grown old the same way. He'd have liked that. At the same time, he wished he'd known Kate forty years ago. He imagined she cut quite a figure then.

She still did.